# The Women's March

# The Women's March

### A Novel of the 1913 Woman Suffrage Procession

## Jennifer Chiaverini

**HARPER LARGE PRINT**

*An Imprint of HarperCollinsPublishers*

THE WOMEN'S MARCH. Copyright © 2021 by Jennifer Chiaverini. All rights reserved. Printed in the United States of America. No part of this book may be used or reproduced in any manner whatsoever without written permission except in the case of brief quotations embodied in critical articles and reviews. For information, address HarperCollins Publishers, 195 Broadway, New York, NY 10007.

HarperCollins books may be purchased for educational, business, or sales promotional use. For information, please e-mail the Special Markets Department at SPsales@harpercollins.com.

FIRST HARPER LARGE PRINT EDITION

ISBN: 978-0-06-309026-2

Library of Congress Cataloging-in-Publication Data is available upon request.

21 22 23 24 25   LSC   10 9 8 7 6 5 4 3 2 1

*To the women who marched*
*for equality and justice,*
*and those who are marching still*

# The Women's March

# Prologue
# October 19, 1912

## BROOKLYN, NEW YORK

### Wilson

"On behalf of the Democratic Campaign Committee of Kings County," declared the tall, fair-haired Scotsman behind the podium at center stage, his powerful brogue rising dramatically over the cheers of the assembled throng, "it is my great honor and privilege to welcome the former president of Princeton University, the current governor of New Jersey, and the future president of the United States, the honorable Woodrow Wilson!"

The cheers rose to a roar as Wilson emerged from the curtained wing and crossed the stage to meet Chairman McLean at the podium, the smells of tobacco, damp wool, and perspiration wafting from the audience almost as blinding as the glare of the footlights. The venerable theater was packed to the rafters, attesting to McLean's ability to muster up voters as well as Wilson's own renown as an orator and statesman. When he and his entourage had arrived at the Brooklyn Academy of Music not long before, their driver had been obliged to halt half a block away, the automobile's progress impeded by a crowd of hundreds holding tickets aloft and pushing their way into the packed front vestibule. A team of police officers had been obliged to clear a path from the automobile to a side entrance. As Wilson shook McLean's hand and murmured his thanks, he noted with satisfaction that those same eager men now filled every seat and spilled over into the aisles, applauding, waving their hats in the air, shouting his name.

He hoped their enthusiasm would carry them to the polls come November 5—not only these wildly applauding men, but also vast droves of voters of a similar temperament, all dissatisfied with the incumbent, hankering for change, but wary of radicals. Wilson was their man.

He took the podium, raised his hands, and nodded to one section of the house and then another, modestly acknowledging their ardent welcome while also seeking order, mildly surprised to see a few ladies scattered among the gentlemen. As soon as his audience had settled down, he launched into his stump speech—well practiced by now, so late in the campaign, but even more urgent than when he had first announced his candidacy. Their democracy was failing ordinary Americans, he warned. All governmental power was monopolized by a few corrupt men who controlled the system utterly and for their own benefit. Yet an even greater monopoly, rarely mentioned elsewhere in the campaign, threatened to—

"What about votes for women?" someone interrupted from the balcony. It was a woman's voice, full and musical, with an Irish lilt.

Wilson abruptly fell silent as heads craned and murmurs arose, a ripple of confusion and annoyance and disgust. Stepping out from behind the podium and approaching the front of the stage, Wilson scanned the upper seats until his gaze fell upon a fair, auburn-haired woman dressed in a purple shirtwaist and a hat adorned with a yellow feather. She awaited his response, her gaze fixed on his, determined and utterly devoid of deference. And yet there was something warm and appealing in her expression too; slender and apparently in her midthirties, she would probably be quite pretty if she smiled.

"What is it, madam?" he called up to her over the grumbles of the crowd.

"You say you want to destroy monopolies?" Her eyebrows rose, signifying the innocence and eminent rationality of her query. "I ask you, what about woman suffrage? Men have a monopoly on the vote. Why not start there?"

The audience snickered. "Sit down," someone groused loudly from the back.

"Woman suffrage, madam, is not a question for the federal government," Wilson explained patiently, clasping his hands behind his back. He felt almost as if he were back at Bryn Mawr, addressing a class of lovely but tragically uncomprehending female pupils. "It is a matter for the states. As a representative of the *national* party, I cannot speak to this issue."

"But I address you as an American, Mr. Wilson," the woman persisted. "Since you seek to govern all these *united* states, surely you can tell us where you stand."

The crowd's growing dissatisfaction manifested in mutters and glares, in impatient shifting in seats. "Let us not be rude to any woman," Wilson reminded them, silently adding, *No matter how unwomanly she may be.* To the offender herself, he replied firmly, "I hope you will not consider it a discourtesy if I decline to answer those questions on this occasion."

"But I do consider it discourteous, Governor, and

worse." She put her head to one side, curious. "Unless you mean to say that you have no opinion whatsoever?"

"Throw her out!" a deep voice bellowed just beyond the footlights, cutting off Wilson's reply.

A few rows behind that fellow, another man rose from his seat, cupped his hands around his mouth, and shouted toward the balcony, "Why don't you go to your own meeting, girlie?"

A roar of laughter followed.

"Go home and mind the babies!"

"Put her out! Where are the police?"

Wilson could have answered that. From his ideal vantage point, he easily spotted three grim-faced, gray-uniformed officers working their way down the aisles of the crowded balcony toward the woman. With them was a man in a well-cut dark suit, perhaps in his fifties, with Germanic features and an imperious manner, as if he were accustomed to having his orders obeyed. He said something to the woman and made a cutting gesture with his forearm; she threw him a retort over her shoulder. Then her gaze returned to Wilson's and held it, despite the jostling of the increasingly disgruntled men surrounding her.

This could get ugly, Wilson realized. It would play very badly in the press.

"Now, gentlemen, let us remain civil," he urged, concealing his own rising annoyance. Why did she not simply sit down? "I'm sure the lady will not persist when I positively decline to discuss the question now."

He gestured for her to take her seat—and yet still she stood, waiting for him to satisfy her question, as if he had not made it perfectly clear that no answer would be forthcoming. Just then the policemen reached her. To Wilson's consternation, they seized her by the arms and waist, lifted her roughly, and wrestled her from the hall through a fire exit against a backdrop of jeers, hisses, and blistering insults.

"Gentlemen, it is very much against my wishes that the lady has been ejected," Wilson protested, although he doubted he could be heard above the din. "I respect her right to put questions to me, however inopportune."

Inopportune? Better he should say potentially disastrous. He of all men did not quake before difficult questions, but he simply could not afford to answer that particular one, not with Taft and Roosevelt and Debs snapping at his heels, ready to drag him down at the first sign of weakness. Of course he had an opinion on woman suffrage, one shared by the vast majority of southern men: he was definitely and irreconcilably opposed to it. The social changes woman suffrage would entail would not justify whatever small gains might be accomplished. But he could not say so aloud, not with the press standing by with pencils hovering over pads and so many voters yet undecided. Better to evade the question by insisting it was a matter of states' rights, beyond the purview of a presidential candidate.

"I would like to have your attention," Wilson addressed the restless audience, raising his voice but refusing to shout, "while I recover the thread of what I was saying."

The crowd soon settled down, and Wilson continued his speech precisely where he had left off, describing what he considered to be the worst monopoly of all, the influence of powerful interests upon the government. Thereafter the only interruptions were welcome bursts of applause.

When he finished speaking, he barely had time to take a few dignified bows before the candidate for lieutenant governor replaced him at the podium. A moment later his aides were hustling him off the stage, into his topcoat, and outside to the automobile, which waited, engine rumbling, to speed them off to his next engagement.

"Who was that obnoxious woman?" he asked irritably as they settled themselves in the vehicle and the driver swiftly set off for Carnegie Hall, across the East River and north to midtown Manhattan. Women who spoke in public gave him a chilled, scandalized feeling. Thankfully, his own wife and daughters understood that a woman's place was in the home.

"That harridan? Maud Malone," one of his aides replied. "She's a militant suffragist librarian and a notorious heckler. Just last week she interrupted Governor Johnson's speech at a Bull Moose meeting. She interrupted Roosevelt on the night before the primaries."

Wilson was tempted to ask how Roosevelt had responded, but he could well imagine how the former Republican president, now leader of the breakaway self-proclaimed Progressive Party, would have appeased the harasser with promises he was powerless to fulfill.

"What will become of this Miss Malone?" Wilson asked. The type of woman who took an active part in suffrage agitation was totally abhorrent to him, and yet he did not like to see any lady so roughly handled.

"She'll be escorted to the nearest police station and arraigned, I imagine." His aide offered a reassuring grin. "Don't worry about her. She'll pay her bail and be back home with her piles of books and innumerable cats by midnight."

The youngest of Wilson's aides chuckled, but the most experienced of the three did not even smile. "Don't let this incident concern you, Governor," he said. "Miss Malone, like all those other suffragettes with a penchant for public spectacle, is an irritant, nothing more. She doesn't even have the power to vote against you."

Yes, there was that. Wilson settled back against the soft leather seat and turned his thoughts from the unsettling Irishwoman to his next speech. He was due to take the stage again in less than an hour, and with only seventeen days until the election, he could not allow himself to be distracted by pretty hecklers and their ludicrous propositions.

# 1
# January 1910
## PHILADELPHIA, PENNSYLVANIA

### Alice

A bracing, icy gust of wind threatened to snatch away Alice's wide-brimmed black hat and cast it into the churning wake of the steamship SS *Haverford* as it slowly cruised up the Delaware River, but she clasped her hand to the crown just in time and kept it atop her mass of long black hair, coiled into a loose bun at the back of her head. A few stray wisps tickled her face as she secured the hat pin and returned her hand to the warmth of her fur muff, but her gaze never left the distant pier as the ship approached the Port of Philadelphia. Despite the wintry bluster, Alice would not dream of abandoning her spot at the railing for the comfort of the upper deck's salon, not when she was so close to her destination and the welcoming embraces of those she loved best in all the world.

The *Haverford* had departed Liverpool on January 5, and now, after a stormy, uncomfortable fortnight at sea, it was about to arrive, four days late, on the snow-dusted shores of Alice's homeland. After nearly three years abroad, she wanted nothing more than to bask in the generous affection of her loved ones and to indulge in the comforts of Paulsdale, her family's 173-acre farm in Moorestown, New Jersey, an idyllic, pastoral haven fifteen miles east of the bustling city of Philadelphia, on the opposite side of the Delaware. She had promised her mother and herself that once she was safely home, she would rest, fully recover her health—which had suffered greatly during her last stint in prison—and sort out how to resume her graduate studies. She would be the first to admit that in recent months, she had neglected her formal education in favor of her suffrage work, her life's true cause and calling.

As the ship came into harbor, Alice scanned the crowd gathered on the pier below for her mother and siblings, not knowing who, precisely, had come to meet her, but confident that some beloved family members stood among the throng. The ship's horn bellowed overhead, two long blasts; while sailors and dockworkers tossed ropes and deftly secured knots, the passengers shifted in anticipation as the ramps were made ready for their descent.

Alice was the last passenger to disembark. Although her legs trembled and her gray wool dress, white linen blouse, and black coat felt heavy and loose upon her thin frame, her heart lifted and her footsteps quickened at the thought of the joyful welcome awaiting her ashore. Searching the upturned faces as she descended, she glimpsed her mother, clad in the plain dark dress, dark cloak, and white cap of their Quaker faith. Her fourteen-year-old brother, Parry, stood at their mother's side; catching her eye, he grinned and waved his arm high overhead, rising up on his toes. He must have grown four inches since she had last seen him, and he resembled their late father so keenly that her breath caught in her throat.

Overcome with happiness and relief, Alice made her way through the crowd and surrendered herself to her mother's and youngest brother's warm embraces—but the moment was quickly spoiled when a swarm of reporters descended, shouting her name, gesturing for her attention, interrupting their family reunion with a dizzying onslaught of questions.

"Shall I clear a path through them to the car?" Parry

asked eagerly as their mother drew closer and took his arm. She barely managed a tentative smile for the reporters.

Weary and longing to get out of the cold, Alice was tempted to accept the offer, but she shook her head. Emmeline Pankhurst and her daughters—in fact, any of the courageous, daring British suffragists with whom she had campaigned and suffered during her three years abroad—would have gladly seized the opportunity to promote the cause, so how could she refuse? As much as Alice dreaded public speaking and longed for a warm fire and a hot meal, if an interview would evoke sympathy and understanding for the woman suffrage movement, it would be time well spent.

"Miss Paul," shouted one eager fellow over the clamor of questions, "how does it feel to be back in America?"

"Quite lovely indeed," she replied, with a fond smile for her mother and brother. She longed to see their two middle siblings, Helen and Bill, and hoped they were waiting for her at Paulsdale.

"Tell us, Mrs. Paul," the same reporter queried, turning to Alice's mother, "how does your daughter look?"

"If I'm to be honest—" She ran an appraising glance over her eldest daughter. "Not so well as when she left us to go abroad, I'm sorry to say."

"I'm perfectly fine," Alice answered for herself, gently resting a hand on her mother's arm. "I'm as physically able to wage an equally active campaign in this country as I did abroad, if I find it necessary."

"By 'active campaign,'" another reporter broke in, pencil at the ready, "do you mean the same outlandish tactics you learned with the Brits, breaking windows and wearing disguises and such?"

"Perhaps, perhaps not," Alice replied. "Over there, you have to stand on your head or do some other foolish thing just to attract attention. Suffragettes tried everything to present the cause before the political powers that be, but each attempt met with failure until we resorted to more militant tactics."

"Miss Paul," called another reporter, a woman this time. "Why do you say 'suffragette' instead of 'suffragist'? Dr. Anna Shaw and Mrs. Carrie Chapman Catt prefer the term 'suffragist.'"

"We all called ourselves suffragists once," said Alice. "Eventually the British authorities began referring to those of us with a more activist bent as suffragettes, disparagingly, to distinguish us from our demurer, better-behaved sisters. We've chosen to embrace the title. We understand, as others may not, that we had to resort to unusual tactics to force the authorities to acknowledge the movement. England is reluctant to accept suffrage, and had the suffragettes gone along quietly, we would have been entirely ignored."

A reporter with gray threaded in his dark hair frowned. "Once you were in prison, though, why didn't you just follow the rules? So you suffered in Holloway. Big deal. You brought it upon yourself."

Alice regarded him calmly, unfazed by his hostile tone. "We suffragettes decided more than a year ago to resist prison passively by taking no food and by refusing to obey any of the regulations. Our purpose was to make the situation more acute, and consequently, bring it to an end sooner." Turning to her mother, she added in an undertone, "It is simply a policy of passive resistance, and as a Quaker, thou ought to approve."

Before her mother could reply, another reporter called out a question. More queries followed, most of them about forced feedings and the more lurid aspects of her experiences, but when Alice's voice began to falter, her mother firmly bade them farewell and Parry hefted her two suitcases by the handles, brandishing them like shields, or so it seemed to Alice, as they made their way through the crowd. Flanking her protectively, her mother and brother escorted her away from the docks and out to the street, where Frank Stout, a kindly neighbor whose farm abutted theirs, waited to carry them home in his black Ford Runabout.

"Bill and Helen are waiting for thee at home," Alice's mother said as Mr. Stout started the engine, answering Alice's unspoken question. Alice and her siblings used the formal "thee" and "thou" within the family and with others in their Quaker community, but used the less formal address with people of other faiths.

"I can't wait to see them," said Alice fervently. It had been far too long, and her siblings' letters, while essential to easing her homesickness, had conveyed only a fraction of the happiness and affection she felt in their company. The four siblings had always been close, and they had acquired a deeper appreciation of one another after they had lost their strict but beloved father to pneumonia eight years before. A bank president as well as a gentleman farmer, William Paul had required an orderly and disciplined household in the Quaker tradition, and although Alice could not say that they had been as close as some fathers and daughters, she did not doubt that he had loved her.

At the time of her father's passing, Alice had been a sophomore at Swarthmore College, her mother's alma mater, a Quaker institution where the "thee" and "thy" of the plain people was still spoken, just as it was among her family. Even so, at college Alice had discovered new freedoms: She had been permitted to wear colorful clothing, unlike the somber, monochromatic dresses and white caps she had grown up with. Music was allowed, and not only hymns; she and her classmates could even dance, albeit only with one another, never with young men. She had begun her freshman year as a biology major, a discipline she had chosen because she knew nothing about the subject and was curious. Eventually she found her interest waning, and by the start of her junior year, a wise and kindly professor had guided her toward social work.

It seemed a natural fit, for Alice had been taught to revere education and social justice almost from birth. After graduating from Swarthmore, she had moved to Manhattan to study social work at the New York School of Philanthropy. A summer toiling on behalf of the suffering indigent at the settlement house on the Lower East Side convinced her that the need was great, but the work was not for her. "I help only one person at a time, one day after another," she lamented to her mother. "It feels like sculpting a block of granite with a hairpin. My best efforts seem to make little difference. I can't truly change anything this way."

Adjusting course, that fall she had enrolled at the University of Pennsylvania to pursue her master's degree in sociology with a minor in political science and economics. After she had completed her degree, the local Quaker community awarded her a scholarship to study at Woodbrooke, a Society of Friends institution in Birmingham, England. Grateful for the opportunity and determined to make the most of it, she spent a few months in Berlin to improve her German before moving to England to begin her classes at Woodbrooke, to volunteer at the Friends' settlement house, and to enroll in the commerce department at the University of Birmingham, the first woman ever to do so.

It was in Birmingham that she met the woman who would irrevocably change her life.

Though only twenty-seven, Christabel Pankhurst had already won infamy as a firebrand suffragist, interrupting politicians' speeches, provoking the police to arrest her, and invigorating the movement through the Women's Social and Political Union, which she had founded with her mother, Emmeline. On a cold December evening in 1907, when Miss Pankhurst was scheduled to speak on woman suffrage at the University of Birmingham, curiosity compelled Alice to attend. As Miss Pankhurst took the stage, Alice observed that she was the very antithesis of the usual cruel caricature of the suffragette—delicately beautiful, with fair skin, rosy cheeks, wide-set blue eyes, a sweet expression, and softly curling dark hair. As to the quality of her voice, Alice learned nothing. To her shock and indignation, when Miss Pankhurst took the podium, she was greeted by a chorus of deep bellows and jeers from the mostly male audience. Unable to make herself heard, she was obliged to quit the stage.

The male students had little time to savor their triumph. Appalled by their lack of decorum, the university administration invited Miss Pankhurst back to campus, but for her return engagement, a revered professor introduced her with a profound apology for the rude welcome she had received on her previous visit. The abashed young men remained silent throughout, but whether they were truly contrite or merely afraid to provoke their professor's ire, Alice did not know.

As for herself, she was enthralled.

Miss Pankhurst's insightful, affecting discourse illuminated the connection between women's disenfranchisement and the vast host of ills that tormented their sex, from forced dependence to poverty to sexual exploitation and on and on. Her truths stirred something deep within Alice's heart, something that as a Quaker she recognized as a Concern, the same heightened awareness that had compelled her forebears to embrace nonviolence and abolition.

From that day forward, Alice was a heart-and-soul convert to the cause.

She joined the militant suffragists in frequent marches, demonstrations, and demands for an audience with the prime minister. She participated in outdoor rallies and distributed handbills. On a beautiful, sunny Sunday in June 1908, she donned a white dress and striped sash—purple for dignity, green for hope, and white for purity—and traveled to London to join the largest suffrage demonstration in the city's history. Suffrage advocates in seven one-mile processions strolled and sang and held banners proclaiming VOTES FOR WOMEN as they wound through the streets and converged on Hyde Park, where Christabel and Emmeline Pankhurst and others addressed the crowd from seven platforms. Tens of thousands turned out for the event, which was almost universally regarded as a tremendous success.

And yet Prime Minister Asquith was unmoved. Though the suffragists expected some substantial response to the overwhelming evidence of public support for the cause, instead he declared that he had no plans to add equal suffrage measures to an upcoming reform bill.

Outraged and indignant, the women refused to be deterred.

Soon thereafter, a pair of suffragists hurled rocks through the windows of 10 Downing Street and were arrested. Similar provocative acts led to more arrests. Alice threw no stones, but she attended rallies, worked as a street newsie selling the WSPU's newspaper, and delivered impromptu speeches in parks, on street corners, and on tube platforms. Though she struggled to overcome her stage fright, to make ends meet, and to balance her studies with her activism, she was absolutely certain that the sacrifices were justified.

Her work for the cause impressed the movement's leaders, but she did not realize how much until she received a letter inviting her to join a special deputation to Parliament led by Emmeline Pankhurst. "It is quite probable that you would be under some danger of being arrested and imprisoned," the letter warned, "so you must not accept this invitation unless you were willing to do this."

Alice had heard dreadful tales of Holloway Prison from sister suffragists who had been confined there, and the thought of its horrors made her heart pound and her mouth go dry. The uncomfortable uniforms of coarse, scratchy fabric worn over pinching antique corsets. The rough, forcible body searches by belligerent matrons. The wooden planks that served as beds in the small, cramped, cold, stifling cells. The foul, repulsive meals of watery gruel, thin slices of bread, lard pudding, and greasy potatoes. Outdoor exercise limited to slow marches around the prison yard three times a week, with a distance of nine feet between each prisoner and conversation absolutely forbidden. Yet as terrible as enduring such trials would be, what Alice dreaded most was the effect upon her friends and family back in the States, especially her mother. They would consider her arrest a shocking disgrace. How could Alice risk inflicting such shame and embarrassment upon them? And yet, how could she not agree to pursue equality and justice wherever her heart led her?

On the evening of June 29, 1909, Alice joined two hundred suffragists in a march down Victoria Street to the House of Commons. A rider on horseback and a drum and fife band playing "La Marseillaise" led the way past thousands of eager onlookers who lined the pavement in hopes of witnessing a spectacle. The protest had been announced days before, and, noting that there was "a reason to think that an unusually large number of persons may be anxious to come into Parliament-square," Scotland Yard had issued a warning to the public "of the danger necessarily created by the assembling of a large number of persons in a restricted area." That very day, the afternoon papers had reported that the House had debated whether to allow the delegation to address them, with one member demanding that the leaders be admitted if they agreed to behave in an orderly manner, and most other MPs retorting that he proposed the impossible. The matter had been dropped, unresolved. Ominously, or so it had seemed to Alice, a related article in the *Globe* announced that "Large bodies of police, on foot and mounted, will be held in reserve on duty or at hand to prevent any raid on the Houses of Parliament by Suffragettes to-night."

From some distance away in the middle of the march, Alice saw that the latter report was all too true. Outside the entrance to St. Stephen's Hall, three thousand police officers stood in precise lines six men deep, awaiting the suffragists' deputation and their hundreds of companions. When Emmeline Pankhurst and seven other WSPU leaders approached Chief Inspector Scantlebury and requested admittance, he handed Mrs. Pankhurst a letter, explaining that he did so according to the explicit instructions of Mr. Asquith's private secretary.

Mrs. Pankhurst quickly skimmed the page. "The prime minister sends his regrets," she said, her mellifluous voice carrying over the crowd, "but he declines to meet with us." She threw the letter to the ground.

Another officer attempted to come between her and the chief inspector. "You must go away now, madam," he said.

Mrs. Pankhurst's brows arched over large, warm, expressive brown eyes. At nearly fifty-one, she was lovely and eloquent, and she delivered her speeches in a low, conversational tone interspersed with humor. "If we agree, Inspector Jarvis," she said, no trace of humor evident now, "would you carry a message from our deputation to the House?"

"No, I will not."

"Then we shall not leave." Then, as the deputation had previously planned, Mrs. Pankhurst slapped Inspector Jarvis lightly on the left cheek.

"You must not do that, Mrs. Pankhurst," he said grimly. "I ask you again to clear the square."

She replied with a second slap to his right cheek. Another woman snatched off his cap and flung it to the pavement.

Immediately other officers sprang forward, arrested the eight leaders, and led them away. Alice and her companions recognized this as their signal to rush the police lines. Forward they charged, twelve at a time, one group holding themselves ready while those ahead of them were seized by the shoulders or throats and flung to the ground. Chaos erupted. Mounted police rode into the crowd of women, knocking some aside, trampling others. For more than an hour the women pressed forward, dodging the horses' hooves, struggling to force their way to the door, crying out as blows rained down upon them. Nearby, other protestors flung stones wrapped in suffrage petitions through the windows of government offices.

The police arrested the women in droves, Alice among them. Bruised, bloodied, their hair in disarray and clothing torn, more than one hundred protestors were dragged off to the Canon Row station house, where they were held for hours, crowded into cells and made to sit on the cold, hard floor until they could be processed. It was after midnight when they were finally released with orders to appear before the magistrate at the Bow Street Magistrates' Court promptly at nine o'clock that morning.

In the trial that followed, the charges against Alice and most of the other marchers were dropped, but the leaders were fined five pounds apiece and warned that they would be sentenced to a month in prison if they defaulted. They adamantly refused to pay what they regarded as unjust and illegal fees, so off they went to Holloway, where they demanded to be treated as political prisoners and refused to eat. Disconcerted, and unwilling to starve women to death, the authorities soon released them.

All that summer, Alice joined in marches, protests, petition drives, and ingenious albeit unsuccessful attempts to circumvent security and call on the prime minister at Parliament or at 10 Downing Street. On

July 30, at a protest in Limehouse where Chancellor of the Exchequer Lloyd George was speaking, Alice was arrested again. This time she was convicted of obstructing the police and sentenced to a fortnight in Holloway Prison.

It was as dreadful as she had been warned.

"Undress," the warden barked after Alice and twelve fellow protestors were herded into the prison. Trembling, remembering her training, Alice said nothing, but linked arms with the other women and stood with their backs against the wall. The warden raised a silver whistle to his lips, sounded a piercing blast—and suddenly the prison matrons swarmed upon the prisoners, tore off their clothes, and thrust bundles of prison garb at them. The prisoners refused to wear the uniforms, so they sat naked on the ground, shivering and vulnerable, covering themselves with their arms as best they could. Two hours later, two matrons grudgingly distributed blankets.

"We demand to be treated as political prisoners," said Alice shakily, wrapping herself in the coarse cloth. "We should be permitted to wear our own clothes, to receive mail, to see visitors, to read books and newspapers—"

"Be grateful for what you have," snapped the older matron. "It could easily be taken from you."

Alice waited until the two matrons had moved off before glancing over her shoulder in hopes of catching the eye of her friend and comrade Lucy Burns, who was grumbling under her breath and adjusting her own blanket to cover as much of her pale, freckled skin as possible. They had met for the first time at the Canon Row jail, for they both had been among the protestors arrested in the tumult following the WSPU march on the House of Commons.

As the prisoners had milled about the station house awaiting processing and release, Alice's attention had been drawn first by the unknown suffragist's red hair and friendly smile, and then by the American flag pin on her lapel. Intrigued, and perhaps a bit homesick, Alice introduced herself, and as the evening passed, the two expatriates sat side by side on a billiards table, sharing stories. Where Alice was dark-haired, pale, and slight, Lucy was tall, robust, and ruddy-cheeked. Alice was the eldest of the Paul siblings, while Lucy was the fourth child of eight of an Irish Catholic family from Brooklyn. Lucy was six years older than Alice and had a warm, generous, ready smile. Alice was reserved and quiet, and she knew, to her regret, that some acquaintances found her aloof or cold. Her family and intimate friends knew better.

For all their superficial differences, Alice and Lucy

had much in common, including strong wills, parents who championed education for daughters as well as sons, advanced degrees from prestigious universities, and a steadfast devotion to the suffrage movement.

That same devotion had now landed them in prison yet again.

When Lucy did not glance up, Alice surreptitiously tapped the floor to attract her attention. Much of Lucy's red hair had come loose from its long, coiled braid, and it spilled over her left shoulder as she glanced up at the sound of Alice's fingertips on stone. "It's rather stuffy in here, don't you think?" Alice murmured.

Lucy regarded her, perplexed. Despite the summer heat outside, the stone floor beneath them was as cold as it was hard, and the walls radiated a dank, gloomy, institutional chill. "It's oppressive, if that's what you mean," she quietly replied, her Brooklyn accent wry.

Alice inclined her head to indicate a low bank of windows on the opposite wall. "I mean that the ventilation could stand some improvement."

"That it could." Lucy offered a small conspiratorial grin. "We could all use a breath of fresh air."

Keeping a wary eye on the matrons, Lucy reached into her uniform bundle and quietly took out the clogs. Alice did the same with her own bundle, gesturing for the two women nearest her to follow suit. The moment both matrons turned their backs, Alice, Lucy, and their comrades scrambled to their feet, darted across the room, and began smashing the windowpanes. The matrons shouted for them to halt, and when they moved to restrain them, Alice and Lucy dodged their reach, darted to the adjacent wall, and began shattering windows there. Suddenly Alice was struck from behind on the head. She cried out, dropped the clog, and struggled to keep her feet as she was seized around the arms and shoulders and dragged off to solitary confinement.

She refused food, refused to don prison garb, and only lay on her wooden bed wrapped in the coarse blanket, praying and longing for a kind word, for news of her friends. Four days passed. Then, too weak to rise, she was carried to the prison hospital on a stretcher. Two days later, or perhaps three—dazed from hunger, she had lost count—she was given a shot of brandy, bundled into a cab, and escorted home by a grim-faced matron.

A wealthy widow sympathetic to the cause took in Alice and a few others and nursed them back to health. As soon as she felt strong enough, Alice was back at it, marching, protesting, distributing leaflets. Her third arrest came in August, when she and two comrades were charged with inciting a crowd to riot after attempting to break into a meeting in Norwich led by a rising young Liberal Party politician, Winston Churchill. Alice quailed at the thought of returning to Holloway, but rumors that the disconcerted authorities were loath to create any more hunger strikers seemed proven true when they were released with a mere warning. A few weeks later when she and several friends were arrested and charged with creating a disturbance after they attempted to interrupt a speech by Colonial Secretary Lord Crewe at St. Andrew's Hall, they took no chances. They forfeited their bail and set out for Scotland, where the authorities were more tolerant of protestors.

In early November, an irresistible opportunity beckoned them back to England: the Lord Mayor's banquet in Guildhall, with all members of the cabinet in attendance. Security was heightened, but despite the vigilance of the patrolling police, Alice, Lucy, and another friend managed to infiltrate the medieval hall, Alice and her companion arriving early disguised as charwomen, Lucy clad in an evening gown and entering with the dignitaries. When they interrupted the prime minister's speech with shouts of "Votes for women!" they were quickly apprehended and hauled away. Sentenced to a month at hard labor, they followed protocol and demanded to be treated as political prisoners, refusing to wear prison uniforms and to eat.

But Alice soon learned that hunger strikes no longer assured suffragists of an early release.

Twice each day, she was wrapped in blankets, hauled from her cell, and dragged off to an interrogation room, where she was held down in a hard chair by the prison's largest and strongest matron, who straddled her waist and pinned back her shoulders. Two other matrons restrained her arms while a doctor stood behind her, held a towel tightly across her throat, pulled her head back with one hand, and forcibly lifted her chin with the other. Then another doctor shoved one end of a rubber tube up her nostril—she shrieked from the pain—and wedged it inside until it reached her stomach. A matron placed a funnel at the other end, and into it poured milk and liquefied food while Alice struggled helplessly. Nauseous, gagging, she thought she might lose consciousness when the tube was roughly removed and she was dragged back to her cell, head reeling, blood, tears, and mucus streaming down her face.

Sometimes the doctors did not insert the tube correctly on the first attempt and had to try again and again, until Alice felt as if they were driving a stake into her head. Over time her nostrils grew inflamed and they had to resort to a smaller tube, but the pain only intensified and her throat spasmed. The matrons taunted her with reports that news of her disgraceful behavior had reached the papers back in the States, and that her heartbroken mother was desperately petitioning the American ambassador, Whitelaw Reid, to secure her release. They mocked her anew when Mr. Reid declared himself unable to intervene. "Miss Paul was given a fair and open trial and awarded the same punishment which has been repeatedly awarded to English subjects for similar offenses," he told one prominent newspaper.

Eventually Alice was permitted to write letters, and her first was to her mother to assure her that all was well, and she ought not to believe the exaggerated reports in the press. The matrons were kind, Alice had plenty of books to read, and she had in fact gained more than two pounds while in prison. But the lies, meant only to reassure, weighed heavily on her Quaker conscience.

Thus she completed her monthlong sentence. On December 9, the Pankhursts met her as she passed through the prison gates and escorted her to a wealthy suffragist's country estate, where she was tenderly nursed back to health. One glance in her bedchamber mirror discouraged her from taking another. At five foot six, she had always been slender and somewhat fragile in appearance, but she had lost at least ten of her usual one hundred pounds, and her once-lustrous black hair with auburn highlights, though swept back neatly into its usual Quaker bun, looked dull and brittle. Her dark eyes framed by dark brows were as intense and serious as ever, but they were strained and shadowed, and seemed much older than her twenty-four years.

After two weeks in her restful retreat, the outward signs of her grueling ordeal had mostly faded. Only then did Alice feel strong enough to write again to her mother and confess the truth about her horrifying incarceration—the pain, the nausea, the fear, the cold, the loneliness. She also shared the news her family had long anxiously awaited: she was coming home.

And now she was nearly there.

With Mr. Stout behind the wheel, the miles passed steadily, and each glimpse of a familiar landmark—the arched iron bridge over the Cooper River, the red brick schoolhouse she had attended as a girl—made Alice's smile broaden, her pulse quicken with happiness.

Then, at last, through a light veil of swirling snow, Paulsdale came into view, a stately white stucco home at the top of a small hill that curved gracefully down to a sweeping front lawn, so familiar and welcoming that Alice's heart nearly burst with gladness to see it. There, she knew, in the days to come, she could rest, recover her strength, and ponder the onerous question that had clouded her skies throughout the Atlantic crossing.

What next?

# 2

# May 1910

## CHICAGO, ILLINOIS

### Ida

Ida studied her reflection in the mirror as she adjusted her black felt hat trimmed with ostrich feathers and mauve silk ribbons. The collar and lapels of her taupe twill striped skirt suit echoed the mauve hue, as did the sash fitted at the natural waist and the double row of buttons down the front of the jacket. When she had the angle of the wide hat brim just right, she stepped back from the full-length mirror and inspected herself ruthlessly from feather plume to hem, which brushed the instep of her polished black leather boots with curved heels. For a moment her attention lingered on her own face—rounded, with large, wide-set brown eyes; a strong, determined jaw with the slightest dimple in the chin; luminous brown skin that belied her nearly forty-eight years; and a keen, unflinching gaze. Satisfied, she allowed her reflection one nod of approval before taking her purse in hand. The press had been invited to the grand opening, and although Ida had absolute confidence in the suitability of her prepared remarks, with photographers present, her appearance too must be equal to the occasion. She would not give the usual cohort of condescending white reporters any cause to ridicule her, not that they ever needed an excuse to belittle a Black woman if the mood struck them.

Leaving her bedroom, she went downstairs and joined her husband in the front parlor, pleased to see how handsome he looked in his best dark gray suit, plum four-in-hand cravat, and new black bowler hat. Tall and slim, with solemn, intelligent, dark brown eyes; high, elegant cheekbones; a well-shaped, full mouth given to kind words; a tall forehead that suggested wisdom; and a short, neatly groomed beard sprinkled with silver, he looked every bit the distinguished lawyer he was and the judge he aspired to be. He had taken the morning off from work to escort her to the grand opening, a show of support that warmed her heart, for an assistant state's attorney's time was a precious commodity indeed.

"You look lovely, my dear," Ferdinand said, bending to kiss her cheek.

"Thank you, honey," she replied, smiling, basking in his affection. "You look quite fine yourself."

It took a strong, confident man not to be intimidated by a strong, fiercely independent woman, and Ida had met her match in Ferdinand Barnett. He was her elder by ten years, born in Nashville to a freewoman and an enslaved blacksmith who had purchased his and his son's freedom before Ferdinand's first birthday. The family had moved to Ontario, Canada, to evade the reach of the Fugitive Slave Acts, whose adherents often did not discriminate between freeborn, emancipated, or formerly enslaved Black folks when choosing whom to capture in free states and sell down South for a profit. After the Civil War, while Ida was growing up in far-off Holly Springs, Mississippi, Ferdinand and his parents had returned to the United States and settled in Chicago. There her future husband had attended high school, graduated from law school, and been admitted to the Illinois bar in 1878, only the third Black man to achieve that distinction. He had practiced law and edited the *Conservator*, a newspaper focused on social justice and equal rights, and in 1896, he had become Illinois's first Black assistant state's attorney. Of all his accomplishments and excellent qualities, however, what Ida appreciated most were those that made him a devoted husband and father.

As Ferdinand helped her with her shawl, the children bounded into the room, breathless and grinning, but they promptly slowed to a more appropriate pace at the sight of their mother's raised eyebrows. The eldest, fourteen-year-old Charles, held his hands behind his back as he approached. "This is for you, Mama," he said, revealing a lovely white gardenia corsage. "Congratulations."

"And best wishes for a great first day," Herman chimed in, one year younger, gesturing proudly to the corsage. "I picked it out. Papa helped."

"How pretty," said Ida, admiring the fragrant flower, which was set amid a cluster of baby's breath and tied with an aubergine ribbon. "Thank you all."

Nine-year-old Ida Junior offered to help her pin the corsage in place on her lapel, while little Alfreda, all of six years old, looked on intently, a tiny furrow appearing between her brows as she scrutinized her sister's work. Mindful of the hour, Ida kissed the children and bade them goodbye, reiterating instructions for Charles to see his younger siblings and himself safely to school. Then she and Ferdinand set out, her arm nestled comfortably in the crook of his, to 2830 South

State Street, where she would cut the ribbon on the front doors of the Negro Fellowship League Reading Room and Social Center.

The first permanent home for the Negro Fellowship League marked an important milestone in the history of the organization for Black men and boys that Ida had founded about two years before. At the time, she was teaching—and still taught—a Bible study class for young men ranging in age from eighteen to thirty; over one hundred were enrolled, with an average attendance of about twenty-five to thirty week to week. Every Sunday—neatly groomed, shoes shined, and wearing their best suits, their dignity and self-respect evident regardless of their station in life—the young men gathered at Grace Presbyterian Church, where Ida led them in a study of a scripture lesson and a discussion of how to apply its truth to their daily lives.

In August 1908, a race riot had erupted in Springfield, Illinois, after a group of white folks vowed to lynch two young Black men accused of assault and murder. The planned lynchings were thwarted when the white men arrived at the prison only to discover that the sheriff had transferred the alleged culprits out of the city for their protection. Enraged, the vigilantes unleashed their fury upon Black neighborhoods. Over three terrifying days and nights, a mob of five thousand white citizens and European immigrants attacked Black families in their homes, murdered them in the streets, and destroyed their businesses and residences. The state militia was called in to subdue the rioting, but even so, at least sixteen were killed, most of them people of color and white folks accused of being Black sympathizers.

As a longtime anti-lynching activist who had written numerous papers on the scourge and had lectured throughout the United States and Great Britain, Ida was no stranger to the horror of mob violence against her people, yet she was shaken to know that this latest outbreak had taken place in the North, in the hometown of the Great Emancipator, Abraham Lincoln, only two hundred miles southwest of her own home. For reasons she could not fully explain, she was especially haunted by the story of an elderly Black resident who had been married to a white woman for more than twenty years. His distraught wife and children had been unable to prevent a group of angry white neighbors from bursting into their home, hauling their beloved patriarch outside, and hanging him in their own front yard.

For days, Ida brooded over her feelings of helpless impotence, which she hated; her apprehension that lynchings could become as commonplace in the Middle

West as they had long been in the Deep South; her frustration that Black folks had no group or organization in place to coordinate a forceful response; and her outrage that no condemnation, no new laws, no response of any kind seemed to be forthcoming from the dithering politicians at the Illinois state capital.

One Sunday, as she walked to Grace Presbyterian Church to teach her class, she had found herself unsettled and angry at the sight of dozens of Black folks parading about in their fine Sunday clothes, carefree and smiling as they enjoyed the summer sunshine, apparently unconcerned about the murderous turmoil unfolding elsewhere in their state. Her emotions spilled over into her lesson, which became a passionate, indignant denunciation of their people's ostensible apathy. "We should be rousing ourselves to see that something like this never happens again," she declared. "We can't allow this unlawful behavior to go unchallenged."

"Yes, ma'am, it's terrible," replied one of the older students as his classmates nodded, "but what can we do about it?"

"You could at least gather together and ask yourselves that question," she countered. "The fact that no one seems concerned is as terrible a thing as the riot itself."

"Our leaders should be taking action," another young man said.

"Indeed they should, but that doesn't absolve you of your responsibilities." Ida's gaze took in the rest of the class. "Or any of you. Don't leave it up to some other designated leader."

"It's not that we don't care," a younger student said, "but we don't even have a place to meet."

"Well, then, I hereby invite you to meet at my home this afternoon," said Ida, "if any of you truly do desire to come together."

Only three of the thirty students who were present to hear the invitation took her up on it, but Ida considered that a promising start. After a long and somber but impassioned discussion, they concluded that they ought to organize a formal group to discuss issues relevant to the Black community, to work out solutions to their common troubles, and to speak with a unified voice when necessary. When one of the students expressed doubts about the feasibility of their plan, Ida urged each of them to bring one additional person to a second meeting in a week's time. At that meeting, Ida assigned the same task to the six young men in attendance, and did the same the following week to the dozen present. Within a few weeks, the organization that would become the Negro Fellowship League had scores of members, a strong foundation, and ambition to grow.

On the whole, Ida found that the young men of the League were ambitious and hardworking, determined to make the most of themselves in a world often set against them. Although they hailed from different parts of the country, most came from good families and many were well educated. Some studied medicine or law by day and earned their keep by working night shifts at various menial jobs.

After months spent in comradeship and theoretical discussion, Ida urged the young men to turn their attention to practical applications, such as the increasing number of young men of color who stumbled or were pushed into Chicago's criminal justice system. Black men had begun to fill prisons in such disproportionate numbers that Ida, increasingly concerned and skeptical, made multiple trips to the Illinois State Penitentiary in Joliet to interview incarcerated men of color. She learned that many of those unfortunates had been newcomers to Chicago, migrants who had fled the oppressive Jim Crow South for the promise of a better future in the North. When they had first arrived in the city, penniless and friendless, with no jobs and no place to call home, they had gravitated to State Street and its saloons and gambling dens, where too many eventually ran afoul of the authorities. The police never lost an opportunity to haul the Black men away and thrust them before unsympathetic juries and merciless judges.

"How differently their lives might have turned out if they had found a warmer welcome in our city," Ida reflected at a meeting of the Negro Fellowship League in her parlor, which could no longer comfortably accommodate the gatherings, though no one complained. "We need to build some sort of lighthouse on State Street, where we can keep watch for these lost newcomers and extend them a helping hand."

"It sounds like a fine idea," said one young man, an aspiring lawyer. "Almost like the YMCA, not that I'd know that from personal experience."

A wry chuckle went up from the group. Ida knew that many of them had tried to cross the thresholds of various branches of the Young Men's Christian Association, only to be promptly shown that they were not welcome.

"Our lighthouse would be more than that," said Ida. "Amid all the temptations of State Street, we could establish a comfortable, up-to-date library and put a consecrated man in charge of it. One of his duties would be to visit the saloons and pool rooms several times a day, distributing cards to the young men he found there and inviting them to the reading room, where they could spend their idle hours in self-improvement. We could provide them with inexpensive meals and lodgings, and help them find work. Think of how meaningful this assistance would be, how much it would help these young men find their footing before they go too far down the wrong path."

"I agree that the need is great," one of the longtime members said, "but how would we pay for this sanctuary?" He glanced around the room for confirmation as murmurs of reluctant agreement rose. "We don't have that kind of money."

"We wouldn't have to do everything at once," Ida pointed out. "We could start with the reading room and grow from there." Judging from their expressions that they were warming to the idea, she added, "If you can find the right man to run our center—and I'd strongly recommend a young minister—I'm confident that I could raise the money."

The consensus was that they should proceed.

Over the course of several months, Ida found a wealthy benefactor who agreed to pay the rent, operating expenses, and director's salary for one year, after which Ida intended for the center to be self-sustaining. She located a suitable building for rent on South State Street and signed the lease, over the objections of some members who believed the neighborhood was unsavory and beneath their dignity. "Where else should we be," countered Ida, "but where the need is greatest?"

She knew from firsthand experience that people could not always get to the places where they could find education, guidance, and all the other things folks needed to climb out of poverty and improve their lives. Often, even the distance of a mile or two was too vast to cross, and the resources had to be brought to the people who needed them, where they were. From the time Ida was quite young, she had seen how bridging that gap often meant the difference between struggle and success.

Like Ferdinand, Ida had been born into slavery—in Holly Springs in July 1862—but unlike her husband, she had lived as a slave until slavery's end. Her father, Jim, had been born on a plantation in Tippah County, the son of the master and one of the women he enslaved, Peggy. Mr. Wells and his wife, whom the enslaved called Miss Polly, had no children, so Mr. Wells directed his paternal attention toward his firstborn son, perhaps even loving him, in his way. Although Miss Polly was considerably less fond of Jim, he was spared the worst of slavery's cruelties, and was never beaten or threatened with the auction block.

As the years passed, Jim became his father's most trusted companion. When he was eighteen, Mr. Wells apprenticed him to Spires Boling, a master builder and architect, to train as a carpenter. Mr. Boling enslaved nine people on his Holly Springs estate, in a home he himself had designed, a white two-story Greek Revival residence with five bays and octagonal columns on the portico. His enslaved staff included a gifted cook, Elizabeth Warrenton, born in Virginia to an enslaved mother and, so she had been told, a freeborn half-Indian father. Lizzie was still very young when she and two of her sisters had been sold to slave traders and taken to Mississippi, where they had been auctioned off to three different masters. Lizzie was a devout Christian, and she had memorized so many Bible verses from hearing them at services that maybe she didn't really need to be able to read the scriptures, but she longed to nonetheless.

In time, the carpenter and the cook fell in love and married in the manner of their people, and married again at the courthouse when freedom came. After the war Mr. Boling urged his skilled apprentice to stay on as a tenant and paid employee, an agreement Jim kept until they had a falling-out two years later, when Ida was five years old. By that time, Black men had been granted the vote, and Mr. Boling adamantly insisted that Jim vote as he himself did. Jim refused. He went off to the polls to cast his ballot as he saw fit, and when he returned, he found himself locked out of the carpentry shop. Rather than beg his employer for forgiveness, Jim bought a new set of tools, rented the house across the street, settled his young family into it, and opened his own carpentry business, never again to call any man boss or master.

From a very early age, Ida and her siblings understood that their duty was to go to school and learn all they could, the better to make something of themselves when they were grown. A year after the war, the Freedmen's Aid Society had established Shaw University, a school for colored folks only a few blocks from their home. Ida's father was one of the trustees, and all the Wells children attended as soon as they were old enough. Ida's mother did too, so she could at last learn to read her beloved Bible. Lizzie was a loving mother but a strict disciplinarian, enforcing Sunday School attendance and devotions on the Sabbath and assigning chores around the house, tasks the children were expected to perform promptly and to perfection. Sometimes she would tell them about the beatings and hunger she had endured in slave times, and of the perpetual loneliness of not knowing where her people were or how to find them. As harrowing as her stories were, Ida always had the sense that her mother was holding back the worst of it.

In contrast, Ida's father confided little about his slavery years, except to explain his parentage. Perhaps he thought his children were too young to understand. Perhaps he thought his wife's stories were enough, especially since the children only had to look across the street to the Boling residence to see where much of his history had unfolded.

A single incident was burned into Ida's memory, one scene from which to extrapolate and reconstruct her father's first thirty years. Ida was ten years old when her father's mother, Peggy, came to Holly Springs for her annual visit. Peggy and her husband had acquired a sizable plot of land during Reconstruction, and every year after the harvest, they brought their corn and cotton to market. Peggy also brought small gifts for her grandchildren, and sausages and cured meats from the season's hog butchering for her son and daughter-in-law.

One afternoon, Ida was studying her history schoolbook in the shade of a tree when she overheard her father and grandmother speaking as they strolled nearby, unaware of her presence. "Jim," her grandmother said, "Miss Polly wants you to come and bring the children. She wants to see them."

"Mother, I never want to see that old woman as long as I live," he replied, a sting of venom in his voice. "I'll never forget how she had you stripped and whipped the day after the old man died. I guess it's fine if you choose to take care of her and forgive her for what she did to you, but if it had been up to me, she would have starved to death."

Ida froze, thunderstruck, hoping they would say more, but they had walked beyond her hearing. She was not too young to not understand that the old man—the white grandfather she had never met—had taken her grandmother without her consent, as masters had always done in slavery days. She also understood that Miss Polly could not punish her husband for straying, so she had taken her revenge on the unwilling woman, although Miss Polly had been obliged to wait until after his death to do it.

Ida trembled with rage whenever she recalled that accidental glimpse into her grandmother's past, which she did every time Peggy came to visit, or when Ida, as the eldest grandchild, was permitted to visit her grandparents' farm on her own. Through the years the temptation to ask about Miss Polly's hateful vengeance grew, but so too did Ida's awareness that there were some things the younger generation could not ask their elders, secrets too painful and shattering to share.

In the years that had passed since then, from time to time Ida would find reason to pause and wonder how dif-

ferently her life might have unfolded if the Freedmen's
Aid Society had not established Shaw University—now
a thriving college called Rust University—a few blocks
from the family's home. Would she have acquired an
education in some other way? Perhaps, since her parents had so avidly wanted schooling for their children,
but their education would have been far more difficult
to come by and almost certainly would have been delayed.

The young men who would benefit from the Negro
Fellowship League Reading Room and Social Center
had never lived a day enslaved, but that did not mean
they enjoyed full freedom and equality. Lynching
thrived throughout the South and increasingly elsewhere, an insidious and terrible scourge wielded to
assert white supremacy. Disgraceful state voting laws
made a mockery of the Fourteenth and Fifteenth
Amendments, abridging the rights of Black men, American citizens, by denying them the vote and depriving
them of life, liberty, and property without due process
of law.

Disenfranchisement and lynching were white supremacy's cudgel and scythe. To colored folks, education, organization, strength of numbers, and the vote
were both shield and sword, and Ida would do all she
could to arm her people.

# 3
# March 1912

## Maud

Maud Malone often mused that she learned more about the disparity between privilege and poverty in New York City by walking from her home on West Sixty-Ninth Street to her job on the Lower East Side than from all the books written on the subject—and that was no small thing, for she was a librarian and knew every relevant book worth reading.

Five days a week, she glimpsed millionaires' pampered wives draped in furs and silks and jewels emerging from storied mansions and gliding gracefully into luxurious automobiles, with drivers, maids, and doormen attending to their every need. She noted clerks in suits, shopgirls in smart dresses, and tradesmen in overalls hurrying eagerly to work on some mornings, trudging resignedly on others. She observed thin, hollow-eyed mothers in threadbare, made-over dresses studying a grocer's wares with poorly concealed worry and despair, empty market baskets dangling from the crook of an elbow. Other women gathered on stoops gossiping with friends, keeping watchful eyes on packs of children—hair tousled, faces smudged, noses running, clothes patched and repatched—as they played and jumped and shouted on the sidewalks and in the gutters, momentarily forgetting their empty bellies or absent fathers. In a few years, how many of those children would be toiling in sweatshops or stuck inside squalid, fetid tenements laboring over piecework, all to keep bread on the table and coal in the scuttle one day more?

New York City fairly overflowed with abundance, but wealth and opportunity alike were so appallingly, cruelly, lopsidedly distributed that it defied understanding. As for herself, Maud was certain that even if she sank into the most comfortable featherbed, her belly stuffed with the finest quail and wine and cake, she would never be able to sleep at night knowing that she had spent the day overindulging every appetite while others scrounged for crumbs and shivered in the cold.

Not that Maud was in any danger of suffering from excessive wealth. Her own apartment at 231 West Sixty-Ninth Street was comfortable enough, a rare jewel of an affordable two-room flat incongruously tucked away in a neighborhood of lovely town houses well beyond her means. Her librarian's salary was just enough to cover her rent, utilities, and food for herself and her two cats, Scylla and Charybdis, and the occasional night at the theater or a first edition of a beloved classic novel.

Yet for all its cozy simplicity, her apartment was the grandest place she had ever called home. Her elder siblings pursued more lucrative careers and enjoyed more gracious residences, but none of the five living Malone siblings ever forgot that they had grown up in one small, overcrowded rowhouse on South Second Street in Brooklyn. Their late father, an Irish immigrant, had been a doctor; their late uncle had been a beloved neighborhood priest and longtime rector of Saints Peter and Paul Parish. The two brothers had received classical educations back in Ireland, and after immigrating to the United States, both had toiled in their own ways to improve the lives of their less fortunate neighbors, eventually founding the New York Anti-Poverty Society to promote social justice and social change. It was little wonder that the Malone children, sons and daughters alike, had been encouraged to pursue their educations and had chosen careers that served the public good—lawyers, doctors, government workers, and one strong-willed, indisputably independent librarian.

One who would arrive ten minutes early for work that day, Maud noted with satisfaction, glancing at her watch as she took a shortcut through Seward Park. She would be punctual despite a delay crossing Houston at Bowery, slowed by a crowd that had gathered to gawk at a horse-drawn-wagon-versus-automobile collision. Thankfully, the horse had apparently suffered no harm, but the same could not be said for the delivery wagon, which had lost a wheel and had spilled a dozen or more sacks of flour and cornmeal into the street. While the drivers argued, Maud observed a trio of scrawny urchins stealthily heft a twenty-five-pound sack of flour from the gutter and spirit it away. It occurred to Maud only after she crossed the street and had moved on that she probably should have shouted a warning to the grocer instead of admiring the thieves' pluck. If the boys had not looked so undernourished, perhaps she would have.

When the Seward Park Library—*her* library—came into view, she felt her mouth curving into a smile, the pangs of her guilty conscience fading. The four-story, red brick Renaissance Revival building, one of sixty-five branches of the New York Public Library founded by the impossibly wealthy industrialist Andrew Carnegie, had become almost a second home to her since it had opened two and a half years before, and she adored its every elegant detail and unexpected quirk. The high ceilings, the curved windows, the abundant stacks, the warren of offices, the busy repair and restoration workshops—nearly every space held a fond memory of books discovered, readers inspired, useful work accomplished, or engrossing conversations shared.

She entered through the employees' entrance off the alley, slipped out of her coat, and stopped by the staff lounge for a cup of coffee, where she found her good friend Anne on her way out. Tall and slender, with chestnut brown hair and a thin, patrician nose, the senior reference librarian usually wore smart dress suits on a spectrum of dove gray to black, accessorized by a single item in a vivid primary color; today it was a brilliant red silk scarf draped around her neck and tied in a stylish bow on her left shoulder. "Good morning, Maud," Anne greeted her. "Will you be joining the girls for bridge tonight?"

"I can't," said Maud, sipping her coffee. "I hate to miss the fun, but I have a meeting."

"You don't say." Anne crossed her arms and regarded Maud knowingly. "This wouldn't be a date with Colonel Roosevelt, would it?"

"What better way to celebrate the eve of the primary?" Maud replied, a hint of mischief in her voice. "He's speaking at six different venues along the East Side of Manhattan and the Bronx this evening, from Apollo Hall all the way to Niblo's Garden. How could I miss such an ambitious spectacle?"

Anne's eyebrows rose. "Are you planning to chase him from one speech to the next?"

"That's tempting, but no. I'll catch up with him at the fourth stop, the New Star Casino." Maud glanced at her watch and saw that she had two minutes to leave her coat and satchel at her desk before she was due at the staff meeting. "You should come with me. It'll be a lark. We can play cards next week."

Anne winced. "My husband wouldn't like it."

Maud wasn't surprised. Anne's husband was an amiable fellow, but he barely tolerated that his wife had kept her job after they married. Overt public displays of suffragist sympathies would be simply too much for him. "The invitation stands if you change your mind," Maud said nonetheless, with a shrug and a smile as she hastened away.

Sometimes—though Maud would admit it to no one but her elder sister—she longed for a bit of romance, a handsome fellow who might admire her, bring her gifts of books and flowers, and take her out to dinner. More often, though, she counted herself lucky that she didn't have to answer to a husband as her married friends did. Have oatmeal and blueberries for supper—why not? Sleep in on a Saturday morning despite household chores beckoning—sure thing! Spend a few minutes of a Monday evening querying a former president and current Republican primary candidate about his views on woman suffrage? Absolutely. Maud had her friends and family for companionship, her cats for adorable dependents, her own income and interests, and the freedom to do as she pleased. She simply could not imagine sacrificing any of that for a man, although she supposed the right man would not expect it of her. Maybe such a man would wander into the Seward Park Library someday and become immediately smitten with her Irish lilt, charming dimple, and deft hand at shelving books, but she wasn't about to put her life on hold until he appeared.

No indeed—she had too much to do. In addition to her career, for more than a decade she had been a devoted suffragist—a "militant suffragette librarian," as one newspaper had called her disparagingly. What a misnomer! There was nothing martial about her demeanor except that she enjoyed marching and gathering like-minded people together to work for a common goal. Was that militant? She hardly thought so.

Yet as any soldier would, she understood the power of numbers and organization. About five years before, she had founded the Harlem Equal Rights League, a woman suffrage organization composed of radical working people, and as its president she had led vigorous campaigns not only in Manhattan but throughout the Five Boroughs. Taking her cues from British suffragettes, one bitterly cold afternoon in December 1907 she had led the first open-air suffrage meeting in the United States, a series of speeches by prominent American and English women activists in front of the Metropolitan Life building on Madison Square. The *New-York Tribune* had called them "Female Revolutionists"—not unkindly—and afterward had declared, "The first gun in the warfare of the American suffragettes for the possession of the ballot was fired" that day.

Such warlike imagery for what had been a cheerful, spirited, good-natured event! Maud understood well that to win over her audience, she must not hector them, but draw them in with humor and amusing banter. She never flinched when skeptical men interrupted her with criticism and jeers, for she could always turn their words to her advantage.

"The place for women is in the home and to cook the dinner," one man had shouted that day in a thick German accent.

"She can get his dinner better if she knows he had good wages to provide it," Maud had replied. "For the sake of her family, she will vote for sensible representatives who will create jobs with good wages. Besides, a woman can't spend *all* her time preparing dinners. Nor is all the cooking done by women. Look at the hotels and restaurants around here where cooking is done by men."

"You tell 'em, Miss Malone!" a woman had cried out, sparking applause.

"And please do explain how voting will keep women away from home all day, every day." Maud spread her arms, indicating the many men in the audience. "You all have the vote, and yet that hasn't kept you from your jobs or your homes. Not one of you is obliged to loiter about his polling place except for a few minutes on Election Day. Why should it be different for women?"

"Do women know enough about politics to vote?" a young blond man called out.

"Women know as much as men."

"How do you know?"

"Why, I can tell by looking into your faces," Maud had retorted with a teasing smile, prompting laughter from the crowd. "Perhaps women know *more* than men. If you men know politics so well, why did you choose the men in power right now in Albany?"

"We won't choose all of 'em next time," a man had assured her loudly, and another rumble of laughter had gone up from the crowd.

No, Maud did not mind at all when men questioned and even challenged her. She knew that winning over the men was crucial to the movement's success, as necessary as inspiring the women. In New York, men alone had the ballot, and they alone could vote to extend that right to the other half of the population. She appreciated those who joined woman suffrage organizations and attended suffrage meetings, but their hearts and minds were already won. Only by going out to speak on street corners and in public squares could Maud hope to reach all those other multitudes of men who held the fate of equal suffrage in their hands.

Less than two months after her first open-air meeting, Maud had organized a suffrage parade, the first in the United States. Although the police department had refused to grant them a permit, on February 16, 1908, two hundred suffragists had met at Union Square wearing sturdy shoes and warm coats. But as the band had tuned their instruments and the marchers unfurled banners, Police Inspector Moses Cortright had approached Maud and her special guest, the German-born British suffragette Mrs. Bettina Borrmann Wells, and reminded them that if they proceeded with their march without a permit, they would violate the Criminal Code.

Maud had offered her most charming, eloquent pleas, but although his expression had grown less stony, the police inspector had insisted that he was powerless to grant them permission to demonstrate. "I must insist that you move along," he had said gruffly, waving an arm toward Broadway, their intended parade route. "Move along, quietly."

Maud and Mrs. Wells had exchanged a look. "May we still hold our rally inside the Manhattan Trade School?" Maud had asked. "We already obtained their permission, in case of bad weather."

"There's no law against an indoor meeting on private property," the officer had acknowledged, "as long as you observe the fire codes."

Satisfied, Maud had hurried to the grandstand, where she had called for attention and announced that there would be no parade and no open-air meeting after all. When a chorus of dismay rose from the crowd, Maud had shaken her head and raised her hands to quiet them. "A protest against the disenfranchisement of women will be held at once in the Manhattan

Trade School on East Twenty-Third, and all are invited to attend," she had announced. "Please put away your banners and pack up your instruments. We've been ordered to move along quietly, and so we shall—but as a single group, traveling in the same direction."

A ripple of laughter and cheers had passed through the crowd as understanding dawned—they would march their parade straight through a loophole. Maud, Mrs. Wells, and a few other dignitaries had taken their places at the front of the throng, and then, in neat, orderly rows, the women had walked up Broadway toward Twenty-Third Street. They had sung no songs and chanted no slogans, but their ubiquitous yellow "Votes for Women" badges and an occasional green, purple, and white striped sash made their purpose perfectly evident. Their voices had never risen above conversational tones punctuated by the occasional burst of laughter. Police posted along the route had watched them from the sidewalks and had let them pass unimpeded, some even nodding courteously when the marchers smiled and waved. At each major square and intersection, more onlookers had joined the parade, and by the time they reached Madison Square, they had numbered several thousand strong.

Once inside the Manhattan Trade School, the marchers' enthusiasm had burst forth into glad shouts and proud cheers. Each speaker had roused their spirits to greater heights, until the hall had seemed to shake from the fervor of their applause. Afterward, a collection taken up for the cause exceeded all expectations. Thus the unofficial parade had officially been a resounding success, inspiring Maud to expand her endeavors.

For ten days in May 1908, she had traveled by trolley with Harriot Stanton Blatch, daughter of the pioneering suffragist Elizabeth Cady Stanton and founder of the Equality League of Self-Supporting Women, to instruct her in the art of peaceful public protest. In early 1909, Maud had begun an intermittent series of solo protests in Albany, taking the train to the state capital whenever her obligations to the library and the Harlem Equal Rights League permitted. In fair weather and foul, she had paraded around the capitol building carrying a bright yellow banner proclaiming VOTES FOR WOMEN. She had handed out literature and engaged passersby in conversation and debate for as long as they were willing.

She had also reached out to the public via the press. Through the years she had written countless letters to the editors of the major New York papers to advocate for woman suffrage. A few months ago, when she began a campaign of interrupting politicians' speeches, her letters had focused on explaining why she was so determined to get the candidates on the record regarding woman suffrage, even if it meant appearing rude or unladylike. She didn't consider her pointed queries disruptive, but rather essential to a fair democratic process. Didn't voters deserve to know the presidential candidates' positions before they cast their ballots? Shouldn't all citizens be concerned when candidates dodged their questions?

Maud thought so, and she had to believe she wasn't alone.

The day passed swiftly in a pleasant hum of productive work and cordial encounters with coworkers and patrons. At five o'clock, Maud hurried home for a quick supper, freshened up, straightened her yellow suffrage badge on the lapel of her plum suit jacket, and set out for her date with Colonel Roosevelt at the New Star Casino on East 107th Street in Harlem.

She knew that the fate of the former president's attempt to win a third term after a four-year hiatus depended upon securing the Republican Party nomination, and *that* depended upon his success in the next day's New York State primary. Unfortunately for him, the incumbent president, William Taft, his successor, had a vast lead in the delegate count over both Roosevelt and the progressive Robert La Follette. Since La

Follette was sure to win his home state of Wisconsin the following week, Maud agreed with most political observers that Colonel Roosevelt must take New York if he had any hope of surviving the primaries.

Twenty minutes before the candidate was due to take the stage, Maud slipped into the grand hall of the New Star Casino, where about four hundred other men and women had already found seats. Claiming a chair in the third-to-last row on the aisle, she settled in expectantly, exchanging smiles and nods and pleasantries with her nearest neighbors. The room smelled of hair tonic, perspiration, and oil smoke, and it was just a trifle too warm for comfort. Onstage, several important-looking men conversed as they awaited the guest of honor, glancing toward the wings now and then as the minutes ticked by. Maud could have spent the interval rehearsing what she intended to say, but there was no need. All she intended was to ask a very simple question, one that any qualified politician should be able to answer.

There was a sudden bustle of activity just offstage, a swift but laudatory introduction, and then Colonel Roosevelt himself strode to the podium. The hall erupted in applause and cheers. He looked exactly like his photos, Maud thought as she clapped politely. His expression was fixed and determined as he nodded this way and that to acknowledge the warm reception.

His light brown mustache curved in a rough crescent above his firm mouth, and his pince-nez glasses seemed well anchored in place. He raised his hands for silence, thanked his hosts, and with little preamble launched into a humorous but pointed critique of the absurd primary laws that he seemed to believe had been designed specifically to thwart his campaign. Several of the important-looking men onstage were required to help him unfurl the fourteen-foot-long ballot—unmistakable proof, he declared, of the law's encumbrances upon the right of the people to rule themselves. The audience laughed and murmured at the sight, incredulous, but as their mirth subsided, Roosevelt warned, "Never forget, it's your right to vote they're interfering with."

Maud knew her moment had come. "How about women and their right to vote, Mr. Roosevelt?" she called out, stepping into the aisle and moving to the center of the hall. A familiar chorus of catcalls, hisses, and shouts rose up all around her, but Maud kept her eyes fixed on the former president.

Colonel Roosevelt raised his hands for silence. "Madam," he said courteously, "I believe that you women should be allowed to vote to determine whether or not you shall have your suffrage."

Something light struck Maud in the back of the head; she realized it was only a ball of crumpled paper when it rolled past her feet down the aisle. She had endured worse. So Roosevelt believed women should be allowed to vote to determine whether they could have the vote? That was a reply devoid of an answer if she had ever heard one. How would such a vote have any legal standing? What would he do about woman suffrage if he became president? "Mr. Roosevelt," she said again, her voice carrying clearly above the din, "do you believe women have the right to vote?"

The audience groaned and muttered disapproval. Other paper missiles flew and struck their mark, but Maud held her ground.

"Sit down," one of the dignified-looking men shrilled, spittle flying, looking quite a bit less dignified as he strode to the edge of the stage, shaking his finger at her.

"You've promised the people a square deal, Mr. Roosevelt," she reminded the former president, raising her voice to be heard. "This is no square deal for women."

Men bolted to their feet, outraged. Shouts and jeers and curses broke out, thunderous.

"Let me handle this," Roosevelt shouted, looking around the hall, waving his arms, scowling. "Sit down! Sit down! Sit down!"

The first two commands were directed to the audience, the last to Maud alone. No one obeyed.

Suddenly Maud felt hands seize her shoulders roughly from behind; twisting about, she glimpsed a gray policeman's uniform and an angry scowl. The officer dragged her down the aisle and tried to force her back into her seat, but when she would not submit, he grabbed her around the waist and wrestled her toward the double doors of the entrance.

"Be quiet, all of you," she heard Roosevelt say as she was propelled out of the hall and into the lobby, still struggling to free herself. "That was probably a put-up job on the part of the opposition. They've singled me out for attack, but they won't prevail!"

The doors swung shut behind Maud and the officer, muffling the crowd's earsplitting roar of approval.

"You're lucky I don't arrest you," the officer gritted through clenched teeth as he dragged Maud to the exit and shoved her outside to the sidewalk. "This was no way for a lady to behave. What do you have to say for yourself?"

Panting, Maud straightened her suit jacket, tucked loose locks of hair behind her ears, and adjusted her hat. "Which way to the next hall?" she retorted.

Glowering, the officer slammed the door shut.

Maud rested her hands on her hips and caught her breath, pondering the closed door. It would avail her little to storm this same bastion again tonight, and Roosevelt's entourage would be keeping watch for her at the Lenox Assembly Rooms and the other remaining stops on the tour. Her taunt for the officer who had ejected her notwithstanding, she would call it a night. She had made her point. Candidate Roosevelt was unlikely to forget her, or her demand for answers.

She would have a few new bruises in the morning, but no regrets. Insults about her so-called unladylike behavior would not discourage her. She was absolutely resolved to continue putting her questions to all the men who wanted to govern her without her consent. Until she had a voice in this democracy, she would persist, let the consequences fall upon her as they may.

# 4

# June–July 1912

## PHILADELPHIA AND NEW YORK CITY

### Alice

Two weeks after defending her doctoral dissertation and receiving her Ph.D. in sociology from the University of Pennsylvania, Alice accepted an invitation to lunch with one of her professors, Dr. Carl Kelsey. At forty-one, he was the youngest full professor in the department, and during Alice's two years at Penn, she had found him especially encouraging and generous to graduate students like herself.

"I must congratulate you on your excellent examination," he said after they perused the menus and placed their orders. "It was beyond question one of the best I've ever seen."

"Thank you, Dr. Kelsey," said Alice, pleasantly surprised. She had become unaccustomed to praise, considering that the campus was full of equally brilliant young scholars and that some gray-bearded professors barely acknowledged that she, a mere woman, was in the room. "The work was a pleasure, since I find the subject so compelling. The history of women's legal status in the United States, and in Pennsylvania in particular, has interested me ever since I was studying social work at Swarthmore."

"Your many years of toil have certainly borne fruit," the professor replied, smiling. "May I ask what your plans for the fall term are? Are you in line for an assistant professorship anywhere?"

His tone was so hopeful that Alice hated to disappoint him. "I've considered pursuing an academic career," she admitted, trying to keep her smile in place, "but I haven't found a suitable faculty position anywhere."

It would have been more accurate to say that she had inquired with many colleges and universities throughout New England and the mid-Atlantic region, but her letters had yielded only a handful of polite rejections and not a single interview. But although academia had not beckoned, she had received several intriguing offers from suffrage organizations. Harriot Stanton Blatch had asked her to become the first paid organizer for the suffrage group she had founded, recently renamed the Women's Political Union. The Ohio Woman Suffrage Association wanted her to lead their campaign for a state constitutional amendment granting women the right to vote, an effort they promised would be exciting, challenging, and, with Alice at the helm, inevitably triumphant. Only yesterday, a member of the executive committee of the National American Woman Suffrage Association—NAWSA, or "the National," as it was more familiarly known—had promised her complete autonomy if she took charge of organizing their open-air meetings. The most tempting offer had come from the Pennsylvania Woman Suffrage Association. The National would gather for its annual convention in Philadelphia in November, and to welcome the delegates from around the country, the state's suffrage leaders hoped to put on a grand parade to rival those Mrs. Blatch staged every spring in New York City. Since Alice had acquired a reputation as an inventive, capable, tireless organizer, they believed she was the ideal person to take charge of the event.

Alice thought a parade was a marvelous idea, and she was pleased that Mrs. Dora Lewis herself had written to offer her the job. The wealthy, widowed Philadelphia activist had been involved in causes from prison reform to the shirtwaist strikes, and she was renowned for her unfailing commitment to women's rights and the labor movement. Alice had met her a few months after her return from abroad, when she had joined the Philadelphia Equal Franchise Society. She and Dora had become better acquainted in the summer of 1911, when Alice and her comrade Lucy Burns had come to Philadelphia in hopes of energizing the city's timid suffrage movement. From July through September, Alice and Lucy had directed Philadelphia's first open-air suffrage meetings, had led overnight sorties to chalk suffrage slogans on sidewalks throughout the city, and—the pinnacle of their summer campaign—had organized a glorious rally on Independence Square. On the last day of September, before a crowd of more than two thousand eager, cheering spectators, eighteen renowned suffragists had proclaimed woman's inalienable right to vote from five stages bedecked in red, white, and blue bunting and flowers. Among the illustrious speakers were Alice herself; Dr. Anna Shaw, president of the National; and Inez Milholland, the famously wealthy, beautiful, and popular activist, a Vassar alumna and the first woman graduate of the New York University School of Law.

Dora Lewis had participated in many of the events of the summer campaign, and in the brief time they had been acquainted, Alice had come to admire and respect her boundless energy and moral courage. The thought of resuming their partnership by accepting the post with the Pennsylvania Woman Suffrage Association appealed to Alice very much. She had been on the verge of accepting the position when, after an exchange of letters describing her preliminary ideas for the convention parade, the National had rejected her suggestion to include floats. The executive board had offered no explanation for their ruling, which to Alice had seemed wholly arbitrary; floats would not violate any local ordinances or create any logistical snarls that she could not untangle. Dora had promised to appeal to the board, but when the officers proved intractable, Alice's interest in the job had waned. The idea of organizing a half-hearted, diminished parade had held no appeal for her, nor had she relished the thought of enduring any ongoing overreach and interference from the National, a wholly separate entity. Yes, it was the National's convention, but it was the PWSA's parade, and they ought to be free to arrange it as they saw fit. If Alice were the director, she could not imagine running things any other way.

Although Dora was the chair of the committee arranging the convention, she had been powerless to veto the National's decision, but she had tried valiantly to persuade Alice to take the job despite her misgivings.

"If we can't have floats, we could try and make up for that deprivation by having plenty of music, don't you think?" Dora had cajoled in a heartfelt letter. "Banners could be a very affecting substitute. We need the parade, and you are the one person to manage it."

Alice enjoyed praise as much as the next person, but her love of truth and her Quaker humility would not allow her to believe that she was irreplaceable. She also could not agree that banners, which were inevitably smaller and simpler, were as striking and effective as floats. In the end, reluctant to disappoint an activist she so admired but unable to compromise her artistic ideals and rhetorical vision, Alice had declined the job.

But that left Dr. Kelsey's question unanswered. Alice's heart's desire was to devote herself to the suffrage cause, but what role she would take and what path she would follow remained indistinct.

Contemplating Dora Lewis's proposal had evoked warm memories of that exciting summer in Philadelphia, and Alice found herself revisiting them again and again. Until that momentous season, the city's suffragists had never attempted so bold a campaign. Even as the summer had waned, and the days had grown shorter and the leaves had begun to turn, the women's excitement and ambition had caught fire, fed by the fresh winds of success.

Yet to Alice, one year later, those flames seemed more like smoldering embers. From the frequent letters they exchanged, she knew Lucy felt the same. As pleased as they were with the rekindled energy of suffrage groups in Philadelphia, New York, and elsewhere, tangible progress trudged along with unbearable slowness.

"I would admire the National's single-minded commitment to separate campaigns to amend individual state constitutions if it didn't blind them to other possibilities," Lucy wrote one summer day. "Can't they see that the process is difficult in some states and virtually impossible in others?"

Alice wholeheartedly agreed. Amendment laws varied from state to state, but as she lamented to Lucy, they were all maddeningly tortuous, with requirements for referenda and legislative approval and high voter majorities for passage. Some states also imposed unreasonable punishments for measures that failed. One particularly vexing law, enforced in seven states, prescribed that if an amendment did not pass, it could not be proposed again for up to ten years, which required suffragists to determine the timing of their campaigns very carefully. If they misjudged the temperament of the voters and pushed for an amendment too soon, they could set back their state's movement a decade. If they waited until everything fell into place and victory was certain, they might wait forever.

By the time Alice had finished writing her dissertation, she and Lucy had concluded that equal suffrage would never become the law of the land unless suffragists abandoned their attempts to win the vote state by state and instead focused on passing a federal constitutional amendment.

It wasn't an outlandish concept; it wasn't even original. A federal amendment stating that the right of citizens of the United States to vote must not be denied on account of sex had been proposed as far back as 1878. Suffragists of the era had referred to the measure optimistically as the Sixteenth Amendment, but so much time had passed that an entirely different amendment with that designation had been passed by Congress in 1909. It was still awaiting ratification, as was the Seventeenth Amendment, passed earlier in 1912. Perhaps, Alice dared hope, the woman suffrage amendment could become the Eighteenth Amendment, or the Nineteenth.

She knew that the only way to hasten that glorious day would be to marshal the resources of the major national suffrage organizations—which meant persuading their stubborn, skeptical leaders.

Two weeks after her luncheon with Dr. Kelsey,

Alice was no closer to landing a job, but she at least had made plans for her immediate future. She and Lucy had agreed to meet in Manhattan to call on Mrs. Mary Ware Dennett, the secretary and administrator of the National. If they could convince her to approve a reinvigorated campaign for a federal amendment, they could more easily win the support of the organization's other leaders, who controlled access to essential resources and influence.

Early on the morning of July 15, Alice boarded the train to Manhattan and spent the ride looking over her notes and silently rehearsing her appeals. Lucy, who had a much shorter journey from her home on Long Island, met her at the station. As Alice descended from the train, she easily found her longtime comrade waiting on the platform, her striking red hair setting her apart from the crowd.

Lucy's face brightened as she caught Alice's eye, and she quickly made her way through the crowded platform to join Alice as she disembarked. "Good morning, Miss Paul," said Lucy, smiling. She wore a pale green walking suit trimmed in maroon ribbon, with a band of the same hue adorning her tan felt hat. Alice's own attire was in the more subdued shades of dove gray with lavender trim, a preference born of her Quaker upbringing.

"Good morning," replied Alice, checking her watch to be sure that it was indeed still morning. "Goodness, it's later than I thought. Mrs. Dennett agreed to see us at noon?"

"Yes, and if we walk briskly, we'll make it to her office with minutes to spare." Lucy indicated the direction with a tilt of her head, and they set off side by side, their strides nearly matching despite their difference in height. The National's headquarters were in a posh suite of offices on Fifth Avenue, paid for by a wealthy benefactress, Mrs. Alva Belmont. After divorcing the immeasurably wealthy William K. Vanderbilt, a scandal that had rocked New York society, she had married Mr. Oliver Belmont, a wealthy banker and former U.S. congressman. After his death in 1908, Mrs. Belmont had devoted herself to charitable works and noble causes, including woman suffrage. She was a life member of the National, and in addition to paying the rent for their headquarters, she also sponsored the organization's press bureau, which kept their mission— and her own name—in the headlines. She would be an important ally, if Alice could meet her and win her over.

As they walked along, Alice and Lucy discussed strategy, which points to emphasize and which were unlikely to make a favorable impression. "Perhaps we should have brought gifts to charm Mrs. Dennett," Alice suddenly realized, too late to do anything about it. "Flowers for her, a box of cigars for her husband—"

With a gasp, Lucy abruptly seized her arm and brought them both to a halt. "When Mrs. Dennett greets us, it would be best if we didn't mention Mr. Dennett," she warned. "Don't ask after his health, or express hope that he is well, or any of that."

"Why not? Is there no Mr. Dennett?" Perhaps the National's secretary had adopted the title of "missus" as an honorific, which was not unheard of for unmarried women of a certain age.

Lucy shook her head. "There is a Mr. Dennett, but Mrs. Dennett might very well wish there weren't. She and her husband are estranged due to his affection for another woman."

"Oh, goodness."

"Yes, that'll do it, won't it? Mr. Dennett is an architect, but Mrs. Dennett is an accomplished artist and designer in her own right," Lucy explained as they continued on their way. "She cofounded her husband's architecture and interior design firm, although he gets all the credit. A few years ago—1908 or 1909, I think— while Mr. Dennett was working on a house for a certain Dr. and Mrs. Lincoln Chase, he and Mrs. Chase fell madly in love. When Mrs. Dennett discovered the affair, she wrote Mrs. Chase a heartfelt letter pleading with her, as a wife and mother herself, to end the relationship, but Mrs. Chase adamantly refused. Soon after that, Mr. Dennett moved out of the family home and moved in with his lover and her husband."

Incredulous, Alice paused before the elegant front entrance of the National's building, all rusticated blocks of stone in the neoclassical style. "He didn't."

"Oh, yes, he did."

When the doorman opened the door for them, Alice gestured for Lucy to precede her into the lobby. "And Mr. Chase didn't protest?"

"On the contrary, he seems to have taken it in stride. Apparently the three of them have been living happily together all these years as a ménage à trois. They've been rather frank about it in the press, and it's quite the scandal." Lucy lowered her voice. "Especially now that Mrs. Dennett has sued for divorce."

"The poor woman." Alice sighed and shook her head as they continued across the lobby. "It's unfair how her reputation will suffer for this, although she did nothing wrong. You said the Dennetts have children?"

They stepped into the elevator. Lucy gave the attendant the number of their floor, and with a jerk and a clatter of metal, they began to rise. "Two children yet living, both sons, about seven and eleven. I met them once at a march. They're staying with their mother in the family home, but word is that Mr. Dennett wants custody."

"And as the father, he'll likely get it." So demanded the law: a father was granted custody by default unless he was deemed entirely unfit, and most courts required a high standard of proof. That was only one of many divorce laws that kept women trapped in unhappy or abusive marriages, for most mothers would submit to humiliation and even broken bones rather than be parted from their children. If women had the vote, lawmakers would be obliged to take their concerns more seriously—and how profoundly the lives of women and their children would improve after that.

Upstairs, as soon as they entered the National's main office, Alice recognized several suffragists she knew well among the clerks, managers, and volunteers bustling about. She and Lucy spared time to greet a few acquaintances before an assistant escorted them to Mrs. Dennett's office, where the woman herself welcomed them graciously, her voice touched with a distinctive Boston Brahmin accent. She wore her light brown hair in a braided coil with a few gently curling strands framing her face, and a russet-and-amber paisley silk headband added a note of artistic whimsy to her simple plum silk day dress.

They had no sooner settled into their chairs than the assistant returned with coffee and slices of a delicious lemon tart. "Your reputations precede you," Mrs. Dennett remarked as they enjoyed their refreshments, her tone expressing neither approval nor censure. She looked to be about forty, and her brown eyes regarded them appraisingly through round wire-rimmed glasses.

Lucy smiled and inclined her head as if acknowledging a compliment, although Alice knew she was too perceptive to miss the deliberate ambiguity of Mrs. Dennett's words.

"Then you're aware of how deeply committed we are to woman suffrage," said Alice. "We both learned a great deal working alongside Mrs. Pankhurst and the Women's Social and Political Union in Great Britain, and since our return from abroad, we've adapted British suffragist tactics to our marches and demonstrations here in the States."

Mrs. Dennett sat back in her chair, cradling her coffee cup in her hands. "Some of those British tactics require a great deal of adaptation indeed." She sipped, regarding them coolly over the rim. "Breaking windows? Charging police officers? Such radical behavior is simply not acceptable on this side of the Atlantic. It would turn public opinion entirely against us, undoing decades' worth of hard toil and steady progress."

"We would never advocate breaking windows here," said Lucy, looking shocked at the very idea, though Alice knew she had shattered many a pane in her day. "It's a time-honored tradition in England, but Americans wouldn't stand for it."

"Nor should they be expected to."

"What we propose is a change of focus," Alice broke in. "After years on the front lines of the movement, and after much careful study, we believe that the time has come to concentrate our efforts on an amendment to the federal constitution."

Mrs. Dennett paused, then deliberately set her coffee cup down on her desk. "The National already has a Congressional Committee," she said. "Mrs. William Kent, the wife of the California congressman, has led its efforts for a federal amendment quite ably for several years."

"I'm sure she has," said Lucy, smiling, "which is all the more reason to give her more support."

"Imagine how much more Mrs. Kent could accomplish if the National shifted some resources from individual state campaigns to the congressional campaign," said Alice. "The process of amending individual state constitutions has indeed been steady, but—I trust you'll agree—regrettably slow and often fruitless. Some states are so adamantly opposed to equal rights that they'll never give women the ballot unless compelled to by federal law. The great difficulty colored men have had voting in the South is proof enough of that."

Mrs. Dennett inhaled deeply, frowned, and gave an almost imperceptible nod. Encouraged, Alice and Lucy took turns pleading the case for a rejuvenated push for a federal amendment. With facts eloquently presented, and the potential obstacles realistically acknowledged, they explained why this was the most promising course if they hoped to achieve equal suffrage for all women throughout the United States within the decade.

Mrs. Dennett listened impassively, rarely posing questions, frowning more often than she nodded. Thus Alice was disappointed but not surprised when, after they concluded their proposal, Mrs. Dennett sighed and shook her head. "I can see well enough that you girls thought long and hard about this, and I'm sure your hearts are in the right place," she said. "However, your proposal is, frankly, rather foolish. Our state campaigns have won women the ballot in several western states, and we have great hopes for Kansas and Arizona later this year and Illinois and New York in the spring. With victory so near, we could not possibly divert resources from those efforts to support a federal campaign that thus far has made little headway."

Alice kept her expression carefully neutral. It stung to hear their plan called foolish, and the administrator's disdain for a federal campaign contradicted her earlier praise of Mrs. Kent. "Perhaps if we shifted a minimum of funding from the state campaigns to the Congressional Committee," she ventured, "and made up the shortfall with new donations, and mustered new volunteers—"

"I'm afraid it's simply out of the question," said Mrs. Dennett, holding up a hand to forestall further argument. "It is clear to me that you young ladies advocate a campaign of militancy, which you no doubt learned from Mrs. Pankhurst and, now that you are home, must endeavor to unlearn. Your passion, properly directed, will be of great value to the cause, and I strongly encourage you both to get involved with your state campaigns. This is the National's course, and we must commit to it and remain steadfast."

She rose and reached across the desk to shake their hands. If they needed another sign that the interview was over, the smiling assistant immediately returned to escort them from the office.

"If a campaign for a federal amendment is so foolish," said Lucy as they left the building and paused on the sidewalk to reflect, "why have a Congressional Committee at all?"

"To keep a presence in Washington, I suppose—although from the sound of it, their primary occupation is to host teas for congressional wives." Inhaling deeply, Alice squared her shoulders and considered her options. "Well, so much for winning over Mrs. Dennett. Still, I've come all this way, and I don't want to return home with nothing to show for it. There must be someone else we can talk to. Is Dr. Anna Shaw in the city?"

"I don't know, but maybe we shouldn't overreach. Mrs. Dennett would never forgive us for going over her head to the National's president." Lucy cupped her chin with her hand, thinking. "There *are* other suffrage groups in New York who might support us. They might not be as esteemed as the National, but some influence is better than none."

"There's the Women's Political Union," said Alice. "I'm acquainted with their president."

"You know Mrs. Blatch?"

"Not well, but yes. During my last term in Holloway, she wrote countless letters appealing for my release, and after I returned from Britain, she invited me to speak at several suffrage meetings." She had also offered Alice a job, which Alice had declined. With any luck, Mrs. Blatch would not hold that against her.

"Their headquarters is on the Lower East Side," Lucy said. "We could be there in no time. Shall we?"

Alice agreed, and they set off through the city, their footsteps quickened by purpose. As the daughter of the renowned American suffrage matriarch Elizabeth Cady Stanton, Mrs. Blatch was a lifelong activist, her commitment to woman's rights and other social reform movements never faltering despite the obligations of her marriage to a British businessman and motherhood. When the family had returned to the States after many years in Great Britain, Mrs. Blatch had served in various suffrage organizations before founding the Equality League of Self-Supporting Women, a suffrage group comprised of nearly twenty thousand factory, laundry, and garment workers. With her fellow New York activist Maud Malone, she had organized suffrage parades and open-air meetings throughout the Five Boroughs, earning them the disdain of more conservative suffrage leaders, who feared that such unladylike displays would provoke enmity from the public. More recently Mrs. Blatch had renamed her organization the Women's Political Union.

"I have it on very good authority that Mrs. Blatch has broken with the National," Lucy confided, lowering her voice as they approached their destination.

"Apparently she declared it moribund and claimed that its officers are more concerned with internal politics than with advancing the cause."

"Let's try not to take sides, or at least not to express any favoritism publicly," said Alice. Still, unlike Mrs. Dennett, Mrs. Blatch would surely not dismiss their proposal as "a campaign of militancy." She seemed to have a penchant for militancy herself.

The headquarters of the WPU were located on a bustling street on a crowded block full of shops and tenements. As they strolled along the sidewalk checking the building numbers, Alice heard a jumble of languages and breathed in the aroma of the cooking of many distant lands, sharply cut, when the breeze shifted, by the fetid stench of a sewer. The familiar mixture of sounds and smells evoked vivid memories of her term with the School of Philanthropy, when the ideals that had led her into social work had crashed headlong into reality—the enormous need, the omnipresent suffering, the humbling realization that her work, though grueling, could do little to change the deeply flawed, oppressive system that kept her clients in misery. But if she could help win the vote for women, and the women in this neighborhood and others like it could use the ballot to improve their lives and their children's lives— that would achieve real and enduring progress.

The WPU's headquarters were on the ground floor between a tailor's shop and a kosher butcher, smaller and more humbly furnished than the National's but equally busy and infused with an air of confident resolve. Mrs. Blatch herself welcomed them into her office, petite and bespectacled in her midfifties, attired in a lovely tailored suit of rose silk with chemise detailing. She queried them about mutual acquaintances among the British suffragettes for a good twenty minutes before Alice could broach the purpose of their visit. Unlike Mrs. Dennett, Mrs. Blatch listened with keen interest, and by the time Alice and Lucy finished arguing their case for a federal amendment, she was nodding and murmuring assent.

But when Alice asked for the support of the WPU, Mrs. Blatch too sighed and shook her head. "You have our moral support, of course," she assured them, "but I'm afraid we cannot provide you with any funding or volunteers. We are absolutely focused on our own state referendum, which will be upon us before we know it. I cannot even begin to describe the vast amount of work that must be accomplished between now and then. We cannot divert from our path."

"I see," said Alice, struggling to conceal her disappointment. Mrs. Blatch had seemed so convinced that a federal amendment was the best way forward.

"After our referendum, we shall be in a better position to help you," the older woman added. "If we win the vote for the women of New York State, we'll support you with our ballots. If the measure fails—God help us—we may conclude that a federal amendment is our only hope, and our many experienced campaigners will hasten to your side."

"With respect, the New York referendum isn't scheduled to come before the legislature until 1915," said Lucy. "Three years is a long time to wait when we need assistance so urgently."

Mrs. Blatch paused, considering. "I suppose there is something else I could do. Have you young ladies had the honor of meeting Miss Jane Addams?"

"I haven't," said Alice, "but I've heard a great deal about her work on behalf of the poor in Chicago. I have all the respect and admiration in the world for her."

"I believe she's the current vice president of the National," Lucy added.

Mrs. Blatch nodded. "Yes, indeed. She's also my dear friend. This is what I can do: I'll write a letter of introduction for you to Miss Addams. I'm certain she'll agree to meet you and listen to your proposal. Were you planning to attend the National's convention in Philadelphia later this month?"

"We wouldn't miss it," said Lucy, shooting Alice a

quick glance, seeking confirmation. Alice discreetly nodded.

"Perfect. Miss Addams will be there too, so I'll arrange a meeting. Plead your case to her as well as you did to me, and I'm sure you'll win her over. And after you obtain the support of someone so admired, respected, and well placed—" Mrs. Blatch smiled and lifted her hands. "Anything could be possible."

She rose then, bringing the interview to an end. Alice and Lucy quickly stood, shook her hand, and thanked her profusely.

Outside on the sidewalk, Lucy smiled and clapped Alice on the shoulder. "Well done, Miss Paul."

"Well done, Miss Burns," replied Alice, smiling back. "Now all we have to do is get ourselves invited to the convention."

# 5
# October 1912

## CHICAGO, ILLINOIS

### Ida

The door had been left ajar between the comfortable parlor where Ida Bell Wells-Barnett waited and the grand ballroom of the Hotel La Salle, so the rising murmur of voices and rustle of skirts and scraping of chairs assured her that she would soon address a full house. Still, a twinge of misgiving diminished her satisfaction. She knew that in the crowd of hundreds she would glimpse only a few faces as dark as her own, and those would belong not to members of the Women's Party of Cook County, but to members' friends and special guests. The group's bylaws did not exclude women of color, or else Ida never would have agreed to do the lecture, but Black women were not exactly encouraged to join either.

Ida sighed. *Steady and incremental change,* she reminded herself; an echo of her husband's oft-repeated strategy for progress. Tireless strides ever forward would lead them to the ultimate goal of equality and justice for all—women and men, Black and white.

So much depended upon the outcome of the upcoming presidential election, perhaps more so than any election since 1860. On the Republican side, the incumbent, President William Taft, had emerged victorious from the party's national convention in June, but the choice was bitterly contested. In some states, the delegates had been chosen by popular vote, and in others they had been selected by state conventions. Former president Theodore Roosevelt, who had won far more elected delegates than either of his rivals, nonetheless lost the fierce political battle to claim the handpicked state delegations. Accusing the Republican political machine of fraud, Roosevelt and his followers had broken away to create a new Progressive Party, and at their first national convention in Chicago in August, they had chosen Roosevelt as their nominee. Both men would now vie against the Democratic nominee, New Jersey governor Woodrow Wilson, and the Socialist candidate, Indiana labor activist Eugene V. Debs, to become the twenty-eighth president of the United States.

It was that momentous election that had brought Ida to the meeting of the Women's Party of Cook County that evening.

She glanced at her notes, although by now she knew her speech by heart. Indeed, it was from her heart that she always spoke, whether the subject was woman suffrage and the upcoming election, as it was this afternoon, or calls to rescind the Jim Crow policies of her native South, or demands to end the horror of lynching—murder and the fear of it wielded as weapons by unscrupulous whites to keep Black folks subordinate and afraid. White men who resented Ida's outspokenness had threatened her life time and again, but she would not be silent.

No doubt those white men would be disgusted and outraged if they knew that even now, hundreds of white women eagerly awaited her remarks, that they had come especially to hear the hard-won wisdom of a fifty-year-old Black woman, born into slavery, now an acclaimed international speaker. Those same women were determined to seize the vote for themselves, and the opinions Ida helped shape today would influence the elections in the years to come—though not, unfortunately, the presidential contest only days away.

Ida had influenced and educated throughout her career, first as a schoolteacher for Black children in Tennessee, with shorter stints in Missouri and California. She had still been a Memphis schoolteacher when she'd embarked on a second career as a journalist, beginning with church papers and moving on to several weeklies produced for mostly Black audiences. When at the age of twenty-five she was offered an editorship with a Memphis newspaper called the *Free Speech and Headlight,* she accepted the position and also purchased a one-third interest in the paper so that she would join as an equal partner with the two men who had hired her. Within three years Ida had shortened the name of the newspaper to *Free Speech,* had vastly increased the readership, and had outraged the white community with scathing editorials denouncing their tolerance of lynching and questioning the legitimacy of a legal system that had been built on discrimination.

For three years, the *Free Speech* thrived. Ida was happy in the knowledge that the newspaper benefited the Black community and that she could make a living doing work that she loved. Often the pursuit of a story or a new business opportunity called her out of town, but she enjoyed travel, and with no husband or children to miss her, she had always been willing to pack a bag and take the train wherever duty summoned her.

She had been campaigning for new subscriptions in Natchez, Mississippi, when back home, three men of color, including one of her dearest friends, were killed in a horrific lynching.

Thomas Moss, Calvin McDowell, and Henry Stewart owned a popular, successful grocery store in the predominantly colored district known as the Curve due to a sharp turn in the streetcar line there. Thomas was also a mailman—his route included the *Free Speech* offices—so he worked at the grocery at night while his partners took the day shifts. He and his wife were Ida's best friends in Memphis, and she was the godmother of their only child, a daughter. Until Thomas and his partners launched their store, a white grocer had held a monopoly on the trade in the district, but many local residents knew the three Black men from church or clubs and soon became loyal customers of the People's Grocery Company instead.

One day in early March of 1892, a group of Black boys and white boys were playing marbles on the sidewalk near the grocery when they fell to quarreling. A fistfight broke out, the Black boys triumphed, and the white boys fled home. Furious, the father of one of the white boys returned with a whip and began flogging the eldest and presumed leader of the Black boys. At the sound of his cries, the boy's father came running to protect him, and soon several other Black men threw themselves into the fray, subduing the man with the whip and the other white men who rushed to his defense. Bitter in defeat, the man with the whip and the white grocer arranged for a warrant to be sworn for the arrest of the Black men, including Thomas and his partners.

The Black men were charged minimal fines and dismissed, but what colored folks regarded as yet another unfair punishment, unsympathetic whites saw as outrageously lenient. Rumors soon swept the Curve that white men were planning to come the following Saturday night to "clean out" the People's Grocery Company. Thomas and his partners stationed several armed men in the grocery's back rooms, hoping their presence would be enough to deter an attack.

At ten o'clock that night, while Thomas was working on the books and Calvin and a clerk were waiting on a few last customers before closing up, a group of white men broke in through the back door. The guards immediately fired upon them, wounding three and scattering the others, who fled to the police.

The next morning, the city's newspapers—with the

exception of Ida's *Free Speech,* which took a very different tone—brandished lurid headlines above reports of how "officers of the law" had been wounded "while in the discharge of their duties, hunting up criminals" whom they had been told were harbored in the People's Grocery Company, "a low dive in which drinking and gambling were carried on: a resort of thieves and thugs."

Early that same morning, police had raided dozens of homes in the Curve, hauling hundreds of Black men from their beds and breakfast tables and locking them up "on suspicion." Throughout the day, white folks were allowed into the prison to view them, as if they were dangerous animals in a zoo. As the days passed, tensions rose as the people of Memphis, Black and white alike, waited to see whether the wounded white men would live or die. All the while, members of the Tennessee Rifles, a Black militia regiment with a nearby armory, stood guard over the prison to prevent a vigilante mob from descending upon their captive brothers.

On Monday, March 8, when the wounded men were declared out of danger, a great wave of relief swept through the Black community. Believing the crisis had passed, the Tennessee Rifles stood down. But the following night, under the cover of darkness, a few white men were allowed into the prison. They seized Thomas and his partners from the cells where they lay sleeping, hauled them onto the switch engine of a railroad that ran past the jail, and transported them a mile north of the city limits. There the white vigilantes brutally shot them to death.

On Wednesday, morning editions of the city's papers were delayed in order to cover the overnight murders, although the white press did not call them that. Reporters described the condition of the bodies in such gruesome, heartbreaking detail that Ida knew they had either interviewed the killers or had been invited along to witness the lynchings. They had also recorded Thomas's tragic final moments, as he had begged for his life for the sake of his wife, daughter, and unborn child. When asked if he had any final words, he had shaken his head and replied, "Tell my people to go west. There is no justice for them here."

Shocked and horrified, colored folks gathered around the People's Grocery Company to mourn and to comfort one another, but despite their acute anger and grief, no one proposed to return violence for violence. Nevertheless, rumors that Black people were massing in the Curve prompted a judge of the criminal court to issue an order for one hundred armed men to go to the district and "to shoot down on sight any Negro who appears to be making trouble."

Gangs of white men eagerly armed themselves and rushed out to the Curve, where they began indiscriminately firing upon any cluster of brown faces they saw. As colored folks fled, the white mob tore into the People's Grocery Company, gorging on food and drink, snatching up whatever goods they could carry away, destroying all that they could not eat or steal.

Thus the white grocer triumphed over his Black competitors.

By the time Ida returned from Natchez, her dear friend Thomas and his partners had already been laid to rest. Grief-stricken and outraged, Ida wrote a blistering editorial in the *Free Speech* in which she accused the entire white community of Memphis of complicity in the men's murders for ignoring the increasing violence and lawlessness against their Black neighbors that had culminated in this terrible act. "The city of Memphis has demonstrated that neither character nor standing avails the Negro if he dares to protect himself against the white man or become his rival," she wrote. "There is nothing we can do about the lynching now, as we are outnumbered and without arms. . . . There is therefore only one thing left that we can do: save our money and leave a town which will neither protect our lives and property, nor give us a fair trial in the courts, but takes us out and murders us in cold blood when accused by white persons."

Her exhortation, a furious echo of Thomas's last words, affected her city more profoundly than she could have imagined. Hundreds of colored folks sold their homes and businesses, packed up their belongings, and left Memphis for more peaceful regions. Two prominent pastors took their entire congregations west. Those who stayed behind stopped riding the streetcars and took their business to friendlier establishments in nearby towns. Memphis shopkeepers fumed as they counted their dwindling receipts, but their consternation was nothing compared to that of the white ladies who found themselves suddenly without household help.

One afternoon six weeks after the lynching, Ida and her colleagues were working at the *Free Speech* when the superintendent and treasurer of the Memphis Street Railway Company called at the office and asked if they would consider writing an article or two encouraging colored people to resume riding the streetcars.

"Why come to us with this?" Ida asked, more indignant than curious.

"Because you have great influence with the Negroes, of course," said the superintendent.

"Colored people have always been our best patrons," the treasurer said, "but recently, there has been a marked decline in their patronage."

Ida sat back in her chair and folded her arms. "And why do you suppose that is?"

"We don't know," said the treasurer, shrugging weakly. "We hear that Negroes are afraid of electricity."

"Please assure your people that electric streetcars are perfectly safe," said the superintendent. After an almost imperceptible nudge from his companion, he added, "And tell them that any discourtesy toward them will be punished severely."

Ida could barely contain her scorn. "You blame this downturn on a fear of electricity? Memphis streetcars have been electrified for more than six months, and you haven't noticed a slump until now."

"Well, whatever the cause, we need more riders paying fares," said the treasurer, peevish. "If we don't find the reason for the decline and a remedy for it, the company will hire other men who will."

Ida rose and fixed a steely gaze on the men. "So your own jobs depend on Negro patronage?"

Both men flushed scarlet. "Look here," said the superintendent, scrambling to regain his composure.

"When the company installed electricity last fall—at a cost of thousands of dollars—Negro labor got a large share of it in wages for laying tracks, grading the streets, and so on. It's only fair that they should give us their patronage in return."

"They were doing exactly that until six weeks ago. You can't seriously expect me to believe that you don't know the cause of the decline. You know very well that six weeks ago, three good Black men were lynched in Memphis."

"But the streetcar company had nothing to do with that," the treasurer protested. "It's owned by northern businessmen."

"And run by southern lynchers. Did you know Tom Moss, the letter carrier?"

After a reluctant pause, the men nodded.

"A finer, more decent man than he never walked the streets of Memphis," Ida declared, furious and heartbroken, a tremor in her voice. "He was beloved by all, yet he was murdered in cold blood, all because he defended his property from attack, as is any man's right. Every white man in town knew what was planned, and by doing nothing to prevent it, they consented to the lynching. The way Black folks see it, that makes them as guilty as those who fired the guns. Why should we give you our hard-earned money? Why shouldn't we leave this town and never look back? No one has been arrested or punished for this terrible crime, nor will anyone be, not soon, not ever."

"I'm no murderer," protested the superintendent. "If you Negroes want the guilty men punished, don't accuse the whole town. Go find the killers yourselves."

"As if we could," Ida retorted. "Word is that the criminal court judge himself was one of the lynchers. Suppose we had the evidence. Could we present it before that judge? Or to a grand jury of white men who permitted this crime to happen? Or could we force the reporters who wrote up all those eyewitness accounts to testify?"

The men, greatly discomfited, would not answer her directly. Instead they repeated their hope that she would use her newspaper to encourage her people to ride the streetcars again, where they would be treated with utmost courtesy. Before the door closed behind them, Ida had already decided to publicize their request, all right, but not in the way they wanted. Instead she sat down, seized pen and paper, and swiftly recorded their conversation before she forgot a single detail. She published the transcript on the editorial page of the next issue of the *Free Speech,* and in a sidebar, she urged her readers to stay off the streetcars. Since appealing to their white neighbors' sense of basic human decency had little effect on their behavior, Black folks must strike where it really hurt: their pocketbooks.

The streetcars rattled along half-full, and more and more Black families left Memphis, vast numbers settling in Oklahoma. The other Memphis papers attempted to slow the exodus of customers and servants by printing alarming tales of the hardships, deprivations, and disappointments suffered by those who had emigrated—starvation, attacks by hostile Natives, stubborn soil that refused to yield crops. "Stay among friends where there are no such dangers," one editor urged, echoing dozens of similar appeals in the white press.

One day, Isham F. Norris, a former member of the Tennessee state legislature and distant kin of Ida's by marriage, encouraged her to travel to Oklahoma, to learn the truth firsthand and to write about it for the *Free Speech*. It was certainly a newsworthy investigation, so she took the train to Kansas City, Missouri, joined up with a group of settlers, and headed southwest. For three weeks she journeyed through the territory, submitting weekly reports to her paper describing the new, thriving towns and boundless opportunities. Ida was so impressed with what she saw that when she returned to Memphis, she proposed moving the *Free Speech* to the territory, but her partners objected and she could not afford to buy out their shares.

She settled back down to work, writing and editing, letting no one forget the grave injustice done to Thomas and his partners, reporting on other similar cases throughout the South. In the third week of May, she traveled to Philadelphia to attend the general conference of the African Methodist Episcopal Church, her first visit to the East, a trip long in the planning. After the conference, she continued on to New York City to meet Thomas Fortune, editor of the *New York Age*, with whom she had long corresponded.

"It's taken us quite a while to get you to New York," he remarked when he met her at the station. "Now you're here, I'm afraid you'll have to stay."

"I don't see why that follows," said Ida, amused, admiring the busy urban scene as the porter loaded her bags onto the carriage. How tall and bustling New York City seemed compared to Memphis, so full of energy and ambition!

Mr. Fortune offered her his hand and assisted her into the carriage. "After the rumpus you've kicked up, I should think you wouldn't venture south again."

"I confess I have no idea what you're talking about."

"Haven't you seen the morning papers?"

Suddenly apprehensive, she told him she had not.

He left her for a moment and returned with a copy of the New York *Sun,* folded open to an Associated Press dispatch from Memphis. Ida read, heart pounding, of how a "committee of leading citizens" had gone to the office of the *Free Speech* on the evening of May 27 and had run her friend and partner J. L. Fleming out of town. They had ransacked the offices, destroying type and presses and furnishings, and had left a note declaring that any attempt to resume publishing the paper would be considered an offense punishable by death.

The article ended by noting that the paper was owned by a colored woman, Miss Ida B. Wells, a former schoolteacher currently traveling in the North.

For a long moment, Ida felt anger and shock constricting her chest until she could breathe only in quick, shallow gasps. The *Free Speech*—her paper, her livelihood, her voice. Friends had warned her that she was putting her life in danger by continuing to demand justice for Thomas Moss and the other two men, and by refuting the white paper's lies about Oklahoma, and by urging colored folks to walk with dignity rather than ride the streetcar in comfort. She had bought a pistol weeks ago, determined to die fighting rather than cowering in a corner in fear. If she had to die, if she could take just one lyncher with her, that would even up the score a bit. But her enemies had attacked while she was away, denying her the chance to defend what was hers.

When the initial shock faded, she telegraphed her lawyer and begged for word of her partners. Soon thereafter she received a flurry of telegrams and letters assuring her of their safety and emphatically warning her not to return to Memphis. White men were watching the trains, white men who had vowed to kill her on sight. Alerted to the threats, Black men had organized themselves to protect Ida should she return. She knew that if she went home, it would mean more bloodshed, more widows, more orphans. What choice did she have but to stay away?

Resigned to her exile, she remained in New York, joined the staff of the *New York Age,* and continued to wage war against lynching and lynchers. Those hateful men had destroyed her paper, in which she had invested all her savings from her years as a schoolteacher, every dollar she had in the world. They had threatened her life for exposing their lies and wrongdoing; she owed it to herself and to her people to tell the whole truth.

At the end of June, the *New York Age* ran a front-page, seven-column article she had written describing many lynchings of Black men accused of raping white women. She provided ample evidence, meticulously gathered and evaluated, that the alleged assaults had never occurred or were actually ongoing consensual relationships intolerable to white society. This report and those that followed soon attracted an avid following. She began receiving invitations to speak at church groups and civic organizations, and, determined to raise awareness and thereby promote change, she accepted as many as she could. As her fame grew, she was introduced to a man she had long admired: the great abolitionist, activist, and author Frederick Douglass. Their professional friendship grew, and in November, he arranged for her to speak at the Metropolitan AME Church in Washington, D.C., before a packed house, the largest audience she had ever addressed.

Her lectures took her more frequently away from New York, and increasingly far. As the years passed, she completed several cross-country tours in the United States and two in Great Britain, one for three months in 1893, and another for six months in 1894. As she traveled through England, Scotland, and Wales, she observed with great interest the progressive activities of the women there, their passionate resolve to win the vote, their tireless determination to endure whatever they must to achieve equality.

Between her two voyages abroad, Ida had spent many months in Chicago investigating the Chicago World's Fair, specifically how Black Americans had been excluded from it, despite numerous applications from individuals as well as from Black organizations. In this work she was advised by Mr. Douglass, who introduced her to Ferdinand L. Barnett—a remarkable Black man, dignified, educated, handsome, and righteous. He was the publisher of the *Conservator*, the first Black newspaper in Chicago; a lawyer; an aspiring politician; and the widowed father of two young sons. Together she, Mr. Douglass, and Mr. Barnett wrote an eighty-one-page booklet exposing why Americans of African descent and their culture had been deliberately excluded from the World's Columbian Exposition of 1893. It was a daring and revealing work, and Ida was quite proud of it.

During her second tour to Great Britain, Ida stayed in touch with her two fellow authors, as well as with the editors of several prominent Chicago newspapers. While she was abroad, the *Chicago Tribune* published several articles comprising her observations of the British suffrage movement and the British people's response to her lectures about lynching in America. The *Inter Ocean* ran her dispatches in a regular column titled "Ida B. Wells Abroad." Upon her return to the States, weary and longing for a permanent home after too many itinerant years, she decided it made perfect sense to settle in Chicago. She told herself she had chosen that city for its many promising journalism opportunities and for the active women's clubs that could help her promote her causes, but it was also for Mr. Barnett, who had become her own dear Ferdinand. They fell in love, and—after Ida postponed the wedding three times due to her rigorous lecture schedule—in June 1895, they married.

In the seventeen years since then, Ida had become the stepmother of two and the mother of two fine sons and two brilliant daughters. In 1901, she and Ferdinand had bought a home at 3234 Rhodes Avenue, most likely becoming the first Black family to move east of State Street. Although most of their white neighbors greeted them with more indifference than hostility, the family next door would rise from their seats on their front porch whenever the Wells-Barnetts appeared, mutter and shake their heads in disgust, and withdraw huffily into their house, punctuating their disgruntlement by slamming the door.

Although Ida had withdrawn from the public sphere when her children were very young, she had continued to write, and to speak out against lynching and in favor of universal suffrage. She had created the Negro Fellowship League in Chicago, and with Dr. W. E. B. Du Bois she had founded the National Association for the Advancement of Colored People. Working alongside strong, brave Black men and women to improve the lot of their people, she had become convinced that the vote was essential to achieving equality, dismantling systemic racism, and ending forever the horror of lynching.

That was why she had gladly accepted the invitation from the Women's Party of Cook County to address them on the subject of the upcoming election. The women awaiting her in the lecture hall could not vote, not yet, but they could influence the men in their lives, and since they had asked for her opinion, she would readily share it.

To her the choice was clear. For more than a generation, the Party of Lincoln had consistently shown the greatest commitment to women's rights, to education for all, to social justice and social reform, and most important, to legislation protecting the rights, the liberty, and the very lives of people of color. Other leaders within the Black community, Booker T. Washington foremost among them, insisted that Theodore Roosevelt and his new Progressive Party would do more for their people than President Taft ever had, but Ida was deeply skeptical that they had any genuine interest in lifting up women or colored folks. She doubted Roosevelt would give equal suffrage a passing thought if not for the fact that women in six western states already had the ballot, and he craved their votes. As for Woodrow Wilson, he adored a certain type of docile female and despised all others, and although Eugene Debs's heart was in the right place, as the leader of a fringe party, he was tragically unelectable.

If American women wanted to win the vote for themselves, they first had to help win a second term for President Taft. That was what she would tell the eager ladies who awaited her in the adjacent ballroom. The election was the first battle of the new war for suffrage that they simply must win.

She had been preparing for this fight for her entire life, and she would not fail.

# 6

# October 1912

## NEW YORK, NEW YORK

### Maud

"What about votes for women?" Maud called out from the balcony of the Brooklyn Academy of Music.

On the stage below, Governor Woodrow Wilson abruptly fell silent. From balcony to orchestra, members of the audience craned their necks to see who had so rudely interrupted the candidate's speech. Maud knew she would be easy to spot in her distinctive purple shirtwaist and hat adorned with a gold feather, especially since she was standing in the middle of the row, obstructing the view of those seated behind her. But they were not the only people muttering in confusion and annoyance and disgust. She hoped at least a few of the silent men and women with their gazes fixed on the Democratic nominee were on her side, awaiting an answer to her perfectly reasonable and relevant question.

Stepping out from behind the podium, Governor Wilson approached the front of the stage and scanned the upper seats until his gaze locked on hers. She waited, raising her eyebrows inquisitively to encourage him to respond. Former president Theodore Roosevelt had replied to a similar query on the night before the New York State primary; although his answer had been unsatisfactory, at least he had offered one. Not so Governor Hiram Johnson of California, Roosevelt's vice presidential running mate. When Maud had interrupted his speech at Carnegie Hall earlier that month, he had parried her questions with repeated demands that she wait until after he had finished his speech. When she refused, he had sent four committee men wading into the crowd to seize her and throw her out of the theater. They had torn her favorite gray walking suit, broken her glasses, and left her with painful bruises on her arms and back and hips. What would Governor Wilson do?

She held her breath as he prepared to speak.

"What is it, madam?" he called up to her over the grumbling crowd.

She exhaled, disappointed. How anticlimactic to

pretend that he had not heard the question. "You say you want to destroy monopolies," Maud called back. "I ask you, what about woman suffrage? Men have a monopoly on the vote. Why not start there?"

The audience laughed, low and belligerent. "Sit down," a man shouted gruffly a few rows behind her.

Governor Wilson clasped his hands behind his back, the picture of didactic patience. "Woman suffrage, madam, is not a question for the federal government. It is a matter for the states. As a representative of the *national* party, I cannot speak to this issue."

"But I address you as an American, Mr. Wilson," Maud persisted, ignoring the audience's glares and muttered oaths, the impatient shifting in seats. Surely some of them agreed that he ought to just answer the question. "Since you seek to govern all these *united* states, surely you can tell us where you stand."

Governor Wilson looked around at the increasingly restless audience. "Let us not be rude to any woman," he entreated them before returning his attention to Maud. "I hope you will not consider it a discourtesy if I decline to answer those questions on this occasion."

"But I do consider it discourteous, Governor, and worse." She put her head to one side, studying him, genuinely curious. "Unless you mean to say that you have no opinion whatsoever?"

"Throw her out!" a deep voice bellowed somewhere below, close to the stage.

"Just answer the question," cried a woman, somewhere near. Would her voice carry all the way to the stage in that din?

In the center of the house, a young man rose from his seat, cupped his hands around his mouth, and shouted toward the balcony, "Why don't you go to your own meeting, girlie?"

A roar of laughter followed. "Go home and mind the babies!" another man shouted.

"Put her out! Where are the police?"

In her peripheral vision Maud spotted figures approaching her; she glanced to her left and found three grim-faced, gray-uniformed officers and a man in a well-cut dark suit drawing near. The civilian looked to be in his fifties, with Germanic features and an air of command. "If you don't take your seat, madam," he barked, gesturing sharply, "I will order you arrested. You could get thirty days in prison for this!"

"I've done nothing to deserve arrest," Maud protested. "Any citizen has the right to question the men who seek to govern us."

"Now, gentlemen, let us remain civil," Wilson urged, although Maud could barely make out his words, so raucous had the audience become. "I'm sure the lady will not persist when I positively decline to discuss the question now."

He gestured for her to take her seat, but she stood fast, her eyes fixed on his, waiting for him to reply. Meanwhile, the scowling officers awkwardly made their way between the rows toward her, past the seated spectators, tripping over feet and handbags.

"Why don't you answer, Governor Wilson?" another voice called out, some distance away.

Then the policemen seized Maud by the arms and waist, lifting her roughly. As jeers, hisses, and blistering insults rose in a cacophony of condemnation, they wrestled her down the row and up the aisle to the back of the balcony, where they hauled her outside through the fire exit. Stumbling to keep her feet on the narrow landing of the fire escape, she wrenched one arm free, seized the railing to steady herself, and shivered in the sudden chill. "My coat and hat," she managed to say, stepping toward the door.

The man in the dark suit grabbed her arm again. "We'll get them for you," he snapped. He gestured for one of the officers to fetch her coat and hat, and by the time he returned with them, the others had propelled her down the fire escape ladders to the pavement. They released her arms only long enough to let her put on her coat, which looked as though it had been knocked from her seat and trampled underfoot. Judging by the footprint and crushed crown, someone had definitely stepped on her hat. The yellow feather trembled forlornly in the breeze.

The men loaded her into a patrol wagon and took her to the station house on Adams Street, where she was processed and charged with disorderly conduct. She was disconcerted to overhear that the man in the dark suit was none other than Chief Magistrate Otto Kempner, a judge renowned for his strict interpretation of the law and utter lack of a sense of humor.

Her heart plummeted at the realization, and sank lower yet when the doors of her solitary cell clanged shut behind her and the guard turned the key with a solid, irrefutable thunk.

Breathing deeply to steady her nerves, Maud threw her shoulders back and examined her surroundings. Her cell was surprisingly clean, with cinder-block walls; a high window with an iron grate; a single bulb fixed to the ceiling; a bucket in the corner, the purpose of which she preferred not to contemplate; and a wooden cot draped with a threadbare wool blanket. A pungent smell like burnt cheese hung faintly in the air, its source unknown and perhaps better left undiscovered.

She tested the cot, found it less uncomfortable than she had expected, and settled down to await whatever might come next. From some distance away she heard voices raised in argument, and she passed several long minutes contemplating whether it was better to be lonely and bored in safe solitude or to have companions, albeit belligerent, hardened criminals, whose stories might help pass the time.

She had just decided that she would rather have dangerous company than none at all when a guard strolled up to her cell and addressed her through the bars. "Your lawyer's here," he said flatly.

She sat up straight and smoothed her skirt. "My lawyer?"

"Yeah. Sylvester Malone, your lawyer."

"Oh, of course." Her eldest brother was indeed a lawyer, but she had never really thought of him as *her* lawyer. She supposed she would need a lawyer's services, but Sylvester would probably arrange for someone more objective to take her case.

The guard eyed her with faint reproach as he selected a key from the heavy ring at his belt. "He's offered to post your bail. You're free to go."

Relief flooded her, and yet she hesitated. "Tell him to come back tomorrow morning."

He paused with the key in the lock. "Beg pardon?"

"Tell him to come back for me tomorrow." She remembered to add, "Please ask him to check on my cats in the meantime."

She was obliged to repeat herself twice before the dumbfounded guard left with the message, shaking his head and muttering under his breath about the unpredictable foolishness of women. She could well imagine how the news of her delayed departure would exasperate Sylvester, her elder by eleven years, as passionate as she was about social justice and women's rights but far more conventional in the way he expressed it. Though he might not approve of her choice, he would understand that it wasn't that she enjoyed being locked up like a common crook. Later she would explain that since she was there already, she thought she should partake of the overnight experience, for the purpose of empirical study.

Her choice seemed rather whimsical and foolish the next morning, after a sleepless, uncomfortable, lonely night. When Sylvester arrived to post her bail at eight o'clock sharp—head and shoulders taller than herself, but with the same dark auburn hair and clear blue eyes—it was all she could do not to sprint for the nearest exit. She managed to linger long enough to complete the necessary paperwork, including a form acknowledging her obligation to appear before the magistrate three days hence. Upon her release, her brother escorted her to his home on West 147th, where her mother and elder sister, Marcella, greeted her with such warmth and sympathy that tears sprang to her eyes.

No sooner had she washed, changed clothes, and had a bite to eat than friends began dropping by to praise and comfort her. Reporters called too, eager for her story.

"I don't in the least regret my attempt to make Governor Wilson declare his attitude on the suffrage question," she replied as she poured tea for a newcomer. "I maintain that I was not in the least disorderly. I rose in a perfectly dignified and businesslike manner and asked the Democratic candidate for president whether he believed in giving the vote to the women of the country, and he replied that it was not a national question." She shook her head, laughing lightly. "It's a question that is agitating thousands of women in every state in the Union. If that's not a national question, I don't know what is."

"Brava, sis," declared Marcella, seated beside her, her dark eyes flashing a challenge to their visitors, daring them to disagree.

"Why do you persist in heckling these gentlemen?" queried a bespectacled young reporter with a crisp part down the center of his slicked-back brown hair. "It never ends well for you."

"My objective is simply to make them go on the record. If Governor Wilson had said, 'No, I don't believe in giving the vote to women,' I would have taken my seat and kept quiet, just as I would have had he declared himself a friend of the suffrage cause."

"Will you promise never again to disturb a meeting if the magistrate lets you off this time?" another reporter asked.

"How could I?" replied Maud, incredulous. "I don't know what I might be required to do in the future in the interest of our struggle for political equality, and I certainly won't bind myself by any promise."

The journalists, eagerly jotting notes, had seemed especially pleased with that answer, hinting as it did of future spectacles worth reporting.

But that was yesterday's bravado, and hours after her audience departed, Maud felt only a faint, lingering warmth of its fire.

On the day of her court appearance, Maud arranged her auburn tresses into an attractive, dignified twist and dressed as she would have for any autumn Wednesday at the library, albeit with extra care to smooth wrinkles and remove stray threads. Her steel-gray suit of worsted wool with plum trimming was not her newest, but it was her favorite, the jacket fitting perfectly snug over her crisp white blouse without constraining her arms, the extra pleats in the straight skirt allowing for brisk walking and the sort of bending and stretching required to retrieve and replace books along the entire span of the stacks.

"Will you wear your 'Votes for Women' sash too?" Sylvester inquired over lunch, fighting to hide a grin. "It *is* part of your standard protest uniform, after all."

Maud pretended to consider it. "I think not," she said, shaking her head. "The bold colors wouldn't suit this demure, tailored ensemble. Besides, the sash is reserved for weekends and parades." She patted the yellow woman suffrage button pinned to her lapel. "This adornment must suffice."

Sylvester chuckled, but Marcella fixed them with a familiar look of warning. "Leave the jokes at home, both of you," she advised. "Magistrate Kempner doesn't like comedy in his courtroom, nor does he approve of outspoken women."

Marcella would know. Like Sylvester and their second-eldest sibling, Lawrence, she too was a lawyer.

"I'm aware of his opinion of women who dare to speak in public," said Maud. "We didn't have much time to chat that night in the balcony when he had the police haul me out, but *that* he made perfectly clear."

"So you'll behave yourself?"

"I can't promise not to speak my mind—especially if I swear to tell the whole truth—but I promise, no riddles, limericks, or heckling. Not today."

Sighing, Marcella turned to their brother. "I wish you and James Kohler good luck. It's a daunting task, keeping our baby sister out of jail."

*Baby sister indeed,* Maud thought, indignant but amused. "Thanks for hiring him, by the way," she said. Her wealthier siblings were instinctively generous and never made her feel indebted. Helping one another was just something they did in the Malone family, without expectation of anything in return.

"We all chipped in," said Marcella. "Ma too. She took up a collection at her quilting bee."

"I could've used one of their quilts in my cell," Maud said, frowning with distaste as she recalled the hard wooden cot and scratchy wool blanket.

"Next time," said Sylvester, grinning.

"Pray there isn't a next time," said Marcella firmly, shooting them each a sharp look.

"Oh, I do," said Maud, and she meant it. She knew that her night in jail, as unpleasant as it had been, had been a day at the park compared to what British suffragettes endured in prison on behalf of the cause, what American women convicted of serious crimes suffered every day here at home, what she herself might face if the hearing went against her.

Marcella was due at an arraignment, so Sylvester alone accompanied Maud to the Temple Bar Building in Brooklyn. In a private conference room, they met briefly with James Kohler before reporting to the courtroom of Chief Magistrate Otto Kempner for her two o'clock hearing. Among all the reporters and avid spectators, it was comforting to find two friends and respected suffragists, Dr. Mary Halton and Miss Mary Donnelly, seated with a half dozen or so other ladies in the front row. She longed to speak with them, but her friends had only a brief moment to throw her a few sympathetic, encouraging glances before Magistrate Kempner entered and called the hearing to order.

Maud's lawyer began by asking the court to immediately dismiss the complaint on the grounds that it was inappropriate for Magistrate Kempner to preside. "Police records show that you were present at the Brooklyn Academy of Music that evening, Your Honor, and that it was you who ordered the police to arrest her," said Mr. Kohler, his manner respectful but insistent. "That alone is cause for this case to be dismissed."

Magistrate Kempner regarded Mr. Kohler over the

rims of his glasses. "Are you saying that you don't believe I can be fair and impartial?"

"Not at all, Your Honor, but the appearance of any bias would be grounds for your ruling to be overturned on appeal. Let us spare the courts and my client that ordeal."

"Understood. Motion dismissed." Kempner banged his gavel. "Call the first witness."

Mr. Kohler had warned Maud that his motion would likely fail, but her heart still sank a bit as the first witness took the stand. Mr. Lohman, an advertising agent for the Academy, seemed a curious choice for the prosecution, for he confirmed only that he had attended the meeting, that he had seen people "jumping and hollering," but that he "never heard the lady say a single word." The second witness, a Mr. Senft, proudly and with great theatricality described how, after Miss Malone had "asked her woman suffrage questions and kept on asking after Governor Wilson declined to answer," he had left his box seat to help the officers as they "pulled and pushed" her from the building. "The whole audience," he declared, "especially the ladies, joined in the mad demand to have that unruly suffragette put out."

Maud muffled a sigh. That was *not* what had happened. She had distinctly heard several people call out to Governor Wilson to answer her question, and several more had admonished the officers for handling her so roughly. As for Mr. Senft, she had no memory of him at all.

Mr. Andrew McLean, chairman of the ill-fated meeting, was the next to take the stand. A courtly, learned gentleman with a Scottish brogue, he offered a blessedly restrained and accurate version of what had unfolded in the auditorium. After his testimony, Officer Dubois and Lieutenant Wold of the 146th Precinct took turns describing her arrest.

Then Maud was called to the stand.

After confirming her name and residence, and less readily acknowledging her age, Maud braced herself for more difficult questions. "Did you go to the Academy willfully to disturb that meeting?" the magistrate demanded.

"*I* didn't disturb the meeting," she replied.

"But you have a history of doing so," said Kempner, proceeding to query her about several incidents from the past few months. He fixed his stern gaze alternately upon her and on the thick stack of papers on the high desk before him, his brow furrowing ever deeper while she calmly and succinctly answered his questions. As she described the incident at Carnegie Hall a fortnight earlier, when she had interrupted the Progressive Party's candidate for vice president, Kempner suddenly interjected, "Do you mean to say that it took five policemen to put you out of that hall?"

Maud glanced down at the yellow suffrage button given pride of place on her lapel. "They seemed to think it did." That had not been the first time she had been dragged out of a political meeting for questioning the speaker, but never before had she been left with cuts and bruises.

Kempner sat back and glared disapproval down from the bench, but Maud relaxed a trifle, knowing that it was now her own lawyer's turn to pose questions. Mr. Kohler asked her to describe what had happened on the evening of October 19, which she did, in a perfectly reasonable, conversational tone, remembering Marcella's warning to avoid humor.

After she finished, Mr. Kohler nodded thoughtfully. "Miss Malone, have you ever carried bricks or stones or baseballs into a meeting?"

"Of course not," she replied. "I just ask candidates what they think about woman suffrage, and if I am given an answer, yes or no, I sit down."

"And if you are not given an answer?"

"Then I keep on asking until they give in or I am put out," she said. "My purpose is to make it a political issue, which any reasonable person would agree it certainly is."

Eventually she was excused from the stand, and the magistrate withdrew to ponder the evidence. She thought she had represented herself well, and from her lawyer's demeanor and her friends' delighted smiles, it seemed they did too.

Unfortunately, when the hearing resumed, she learned that Magistrate Kempner had not been impressed.

"What you did at the Academy of Music on Saturday night was not only unlawful, but, in my judgment, in very bad taste," he declared, regarding her severely. "At the risk of creating a riot, you persisted in disturbing that meeting. Your course is that of a willful and malicious lawbreaker. You have proceeded, arbitrarily and brazenly, to ride roughshod over laws and customs."

Even if Maud had been permitted to reply then, she would have been speechless.

"You disgraced yourself and injured your cause," the magistrate continued. "If there were refined and cultured suffragists of your sex in that audience, they must have felt ashamed."

A hiss went up from the front row. Maud supposed it was her friend Mary Donnelly.

Magistrate Kempner spared a warning look for the ladies before turning back to Maud. "You are one of the scatterbrained, loose-tongued, ill-mannered viragoes whose methods impede the suffrage cause, as do the actions of the window smashers in England. To such as you is due the increase in the number of dangerous cranks, yes, and the bullets in the bodies of our governors and presidents."

A gasp rose from the courtroom, and Maud felt her breath catch in her throat. Everyone there understood the reference to the attempt on Theodore Roosevelt's life at a campaign event in Milwaukee earlier that month. A would-be assassin had shot him as he had entered the auditorium, but although the bullet had lodged in the muscles of his chest, a thick folded manuscript in his breast pocket had prevented it from penetrating the lung. Wounded, he had nonetheless taken the podium, and with blood seeping through his shirt, he had said, "Friends, I don't know whether you fully understand that I have just been shot, but it takes more than that to kill a Bull Moose." He had then proceeded to deliver his speech as planned, all ninety minutes of it, before he left the stage and accepted medical attention.

How could Magistrate Kempner accuse her of inspiring assassins like that dreadful man who had attacked Mr. Roosevelt? Her questions were straightforward and fair, and all the violence done that night had been inflicted *upon* her, not *by* her. Such hyperbole, to equate the public questioning of a political candidate with inciting murder!

Maud fought to compose herself as the magistrate rendered his decision: She would be held over for trial at the Court of Special Sessions in lieu of $500 bond. Librarians did not typically carry that kind of money around in their pocketbooks, but Sylvester had come prepared. "I proudly pay her fee, for future generations will remember my sister with gratitude," he declared, handing the cash to the bailiff. "Speeches like the one Magistrate Kempner just made are buried in dusty volumes. My sister's actions will go down in history."

Maud's heart warmed with gratitude as the women in the front row applauded with great enthusiasm. Speaking close to her ear under the clamor of voices, Mr. Kohler assured her that he would file another motion to have the case dismissed, but while they awaited a decision, he would prepare for her trial. Sylvester put his arm around her shoulders, and as they left the courtroom, the suffragists hurried to gather around her, to shake her hand and tell her how brilliant she had been, and how absolutely insufferable the magistrate. Dr. Halton vowed to have her own lawyers investigate the legality of Magistrate Kempner's presiding that day. Maud smiled and thanked her; it wouldn't hurt to have other legal opinions supporting the motion that the magistrate had so peremptorily dismissed.

Sylvester and Mr. Kohler flanked Maud as they made their way to the exit, but that was not enough to discourage the press, who swarmed them on the court-house stairs and assailed them with questions.

"Mr. Kohler, how do you feel about this decision?" one man called.

"I have nothing to say," Mr. Kohler replied shortly, shifting his torso to block Maud from view.

"Have you learned your lesson, Miss Malone?" another shouted. "Are you going to lie low from now on?"

Astonished, Maud halted so abruptly that her two gallant escorts almost stumbled. "Of course not," she exclaimed. "I've already arranged to speak at an open-air suffrage meeting tonight at Columbus Circle. Now, that's a story worth reporting. I hope to see you all there."

Bidding the press farewell with a jaunty wave, she linked her arms through her brother's and her lawyer's and hurried off before any of the reporters noticed the quiver in her voice or the strain in her eyes. Let no one mistake momentary fatigue for wavering resolve. It was not against the law to ask questions, and she would not be silent.

# 7

# October 1912

## PHILADELPHIA, PENNSYLVANIA

### Alice

With scarcely more than a month to go before the opening ceremonies of the National's annual convention, Alice had yet to secure a place with an official delegation. Without that status, it would be very difficult to take advantage of Mrs. Blatch's letter of introduction to Jane Addams, and without Miss Addams's recommendation, Alice would be in no position to convince the National's leaders to shift resources from individual state campaigns to the congressional campaign. Despite her renown—or infamy—as a suffragist, she was too young, too new to the National, and, some would argue, too radical to be trusted with such strategic decisions.

Even so, and even among her critics, Alice remained much in demand as a suffrage speaker. Although she had no part to play in the convention's official proceedings, she had been invited to speak at a rally on opening day at Independence Square, the same place where she and Lucy had concluded their successful summer campaign so triumphantly the previous September. As a dues-paying lifetime member of the National, Alice readily agreed to participate. The role wouldn't grant her access to the executive meetings where the policy decisions would be made, but the event would give her the opportunity to mingle with the decision-makers. She might even use her speech to enrich the soil, to prepare it for the seeds of her proposal to reinvigorate the campaign for a federal constitutional amendment.

Yet the real prize, a place with an official delegation, eluded her. She pursued one lead after another, but as time passed and nothing came through, she realized that Lucy might have to approach Jane Addams alone. It was a stroke of tremendous good fortune that Lucy had obtained what Alice still sought. In August, Mrs. Blatch had invited Lucy to join the delegation of the New York branch of the Women's Political Union. She would have included Alice too, if she were a New Yorker, but the WPU had nothing to offer her, and the New Jersey delegation was full.

One misty morning as Alice, Parry, and their mother were in the garden harvesting acorn squash, butternut, and pumpkins, their mother waited until Parry had moved some distance away down the rows before observing, "If thou had taken the job with the Pennsylvania Woman Suffrage Association, thou would be settled in Philadelphia by now. As the director of the welcoming parade, thou surely would have been introduced to all the important people thou are trying to meet now."

"That has occurred to me," Alice admitted ruefully, setting down her heavy basket to work a knot out of a muscle in her left shoulder. Although the cool air carried the scent and feel of autumn, she perspired in her plain linsey-woolsey work dress. "What's more, if I'd accepted the job offer from the National, I would've proven myself by now. The members of the board would have seen for themselves how capable and committed to the cause I am. If I broached the subject of strengthening the campaign for a federal amendment, they would have listened to me as a colleague rather than some meddling upstart."

Her mother studied her for a moment, kindness and understanding etched in every soft line of her face. "Perhaps, but those were not the positions thou wanted."

"No, they were not." Sighing, Alice bent, knife in

hand, to cut through the thick stem of another perfectly full, ripe butternut squash. She could almost taste it, roasted and sprinkled with maple sugar, a glorious autumn dish she looked forward to from the moment they sowed the seeds. "But either one would have brought me closer to the position I *do* want."

If only she'd had the foresight to realize that before she had declined the offers. Instead, she had little choice but to continue to seek a place with a delegation, or leave it all up to Lucy, which was not what either of them wanted. They worked brilliantly as a team, as they had discovered in the months they had labored shoulder-to-shoulder in the United Kingdom. As they saw it, official ranks and titles didn't matter; they would divide up the work according to which tasks best fit their talents and inclinations, as they had always done. What *did* matter was that they both be present to make their case to Miss Addams and the National's officers and whomever else needed convincing, because the two of them together were more persuasive than either of them alone. That opportunity would be lost if Alice couldn't even get into the room.

When she described her quandary in a letter to William Parker, a dear friend and former graduate school classmate who had taken a job on Wall Street after graduation, he promptly replied with a solution he figured would suit them both: she should become a New Yorker. If she moved to Manhattan, she would be eligible for Mrs. Blatch's delegation, she would discover that the opportunities for a girl with a Penn doctorate were innumerable, and they could see more of each other. "I'd like to take you out to dinner at a little Hungarian place I know," he wrote, his eagerness evident in the quick strokes of his pen. "You may recall I spoke of creating an intellectual salon. Perhaps one day soon you will grace it, and will be amused and warmed by the glow of all the good spirits."

Alice liked Will very much. When they were students together, she had enjoyed his company, his warmth and kindness, his intellectual curiosity, his clever humor. She smiled whenever she recalled his endearing loping stride as they crossed the quad on the University of Pennsylvania campus side by side, and the way his light brown hair glowed bronze in the sunlight.

If she moved to New York, she could find a modest apartment and useful work with one of the city's prominent suffrage organizations, or perhaps a faculty position with a college or university. She and Will could see each other often. If their fondness deepened, her life might take an unexpected and perhaps rather wonderful turn. But—she had seen it happen to others—marriage and motherhood would inevitably draw her time and attention from career and cause, at least for the short term. Would a life with Will be enough to make up for all she would sacrifice to be his bride?

She checked herself. Will had never implied that he intended to propose someday. Perhaps he was only offering career advice and a solution to her dilemma, as any thoughtful friend would. But in her heart, she knew there was more to his suggestion than that. She understood implicitly that he wanted her to move to New York to be near him, and if she was completely honest with herself, she found a certain reassurance and comfort in his unspoken promise.

But other dreams for the future beckoned too.

As a brilliant flood of autumn color washed over the home farm, Alice continued to exchange fond letters with Will—but not only with him, for her correspondence with Lucy and other suffragist friends went on as lively as always. Ever more frequently, she found herself contemplating a trip to New York. She had a long-standing invitation from Lucy to stay at her home on Long Island and speak at several open-air meetings in the Five Boroughs; while she was there, Alice could inquire about professional opportunities in the city, spend a day with Will, and consider whether she ought to make a more permanent move.

She had not yet made up her mind when she received an unexpected invitation to call on Mrs. Dora Lewis, the wealthy Philadelphia widow and longtime activist who was in charge of organizing the National's annual convention in late November. They had not corresponded since Alice had declined the job offer with the Pennsylvania Woman Suffrage Association, and she was relieved to see that their friendship apparently had not suffered for her refusal. She wondered why Dora wanted to see her "at her earliest convenience," as she put it, which suggested some urgency. Had another position with the PWSA become available? If so, why not say so? Why send such a tantalizingly vague letter?

Alice mulled over the three invitations—Dora's, Lucy's, and Will's. Even though she could conceivably accept all three, she sensed that the one that drew her most powerfully in this moment would reveal something important about what her heart most desired.

In the end, she took pen in hand and wrote to tell Dora she would be pleased to call on her two days hence.

The Paul family farm in New Jersey was only fifteen miles east of Philadelphia, and she had come to know the city and its suffragists especially well during graduate school and from the suffrage campaign of the summer of 1911. Even so, this would be her first visit to Dora's gracious home, a four-story brick town house on Pine Street near Rittenhouse Square. A maid answered the door, but Dora herself appeared immediately thereafter, her smile warm and welcoming as she took Alice by both hands and brought her inside. She wore a graceful tea dress of fawn-colored silk trimmed in ivory lace, with a square neckline that showed off a lustrous string of pearls, their glow echoed in her pearl drop earrings. Her fine blond hair was arranged in a loose Grecian knot encircled by a braid, but although her manner and voice were gentle and calm, an indomitable light shone in her clear blue eyes.

"It's so good of you to come," Dora said as they seated themselves in the parlor, a bright, sunny room that kept the old-world Victorian décor from seeming fusty.

"The pleasure is mine," Alice replied. "I was delighted to receive your letter."

Over tea, delicate cucumber sandwiches, and fine strawberry tarts with cream, they chatted first about their families—Dora had one daughter, Louise, a year older than Alice, and two sons, Robert and Shippen, one studying medicine and the other law—but the conversation soon turned to their shared passion, woman suffrage.

"I understand that you've been reviving interest in a federal amendment," Dora remarked as she refreshed Alice's cup.

"I hope I'm doing so," said Alice. "I've certainly tried, but the response has been mixed."

Dora smiled. "I imagine it ranges from indifference to utter contempt?"

"Something like that, yes." Alice paused to reflect. "That's not entirely true. There *is* keen interest in a federal amendment out there, but not necessarily in the hearts of those who lead our most influential organizations."

As Dora listened intently, Alice explained why she thought it was absolutely necessary to redirect the National toward a nationwide effort, even though four more states were likely to pass universal suffrage measures in the upcoming election, with opportunities in other states to follow in the spring. More ruefully, she described her and Lucy's trip to New York and the mixed results of their attempt to persuade Mary Ware Dennett and Harriot Stanton Blatch to influence the movement's leaders on their behalf.

"You would have greater influence yourself—and a better chance of success—if you were appointed to the National's Congressional Committee," Dora remarked when Alice had finished. "Better yet, you should lead it."

For a moment Alice was struck speechless. "What about Elizabeth Kent, the congressman's wife? Isn't she still the chairwoman?"

"Yes, but I've heard she wants to step down." Although they were alone, Dora lowered her voice and added, "Just between us, I believe you would be more effective."

"I'd be delighted for the opportunity to prove you right."

"Mrs. Blatch's letter of introduction to Jane Addams will open doors for you," Dora mused, cupping her chin with her hand, "but it would be helpful if you were part of your state's delegation."

"I inquired, but I was too late. The New Jersey delegation was already complete."

"In that case, would you accept an appointment as my assistant instead?"

"Gladly," said Alice, delighted. "What would that mean? How would I assist you?"

"Oh, I'll find work for you, never fear, but your real mission at the convention will be to lobby for the Congressional Committee chairmanship." Dora regarded Alice steadily, with a look both wise and kind.

"I trust you'll make the most of your office, should you win it. We stand poised at a crucial moment in history. We shall require a singular, extraordinary effort to command the attention of those in power so they can no longer nudge us into the margins. Teas for politicians' wives and once-a-year appeals to Congress will not do it."

"They certainly haven't sufficed so far," said Alice. A singular, extraordinary effort—she and Lucy had long debated this very thing, but neither thought they should emulate the window-smashing, police-charging tactics they had learned from British suffragettes. The American people would denounce them, politicians would disavow them, and they would lose whatever moral authority they had.

Yet they must do something—something new and unprecedented, something magnificent—to herald the launch of their newly reinvigorated national campaign, to capture the attention and the imagination of the public, the politicians, and the press alike.

Their message to the world would be simple and clear: Whoever won the upcoming presidential election, suffragists were not going away. If anything, they had finally fully arrived, and they demanded to be heard.

# 8

# November 1912

## CHICAGO, ILLINOIS

### Ida

On the morning of Election Day, Ida saw her husband off at the front door earlier than usual. His polling place was on the way to the state's attorney's office, and he intended to vote before reporting for work.

"By the next presidential election, you'll be able to cast a ballot too," Ferdinand predicted, stroking her head and kissing her, pressing his cheek to hers. He knew what a bitter affront this was to her, to be denied the right to choose who would represent her in government, who would make the decisions that would affect her life in countless ways. Hadn't the American colonists fought a war with England over this very matter?

The insult stung all the more when she considered how diligently certain candidates had courted Black voters and appealed to women of color to assist their campaigns. Although Black women could not vote in most states, savvy politicians understood well how their voices inspired and influenced the men in their families and communities.

Later that morning, in fact, as soon as Ida saw the children off to school, she would set out for her first speaking engagement of the day, a rally for President Taft at a plaza on the South Loop. At noon she would address a luncheon for the Women's Party of Cook County, and after that, she would report to the Negro Fellowship League to help direct their efforts to get out the vote. The night before, she had advocated for President Taft at a program sponsored by the NAACP. Her colleague W. E. B. Du Bois had made the case for Woodrow Wilson, who had vigorously sought the Black vote and had shaped his platform accordingly, while Ida's friend and fellow suffragist Jane Addams, the tireless social reformer and leader of the Chicago branch of the NAACP, had spoken on behalf of Theodore Roosevelt. Offstage, both before and after the debate, each speaker had tried to persuade the other two to switch their loyalties, wielding humor and tact so their friendship would not suffer. Whatever the outcome, on November 6 they would again be united in purpose, working together on behalf of people of color, women, and the disenfranchised.

Ida knew that she had chosen the candidate most likely to promote the causes dearest to her, and that her ordinarily wise and reasonable friends were tragically mistaken. Although the Republicans sometimes fell short when it came to fulfilling the promises made during Reconstruction, no one had done more for people of color than the Party of Lincoln. Often that meant simply staying out of the way and not creating impediments as Black folks strove to improve their own lives and to create a more promising future for their children. Ida suffered no illusions that any politician was going to look out for her, to smooth the rocky path before her and guide her around obstructions. From the time she was quite young, she had known that if she wanted anything in life, she would have to work for it.

She was only sixteen the summer that lesson was seared into her memory forever, the summer her childhood ended.

As the eldest child of the family, she was sometimes permitted to visit her grandmother's farm without any of her siblings. Although she was sent to help her grandmother, uncle, and aunt pick the first fall cotton—hot, backbreaking, finger-aching work—the change of scene, the freedom from minding her seven younger siblings, and the attention of her doting elders felt like a holiday. In August 1878, she had been at her grandmother's snug, tidy cottage about a week when word came that yellow fever was ravaging Memphis, about fifty miles northeast of Holly Springs. Terrified residents were fleeing the city, but most other towns, having learned hard lessons from past epidemics, had set up roadblocks and refused to take in the refugees. The mayor of Holly Springs, however, welcomed them gladly, not out of altruism but because they would fill the town's hotels and boardinghouses, feast in the restaurants, quench their thirst at the taverns, and buy necessities in the shops. It was in the best interest of the town's economy, he had proclaimed, to gather up this windfall despite the risks.

Ida felt a chill as she and her elders absorbed the news. She must have looked sick from worry, for her uncle clapped his hand on her shoulder and said, "Don't fret. Your father's a clever man. He surely took the family out into the country at the first sign of trouble."

"That's exactly what he'd do," said her aunt, nodding for emphasis. "No doubt he's at your aunt Belle's place this very minute."

Ida felt her anxiety ease. Yes, of course her mother's

sister would have urged them to come, and her parents would have loaded the younger children into the wagon and left the city as soon as the danger became evident. Her grandmother's farm was so remote that mail delivery was irregular at best, so it was not at all strange that Ida had not yet received a letter reassuring her that all was well.

Ten days passed, each one bringing new rumors that the disease was sweeping through the state, that it had cut through Holly Springs like a scythe. The people were fleeing, scattering; some trudged along the dirt road that wound past her grandmother's place, but they did not approach the house and Ida dared not run after them in case they carried the fatal miasma on their clothes or in their breath.

One afternoon, Ida was at the pump fetching water to carry out to her elders in the cotton fields when she heard a loud pounding on the gate. Setting down the bucket and dipper, she walked around the corner of the house, shaded her eyes with her hand, and spotted three men on horseback on the other side of the fence. After a moment, Ida recognized them as her next-door neighbors from Holly Springs, good friends of her parents. Although her grandmother had warned her that until the epidemic subsided she should not invite refugees into the house but should take necessities out to them instead, Ida was sure an exception could be made for people she knew. She waved her arm and called out a welcome, and the three men opened the gate and rode up to the house.

Ida met them on the front porch and escorted them inside to the parlor, inviting them to sit and asking about their health and offering them refreshments in such a stream of chatter that they scarcely had time to reply. "Do you have any news from home?" she asked breathlessly, looking from one somber face to another.

One man rose, took a letter from his coat pocket, and held it out to her. "My wife received this letter yesterday." He cleared his throat roughly, betraying his reluctance. "I'm so sorry, Ida."

Ida studied him for a moment, uncomprehending, before she roused herself and took the folded paper. She did not know who had written the letter, which began with an account of the disease's swift and merciless course through Holly Springs. Then words at the bottom of the first page leapt out at her: "Jim and Lizzie Wells have both died of the fever. They passed within twenty-four hours of each other. The children are all at home and the Howard Association has arranged for a neighbor woman to stay and look after them. Send word to Ida."

She could read no further.

Her grandmother's cottage, always a place of happiness and refuge, suddenly became a house of mourning. Ida wanted to rush home to her younger siblings, but yellow fever lingered in the town, and her grandmother, aunt, and uncle refused to let her go. Only three days later, when a doctor tending the children wrote to say that she ought to come home at once, did her grandmother reluctantly consent.

Her uncle took her to the nearest town on the railway line, but when she tried to purchase a ticket to Holly Springs, everyone at the station urged her not to go. "You go in there fresh from the county, and you'll fall victim at once," the ticket agent said.

"It's better you stay away until the epidemic is over," said the conductor. "If you fall sick yourself, how will you take care of the younger children?"

The ticket agent nodded grimly. "That's if any of them are still living by the time you get there."

Suddenly queasy, Ida pressed a hand to her waist to steady herself. "I must get home. My brothers and sisters need me. The doctor told me I should come."

The conductor dismissed that notion with a wave of his hand. "No Holly Springs doctor would have told you that. This one must be some stranger brought in for the emergency and eager to be gone again, with no real concern for the folks left behind. If you'd heard the stories we have, you wouldn't even think of going there."

Soundly chastised, Ida wavered. It was true she hadn't recognized the doctor's name. As other station workers piled on more warnings, she agreed to stay. She asked for paper and pen and found a quiet corner to write a letter home explaining her delay, but as she wrote, she thought of her next-eldest sister, Eugenia, crippled from a strange growth in her spine that had bent her nearly double and pinched her spinal cord, paralyzing her from the waist down. She could not walk, nor properly care for the younger children, especially nine-month-old Stanley.

Ida was the eldest. With her parents gone, the family was her responsibility. She had to get home.

Discarding the unfinished letter, she returned to the ticket booth and insisted on buying passage to Holly Springs, only to be told there were no more passenger trains running. A freight train was heading that way, and she could ride in the caboose. Before the agent could change his mind, Ida quickly agreed, paid the fare, and hurried outside to the platform where the train was waiting.

A conductor stood by to help her aboard the caboose, which was draped in black. "That's in mourning for two of my fellow conductors who died of this yellow fever," he told her as she studied the somber bunting. "You're making a terrible mistake, going to a town where so many have succumbed."

"Why are you running the train when you know you're as likely to get the fever as your two predecessors?" Ida countered.

He shrugged. "Somebody has to do it."

"That's exactly why I'm going home," said Ida. "I'm the oldest of seven living children. There's nobody but me to look after them now. Don't you think I should do my duty too?"

He hesitated, then extended a hand to help her aboard. "Goodbye, then, miss, and good luck to you."

The journey home was uncomfortable and felt interminable. When at last she arrived, the Holly Springs stationmaster regarded her in shock as she disembarked. "You shouldn't get off here," he said. "Stay on board and ride on to the next town."

"I live here," she replied shortly, hefting her bag.

She left him on the platform still calling protests after her. In front of the station, she looked for a cab, and when none could be found on the deserted street, she headed home on foot. A neighbor passed her along the way and offered her a ride in his wagon, but after expressing his condolences, he spent the last half mile chiding her for coming home. When she arrived, she met the woman appointed to care for her siblings just on her way out; she scolded Ida too, then told her that all of the children except Eugenia had come down with yellow fever. Five-year-old Annie and the eldest boy, James, were still in their sickbeds, but the others had recovered. All except baby Stanley, who had died four days before.

Blinking back tears, Ida thanked the woman and hurried into the house. "What are you doing here?" exclaimed Eugenia from her usual place on the sofa between the window and the fireplace, cold and swept clean now, in the height of summer. Her voice was as reproachful as the stationmaster's had been, but her relief was obvious.

When Ida returned from checking on the other children, Eugenia quietly and tearfully told her about their parents' last days, how her father had gone around the neighborhood nursing the sick and making coffins for the dead, how their mother had cared for the children until she had collapsed onto her sickbed. Their father tended her until she passed, though he too had already fallen ill. Before he perished he told Eugenia that he had saved up more than three hundred dollars, which he had entrusted to their family doctor when he last visited. It would be held in the safe in the Masonic Lodge downtown until Ida could retrieve it.

Even as Ida silently thanked her father for his foresight and marveled at the amount he had been able to put aside, she knew that even if she was frugal, three hundred dollars would not support a family of six for long. She would have to leave school, find a job, and arrange for someone to look after the children while she worked.

She soon learned that her father's Masonic brothers had other plans.

One Sunday afternoon, a group of Masons called to inform Ida of the arrangements that had been made on the children's behalf. Two men's wives longed for a little girl, so Annie would go to one family and Lily to the other. Two other men, both carpenters, each offered to apprentice one of the boys, and would provide for all their needs. The Masons had unanimously agreed that Ida was old enough to fend for herself.

"What about Eugenia?" asked Ida when they had finished.

The brothers exchanged guarded looks. "She must go to the poorhouse," one of the men said carefully. "She is a cripple and helpless, and no one has offered her a home."

Ida inhaled deeply, steadying herself, remaining calm. They had not even consulted her. They were scattering her family, and not one of those well-meaning men had asked how she felt about that. The very thought of her beloved Eugenia abandoned to a poorhouse where she would be unloved and neglected set her blood to boiling. It would not happen, not while she had breath in her body.

"I thank you for your concern," she said, "but you're not going to take any of my brothers and sisters anywhere. My mother and father would turn over in their graves if they knew their children had been scattered like leaves on the wind." She gestured, taking in the four walls surrounding them. "My parents owned this house, and now it's mine, and if you good men can help me find work, I'll take care of the children."

"You're a schoolgirl," one of the men protested. "You've never even had to care for your own self. You have no idea what it is to raise a family."

"I've been helping my mother mind the children for as long as I can remember."

"It's not the same," the first man said. "You're sixteen, right? You're too young to take on all alone what a father and a mother do together."

But Ida was adamant. Eventually she wore them down, and they agreed she should take responsibility for her siblings and promised to help her find work. Two of the men were chosen to be the children's legal guardians until Ida came of age.

Before long, a few of the Masonic brothers returned to tell her that after much consideration, they thought it best that she become a teacher. A small school in the countryside would not object to her youth and inexperience as long as she earned her certifications, which a bright girl like her ought to be able to do. It sounded like a reasonable plan, so Ida sat for the examination and earned her credential. With her guardians' help, she was hired to mind a small school six miles outside of town, for which she would be paid twenty-five dollars a month. An old friend of her mother's agreed to stay at the house to care for the children while Ida was away.

When the fall term began, Ida let out the hems of her dresses and put up her hair so that she would look more like a young woman and less like a schoolgirl. Every Monday morning she rose early and rode a mule six miles out into the countryside to the schoolhouse. She boarded with a student's family during the week, and every Friday afternoon she rode the mule back to Holly Springs. Saturdays and Sundays passed in a rush of washing and ironing and cooking, and escorting the children to church, and checking up on their progress in school. Her students' parents, aware of her circumstances, kindly offered her fresh eggs and butter to take home to her siblings. Between their generosity, her father's savings, and her wages, Ida managed and the children thrived.

So it was that from the time Ida was barely on the cusp of womanhood, she had learned that she could not count on other people to manage her affairs as well as she could herself. That principle applied less to kind-hearted friends and family than it did to politicians, and yet it was essential to have intelligent, ethical people in office so that the rich and the powerful did not exploit everyone else, and so that the majority could not tyrannize the minority. Ida also understood that she had an irrevocable responsibility to look out for her own, whether that meant her orphaned younger siblings or the Black community.

That was why Ida spent the fifth of November campaigning vigorously for President Taft. By no means did she suffer under the illusion that he was a perfect man, but as far as colored folks were concerned, he was the best of the four candidates.

After the polls closed, she awaited the campaign results with increasing apprehension as rumors of a Wilson landslide sped through the city. To her chagrin, when the final results were announced, the rumors proved all too true. Woodrow Wilson had won forty states, including Illinois, to Roosevelt's six and Taft's two. It was a thoroughly humiliating defeat for Taft.

No incumbent president had ever performed so poorly while seeking reelection, in both the popular vote and the Electoral College.

While the results of the presidential race disappointed Ida and Ferdinand, the down-ticket races brought both good tidings and bad—and the bad struck very close to home. Voters who came out to support Wilson also sent more Democrats to the Illinois General Assembly, and they elected the Democrat Edward Dunne as governor. A few days after the election, Ferdinand came home from work looking discouraged and angry, but his voice was calm when he told her that in the wake of the Republican losses, the timbre at the state's attorney's office had changed drastically, and he thought it prudent to resign.

"Never mind," said Ida stoutly, taking his hat and coat. "You'll build up your private practice again. We'll be fine."

She spoke with greater heartiness than she felt. Even though she had absolute confidence in her husband, his resignation, though necessary, was an unexpected blow.

Yet amid the disappointment and unsettling developments, she found hope. On Election Day, four more states had passed equal suffrage measures—Kansas, Michigan, Arizona, and Oregon. In Illinois, the candidates newly elected to the state legislature included two Progressive Party senators and twenty-five representatives to the House, all of whom had declared for woman suffrage during their campaigns.

For the Illinois state suffrage movement, the future had never looked brighter.

# 9
# November 1912

## NEW YORK, NEW YORK

## Maud

Maud had hoped that Theodore Roosevelt and the Progressive Party would sweep every voting district from Maine to California, so when the presidency went to Woodrow Wilson instead, she allowed herself a brief period of mourning, and then got back to work on her defense. Wilson's victory offered a silver lining: since he had won decisively, no one could argue that her persistent questioning at the Brooklyn Academy of Music had done him any harm.

She wondered if that would make any difference to the judges.

Ever since Magistrate Kempner had held Maud over for trial at the Court of Special Sessions, her lawyer had diligently prepared to confront a more rigorous prosecution. Mr. Kohler had found a witness among the attendees that night who would testify that she had not caused a disruption, but rather had posed questions to the candidate in a perfectly dignified manner. Mr. Kohler had also issued a subpoena to Woodrow Wilson asking him to appear before the court, but the president-elect had not been in the state of New York for the past ten days. Although several process servers were keeping a sharp eye out for him at his usual haunts, so far he had managed to evade the summons, and it was very unlikely that he would testify.

In the meantime, Maud did all she could to put her case before the court of public opinion. She granted several interviews with respected journalists and wrote numerous letters to the major New York City newspapers. She had no idea if a groundswell of popular support would sway the judges, but she had to try. It occurred to her that the judges might be inclined to weigh the evidence more thoroughly if the courtroom was filled with friendly observers. And if a few hostile antisuffragists showed up too, their jeers and nasty looks might evoke sympathetic indignation. It was worth a try.

Notice of the upcoming trial had already appeared in the papers, but in order to ensure a full gallery, Maud drew on her sense of humor and her penchant for the element of surprise and sent out dozens of personal invitations. On creamy ivory cards framed in sky blue, appropriate for any fine society event, she typed up a cordial message that was both a request for the honor of one's presence and a press release.

THE PUBLIC IS INVITED TO ATTEND THE TRIAL OF THE PEOPLE VS. MAUD MALONE, TO BE HELD TUESDAY, NOV. 12, 10 A. M., AT THE COURT OF SPECIAL SESSIONS, ATLANTIC AVENUE AND CLINTON STREET, BROOKLYN. THE CHARGE IS WILLFULLY DISTURBING A PUBLIC MEETING. THIS IS A MISDEMEANOR, THE PUNISHMENT FOR WHICH IS ONE YEAR IN PRISON OR $500 FINE. ON OCTOBER 19 AT A MEETING AT THE ACADEMY OF MUSIC, THE DEFENDANT GOT UP IN HER PLACE AND ASKED MR. WILSON, "WHAT ABOUT WOMAN SUFFRAGE?" SHE WAS THROWN OUT AND ARRESTED. MEN HAVE ALWAYS QUESTIONED CANDIDATES AT POLITICAL MEETINGS. WHY NOT WOMEN?

## C. O. T. A. S. MAUD MALONE.

C. O. T. A. S., a whimsical substitute for the traditional RSVP, meant "Come Over Tuesday and See." Maud knew the cleverer recipients would understand.

She mailed the invitations to friends, supporters, famous suffragists, and the best newspaper reporters within a reasonable train ride of Brooklyn. With any luck, the journalists would not only attend the trial but also report on the invitations ahead of time, increasing their reach.

On Tuesday morning one week after Election Day, Maud dressed with care in an embroidered brown shirtwaist and long flared skirt, a stylish purple velvet hat, and a white corsage. Her only other adornments, besides the silver wristwatch and pebble eyeglasses she wore everywhere, were her favorite yellow "Votes for Women" badge and an enameled tin brooch with a miniature portrait of Elizabeth Cady Stanton.

Although she was eager to make her case before the court, she felt a trifle nervous now that the day had come. She said little as her brother Sylvester escorted her to the courthouse. Her lawyer met them in the vestibule, where they conferred about the procedure as they awaited their summons into the courtroom. They waited, and waited, and eventually were informed that there would be a four-hour delay, no explanation given. Deflated, concerned that the audience she had tried so hard to muster up would vanish rather than linger, Maud nodded consent when Mr. Kohler suggested that they find a quiet restaurant and continue their conversation over lunch.

When they returned a few minutes before two o'clock, Maud's spirits rose at the sight of a long queue of spectators filing into the courtroom. Among them she recognized several loyal friends, some acquaintances from suffrage meetings, and many a yellow "Votes for Women" badge pinned proudly to a lapel. As she entered and walked down the center aisle flanked by her brother and her lawyer, she spotted her friend Mary Donnelly seated a row back from the defense team's table. When Maud caught her eye and smiled, Mary nodded soberly, her expression resolved.

The defense and prosecution were seated, every space in the gallery was filled, the clerks took their places, and still the judges did not appear. "They must be having a good luncheon," Maud overheard a man remark, and she would have laughed aloud except at that moment Justices Howard Forker, John Fleming, and Cornelius Collins finally strode in, stern and imposing in their black robes.

After the perfunctory rites and opening statements, a young man named James Byrne was called to the stand. Maud clasped her hands together in her lap, suddenly anxious. She had never seen this fellow before, and although Mr. Kohler had summoned him, he might have a damaging tale to tell. A few minutes into his testimony, however, Maud breathed a faint sigh of relief. His description of the incident was accurate and unembellished, although if, as he claimed, he had indeed "hastened to the lady's side to protect her when the audience began to rough-house," she had not noticed it. Of course, her gaze had been fixed on the recalcitrant man on the stage below.

When white-haired Justice Fleming asked if the militant suffragette Maud Malone had caused any harm that night, Mr. Byrne shook his head. "No, sir," he said emphatically, "nor would I say she was particularly militant. The lady didn't hurt a single person, or a chair, or a curtain, or anything at all in the Academy of Music."

The justices frowned as if they had expected a very different answer.

The next witness was Frederick Lohman, advertising agent, whom Maud remembered from her previous hearing. He approached the stand with a more confident stride than before, was sworn in, and took his seat, but then his gaze caught Maud's and his resolve seemed to waver. She smiled, and he smiled weakly back, and with much throat-clearing and blushing, he briefly summarized the events as he recalled them, without uttering a single critical word about her. In fact, he concluded, "I didn't hear the lady open her mouth at that there meeting."

Maud winced. She *had* spoken at the meeting; that was never in question. Would the justices believe Mr. Lohman lied? No, perhaps not. Perhaps the important point was that she could not have caused a terrible disturbance, if a member of the audience had not even heard her.

Sylvester leaned closer and murmured, "I think Mr. Lohman fancies you."

"Hush," she whispered back.

Next, Mr. Senft made a return appearance, as theatrical and condemning as his October debut. He improvised on his original performance in several significant ways. First, he claimed that he had put her out of the meeting so vigorously that he had fallen down the aisle and barely escaped serious injury. Second, he swore that he had not treated Miss Malone roughly at all, but had merely put his hand on her arm and asked her to sit down. "The lady told me I had no right to touch her," he said, his bravado fading a trifle. "I rather thought maybe I hadn't, so I removed my hand."

The third variation was the most surprising. As his last question, Mr. Kohler asked Mr. Senft if he was against woman suffrage. "No, sir. I'm not," he declared, shaking his head vigorously. "I'm in favor of it. I just don't believe in what some of these suffragists do."

After that curious turn, a new player took the stage. Herbert Swin, the superintendent of the Academy, testified that he was in his office when word came to him that there was trouble in the auditorium. "I went upstairs and saw a woman—*that* woman, the defendant—standing in the balcony," he said, inclining his head Maud's way. "Many other people around her, most of them women, were yelling, 'Shut up!' and 'Put her out!'"

"What did you do when you observed this disturbance?" asked Mr. Kellogg, the prosecuting attorney.

"Well, I figured it was my duty to make sure the lady didn't get hurt and that the lady didn't hurt the Academy or any of its fixtures. So I went up there and told her that she must be quiet or leave. I cautioned the ushers not to touch her, as she was waving her arms around violently."

*Oh, honestly.* Maud resisted the impulse to roll her eyes.

"What happened next?" Mr. Kellogg prompted.

"Magistrate Kempner came along and told her she would be arrested unless she sat down. She didn't, so the police took her out the fire escape."

Eventually Mr. Swin was dismissed, and the judges summoned Maud to the stand.

They interrogated her in turns, Justice Collins more harshly than his colleagues, as if he were Woodrow Wilson's dearest friend and took the incident as a personal affront. Justice Forker seemed most interested in extricating from her a tearful admission that she regretted not taking her seat immediately after asking her question. "Are you not sorry you were so persistent?" he asked, seeming genuinely baffled.

"No, Your Honor, I'm not sorry," she replied. "I didn't go to the meeting with the intention of disrupting it, but I was determined to hold my ground until I got an answer, one way or the other."

Curiously, all three judges seemed fixated on this particular point, and each pressed her from different angles as if searching for the hidden catch that would release the lid on her composure and allow shame and remorse to come billowing out. But although she felt beleaguered by the incessant barrage of questions, she could not give them what they apparently wanted. She firmly believed she had done nothing wrong that evening, but had only exercised her right to free speech as the First Amendment granted. She could not pretend to feel ashamed.

"How long did you stand up after you asked Governor Wilson, 'What about woman suffrage?'" Justice Fleming demanded.

"I was standing about ten minutes," Maud replied.

He smirked. "According to the common notion of time, or according to a woman's notion?"

The three justices laughed, and about half the courtroom joined in. Maud raised her eyebrows and regarded the judges with mild surprise. Did they consider this trial a nuisance or a lark? They seemed unable to decide exactly why to dislike it, only that they should.

Evidently it was the former, for Justice Fleming's mirth was short-lived. "What did Governor Wilson do," he asked, eyes narrowing, "when Mr. Senft put his hand on your arm and the other men attempted to escort you out?"

Escort? Maud smothered a laugh. The judge made it sound like the men had gallantly taken her outside for a breath of fresh air to cure a feminine swoon. "Governor Wilson called out from the stage, asking them not to be rude to a lady, and said I had a right to ask my question. He said suffrage was a state issue and not a national issue, and so he would not answer. I replied that I wanted to know why he didn't consider it a national issue. I thought it was very ignorant of him not to know it most definitely is one."

A low murmur of reproach went up from some of the men in the audience; that and her lawyer's carefully fixed expression warned her that she might have gone too far. *Very well,* she told herself, chagrined. No more calling the president-elect ignorant, even if he was.

Justice Collins glowered down at her. "Did you, when you persisted in standing at your seat after Governor Wilson had said that he could not discuss the question with you then—did you hear Magistrate Kempner say, 'If you don't sit down I'll order your arrest'?"

"I heard him say that it would cost me thirty days if I did not."

"Then you concede that you had ample warning," said Justice Collins, triumphant. "You ought to have taken your seat after Governor Wilson announced that he would not answer you. Your sole purpose was evidently to force him into a statement about woman suffrage, and by remaining on your feet after calls from the audience and the chairman of the meeting to take your seat, you provoked members of the audience to disorderly acts."

"Much of the audience had seemed very much provoked," Maud acknowledged, "but I deny that I caused them to act as they did. They're entirely responsible for their own behavior—but really, there's no telling with such men. They go around and around like windmills when a woman's voice is heard in one of their meetings. It would be awfully funny in another context."

A light ripple of laughter went up from the gallery, but the judges were clearly unamused. When Maud was dismissed from the stand, they withdrew to their chambers to ponder the evidence.

"They won't need long," said Maud glumly to Sylvester, rising and working the strain from her shoulders. "I think they made up their minds before they called the court to order."

"Maybe that's why they took such a long lunch," Sylvester remarked.

When Maud laughed, Mr. Kohler regarded them with utter disbelief. Maud apologized and assured him that this was just their Irish sense of humor at work, and that they both took the proceedings very seriously. She broke off abruptly when a man behind her muttered, "Six months in jail, O Militant Maud."

He had leaned forward so close that she had felt his breath on the nape of her neck. Instinctively, she swatted him away as if he were an insect, but before she could turn around and chide him, she saw Mary Donnelly approaching, her pretty face flushed with anger and indignation.

"Those dreadful men," she murmured icily, glancing over her shoulder at the door to the judges' chambers. "Their smug laughter makes me ill."

"It makes me quite upset too," Maud admitted. "I'd almost prefer for them to scold me as the magistrate did."

Mary pursed her lips and shook her head. "I'm sure they'll convict."

"Let's not give up hope just yet," Mr. Kohler broke in.

Mary seized Maud's hands and clasped them to her heart. "If they fine you, don't pay. Go to jail instead. We ladies will march to jail after you. And tonight, outside the prison walls behind which you will be languishing, we'll hold the most wonderful meeting that the cause has ever known. There will be such a commotion stirred up that you will hear it in your cell. And then—"

"All rise," the bailiff intoned. The justices were returning to the courtroom.

Maud felt her heart flutter and she took a deep, shaky breath. Mary squeezed her hands, threw her one last imploring look, and hurried back to her seat. Maud sank tremulously back into her own.

As the justices settled into their chairs and arranged various documents on the table before them, Mr. Kohler rose and asked for permission to address the bench. When they allowed it, he made a passionate appeal for them to dismiss the charges to, as he put it, "save this woman from the stigma of a criminal conviction."

Justice Fleming laughed, and Justice Collins scowled. "We wish to assure the lady," Justice Forker said dryly, "that her past behavior is too much a matter of public record for any finding by this court to be a stigma upon her. Her own long career answers any imputation that a conviction may carry with it."

Maud knew then that the judges had ruled against her.

Thus the verdict delivered moments later came as no surprise: she had indeed been found guilty of the misdemeanor of disturbing a public meeting. "The trouble with you, Miss Malone, isn't that you stood up and asked the question, which is entirely legal," said Justice Forker. "Rather that you continued to stand after asking it, which is a crime in the eyes of the law."

Maud thought it was utter nonsense and drew herself up to protest, but Mr. Kohler's light touch on her arm reminded her that she had yet to hear her sentence. Whatever it was, she had already decided to appeal.

"We unanimously decline to give Miss Malone any additional punishment beyond the decision convicting her," said Justice Collins, glancing at a paper on the desk before him. "The sentence is suspended."

An exclamation of mingled surprise and delight and chagrin went up from the gallery, but Maud was thunderstruck with dismay. She could not appeal a suspended sentence. The case would end right there and then, without President-Elect Wilson being obliged to reply to the subpoena or to express any opinion on the suffrage question at all.

"Your Honors," Maud blurted, bolting to her feet. "Would you please fine me five dollars to strengthen my grounds for an appeal?"

The three men regarded her, incredulous. "We regret that we cannot accommodate you," said Justice Collins wearily, rising. "Court is adjourned."

As the three justices left the courtroom, Maud leaned forward and braced herself against the table, thoughts churning. "I want you to file an appeal," she told Mr. Kohler in a low voice beneath the din. "I know what you're going to say. It will likely be dismissed. Nonetheless, I want you to make the attempt. Please."

He looked as if he might protest, but he sighed and nodded.

President-Elect Wilson had ducked the question long enough. Maud fervently wanted to confront him in a courtroom and put him to question under oath, but if that failed, she would find another way to make certain he could not forget or ignore the matter of woman suffrage.

# 10

# November 1912

## PHILADELPHIA, PENNSYLVANIA

### Alice

On the morning of Thursday, November 21, Alice took the early train into Philadelphia and checked into a Quaker boardinghouse a few blocks from the Witherspoon Building, the venue for the convention. Most of the delegates were staying at the luxurious Hotel Walton on Broad Street, which was said to be as sumptuous as New York's Waldorf-Astoria and only a pleasant five-minute stroll to the convention. But although Alice appreciated comforts, she didn't require luxury, so the frugality and relative calm of the boardinghouse suited her perfectly well.

She had time to settle into her room and review her notes before she set out for Independence Square, bundled warmly in a brown walking suit, a dark gray wool coat, and a black felt hat with a purple, yellow, and white striped band. The day was crisp and bright, with the faint scent of moldering autumn leaves and coal smoke on the wind. She arrived just in time to witness the arrival of the automobile procession, twenty gleaming black cars adorned with "Votes for Women" banners carrying persons of honor, including the National's executive officers. When she realized that this, and this alone, was the parade she would have been in charge of had she accepted the job with the PWSA, she was very glad she had declined. Parades should inform and inspire, not merely transport dignitaries from their hotel to a rally site.

If all went as Alice and Lucy planned, in a few months they would show the world all that a parade could be.

The square had a festive, anticipatory air as hundreds of delegates mingled with the usual noonday crowd that always gathered there in fair weather, and now looked on with curiosity or skepticism. Five platforms had been arranged at different points around the square, from which the three dozen speakers, including Alice, would address the crowd. The program began with a single speaker, Mrs. Dennett, who read a Declaration of Women's Rights from the main platform in front of Independence Hall. How thrilling it was to hear the condemnation of male tyranny and the assertion of women's rights and responsibilities as full citizens while standing before the historic building where the Declaration of Independence and the Constitution had been debated and signed!

Other speakers followed Mrs. Dennett, addressing dense crowds gathered around the stages. Alice was heading for her own venue when she heard a familiar voice call her name and, turning, discovered Lucy Burns making her way toward her through the crowd. "Hello, Miss Paul," she said, reaching out to clasp Alice's hand. "How's the boardinghouse?"

Alice smiled. "Not nearly as opulent as the Hotel Walton, I imagine."

"It's gorgeous," Lucy declared as they continued on to Alice's stage. "The Palm Room must be the most luxurious dining hall I've ever seen, and the roof garden is so lush and beautiful, a bit of summer in late autumn. You should come see it."

"Perhaps I shall."

Alice and Lucy paused near the foot of the steps to the stage while the preceding speaker finished, listening with keen interest, applauding the most stirring lines along with everyone else. Afterward, Boston lawyer and suffragist Teresa Crowley took the stage, nodded formally to Alice, and began to introduce her to the audience. Mrs. Crowley started unremarkably enough by describing Alice's education and work for the cause, but then she went off on a tangent, declaring huffily that she did not approve of "the militant methods of the British suffragettes who taught Miss Paul the tactics she now employs on our shores." It was a strange, undiplomatic barb, quite unsuited to the moment, but when Mrs. Crowley finished and waved Alice up to the stage, she had no choice but to set the insult aside and carry on.

Inspired by the historic setting, Alice had decided to speak about another momentous suffrage demonstration that had taken place there thirty-six years before. In 1876, at a celebration of the nation's centennial, a small band of suffragists had asked to submit a petition granting universal suffrage. "This permission was refused," said Alice, looking out upon the throng of rapt faces, "but led by the redoubtable Susan B. Anthony, the women marched to the square and presented their petition. Then they went to the Chestnut Street sidewalk and held a meeting of their own."

Alice reminded her listeners that four years before that, in Rochester, New York, Miss Anthony had pressured the local registrar into adding her name and those of fifteen other women to the voter rolls, after which she had marched to the polls and cast her ballot. She had been arrested on the spot, and in the trial that had followed, she had been found guilty and fined one hundred dollars. "Miss Anthony never paid that fine," Alice said, her glance lighting upon Mrs. Crowley. "Some might have called her actions extreme. Others might have denounced her as militant. Today, however, I trust that every single woman who longs for the ballot is sincerely grateful to Miss Anthony for her remarkable courage, for doing the bold thing that no one else dared to do."

Mrs. Crowley sniffed and deliberately avoided Alice's gaze.

"Thirty-six years after Miss Anthony's suffrage petition was rebuffed, we stand in Independence Square making the same appeal for full enfranchisement," said Alice, raising her voice to be heard over shouts of affirmation. "Today, American men of African descent and Native American Indian men, once denied the vote, have been granted equal suffrage, and rightly so. Why not women?" Cheers and applause rang out. "Why not us?"

As the shouts and cheers rose ever higher, Alice waved in gratitude and farewell before ceding the stage to the next speaker. Lucy's eyes were bright with merry satisfaction when they reunited at the edge of the crowd. "In the future," she said, "Mrs. Crowley will think better of needling you moments before you must address a crowd."

"I don't object to being called militant," Alice replied. "I simply wish people wouldn't consider the word an insult."

They fell in step together, and as they walked the eight blocks to the Witherspoon Building, they discussed their strategy for the day. President Dr. Anna Shaw would formally call the convention to order at 2:30 P.M., followed by an official welcome from Mayor Blankenburg on behalf of the city of Philadelphia. A few more welcoming speeches would follow, and then reports from executive officers and committee chairs. Later that evening, at a program called Campaign Night, Jane Addams would officiate as Dr. Shaw delivered the President's Annual Address, followed by speeches from the leaders of the four state campaigns that had won woman suffrage in the recent election. Mrs. Lewis had arranged for Alice and Lucy to meet Miss Addams afterward; they could deliver Mrs. Blatch's letter, make their case for a renewed federal campaign, and ask for Miss Addams's support.

From a block away, they spied throngs of well-dressed women bustling through the ornately carved front portal to the Witherspoon Building, eleven stories of white stone with sixteen terra-cotta statues of revered personages from the history of the Presbyterian Church above the entrances. Reporters were milling about too, notepads in hand, pencils at the ready, eagerly buttonholing one delegate or another in search of a pithy, provocative quote. The press was very keen on the suffrage movement regardless of the political perspective of its individual writers, editors, or publishers, and for good reason: editions featuring major suffrage events usually sold out, and ongoing coverage had increased subscriptions throughout the country.

Passing through the bustling front foyer into the main hall, Alice and Lucy found the mood buoyant, even festive, the attendees' spirits soaring in the wake of the four recent state suffrage victories. The hall, rapidly filling with what Alice estimated to be nearly three hundred women, was adorned with large banners bearing suffrage slogans and artwork, and although the NAWSA had no official colors but favored yellow and white, Alice found the traditional suffrage tricolor of purple, green, and white abundant in draperies, bunting, and the women's apparel. On one wall hung an enormous map of the United States, with states shaded in colors according to their status—full suffrage achieved, measures pending, or trailing behind. In a column on the left were listed the names of states where woman suffrage prevailed: California, Colorado, Idaho, Oregon, Washington, Wyoming, and, apparently only recently appended, Arizona, Kansas, and Oregon. Below that— Alice drew closer for a better view, puzzled—it seemed that paper had been pasted to obscure a tenth name.

"Why has Michigan been removed from the list?" Alice wondered aloud.

"Perhaps it's an oversight," Lucy replied, frowning worriedly.

It wasn't until hours later, after the opening session, that they learned from a delegate from Grand Rapids what had happened. Although the initial returns from the November 5 election had indicated that the state suffrage measure had passed by a substantial majority, soon thereafter, opponents had attempted to discard the votes of two counties on a technicality. Although that effort failed, when the final tally came in, the majority had swung inexplicably against the measure. In the demands for recounts that followed, an astounding amount of corruption and voter suppression was uncovered—improperly processed ballots, not enough ballots provided to districts where approval of suffrage was strong, election inspectors assigned to assist illiterate voters marking ballots "no" despite the voter's request to mark "yes," antisuffrage literature left in voting booths.

It was outrageous and appalling, and it provided even more evidence that the state-by-state approach was too tortuous, too slow, and too vulnerable to corruption to remain the National's priority.

This was the case Alice and Lucy made to Jane Addams later that night. Alice had long wanted to meet the venerated suffragist and reformer, whom she deeply admired as the founder of the social work profession in the United States. For decades, the fifty-two-year-old progressive activist had worked on issues essential to mothers and children, public health, and world peace. Hull House, the settlement house she had cofounded on Chicago's Near West Side, served the common good through social, educational, and artistic programs in its working-class neighborhood, and it had become the archetype for hundreds of other similar institutions throughout the country.

Although Miss Addams had promised to meet with Alice and Lucy immediately following the Campaign Night program, so many other colleagues and admirers wanted to speak with her that the two younger women had to wait until the crowd thinned before they could properly approach and introduce themselves. When Mrs. Blatch had arranged their meeting, she evidently had told Miss Addams of their intention to focus on a federal amendment. She must have praised them highly too, for Miss Addams seemed thoroughly familiar with their purpose and asked only for the clarification of a few details.

"Your credentials are impressive," said Miss Addams, giving each of them an appraising glance, "but I believe the other officers would be more inclined to appoint you if you could explain not only why you want to focus on the federal effort—which you do account for quite well—but what you will do differently than your predecessors."

"I intend to do nearly everything differently," said Alice. "Except for the committee's presence in the capital, and the annual lobbying of Congress, the federal campaign will be entirely transformed. It will be focused, energized, and utterly relentless, and we will begin by capturing the attention of politicians and public alike. I intend to launch our new national campaign with a parade in Washington, D.C., on March third, the day before Woodrow Wilson's inauguration."

Miss Addams's dark eyebrows rose. "Interesting timing."

"Ideal timing, I should think," said Lucy, smiling. "Thousands of visitors will flock to the capital for the inaugural events, so we're certain to have an excellent turnout of spectators. The press will cover our parade and spread our message throughout the land."

"The timing suggests that your target is the president-elect." Miss Addams studied them, weighing and measuring. "A curious choice, since the president has no power to amend the Constitution. Amendments are for the Congress to pass and the states to ratify. Shouldn't your focus be on Congress?"

Alice and Lucy exchanged a quick look. "It's true the president can't directly modify the Constitution," said Alice, turning back to Miss Addams, "but he has great political influence over those who can. We believe that if we win the president's support, the strength of his endorsement will persuade the Congress, and the public, to make equal suffrage the law of the land."

"Very well said. I agree that the president has considerable power to shape national discourse, for better or for worse." Miss Addams nodded, smiling. "Thank you, ladies. I'm quite satisfied. I'll wholeheartedly recommend you, Miss Paul, as the new chair of the Congressional Committee, and you, Miss Burns, as her second-in-command."

"Thank you very much, Miss Addams," Alice exclaimed, as Lucy chimed in the same.

"I'll bring the matter up tomorrow afternoon, at the Symposium on National Work," Miss Addams said. "You could be appointed and confirmed by the end of the conference, unless there is some challenge."

Alice and Lucy could not imagine how anyone would challenge a nomination made by the vice president of the National, and they said so. Miss Addams smiled wryly and said that one never knew, and expectations were often overturned when politics entered the scene.

Alice and Lucy parted from Miss Addams relieved and jubilant, and they went their separate ways to seek a well-earned good night's rest.

They met the next morning in the foyer of Witherspoon Hall before the first session opened at ten o'clock. They attended the first two presentations together, but they parted company before noon so that Alice could attend to some clerical work for Mrs. Lewis and Lucy could meet up with the rest of the New York delegation. Alice thought nothing more of Miss Addams's parting remarks until midafternoon, when she fell in with some friends from Pennsylvania on her way to the Symposium on National Work. Her friends broke off their conversation to welcome her, but quickly took it up again as they walked. Their subject was a scandal that threatened to split the National, the possible censure of one of their most beloved officers.

Alice needed a moment to grasp that they were discussing Jane Addams.

"What could anyone possibly have against Miss Addams?" she protested, keeping her voice low.

"There have been some disgruntled whispers about her partisan activity," one friend replied, mouth pinched in worry. "Everyone knows she endorsed Mr. Roosevelt's nomination at the Progressive Party convention, and she campaigned for him, speaking at rallies, in debates—"

"Campaigning isn't against the National's bylaws," said Alice.

"Perhaps not," said another friend, glancing over her shoulder for eavesdroppers, "but it's been an unwritten rule ever since Susan B. Anthony recommended a policy of nonpartisanship, back in the day. Mrs. Harper, the head of the National's press bureau, is incensed, and she's not alone. I've heard rumors that someone may introduce an amendment to our constitution forbidding officers from publicly supporting any particular candidate or party."

Alice felt a stirring of dread. This was not the constitutional amendment she wanted the officers and delegates to be concerned with at the moment.

"Other officers have engaged in similar activities," the first woman said. "Mrs. Dennett and Mrs. Ashley sent letters of support for the Socialist ticket from headquarters using the National's letterhead stationery. If the vice president may be condemned, why not the secretary and treasurer? Why single out Miss Addams?"

Alice shook her head in reply, for anything she said would only be conjecture. Apparently even someone as beloved as Jane Addams could have rivals within the suffrage movement. What would this controversy mean for Miss Addams, and for Alice's hopes for the Congressional Committee chairmanship, which surely depended entirely upon the strength of Miss Addams's recommendation? What would it mean for the future of the National?

The session was called to order. Alice followed the first two reports closely while also taking the measure of the crowd; the mood was heightened, excited, expectant, but nothing seemed amiss. Yet when the agenda turned to congressional work, and Miss Addams approached the podium, a smattering of applause and murmurs of disapproval revealed the fractures in the group's ostensible unity. Uneasy, Alice clasped her hands together in her lap and maintained the appearance of serenity as Miss Addams nominated her for the chairmanship. Mrs. Kent followed up by charmingly stating that she would be grateful to step down, so she asked her dear friends not to put her name forward. After two other candidates were proposed, Dr. Shaw announced that the executive officers would confer and vote by the last day of the convention.

Throughout the afternoon, even as the work of the

convention went on, the controversy simmered. By Saturday morning, it threatened to boil over.

The opening session had barely begun when Mrs. Ida Husted Harper introduced the rumored amendment to the bylaws forbidding officers to lend their influence to any political party, and to require officers to adhere to strictly nonpartisan positions. An exception was made for officers hailing from woman suffrage states, who were permitted and encouraged to participate in elections and to cast their ballots however they pleased. An unscheduled debate ensued, which Dr. Shaw valiantly managed, giving ten minutes to Mrs. Harper, ten to Miss Addams, and three to anyone else who wished to weigh in. By the end of the afternoon, prominent suffragists had taken sides against longtime comrades while hundreds of delegates observed the widening split with astonishment and dismay. In due course Mrs. Harper's amendment was resoundingly beaten, 380 to 38, but the damage was done.

Alice and Lucy kept each other's spirits up as the convention drew to a close. Alice took heart on Monday afternoon when Mrs. Kent, presenting the Report of the Congressional Committee, glanced her way and smiled when she mentioned several new members who would likely join the Washington branch of the National in the months ahead, "under the new chairman."

To Alice's relief, the defeat of Mrs. Harper's amendment and all of the debate that had preceded it seemed to have resolved the conflict. The Thanksgiving Service, an ecumenical program of prayer, hymns, and sermons held at the Metropolitan Opera House on Sunday afternoon, did much to remind them of their common goal, their higher purpose. In the end Miss Addams was not censured; the wealthy benefactress Mrs. Alva Belmont did not quit the National, as she had told a newspaperman she might; and Dr. Shaw was reelected president, although by a smaller margin than before.

And on the last day of the convention, as the delegates were boarding trains and heading home to the four corners of the nation, reinvigorated and newly inspired for the battles to come, the National's officers held their final executive meeting in Westminster Hall of the Witherspoon Building. There Alice was appointed chairman of the Congressional Committee, with Lucy Burns as her second. Conditions for their appointments were imposed, inconvenient but not unreasonable.

After a brief stop home to pack her things and plan, Alice was on her way to Washington.

# 11
# Late November 1912
## CHICAGO, ILLINOIS

### Ida

On the Saturday after Thanksgiving, Ida organized a luncheon feast at the Negro Fellowship
League building for single adults who had no family
in Chicago and had been unable to travel home for the
holiday. Most of the guests were young southern men
who had come north in search of better jobs and relief
from Jim Crow, but a few young ladies attended too, impeccably dressed, arriving in pairs or groups of three.
They sat together at one long table in the middle of the
room, sometimes pretending not to notice the admiring glances of the young men, occasionally rewarding
one or another with a demure smile. Like the majority
of the diners, the menu had southern origins, since Ida

had planned it herself and had included many favorite dishes from her Mississippi childhood—roasted turkey with cornbread dressing, honey-baked ham, potato salad, collard greens, sweet potato pie, and creamed corn.

When the meal was nearly over, Jane Addams stopped by to drop off a box of suffrage literature she had collected at the National American Woman Suffrage Association's annual convention. She stayed to help tidy up the dining room, and while they worked, Jane told Ida about the convention proceedings—the policy debates, the election of officers, the woeful state of the organization's finances, a controversy over the management of the National's official publication the *Woman's Journal,* and a startling scandal with Jane herself at the center.

After her friend told her how she had narrowly escaped censure, Ida had to laugh. "I warned you not to campaign for Teddy Roosevelt."

Jane regarded her wryly. "The problem isn't that I campaigned for *him,* but that I campaigned at all. The National is officially nonpartisan, and therefore its officers are expected to appear so as well, at least in public. I thought it was clear that my opinions were my own, but apparently, I should have done more to avoid giving the impression that I spoke on behalf of the organization."

"I suppose." Ida sighed and shook her head as she wiped down one of the long tables. "But why shouldn't officers campaign for the candidate, or the party, that includes woman suffrage in their platform? For that matter, why doesn't the National speak for itself by endorsing candidates who favor equal suffrage?"

"That's an excellent question." Jane paused from sweeping the floor to consider. "Perhaps because they're afraid of losing support from other parties if they align themselves too closely with one." She fixed her dark, deep-set eyes on Ida knowingly. "It's unfortunate you weren't there to raise that point during the debate."

"I'm not a member of the National."

"You're welcome to join."

Ida laughed shortly. "Maybe, maybe not." She flung the rag down on the table, planted a fist on her hip, and made a sweeping gesture, indicating herself from head to toe. "How many people who look like me did you see at that convention?"

Jane hesitated, resting her weight upon the broom as if it were a walking staff. "Scarcely a handful, I'm afraid. The vast majority of delegates were white, Protestant, Anglo-Saxon, and rather well-to-do, hardly a cross-section of American womanhood."

Ida nodded and took up the rag again, scrubbing the table vigorously. "That's what I'm talking about."

"There were few women of color present," Jane acknowledged. "All the more reason you should have been there, and should be next year. Someone has to speak for Black women or they'll be overlooked, and their concerns will be neglected as policies are formed and become law. The best time to shape the clay is before it goes into the kiln."

Ida inhaled deeply, squaring her shoulders. There weren't many white women who spoke to her on matters of race as frankly as Jane did, but Jane was a rarity, a white, female charter member of the NAACP. The two of them had a comfortable, collaborative friendship that belied their outward differences—Ida, a woman of color born into slavery in the Deep South; Jane, raised in sensible midwestern privilege as the daughter of a founder of the Illinois Republican Party. They were only two years apart in age, and both had spent more than half their lives toiling on the front lines of the struggle for social justice and social change. They understood and respected each other, and Ida did not need Jane to argue her point any further to recognize the urgent truth of it: the suffrage movement could not be the province of wealthy white women alone, or the achievements they made—ostensibly on behalf of all women—might benefit only themselves.

Experience and broken trust had taught Ida not to

put too much faith in white systems of government and law, or in white authorities who promised to help her navigate those systems. The lynching at the Curve had driven that lesson home, but truly, that schooling had begun in her childhood and had never really ended.

Years before her friends had been hauled out of a Memphis jail cell and murdered, and before her beloved newspaper had been destroyed and her life threatened for telling the truth about it, Ida was a young woman raising five siblings on a country schoolteacher's wages and what remained of their father's legacy. After acquiring some teaching experience, and urgently needing to increase her income, Ida had decided to seek a position in a larger school that paid higher wages. Her father's sister, Fannie Butler, encouraged Ida to move in with her in Memphis and teach in a rural Shelby County school while she studied for the qualifying examination to teach for the city school district. Aunt Fannie had been widowed in the yellow fever epidemic, and she had a daughter close in age to Ida's youngest sisters, so she offered to mind Annie and Lily while Ida worked. Aunt Belle offered to take in Eugenia, as well as her brothers James and George, who were old enough to work on the family farm. At first Ida resisted breaking up the family she had fought so hard to hold together, but her elders convinced her that it would be better for everyone in the long run, and that staying temporarily with loving aunts was not at all the same as parceling out the children to strangers.

Soon after moving herself, Annie, and Lily to Aunt Fannie's home, Ida was hired to teach at a school in the town of Woodstock, ten miles north of Memphis. The new position paid a better salary than her first job, and since it was only a short train ride away, she could travel back and forth every day rather than returning only on weekends. Every spare moment not spent teaching, grading assignments, or tending to her sisters she devoted to studying for her city credential.

One soft and balmy morning in May 1884, two months shy of her twenty-second birthday, Ida boarded the early-morning northbound train, mulling over her lesson plans and a possible approach to motivate a struggling student. As always, she purchased a first-class ticket, a comfort in which her improved circumstances allowed her to indulge. She settled into a seat in the ladies' car, took out a book, and was already lost in the pages when the train chugged out of the station.

Before long, the conductor came down the aisle collecting tickets. When Ida passed hers to him, he studied it, frowned, and returned it. "I can't take your ticket here," he said.

Ida thought that was odd, but as the conductor

moved on, she decided not to worry about it. She put the ticket into her satchel and resumed reading.

Eventually the conductor finished collecting the other passengers' tickets, and he returned to Ida. "Maybe you didn't understand me," he said, jerking his thumb over his shoulder to indicate the forward carriage. "You need to go sit in the other car."

"The forward car is a smoker," said Ida. "I cannot abide tobacco smoke. Since I paid for a first-class seat, and I am already comfortably settled here, I shall stay."

"I can't allow that."

Ida fixed him with a stern look and said in her best teacher voice, "The law allows it. Why shouldn't you?"

He scowled and looked as if he might retort, but instead he seized her right arm, tucked his other arm beneath her left armpit, and attempted to haul her out of the seat. She resisted, bracing her feet against the floor and grasping the seat in front of her with her left hand. When his grip on her right arm grew painfully tight, she twisted her head and fastened her teeth into the back of his hand.

He yelped and released her. She slid down the bench away from him toward the window, braced herself more securely, and glared up at him, defiant. He glowered for a moment, then turned and strode away and out the rear of the car. She dared hope she might be permitted to travel the remaining few miles in peace, but the conductor soon returned with the baggageman and another brawny fellow. She did not make it easy for them, but outnumbering and outmuscling her, they managed to drag her from her seat. As they wrestled her down the aisle, several white passengers began applauding and calling out praise to the railroad men; a few gentlemen even stood on their seats to get a better view.

By the time they reached the front of the car, the train had halted at a station. Ida glanced through the filmy window into the smoker car, which was already packed full of white men puffing away on their pipes and cigars and other colored people who had been dislodged from more comfortable places. "I will get off the train now rather than go into the smoking car," she declared through clenched teeth. "Unhand me so I may retrieve my satchel."

At first the men did not believe her—Who would waste train fare? How would she get to her destination?—but in their moment of confusion she wrenched herself free, pushed her way past them, and snatched up her bag. Some of the white passengers cheered as she disembarked, delighted to see her humiliated. When the train started up again, she watched it depart from the platform, fuming. She was breathless, her hair was mussed, and the seams attaching the sleeves of her linen coat had been torn out, but otherwise she was physically unharmed.

She was furious, though, and as soon as she returned to Memphis, she hired a lawyer to bring a suit against the Chesapeake, Ohio and Southwestern Railroad Company.

Months passed as Ida awaited her day in court. One delay followed another, but even as she went about the business of daily life—teaching, studying, caring for her sisters, earning her credential, acquiring a more lucrative job with a school in Memphis—the lawsuit made no progress. Eventually she discovered that her lawyer had been bought off by the railroad, so she fired him and sought another. To her chagrin, the only one who would take the case was a white man, James Micajah Greer, a veteran of the Confederate Army. Defying her expectations, he served her faithfully, and in December, seven months after the incident, her case finally went to trial. Mr. Greer argued that the company had violated two Tennessee statutes: one that prohibited railroads from charging colored passengers a first-class fare and then seating them in second-class cars, and a second that required "separate but equal" accommodations for colored folks and whites. The presiding judge, James O. Pierce, a veteran of the Union

Army from Minnesota, ruled in Ida's favor in the non-jury trial, and she was awarded $500 in damages. She would never forget the headline that appeared in the *Memphis Appeal* the following day: "A Darky Damsel Obtains a Verdict for Damages."

The infuriating pejorative stung, but far less than what was to come three years later. The railroad appealed the case to the state supreme court, and while the new trial was pending, the railroad's lawyers continuously badgered Ida to settle. She adamantly refused, knowing she was right and they were wrong. Yet in April 1887, the ruling of the county circuit court was reversed, and Ida was ordered to pay more than $200 in court costs. "We think it is evident that the purpose of the defendant in error was to harass with a view to this suit," the judge declared, "and that her persistence was not in good faith to obtain a comfortable seat for the short ride."

It was wrong, but it was the law, so Ida indignantly paid the fees.

Twelve years later, Ida learned why the case had garnered so much attention in the press and why the railroad had fought so bitterly on appeal. Although she had not realized it at the time, her case was the first in the South in which a colored plaintiff had appealed to a state court since the Civil Rights Act of 1875 had been repealed by the United States Supreme Court in 1883. If Ida had prevailed, her case would have set a precedent that might have inspired countless similar lawsuits, not only against the railroads but against other institutions that fought ruthlessly to enforce segregation.

This was white justice, as Ida had experienced it. Would the organizations driving the woman suffrage movement do any better, act with any more fairness, if they were not carefully watched?

Ida knew she was uniquely suited to take on that role of observer, reporter, critic, and reformer, but at that moment, in the wake of a disappointing election that had cost her husband his job at the state's attorney's office, and with so many other urgent needs commanding her attention, the very thought of joining the National to instruct all those well-meaning white women in concepts of equality and justice that really ought to be simple matters of decency and common sense exhausted her.

Jane would understand if Ida declined. She knew emotional fatigue better than most people, having endured it herself.

"I couldn't have gone to the convention even if I had wanted to," Ida told her friend, managing a smile. "All my time has been taken up with the Negro Fellowship League and the Illinois state suffrage campaign."

"Of course," said Jane, nodding. "I understand."

Ida was sure she did understand all that was said and unsaid.

"I met a pair of interesting young women at the convention," Jane added thoughtfully. "Miss Alice Paul and Miss Lucy Burns. They made a strong case for shifting the National's focus away from state campaigns toward a renewed push for a constitutional amendment. I helped see to it that they were put in charge of the Congressional Committee. Despite their youth, they've already gained considerable experience on the front lines of the British suffrage movement, which I'm sure will serve them well in this new endeavor."

Ida was intrigued in spite of herself, knowing from her travels abroad what British suffragettes had dared and endured. "I hope those young ladies aren't wasting their time, but I fear they might be," she said. "We both know certain southern states will never vote to ratify an amendment to the Constitution granting women the right to vote. They'll fight it just as they fought the Fifteenth Amendment."

"That amendment eventually passed."

"And yet states opposed to it still manage to find ways to keep Black men from voting."

"States that will not support a constitutional amendment are equally likely never to pass state suffrage amendments," Jane pointed out. "If we rely upon state measures alone, we can be certain that some women will never win the vote, not in our lifetimes, anyway. Yet only three-quarters of the states are required to approve a constitutional amendment for it to become law for the entire country, including the recalcitrant South."

Ida knew that was indeed the crux of the matter. Which approach to equal suffrage was most likely to grant the vote to all women of all races and classes, wherever they happened to live?

A state measure seemed an easier bar to clear than amending the Constitution, just as winning over a state legislature seemed a far less daunting task than wrestling a proposal through both houses of the United States Congress. Yet perhaps those two ambitious young women were onto something. If the hurdle of Congress could be cleared—a fairly significant "if"— thirty-eight states should be easier to win than forty-eight.

That was reason enough to continue the state campaigns. Suffragists must wage war on both fronts, not abandon one to redouble the other. The more states there were where women could vote, the more would swiftly ratify an amendment extending that right to all.

By helping to win suffrage for the women of Illinois, Ida could help secure that right for the women of Mississippi and Tennessee and throughout the South, where the voices of women of color most needed to be heard. It was only a matter of hard work and time.

# 12
# December 1912

NEW YORK, NEW YORK

## Maud

On the first day of December, Maud had planned to meet Harriot Stanton Blatch for a walk through Central Park, but the afternoon was damp and blustery, so they sought refuge in a charming café on Fifty-Ninth Street instead. As they warmed themselves with coffee and éclairs, they discussed how Maud's Harlem Equal Rights League and Harriot's Women's Political Union might collaborate on state suffrage efforts in the year ahead. Afterward, Harriot summarized the highlights of the National's annual convention so Maud wouldn't have to wait for the next *Woman's Journal* for all the details of the debate, decisions, and drama. "You should have come," Harriot scolded her cheerfully. "I could have appointed you a delegate for the WPU."

"Thanks, but the library needed me too badly," said Maud lightly, smiling. Harriot meant well, but sometimes she forgot that women who had to earn their daily bread could not so easily leave town for a week, even for the worthiest of causes. It was an unfortunate truth that working women could not devote themselves exclusively to the suffrage movement the way that women with independent fortunes, generous parents, or indulgent husbands did. Ironically, those who had to schedule their work for the cause around their work for wages needed the ballot even more urgently because their circumstances were more precarious. And if working women didn't navigate the obstacles and show up at protests and speak up at meetings, they risked having their concerns forgotten by their more privileged sisters. To be fair, many ladies of the leisure class fought for equal suffrage precisely because they knew that increased political power would benefit the less fortunate, but far too many considered only how the vote would help women like themselves.

"Amid all the controversy about alleged improperly political behavior," Maud asked, sipping her coffee, feigning nonchalance, "did my name come up?"

Harriot's eyebrows rose. "You mean, after Mrs.

Harper pilloried Miss Jane Addams, did Dr. Shaw do the same to you?"

Wincing, Maud set down her coffee cup and nodded.

Harriot smiled and shook her head. "Never fear. The names of a few other ladies came up, but not yours."

"Thank goodness." Maud sighed, impatient with herself. "I don't know why I care so much. I've had plenty of criticism shouted at me from far rougher characters, and I've always been able to find the humor in it."

"It's one thing to be heckled by some lout on a street corner in Brooklyn, and quite another to be condemned in front of an entire conference of genteel, influential suffragists." Harriot paused, considering. "They probably left you alone because the conflict was about *partisan* activity. Your actions have been decidedly nonpartisan."

"Oh, yes, I pester and interrupt everyone, regardless of political affiliation."

"Still, I understand why you might have worried that Dr. Shaw had seized the opportunity to tell a captive audience what she thinks of you."

"She's already shared her opinion with the entire city of New York," said Maud lightly, forcing a grin. "Why not Philadelphia?"

Maud could joke about it now, but the truth was,

she had been surprised and a bit hurt when Dr. Shaw's interview had appeared in the *New-York Tribune* two days after the trial. "Ignore Maud Malone," the top headline declared in bold capitals, and that was just the beginning.

## IGNORE MAUD MALONE.
### Suffragette Leaders Say She Must Swing in Her Own Orbit.
### DISAPPROVE OF METHODS.
### Dr. Anna Howard Shaw Thinks Turbulent Star Should Join Some Constellation.

Dr. Anna Howard Shaw, president of the National Woman Suffrage Association, feels that if Maud Malone elects to be a votes-for-women comet, shooting around on her lonesome way through space when she might be allied with some nice constellation of suffrage workers, she can't expect these constellations to stop in their courses and back her up when she hits a magisterial planet.

After taking a deep, steadying breath, Maud had reminded herself that Dr. Shaw had not written those startling headlines and silly metaphors. It was entirely possible that she had said something perfectly benign, but the reporter had gleefully spiced it up. Even so, it was difficult to dismiss the direct quotes that followed. Dr. Shaw had been "too busy" to pay any attention to Maud's trial; "I really don't know very much about the case," she had told the reporter, "or about Miss Malone, for it's been a long time since I met her." Although she agreed that woman suffrage was indeed a national question, "when Governor Wilson declined to answer, Miss Malone shouldn't have kept on standing and talking." For someone who admitted that she did not know Maud or her case very well, Dr. Shaw had formed a very firm opinion about both: "Miss Malone is doing things in her own way, and she mustn't look for suffrage organizations or their members to stop their work to rally around her when she gets into trouble. If she won't ally herself with some body of women workers she must be prepared to stand alone in crises and take her medicine."

At that, Maud had laughed aloud, astonished. Apparently she was worse than militant; she was a dangerous, rogue suffragist rampaging beyond the safe confines of the herd.

Unfortunately, Dr. Shaw was too well known and rumors about catfights between suffragists too irresistible for the story to quickly fade. The next day the Batavia *Daily News* picked it up, declaring, "In spite of her strong desire for notoriety, Maud Malone is not to be allowed to become a political issue because the very suffragists whose cause she assumed to champion are too much interested in other matters even to sympathize with her troubles. As a martyr she is a distinct fizzle."

That stung, as did the reporter's presumption that he knew anything about her "strong desires" despite having never spoken to her, but Maud decided to take Marcella's advice and shrug it off. It was, after all, absurd for Dr. Shaw to chide her for not aligning herself with "some body of women workers" when Maud was not only a member but the founder of one such group in the Harlem Equal Rights League. She also had a good laugh the next day at the library when several colleagues presented her with a copy of the *Tribune* article, beautifully framed and adorned with an inscription in elegant calligraphy: *To the brightest star in our constellation, long may you shine!*

Her last lingering hurt feelings were entirely soothed two days later when the *Tribune* published a staunch defense in the form of a letter from Grace Raymond, secretary of the Brooklyn bureau of the Woman Suffrage Party. "Fall in line, ladies!" Miss Raymond indignantly paraphrased Dr. Shaw's criticism. "This declaration of Dr. Shaw is, to say the least, uncharitable and unworthy of a great cause, whose exponents proclaim on all occasions their desire to benefit all women, both socially and industrially, by the aid of the ballot. Can you imagine Dr. Shaw and many other of our American 'leaders' doing anything for 'Votes for Women' that could land them in Raymond Street Jail? Horrors!"

Point by point, Miss Raymond defended Maud's right to question Woodrow Wilson or any other leader or candidate. Furthermore, although Dr. Shaw was correct that "the suffrage organizations did not rally around Maud Malone when she got into trouble," that was their failing, not hers, and they should take no pride in it. As for Maud's methods,

There are many women in this state who believe in militant tactics. They are not women who merely want the ballot, they are women who take time to work along other lines of endeavor, by which they can better the position of other women. Dr. Shaw and many "leaders" adopt the "safe and sane" methods, while others go directly to the factory gates and carry the message of sympathy and cheer to the thousands of women and children who "stand alone," and who toil there for a mere existence. Those women appeal to the voters, too, not alone in

Carnegie Hall, but at the factory and on the street corners. Dr. Shaw should bear in mind that the betterment of the condition of woman is the paramount issue. The vote means nothing unless it be used for that purpose. It would be more consistent for Dr. Shaw and other "leaders" to heckle candidates before the election to office, as Maud Malone did, rather than afterward.

Maud's spirits soared to find herself so completely understood. Miss Raymond was clearly a kindred spirit, so perfectly did she articulate what compelled Maud to march and protest and confront. "Are there classes, too, in the fight for equal suffrage? It seems so," Miss Raymond concluded her letter, echoing Maud's own apprehensions. If the movement was indeed classist, it must not remain so. Equality did not refer only to equality *between* men and women, but also *among* men, and *among* women.

The evening after her conference with Harriot, Maud expected to meet many such wealthy suffragists when she addressed the Political Equality Association as the invited guest of the group's president and founder, Mrs. Alva Belmont, the same benefactress who paid the rent for the National's Fifth Avenue offices and sponsored its press bureau. The lecture at the Political Equality League's headquarters on East Forty-First Street would be open to the public, as Mrs. Belmont had herself announced to reporters. "Miss Malone is going to tell the truth about her recent arrest," she had promised. "She is going to give all the details. And we don't care how many men are in the audience to hear them. It won't be pleasant, but it is time that the truth was known. The improprieties which were perpetrated at the time of her arrest were an outrage."

That same article in the New York *Sun* referred to Maud as "Militant Maud Malone, high priestess of heckling," so she scarcely dared imagine the sort of curiosity seekers that might be drawn to the event. Well, if the hall was filled with antisuffrage hecklers, so be it. How much sweeter the triumph would be when she won them over.

But when Maud took the stage that evening, she looked out upon a decidedly well-dressed, genteel audience, with several gentlemen scattered among the ladies and a few reporters lingering in the back. She began with a humorous, self-deprecating account of her career as a "heckler," including brief sketches of the various policemen who had arrested her through the years. "I have sampled a good many policemen," she reminisced, "but the first one I met was also the politest. It was three years ago at Cooper Union, at a meeting for the candidates running for mayor of New York. Mr. Otto Bannard was onstage when I rose and asked him, as I later asked Teddy Roosevelt and Woodrow Wilson, to explain his position on woman suffrage. The interruption mortified him so much that I would have felt sorry for him except that he refused to answer the question, but instead complained this was an inappropriate place to discuss woman suffrage."

A murmur rippled through the audience. "I know what you're thinking," Maud said, wagging a finger playfully. "You're wondering, as I am, whether politicians would consider *any* place an appropriate place to discuss suffrage. Maybe they could do us all a favor and designate one, or publish a list of places that don't qualify."

While the audience laughed and applauded, Maud picked up her story from where she had digressed. "So, as I said, Mr. Otto Bannard would not explain where he stood on woman suffrage. When I insisted that he answer my question, he lost the thread of his speech and blushed furiously red. At that moment, a police officer approached me and said, 'Madam, the gentleman wishes you to remove yourself.' I told him I thought the gentleman would deign to answer my question if I waited. 'I think not,' the officer replied, with great formality. So we stood there frowning at each other until the other candidates finished speaking, the band played, and the meeting came to an end. Whereupon I did indeed remove myself, untouched and with nary a hair out of place." She mimed primping her curls.

The audience laughed.

"Not so on that October night at the Brooklyn Academy of Music," Maud continued ominously, sighing and shaking her head. The audience hung on her every word as she told them all that had befallen her on the night of her arrest, during her first hearing, and at the trial that followed.

"Afterward, I asked Judge Kempner to shake hands and make peace," she added, provoking a gasp of disbelief from her listeners. "It's true. Indeed I did. He shook my hand, frowned at me studiously, and said, 'Well, you don't look dejected.' 'I'm not dejected,' I replied. 'I'm Irish.'"

Another wave of laughter passed through the audience. At the back of the room, reporters grinned or shook their heads or rolled their eyes, but they all took notes.

Maud then explained how after her hearing she had mailed a marked-up copy of the Constitution to Woodrow Wilson, then vacationing in Bermuda, so he would see that suffrage truly was a national issue. "I have it on good authority that some of President-Elect Wilson's friends wrote up a script of the incident at the Academy," she remarked. "They divvied up the different parts, rehearsed the scene, and recorded it on a phonograph, which he plays for his and his family's amusement." She paused, rueful. "If that's Mr. Wilson's idea of a joke, I think he is quite sadly wrong."

It was a good note on which to end, and so she did, and was rewarded with a standing ovation.

At the reception that followed, many ladies and a few gentlemen approached her with questions and an occasional point of criticism. One dark-haired woman not yet thirty, fashionably dressed in a goldenrod silk voile gown with a crossover bodice and high waist, introduced herself as Rosalie Gardiner Jones, president of the Nassau County branch of the National. Maud recognized her name at once. Her father, a physician, had inherited a great deal of wealth and had earned another fortune in real estate investments, while her mother, who had inherited a fortune of her own, was a notorious antisuffragist.

"I understand that you're a prodigious walker," the younger woman said, regarding Maud appraisingly. She was shorter than Maud, with a broad forehead, wide smile, and small, even white teeth. Her dark eyes offered a gaze that was confident and direct, free of the coquettish mannerisms that usually afflicted New York socialites. Then again, rumor had it that Rosalie had left that life behind, much to her mother's grief and consternation. "I also hear that you're utterly fearless when it comes to challenging men in power."

"Walking is one of my favorite pastimes," Maud replied, "especially if I'm wearing a 'Votes for Women' sash. As for fearless, well, let's just say I'm not easily intimidated by rank or title."

Rosalie smiled. "Then perhaps you would like to join me and a few hardy, dedicated friends on a march from New York City to Albany."

"A march?" echoed Maud, wondering if she had misheard. "On foot? That's about one hundred and fifty miles."

"Yes, it will be on foot, as most marches are, and the distance is indeed that far, with stops for rallies and meetings at towns along the way. When we reach the capital, we intend to call on Governor-Elect Sulzer and encourage him to support the state suffrage referendum."

"That's quite an undertaking. When will you set out?"

"We intend to depart in two weeks, and we hope to arrive within a fortnight."

Maud's hopes plummeted. "I'd love to join you,

but my duties at the library wouldn't permit me to be absent so long." Nor could she afford the lost wages, although she did not say so aloud. What would this wealthy young debutante understand about rent and grocery bills?

Rosalie, perhaps accustomed to getting her own way, was reluctant to accept Maud's refusal, and she wheedled and cajoled and painted an enticing picture of the adventures the intrepid marchers would enjoy. But Maud knew it was impossible, so with great regret, she declined.

"At least come to see us off," Rosalie said, her manner so naturally commanding that Maud had to agree.

So it was that on a bitterly cold December morning, she found herself at the corner of West 242nd Street and Broadway, shivering in her heaviest wool coat, watching enviously from the sidewalk as twenty-six women representing seven different suffrage organizations set out with much fanfare, banners unfurled, drums and fife setting the pace. Rosalie Jones—or General Jones, as her followers called her—led the way with a megaphone and a flag. As the marchers moved off down the block, a mounted police escort flanked them, while a small motorcade of cheering suffragists followed behind. Maud overheard that the cars and the police would accompany them only as far as the city line, leaving General Jones's troops to stride on alone from there.

How Maud longed to go with them, despite the cold, stiff wind in their faces, despite the blisters and fatigue and worn shoe leather that were certain to afflict them all! How proud and brave and determined they looked, and deservedly so. For a moment, as the women shifted, a gap in the lines appeared, a space big enough for one more marcher, existing briefly as both a rebuke and an invitation.

As the procession moved on and disappeared around a corner, Maud vowed that if a similar opportunity arose, she would seize it. Other women risked much more than homes and livelihoods in the struggle for equality. How could she play it safe while they sacrificed on her behalf?

# 13
# December 1912

## WASHINGTON, D.C.

### Alice

In the final hours of the National's annual convention, president Dr. Anna Shaw had agreed to give Alice and Lucy free rein to run the Congressional Committee—but only if they accepted certain conditions. First, they must assemble the rest of their committee by choosing from among respectable, diligent, long-standing members of the National who would be willing to work without compensation. Second, they were not allowed to submit any bills to the National's treasury, nor could they charge anything on credit to the organization's account, but must raise their own funds for an office, staff, and activities.

"You are not to spend even one dollar that you

yourselves did not raise or contribute from your own purses," Dr. Shaw had emphasized, fixing a stern gaze on Alice and Lucy in turn. "Last year, Mrs. Kent had a budget of ten dollars, and she was so clever and frugal that afterward, she returned change to the National's treasury."

"We promise not to spend more than we raise," Alice had said, and beside her, Lucy had nodded. Alice deliberately had not caught her friend's eye, knowing their expressions would reveal the impertinent thought she knew they shared: to have money left over from such a minuscule budget was not a sign of frugality but of inaction.

As parsimonious as Dr. Shaw was when it came to the National's treasury, and as dubious as she had seemed about the wisdom of entrusting the Congressional Committee to two such young women, she had fairly glowed with enthusiasm when Alice had revealed her plan to organize a glorious procession on Pennsylvania Avenue the day before President-Elect Wilson's inauguration. With every detail Alice had shared of her vision, Dr. Shaw's expression had brightened— hundreds of marchers grouped according to their states, hundreds more sorted according to their professions, all attired in capes of varying hues according to their trade. Bands playing stirring, uplifting music.

Beautiful floats depicting significant moments in the history of the suffrage movement. And as a cynosure, a splendid allegorical pageant performed at an important landmark somewhere along the route. "I adore parades," Dr. Shaw had declared, pressing a hand to her heart. "By all means, proceed, with my blessing. I trust you will make it a magnificent spectacle, a procession for the ages."

But Alice must do so without any financial contribution from the National, was Dr. Shaw's unspoken but perfectly understood caveat.

In early December, Alice traveled alone to Washington, D.C., and took a room in a modest boardinghouse on I Street next to the Quaker meetinghouse. Lucy would not be able to join her until the New Year, so Alice's small third-floor bedroom would suffice for a headquarters until she could fill out the committee, gather together a staff of volunteers, and find office space. But first, she needed money.

The National's headquarters had provided her with an alphabetical list of about four dozen registered members, former delegates, and past officers from the capital city, a promising place to start. Alice decided to call on each woman and personally invite her to join the renewed effort to push a federal amendment through Congress. She would remind them that this work had been allowed to lapse since Susan B. Anthony's death, but the time had come to once again take up the beloved matriarch's great task and secure equal voting rights for women throughout the nation.

Bundling up in her warm gray coat and hat, Alice set out on a blustery Saturday morning, the precious list tucked carefully into her satchel among bundles of suffrage literature. Her first stop was only two blocks from her boardinghouse, but when she inquired there, she was told that the woman she sought had moved away and had left no forwarding address. At the next address, the gentleman who answered informed her that the woman in question, his mother, had passed away two years before. So went the morning as Alice visited gracious mansions, proud town houses, and modest apartments, working her way through the list of names and addresses. When she spoke with the perplexed occupants, she discovered that one member after another had either moved away or died.

Evidently the National had furnished her with an outdated list, an unfortunate and exasperating setback, but she decided to press on. Eventually her persistence was rewarded when she called at the home of Emma Gillett, the founder of the Washington College of Law and one of only four women lawyers practicing full-time in the city. Not only was Miss Gillett still among the living, which was delightful enough, but she welcomed Alice in out of the cold, offered her tea, and listened with great interest as Alice explained the purpose of the rejuvenated Congressional Committee. A handsome, sturdily built, flaxen-haired woman of about sixty, Miss Gillett had a commanding presence that no doubt served her well in the courtroom.

"Does your committee have a treasurer?" she inquired when Alice had finished her pitch. "If not, I should be glad to volunteer."

Alice smiled. "And I'm delighted to accept." She retrieved the National's local roster from her satchel and handed it over. "As your first official duty, would you please help me revise this woefully outdated membership list?"

Miss Gillett laughed and agreed, and before the hour was through she had underlined many names to indicate that they were valid, crossed out several others, added a few more, and marked some with question marks. "You should also call on Florence Etheridge, president of the National's D.C. branch," she added, underlining a name twice and marking it with an asterisk. "I'm sure she'll share her roster with you."

"I have an appointment to see her later this week," said Alice. When they had met briefly at the convention, Florence had listened to Alice's proposal for a procession on Pennsylvania Avenue with enthusiasm tempered by uncertainty. As much as she loved the idea, she earnestly explained, she did not know whether it was realistic, especially since they had no money to put on such a grand spectacle.

"After Florence, you should move this woman to the top of the list." Handing the document to Alice, Miss Gillett indicated a name near the center of the second page with a tap of her pen. "Elizabeth Kent, your predecessor. She's an absolute treasure, and she's very influential among the congressional wives."

"I meant to call on her after I had gained a bit of a foothold on my own," Alice admitted. "Certainly after I've set up a headquarters where volunteers can gather. I thought that would make a better impression."

"Mrs. Kent doesn't need you to impress her. She's exceptionally generous, and nothing would make her happier than to help you find your way. You'll understand when you know her better." Miss Gillett paused, thinking. "I know of a vacant suite of offices next door to my own, not too far from the Kent residence. You could tour the office and call on Mrs. Kent— perhaps with the happy news that you've chosen your headquarters—all on the same day."

Alice agreed to see the property but demurred when Miss Gillett offered to accompany her to Mrs. Kent's afterward. They parted soon thereafter, Alice to continue canvassing the potential supporters on the revised roster, Miss Gillett to contact the office's landlord and arrange a tour.

The following afternoon, they inspected the vacant office suite at 1420 F Street Northwest, a rather chilly, dimly lit half-basement flat beneath the Wilcox, Hane, and Company real estate and insurance firm. Its greatest advantages were that it was located on one of the most popular shopping boulevards in the capital, which promised good exposure to the public, and that the rent was only sixty dollars a month. Alice had not yet secured even a dime of that amount, so she asked the landlord for time to consider. He granted her a week.

Satisfied that she at last had something to show for her time in the capital, when she met with Florence Etheridge a few days later and Florence offered to introduce her to Elizabeth Kent, Alice readily agreed.

They called on Alice's predecessor at her gracious Georgian mansion at 1925 F Street Northwest, three blocks west of the White House on the opposite side of the Ellipse from the vacant office Alice hoped to claim as her own, if someone else did not beat her to it. Mrs. Kent welcomed Alice with such genuine warmth and good wishes for her success that Alice chided herself for postponing their first meeting. The California congressman's wife looked to be in her midforties, with keen blue eyes, an open smile, and long, curly brown hair with only a few wisps of silver at the crown. As they conversed, Alice learned that Mrs. Kent was a mother of seven and a devoted conservationist as well as a longtime champion of women's rights. Four years before, she and her husband had donated nearly three hundred acres of coastal redwood forest to the federal government to prevent a Sausalito water utility from building a dam upriver that otherwise would have destroyed it. That year, President Theodore Roosevelt had declared the land a national monument.

Alice wondered, but thought it impolite to ask, why a dedicated activist like Mrs. Kent was so eager to hand over the leadership of the Congressional Committee. In November her husband had been reelected to a second term in Congress, so presumably she was not returning to California. Perhaps she wished to devote more time to environmental issues. Or perhaps experience had taught her that a federal suffrage amendment was a lost cause, although her enthusiasm when Alice described her vision for the suffrage march suggested otherwise. And when Alice told Mrs. Kent about the office suite, so ideally placed and reasonably priced and yet unaffordable, Mrs. Kent immediately volunteered to pay five dollars per month toward the rent. Delighted, Alice thanked her and said that she would sign the lease the next day, confident now that other donors would be forthcoming.

"You must come again soon for tea," Mrs. Kent said to Alice as she showed her to the door. "Would Tuesday afternoon do? I'll invite our most dedicated and diligent suffrage supporters, and among them I'm sure you'll find many volunteers eager to help you organize your procession."

Alice hardly dared to believe her good fortune. "Tuesday afternoon would be perfect. Thank you."

Her spirits rose even higher when Mrs. Kent insisted that Alice join her family for Christmas dinner. Alice had planned on a simple meal alone at the boardinghouse, but this would certainly be more festive, and far less lonely.

As the December days grew shorter, Alice filled every hour setting up the committee's headquarters, organizing volunteers, soliciting donations of funds and goods, and seeking the appropriate permits for the parade, sending out so many letters that she twice had to replace the ribbon in her typewriter. In her quest for permits, she tried to schedule an appointment with police superintendent Richard Sylvester, but he ignored repeated requests until a volunteer's father, a member of Superintendent Sylvester's fraternal lodge, convinced him to see her.

When she was finally shown into his office, she beheld a man in his early fifties, of considerable height and bulk, with silvery-gray hair, penetrating eyes, a thick handlebar mustache, and a well-fed stomach. His erect posture and dark blue uniform, graced with a double row of eighteen brass buttons and gold epaulets, gave him a commanding presence. He welcomed Alice courteously enough, although his manner was one of resignation with an undercurrent of impatience. Yet he listened without interruption, fingers interlaced and resting on his desktop, as she explained her purpose and plans, alluding to the letters she trusted he had read.

When she finished, he shook his head and grimaced. "You don't know what you're asking, miss."

"I'm quite certain I do," she replied mildly.

"Well, you're asking for trouble, that's what. On March third, the city will be filled with men in town for the inauguration the next day—some dignitaries, yes, but also many strangers from all walks of life eager to fill their idle hours."

"Precisely." Alice thought it would be impolitic to mention that the expected 150,000 visitors would include the wives and daughters of the gentlemen who would march in Mr. Wilson's inaugural parade, an ideal audience for the suffragists' message. "What fun is a parade without spectators? We want to draw a crowd."

"Not this crowd. Mr. Wilson is a Democrat and a native Virginian, so his inauguration is sure to bring in droves of southern Democrat riffraff. The location is a problem too. A young lady such as yourself wouldn't know this, but Pennsylvania Avenue runs alongside the Bowery district, full of disreputable saloons and—" Superintendent Sylvester checked himself. "Well, that's bad enough, no need to mention the rest."

"I appreciate your concern, but we're determined to parade on March third," said Alice. "The railroads are offering discount fares on that date, and since most women are financially dependent on their fathers or husbands, we must keep their expenses down."

What she did not add, because she expected he would not understand, was that it was essential for the suffragists to get their message out to the nation and to Woodrow Wilson himself before he became president. He must be put on notice before he took the oath of office that woman suffrage would be a significant issue in his administration whether he liked it or not.

Sylvester shook his head. "Why not March fifth? Many people will still be in the capital on the day after the inauguration, likely even more than will arrive beforehand."

"Then our demonstration would be an afterthought, and that would never do." Alice allowed a small smile. "If, as you said earlier, you're concerned about our procession drawing too large a crowd, wouldn't you rather have us march the day before the inauguration, when you expect fewer out-of-town visitors?"

His frown deepened. "Why not Sixteenth Street? It's half again as broad as Pennsylvania Avenue, and in a much better district. I should think you ladies would prefer to wear your beautiful dresses and pose on your pretty floats in a neighborhood of gracious homes occupied by dignified citizens."

"I must insist on Pennsylvania Avenue." Surely he knew why, but she appended a coda of reasons for emphasis. "Pennsylvania Avenue bears historic significance, and not only because it is the address of the White House. The views are incomparable, and the route from the Capitol west to the Executive Mansion is not only logistically ideal but rich with symbolism. It will also pass the Treasury Building, which is where we intend to stage an allegorical pageant. Its plaza is the perfect stage, and the majestic, columned façade the perfect backdrop."

"The capital is full of places that would be equally

scenic and much more feasible." Superintendent Sylvester sighed heavily and rose, indicating that the interview was over. "I regret that I can't grant you a permit, not for March third and not for Pennsylvania Avenue. Find another date and another location, and I'll see what I can do."

Without acknowledging his suggestions, Alice thanked him for his time and departed, silently fuming. If he assumed this was the end of the matter, he was quite mistaken.

In the days that followed, Alice called on him again and again, sometimes alone, sometimes accompanied by distinguished suffragists, including accomplished professionals, senators' wives, and daughters of military officers. Sometimes Alice was busy with other committee matters and sent a delegation of prominent suffragists in her stead. The superintendent was always willing to see them, but he repeatedly declined their requests with one excuse or another—he was concerned that ruffians would cause a disturbance, due to other inaugural events his men would be stretched too thin to be able to protect the suffrage marchers, and so on. Surmising that he might find other voices more persuasive, Alice wrote to various civic organizations, emphasizing the economic benefits the suffrage march would bring to the city and asking them to advocate on their behalf. According to her sources, within days the police superintendent received letters from the Board of Trade, the Merchants' Association, the Chamber of Commerce, and others urging him to grant the permits. When he showed signs of wavering, she pressed her advantage, writing more letters and scheduling more calls at his office.

On Christmas Day, Alice enjoyed a wonderful dinner with the Kent family and a merry gathering of their friends and neighbors afterward, with delicious food, lovely music, diverting games, and excellent company. Over cups of mulled apple cider by the fireplace, Alice told Congressman and Mrs. Kent about Superintendent Sylvester's obstinate refusal to grant the necessary permits. They urged her not to relent, to keep up the pressure and begin planning for the suffrage parade exactly where and when she wanted it, in anticipation of victory. "He'll surely capitulate by the end of February, if only to stop the onslaught of demands," Congressman Kent predicted, smiling.

As it happened, Superintendent Sylvester gave in much sooner than that, if only in part.

Two days after Christmas, he sent word that Alice could have a permit for March 3, but she must submit a revised application for another route, as Pennsylvania Avenue was strictly off-limits. Alice and her comrades were heartened, but they did not celebrate, knowing that their partial victory mattered very little if they could not secure their preferred route.

Since it seemed that Sylvester had done all he was willing to do for them, Alice decided to go over his head. On the last day of the year, she called together an impressive delegation of suffragists: Mrs. Kent herself; Belle La Follette, the indomitable wife of the progressive Wisconsin senator Robert La Follette; Adelaide Virginia MacDonald, the wife of a prominent doctor; and Alice Chenoweth, the renowned intellectual activist and writer better known by her nom de plume, Helen Hamilton Gardener. Together they called at the office of John Alexander Johnston, West Point graduate, retired army general, and one of three commissioners appointed to govern the District of Columbia. Since the police department was in his purview, he was Superintendent Sylvester's boss and could overrule him.

To the women's dismay, General Johnston was even less inclined to grant the required permits than Sylvester had been. He echoed nearly all of Sylvester's objections and added a few more for good measure. "Perhaps you should consider some other time of the year and some other place," he said, frowning dubiously, as if he was strongly inclined to suggest they abandon the idea altogether.

"We already have the date, sir," Alice reminded him. "All we need is your approval for Pennsylvania Avenue."

General Johnston sat back in his chair and folded his arms over his chest, thinking. "I suppose, seeing as you excellent ladies are so persistent, I could ask William Eustis for his opinion. As chairman of the Wilson inaugural committee, he'd know better than anyone whether your march is feasible, given that he's planning a parade along the same route."

Alice managed not to wince. She knew Mr. Eustis well enough, if only through the mail. She had recently asked him if the suffragists might rent the inaugural grandstands, which he planned to construct on Pennsylvania Avenue for President Wilson's parade. They would be ready in time for the suffrage march, and one would think Mr. Eustis would be glad to offset some of his own expenses by allowing the women to rent them. He had flatly refused.

Satisfied with deferring the decision until Mr. Eustis weighed in, General Johnston bade Alice and her companions a cordial farewell and had his secretary escort them out. Outside on the sidewalk, the women huddled together, burying their chins in their scarves or fur stoles against a scour of icy snowflakes driven by a stiff wind.

"We must give up the avenue," said Mrs. MacDonald glumly. "These men are obdurate, and nothing we say will convince them. We cannot keep pursuing this, or they'll rescind our permit for the date too."

Miss Chenoweth nodded, resigned.

"Let's not abandon all hope just yet," declared Mrs. La Follette, lifting her chin. "Mr. Eustis may side with us, and then General Johnston will have no choice but to grant us the permit."

Alice thought that was highly unlikely, but she refused to acquiesce when the men's objections weren't based on fact or reason, but rather on some vague idea of what was important and what was feminine. "We must have Pennsylvania Avenue," she said, her voice low and calm. "We *will* march where the men march."

Her companions exchanged looks among themselves, until one by one, they nodded, their confidence restored by her steadfast resolve.

# 14
# January 1913
## CHICAGO, ILLINOIS

### Ida

Early in the new year, Ida followed reports about the two different parades being planned for early March in Washington: the official parade to mark Woodrow Wilson's inauguration, and the Woman Suffrage Procession and pageant that would precede it by one day.

She was highly annoyed to learn that Mr. Wilson had prohibited women from participating in his inaugural parade. Would this ban include his own wife and daughters? What about women who had raised funds for his campaign, who had invited his surrogates to address their civic organizations, who had organized get-out-the-vote efforts in states where women had the ballot? If President-Elect Wilson honestly could not think of a single woman who deserved the honor of appearing in his parade, then he clearly had not spent much time pondering the question. Such neglect merited scrutiny and soul-searching on his part—but everything Ida had ever heard about Mr. Wilson suggested that he was not inclined to rigorous introspection. He had always judged others more harshly than himself.

As for the suffrage procession, Ida recognized the names of the two women who were credited with leading the organizing committee—Miss Alice Paul and Miss Lucy Burns, the same pair of interesting young women Jane Addams had met at the National's convention back in November. From the look of things, they had already begun to shift the National's focus to a constitutional amendment. Ida admired the young women's persistence, but she hoped they did not divert attention and resources away from state campaigns where suffrage bills were soon to be brought before legislatures—especially in her home state of Illinois.

In one particularly intriguing article, Ida was surprised to discover that Jane herself, along with Dr. Shaw, Mrs. Carrie Chapman Catt, and other unnamed National officers, would be leading the parade. Jane had not mentioned a word of it to Ida, but that was not Jane's way; she always was too busy advocating for others to boast about honors she received. Miss Paul and Miss Burns were fortunate to have enlisted her, for she would lend dignity and credibility to the event. Ida was certainly far more interested than she would have been otherwise. The next time they met, Ida would ask Jane whether women of color were welcome to participate in the march. She was sure her friend would answer in the affirmative. Jane Addams would not lend her name to any event that excluded Black people.

But while Jane was a woman of formidable character who would never abandon her moral principles for the sake of political expediency, sadly, the same could not be said of all suffragists—including one of the most beloved matriarchs of the American suffrage movement, Susan B. Anthony.

Ida considered herself fortunate to have known Miss Anthony—the real, flesh-and-blood woman, not the mythical figure revered by younger generations of suffragists who had never had the opportunity to meet her before she passed. Even when Ida had known Miss Anthony only from her writings and her reputation, she had admired the pioneering suffragist for her accomplishments, her tireless devotion to the cause, and her directness, her willingness to speak bold truths that others would prefer to ignore.

Yet even Ida would admit that sometimes Miss Anthony had been too forthright, and had spoken bluntly without considering how her words might be interpreted by a diversity of listeners. One particularly infamous incident had taken place shortly after the Civil War, when Ida was still a small child in Mississippi. She had first heard the tale from a newspaper colleague when she was a novice journalist, and had been shocked and disappointed to learn how the pioneering abolitionist and suffragist really felt about giving Black men the vote. It was not until several years later that Ida discovered how the version she had heard—the version most people accepted as proven truth—had in fact been misquoted and taken out of context.

By 1866, Miss Anthony and Mrs. Stanton had resolved to resuscitate the woman suffrage movement, which had fallen dormant during the Civil War. From the remnants of an older group, they had created the American Equal Rights Association, whose mission was to campaign for equal rights, especially the right of suffrage, for all citizens. Unfortunately, they had soon encountered resistance from critics they had expected to be allies, certain abolitionist leaders and prominent Republicans who insisted that the AERA should commit its efforts to winning the vote for Black men, and turn their attention to woman suffrage later, after that formidable battle was won. "I conjure you to remember that this is the Negro's hour," prominent newspaper editor Horace Greeley had told the two women, "and your first duty now is to go through the State and plead his claims." In the months leading up to an 1867 convention to revise the New York State constitution, two other abolitionist leaders, both white men, had urged Miss Anthony and Mrs. Stanton not to squander resources by campaigning to enfranchise everyone, but to focus on winning the ballot for men of color alone. It was far better to gain part of what they wanted than nothing at all, they earnestly explained, especially since, while the vote was *desirable* for women, it was *absolutely essential* for Black men. Indignant, Miss Anthony had declared that she would sooner cut off her right hand than demand the ballot for Black men and not for women.

If Miss Anthony had only known how that remark would startle and offend so many, Ida suspected she would have phrased it differently. She surely wouldn't have permitted the scene to be included in her authorized biography, which is where countless thousands of readers, supporters and critics alike, discovered it. When Ida read the relevant passages, she understood that what Miss Anthony had meant was that she wanted everyone included in suffrage legislation, that the Fifteenth Amendment should enfranchise all citizens, regardless of sex or race. What many people heard, unfortunately, was that Miss Anthony wanted votes for women above all else and thought it was less important to secure the ballot for Black men. As a writer, Ida understood the power of vivid imagery to fix an idea in the mind; if Miss Anthony had not mentioned anything about cutting off her hand, her statement would have been rhetorically unremarkable, and would not have been so often repeated, misquoted, and misconstrued.

Since Ida preferred to judge people by their conduct rather than what others said and wrote about them, she had been willing to give the renowned suffragist the benefit of the doubt. In the years to come, she was very glad that she had, for in the spring of 1895, while she was on an anti-lynching lecture tour of the East Coast, Miss Anthony invited her to stay with her when she passed through New York State. Although Miss Anthony was seventy-five and Ida only thirty-two, in their fortnight together, they became quite good friends.

One Sunday afternoon, Ida spoke at the Plymouth Congregational Church in Rochester, her second appearance in that city. The audience, though welcoming and attentive, was small and predominantly white. The diminished numbers overall did not trouble her; there would have been more people present had she not divided her audience between this event and her lecture at city hall two nights before. It was disheartening, however, to see relatively few people of color. She suspected that more would have turned out if not for the prominent Black leaders, all men, who had criticized her in the press for being too radical in her views, when, they said, "more good could be accomplished with less violent talk." Following so soon after a flurry of editorials in the white southern press denouncing her as a fraud and a crank, the polite condemnation by her own people stung.

Still, a few listeners were better than none, and soon Ida held them spellbound with the heartrending story of the lynchings at the Curve, the death of her friend, the destruction of her newspaper, and the death threats that had forced her into exile. She described a more recent lynching in Pennsylvania, when a white mob had broken into a jail, seized a Black man accused of murder, hauled him to an isolated spot outside the village, and killed him. "It was afterward discovered that a fatal and grossly inhuman mistake had been made," she told her transfixed listeners, a catch in her throat. "Beyond any shadow of a doubt, he could not have committed the crime, but he was a Negro and his death was of no consequence."

As she spoke, she watched their expressions shift in dismay or disbelief as she recited the chilling statistics proving that the scourge was on the rise; she saw them flinch as she displayed photographs of a Black man hanging limp from a noose while boys of about ten years old gathered around the base of the scaffold. It was a grim tale of horrors and heartbreak, but she had to tell it, and they had to hear it, or nothing would ever change.

They applauded her solemnly when she finished, and she glimpsed a few ladies dabbing their eyes with their handkerchiefs.

Next Miss Anthony took the stage, and as if to verify Ida's remarks, she described how surprised and shocked she had been during her recent travels in the South to observe how fiercely "the color line" was enforced. Train stations kept separate waiting rooms for whites and Blacks; some railcars bore placards announcing that they were reserved "for White Passengers only." To her great indignation, at a suffrage convention in a southern city she did not name, Black women had been obliged to crowd into the upper galleries rather than sit among their white sisters in the more spacious and comfortable main house.

"I have always thought Rochester to be the most

civilized spot on the face of the earth," Miss Anthony said, as if musing aloud, "but let us consider how we treat the colored people living among us."

A murmur went up from the audience, a waft of surprise and indignation.

"Why, even the late Frederick Douglass, God rest him, was not given his due." As Miss Anthony's knowing gaze passed over the audience, ladies and gentlemen alike shifted uncomfortably in their seats. "If he had been a white man living in Rochester and had possessed his same powers of oratory, no honor or position would have been denied him. Had he not moved away, I have no doubt that this congressional district would have sent him to Washington as its representative."

A patter of tentative applause went up, but Miss Anthony was not finished. "In the South, so far as the treatment of colored people as servants is concerned, the old masters and mistresses are kinder than a northern master would be—" Interrupted by exclamations of protest, she held up a hand for silence and raised her voice. "So long as the colored people of the South are content to be servants, they will be treated civilly, but the moment they endeavor to rise above that status, they will be condemned. The one thing we people of the North must insist upon is the equal civil and political rights of every person under the American flag."

The audience applauded, many approvingly, others with a chilly politeness. Yet at the reception afterward, everyone treated Ida with utmost respect and courtesy, and if anyone resented Miss Anthony's pointed remarks about northern racism, they said nothing of it within Ida's earshot.

A larger and more diverse audience greeted Ida a few days later when she spoke at the First Baptist Church on Saturday evening. Miss Anthony offered a warm introduction, and Ida launched into her customary speech, well-rehearsed and word perfect by now from continual repeating, but no less impassioned or urgent. She told them how one thousand Black people had been lynched in the decade between 1882 and 1892, sometimes on slight pretenses, often when the victims were known to be innocent. She was describing the second of several specific incidents when suddenly a young, lanky, brown-haired white man stood up, declared himself to be a theological student from Texas, and said in a drawl ringing with challenge, "Do you assume that all negroes that have been lynched in the South since the war have been innocent?"

"I never said that," replied Ida. "I simply claim that they were innocent in the eyes of the law. No man is guilty until found so by trial."

The man frowned, disgruntled, but he took his seat,

so Ida resumed her lecture. Soon she turned to the subject of prohibitions against intermarriage between the races when the Texan again rose, scowling and fairly twitching with agitation. "Do Negroes *want* to marry white folks?" he demanded. "If Negroes are so badly treated in the South, why do they not come north, or go west, or to some other more congenial clime?"

Ida fixed him with an even stare. "They aren't able to emigrate because they're always in debt to their landlords. They're paid not in cash, but in vouchers for provisions that are good only at plantation stores. I'd still be living in the South myself had I not been forbidden to return under the penalty of losing my life."

Before the Texan could reply, Miss Anthony sprang to her feet. "I'll answer that question," she declared, a fire in her eye. "It's because we here in the North don't treat Black people any better than they do in the South, comparatively speaking. *That's* why they don't come here in droves."

A murmur of consternation went up from the audience, but Miss Anthony was not finished. "You'll find proof enough in an incident that occurred in our city only last week. A dance was to be given in the Number Three school to benefit the seventh grade class, and students could purchase a ticket for ten cents." A few members of the audience nodded in confirmation. "Now, it happened that a colored girl in that grade wanted to attend the dance, her mother gave her the money. But when she tried to buy a ticket, her teacher told her that if she insisted on attending, none of the white children would go, and the dance would be cancelled. Thus the poor child was turned away. I believe that this outrage, this utter disregard for fairness and for the feelings of that colored girl, sprang from the same spirit that inspires lynchings in the South."

After a moment of stunned silence, a burst of applause broke out, so steady and sustained that some moments passed before Ida could resume her remarks. As for the Texan who had provoked Miss Anthony's outburst, he folded his arms over his chest, leaned back in his seat, and smirked up at Ida until she completed her lecture and took her bows.

The next morning, when all the Sunday papers reported on the lecture, Miss Anthony's critical remarks caused a stir of indignation and denial throughout Rochester. The following day, while Ida was out shopping with Miss Anthony's sister, the storekeeper approached Ida and asked if she was the Miss Wells who had lectured Saturday evening. When Ida acknowledged that she was, he said, "This morning at the breakfast table my wife and I read what Miss Anthony said, and we both agree that she was very unjust to the North. What do you say about that?"

Ida had quite a lot to say, as it happened, and she launched into a spirited defense of her friend, supported with evidence of segregation she herself had witnessed in northern states, in schools, churches, hotels, and innumerable social events. Flummoxed, the shopkeeper mumbled something that might have been an apology and quickly retreated into a back room.

A few days later, another incident occurred that gave Ida more evidence for her argument that racism did indeed exist in the North. Miss Anthony regularly engaged a stenographer to assist her with her writing, but one morning she had an appointment in the city during their scheduled time. "My stenographer could help you with your correspondence instead," she suggested to Ida over breakfast. "Dictating your letters to her would spare you considerable effort."

Ida gladly accepted the offer.

When the stenographer arrived, Miss Anthony answered the door, already dressed in her coat and hat in her haste to depart, but she lingered to explain the change of plans. Incredulous, the stenographer retorted, "It's all right for you, Miss Anthony, to treat

Negroes as equals, but I refuse to take dictation from a colored woman."

"Indeed!" Miss Anthony replied. "Then you needn't take any more dictation from me, either. Miss Wells is my guest and any insult to her is an insult to me. Since that's how you feel, you needn't stay any longer." When the younger woman simply stood there, wide-eyed and uncertain, Miss Anthony gestured to the door and said, "You heard me. Put on your bonnet and go."

Speechless, the stenographer obeyed.

Ida was heartened by the occasions Miss Anthony had defended her, and she was glad to call such a distinguished veteran of the woman suffrage movement her friend. Thus it pained her deeply when, on the penultimate day of her visit, Miss Anthony told her that sometimes, for the sake of expediency, she was obliged to put the greater good of advancing the cause above her personal views on racial equality.

Troubled, Ida warily asked her for an example.

"I can think of one from very early in the suffrage movement," Miss Anthony replied, her gaze turning inward. "When we called our first convention back in 1848, we invited a great many notable men and women who had publicly stated that women ought to have an equal voice in the government. Frederick Douglass was the only man who attended our convention and stood with us."

Ida nodded. She had known that Mr. Douglass had attended the event, but not that he had been the only man to publicly endorse the meeting.

"He told us he could not have done otherwise, for we suffragists had been among the first to rally to his side when he came among us seeking support for the abolitionist cause. Since that first appearance, he has been an honorary member of the National American Women's Suffrage Association." Miss Anthony rested her chin in her hand, remembering. "At all of our conventions, most of which were held in Washington, he was an honored guest. He sat on our platform and spoke eloquently at our gatherings. But when the National went to Atlanta, I—knowing how southerners feel about Negroes participating in equality with whites—I asked Mr. Douglass not to come."

"You asked him—" Ida drew in a breath. "But why?"

Miss Anthony spread her hands, chagrined. "I didn't want to subject him to humiliation, and I didn't want anything to interfere with bringing southern white women into our suffrage association, their interest being so recently awakened."

"I see," Ida managed to say.

"Not only that, but when a group of colored women came to the Atlanta meeting and asked if I would help them form a branch of the suffrage association among their ladies, I declined to do so, on the ground of that same expediency." Miss Anthony studied her. "You believe I was wrong in so doing?"

"Yes, indeed I do," said Ida without hesitation. "You may have acquired many new white southern women members by disavowing Mr. Douglass and the colored women who sought your help, but what a high price you paid. You compromised your professed belief in the equality of the races, you turned away colored women who were eager to support the cause, and you gave tacit approval to segregation and to white women's prejudices. I—"

When she did not continue, Miss Anthony prompted, "Yes? Tell me."

"I would not have thought you capable of that. It seems . . . so unlike you."

Miss Anthony clasped her hands together in her lap and sat lost in thought for a long moment, frowning pensively. When she at last looked up at Ida, her expression was rueful. "I thank you for always speaking your mind so frankly, even when the words do not flatter me," she said. "I'm always willing to hear all sides of a question. In the future, I hope no one will doubt my commitment to seeing that all women of this country have an equal share in all the privileges of citizenship."

"I have no doubt now," replied Ida. Two unfortunate choices, regrettable though they were, would not tarnish her respect for Miss Anthony's long history of selfless advocacy and activism.

Yet those choices confirmed a dismaying pattern Ida had observed among far too many white women of her acquaintance, women she had toiled alongside, women she trusted as allies. She had seen time and again that at a crucial moment, white women she had considered intelligent, just, and compassionate could suddenly pivot and put loyalty to their race above that to their sex. They would inexplicably take the part of white people who were clearly in the wrong rather than side with people of color, even if it meant compromising their moral principles to do so. Ida wished it were otherwise, but experience had forced her to acknowledge that virtually every white woman she knew might eventually disappoint her in this way. She perpetually braced herself for betrayal, yearning to be proven wrong.

Reminiscing about Miss Anthony and the divisions she had observed in the suffrage movement over the decades, Ida realized that rather than waiting for groups like the National to embrace them wholeheartedly as equals, women of color ought to hold their own suffrage meetings. It was certainly true that Black women had their own unique political and social needs that might not find a place on the agenda of a typical suffrage group, where white women comprised an overwhelming majority. Over the decades, Ida had observed that while women of all races sought the vote in order to gain more autonomy, it seemed that what white women desired most was to be equal to men, whereas women of color saw the ballot as a means to bring about racial equality and to uplift their communities. Far too many white women wanted to elevate themselves while keeping people of color subservient.

Certainly not all white women felt this way—Jane Addams was the first to come to mind, but there were many others, including the friend who offered to assist Ida in early January when she called a suffrage meeting for women of color in Chicago. Belle Squire—an author, music teacher, and suffragist who outraged traditionalists by insisting upon the honorific of "Mrs." although she was unmarried—was the forty-two-year-old leader of the Illinois branch of the No Vote No Tax League, an organization founded on the premise that requiring women to pay taxes while denying them the vote was a form of taxation without representation. For the past few years, Belle had refused to pay property taxes, and after one particularly powerful demonstration, she had inspired five thousand other Cook County women to refuse to pay taxes too. "I am not a tax dodger," Ida had heard Belle explain at many a suffrage meeting, for they frequently shared a stage. "However, I am and will be delinquent until, by the consent of the men running this country, I am regarded as a normal human being who has arrived at the full stature of adult life, and upon whose shoulders rest part of the responsibility of political life with all of its privileges and duties. When that day comes, I will cheerfully pay my share in taxes, but not one day sooner."

On January 5, Ida and Belle led a meeting and panel discussion for women of color at Quinn Chapel at South Wabash and East Twenty-Fourth. The subject was not only how enfranchisement would allow colored women to improve their own lives and those of their loved ones, but also how essential it was for them to organize themselves into suffrage groups and fight for the vote. In their separate addresses, Belle emphasized the indisputable need to create a greater "sisterhood of woman" in their pursuit of the ballot, while Ida spoke about the practicalities of creating civic organizations, a subject she knew well.

During the panel discussion, the women—some solemn and earnest, others smiling and brimming over with enthusiasm—asked such insightful questions about matters both philosophical and pragmatic that Ida's heart warmed with pride. How mistaken Miss Anthony had been to withhold her knowledge and experience from the group of colored women in Atlanta when they had asked for her help years before! What a difference she could have made in a state where the fight for equal suffrage was as daunting as anywhere in the country.

Ida would not make that same regrettable choice. That night's meeting was only the first step. She would not merely instruct others in the mechanics of founding a suffrage group for women of color. She would organize one herself.

With their voices and hands and prayers united for a righteous cause, they could not fail.

# 15

# January 1913

## NEW YORK, NEW YORK

### Maud

Everyone in New York eventually came to the library, so on a snowy afternoon in early January, Maud was not entirely surprised when she glimpsed Rosalie Jones wandering the stacks of the Seward Park branch, looking left and right, searching, but not scanning the shelves. When her eyes met Maud's, she smiled broadly, gave a jaunty wave, and strode purposefully toward her down the aisle between the rows of bookcases, as if she had not come to check out a book at all but to visit the librarian. As she drew closer, Maud realized that was precisely the case.

Maud had not seen Rosalie—or General Jones, as she was known to her followers and increasingly to the press, who adored a clever nickname—since late December, and that had been from a distance, when Maud had been but one of many indistinguishable faces in a vast, cheering crowd. Her regrets that she had been unable to accompany General Jones and her "pilgrims," as they were known, on their suffrage march to Albany had only increased as she had followed their adventures in the papers. As they had approached their destination, Maud had resolved to witness their arrival at the state capital.

On December 28, Maud and her sister had taken an early train to Albany, where throngs of supporters and opponents alike already lined the streets in anticipation of the pilgrims' arrival. The day had been overcast but not too cold, so Maud and Marcella had been perfectly comfortable in their snug wool coats and hats as they linked arms and hurried from the station to the capitol square. Anticipation had filled the air, and their excitement had risen as they had made their way through the crowds down Madison Avenue to Eagle Street and on to State, where Maud had often marched with her yellow banner and placards. How disconcerted she had felt to see scores of people eagerly awaiting a suffrage demonstration where she had so often protested alone, raising awareness in small but steady increments and frequently enduring ridicule. Though the crowds that late December day had seemed to include at least as many gawkers and potential hecklers as they did supporters, by her estimation, it had looked to be a larger audience than she had ever enjoyed on all of her solo ventures combined.

Sometime after four o'clock, the distant sound of cheering and whistling from blocks away had told Maud and Marcella that the pilgrims had entered the city and were approaching the capitol. The shouts and cheers had grown louder until at last General Jones herself had turned the corner of Eagle and State at the head of her intrepid band. The women's fatigue had been evident, but so too their pride, as they had drawn themselves up, thrown back their shoulders, and briskly completed the last few yards of their long and exhausting journey.

The pilgrims had halted before the Hampton Hotel, where a beaming General Jones had raised her hands to settle the crowd while well-wishers and reporters alike swarmed the marchers. "Our task has been accomplished," she called out once the din subsided. "We have done the thing we set out to do. In that thought alone there is much satisfaction, but our success is even greater than that. We have had a chance to talk to the men and women of the rural districts. They have come to know us, and many of them now believe in us and in the cause we represent. Our greatest accomplishment, the greatest good we have done, is apparent when one thinks of the women who now understand us as missionaries of the cause."

"Brava!" a woman had cried out from somewhere in the crowd, followed swiftly by a roar of cheers and applause. Even the dozens of young men, who to Maud's experienced eye seemed the type to have come intending to jeer and catcall, had good-naturedly joined in.

"A spectacular march was necessary to attract attention," General Jones had continued, raising her voice. "I thank all of you who marched alongside us in spirit, including the press, who have done much to spread the word about our mission. I assure you, this shall not be our last march, and I invite all of you—yes, even you fellows in your college scarves over there, I see you— to join us next time, not only from afar but in person. The greater our numbers, the louder our voice, and the more the government must take heed. Thank you!"

Her speech concluded, Rosalie and her pilgrims had gathered for an official photograph, after which they had dispersed to rest until the appointed hour when they planned to regroup and call on Governor-Elect William Sulzer. Maud had longed to remain and witness that confrontation, but no one had known when Mr. Sulzer would receive the delegation. Mindful of the waning daylight, she had reluctantly agreed with

Marcella that they ought to catch the train back to the city and trust that the morning papers would provide a conclusion to the story.

That had been weeks ago, and as far as Maud knew, Rosalie was entirely unaware that she and her sister had been among the cheering thousands who had welcomed the pilgrims to the capital city. So when Rosalie joined her in an aisle in the 323s, Maud congratulated her—in an undertone so as not to disturb nearby patrons—on her successful long-distance demonstration. "Although I missed the march itself," she noted wistfully, "at least I was there for the beginning and the end."

"I'm glad you could be with us on the two most important days," Rosalie murmured warmly, in her own practiced library voice. "Now that we've rested our feet and replaced our worn shoe leather, we have an even grander march in the works. You've heard about the procession the National is organizing in Washington the day before Wilson's inauguration?"

"I have indeed," said Maud. That was a vast understatement. Ever since the event had been announced, she had thoroughly examined every bit of newspaper coverage, hungry for details. Sporadic articles offered tantalizing glimpses behind the scenes—the controversy over the police commissioner's refusal to grant a permit for Pennsylvania Avenue, descriptions of the elaborate allegorical pageant, and director Alice Paul's assurances that the procession would be not merely informative but extraordinarily beautiful. Maud thrilled to learn that women physicians from around the country—condescendingly referred to by one paper as "Doctorettes"—would drive luxury automobiles in the parade. The famous aviatrix Bernetta Adams Miller had promised to bring a message "through the Air from the World," and one prominent float would symbolize greetings from all nations to the women of America. In one part of the parade, marchers would be grouped according to their states, and in another, women would gather according to their professions, distinguished by cloaks of different hues.

Maud could well imagine herself clad in a swirling light blue cloak, striding along proudly with her fellow librarians. "Are you and your pilgrims planning to march in the parade?" she asked Rosalie, hopeful and a bit envious.

"Not only *in* the parade, but *to* it."

"What do you mean?"

"You'll have to come to our meeting to find out." Smiling mysteriously, Rosalie handed her a card. "Thursday evening, seven o'clock sharp. Can I count on you?"

Maud's thoughts raced. "To attend the meeting, yes, but for anything more—"

"Understood. You'll need all the details before you enlist." Rosalie turned to go, but she gave Maud a parting grin over her shoulder. "Don't forget. Thursday at seven. You have the address."

Maud held up the card, a promise that she would not misplace it. "See you then."

Rosalie gave her a mock salute and strode away, the brisk strikes of her boot heels on the marble floor fading as she disappeared into the stacks.

The address turned out to be a gracious town house in Brooklyn, the home of a young suffragist and aspiring lawyer Maud had met before through the Harlem Equal Rights League. More than two dozen women gathered in the parlor, including several Maud recognized as Albany pilgrims. As they waited for General Jones, they found seats wherever they could, teasing and joking as they brushed shoulders and knocked elbows in their effort to make room for newcomers. Spirits were high, and the room was electric with anticipation when at last Rosalie arrived, cheeks red from the cold and eyes bright.

She was still loosening her scarf and shrugging out of her coat as she began to address them. "Thank you all for coming," Rosalie said, smiling around the room, her gaze alighting at least for a moment on every woman's face. "Most of you know why I've invited you here today, but just to be perfectly clear, I hope to enlist you for another march, one even more challenging than our march to Albany, but with all of the greater rewards that greater difficulties bring. By now, I'm sure you've all heard about the glorious suffrage march in the works for the day before Woodrow Wilson's inauguration."

Maud nodded along with the others as a sense of expectation filled the room.

"I propose to march from New York City to Washington, carrying the message of equal rights for women to towns and villages along the way," Rosalie declared. "We'll arrive in the capital in time to join the National's procession, in which we shall march as our own unit, a living symbol of women's unity, determination, resilience, and strength."

Her announcement met with exclamations of wonder and delight. When the women pressed her for more details, Rosalie admitted that her plans were still in the earliest stages, for she had meant to gauge their interest before proceeding. "Judging by your reaction," she said, laughing, "it seems there's no lack of enthusiasm."

"When would we set out?" asked one younger woman eagerly.

"Yes, and how long would it take, do you suppose?" asked another woman, at least a decade older, her brow furrowing.

"I estimate that we could complete the march in eighteen days," Rosalie replied. "We should include at least two additional days to rest or to avoid inclement weather, a lesson learned from our last march. Ideally, we would leave in plenty of time to arrive in Washington with a day or two to recover, meet with the press, call on our representatives and senators, and prepare for the procession."

As the other women peppered Rosalie with questions, Maud tallied the days, calculated the miles, and pressed her lips together to hold back a groan of dismay and disappointment. The march would be roughly 250 miles, depending upon the final route. Twenty days minimum en route, two days of rest in the capital, the grand procession on March 3, and then another day to travel home by train—it all added up to nearly a month, and that was a conservative estimate. She longed to thrust her hand into the air and volunteer, but how could she spare so much time away? How could any working woman? Glancing around the room as her companions chatted excitedly, Maud glimpsed concern and misgivings in the expressions of more than a few.

Some were no doubt worried about whether they were up to a hike of such long duration, while others wondered how their families could manage without them and workplaces tolerate their absence so long.

"I'm leaving for Washington in the morning," Rosalie announced when she had answered all their questions as best she could. "On Sunday I'll call on Alice Paul, and I'm sure she'll give our venture her blessing. After that, Colonel Ida Craft and I will meet with local suffrage leaders along our intended route. With their help, we'll plan our itinerary—the best roads, speaking venues, places to eat, lodgings, local supporters to contact in case of emergency—the multitude of small but significant details that will guarantee our success."

As the meeting drew to a close, more than a dozen women committed to the new pilgrimage on the spot, while several others shook their heads in regret and declined, and some, like Maud, promised to consider General Jones's proposal and respond as soon as possible. Rosalie accepted each reply graciously, but it seemed to Maud that her voice carried a special earnestness when she spoke for Maud's ears alone. "You're a prodigious walker, and a great champion of the cause," she told Maud in parting. "Just imagine if we should have the opportunity to call at the White House on

Inauguration Day after two triumphant marches. Can you just imagine the expression on Mr. Wilson's face when he sees you among the delegation?"

Maud could indeed imagine it, and the thought of standing face-to-face with the president after he had avoided meeting her in court for so many months filled her with righteous satisfaction. If only it were possible.

She spent the weekend weighing her options, but by Monday morning, she glumly concluded that she had no choice but to send General Jones her regrets. She could not afford to take an unpaid leave of absence for a month, and her conscience would not allow her to feign illness. But although she had made her decision, she could not resign herself to it. As she and her colleagues bustled about, preparing to open the library for the day, she told them about Rosalie's proposed pilgrimage. They thought it sounded like a wonderful adventure and were unanimous in their certainty that Maud ought to join in. Their sympathy when Maud lamented that it was impossible took some of the sting out of her disappointment.

At the end of her shift, as Maud packed her satchel and drew on her coat, her fellow librarians gathered around her desk. "We absolutely insist that you join General Jones's pilgrims on this march," said Anne, the senior reference librarian.

"They need you, Maud," added the head of the acquisitions department. "You're the most famous suffrage marcher there is."

"I don't know about that," Maud demurred. "Countless numbers of women have marched and demonstrated and fought for the vote through the years. I'm better known for interrupting politicians and being thrown out of lecture halls."

"Perhaps, but you've become a thorn in Mr. Wilson's side," said Anne. "This particular demonstration wouldn't be complete without you."

"It's all sorted," said the youngest librarian, Sarah, a wide-eyed blonde fresh from Mount Holyoke. "We've worked out a schedule to cover your shifts. The dean of libraries consented. You won't miss a single paycheck."

For a moment, as her colleagues chimed in agreement, Maud was rendered speechless. "It's too much to ask of you," she managed to say, looking around at the half-circle of smiling faces.

"Nonsense," said Anne. "It's only a few extra hours here and there for each of us. We're happy to do it, if it means sending one of our own to represent us in the march to Washington."

"And in the glorious suffrage procession in the capital," Sarah added, beaming. "Say that you'll do it, won't you, Maud?"

"Well—" Overwhelmed, she smiled and blinked back tears of sudden, unexpected joy. "I could hardly refuse, after those fine words. You'd never forgive me. And who knows? Maybe I'll find a way to interrupt Mr. Wilson's inaugural address!"

Everyone burst out laughing, except for Sarah, who regarded Maud with alarm. "Don't risk it," she begged. "They'll arrest you, and we'll never see you again."

"I was only teasing," Maud assured her. "In a crowd that large, I'd never get close enough for him to hear me, anyway."

And what a pity that was, she thought. Now that he was safely elected, Mr. Wilson had no excuse not to declare his position on woman suffrage. Why keep it a big secret? What was he hiding?

She longed to be in the room when he was finally backed into a corner and obliged to explain himself.

# 16

# January 1913

## WASHINGTON, D.C.

## Alice

As soon as Lucy Burns and the other committee officers arrived in the capital in early January, Alice hosted a grand opening of their new headquarters, welcoming members of the press, curious passersby, and dozens of determined women from miles around who had responded to her invitations to volunteer. Alice, Lucy, and Dora Lewis, recently arrived from Philadelphia, took turns escorting visitors on a tour of their below-street-level offices, which they had transformed with fresh paint, colorful banners, dignified portraits of suffrage matriarchs, and plain but functional secondhand furniture. The sight of Alice's office, a space about the size of a generous coat closet tucked away in the back, usually provoked either sympathetic sighs or incredulous laughter.

"You poor dear, you don't even have a desk," exclaimed an elderly suffragist who had worked alongside Susan B. Anthony.

"This table is every bit as good as a desk," Alice replied, patting the well-worn surface. "Better, since it came with the office and didn't cost us a dime."

The older woman raised her eyebrows, skeptical, but said no more.

A few days later, a delivery truck parked in front of their building, blocking the limited sunlight. Alice was speaking with a reporter when she was called to the front door to meet two men in gray coveralls and caps who explained that they had brought a desk for her office. Delighted, Alice led the men past the bustling volunteers writing letters and sorting literature, had them move the old table out of the way, and showed them where to set the desk. It was simple but elegant, narrow but with deep drawers and abundant useful cubbyholes. "But who is my benefactor?" she asked over the sound of typewriters clattering away in the main room.

"There's a letter comes with it," one of the men said, patting the pockets of his coveralls until he found the envelope and handed it to her. All the while, his partner eyed the suffrage banners on the walls, shaking his head and grinning in that infuriating, condescending way of men who found suffragists an endless source of amusement, harmless and politically irrelevant.

When the men departed, Alice returned to the reporter and continued their interview. Afterward, she found a chair that suited the height of the desk, seated herself, and ran her hands over the patina of faint scratches in the varnished, honey-hued oak. The desk was evidently not new, but it had been well crafted and well cared for. It was certainly an improvement over the table, which wobbled and offered the unfortunate hazard of splinters. Settling back, Alice opened the letter, read the first lines—and gasped, astonished, to discover that the desk had once belonged to Susan B. Anthony herself, and was a gift from her longtime secretary. "I read that you intend to carry on Miss Anthony's work," the kind donor had written in thin, spindly script, "and when I heard that your new headquarters is sparsely furnished, I decided that the rightful place for this desk is your office. May you use it well, as Miss Anthony did, to forward the cause."

Alice did exactly that, first penning a thank-you note to the generous erstwhile secretary, and then writing to William Eustis, the chairman of Woodrow Wilson's inaugural committee. She had heard nothing from

General Johnston since their meeting on the last day of December, when he had promised to seek Mr. Eustis's opinion before deciding whether to overrule police superintendent Richard Sylvester's refusal to grant them a permit. Since it seemed no answer was forthcoming from the general and time was of the essence, she decided to contact Mr. Eustis directly. To her surprise, he responded two days later with a public announcement that he saw no reason why the women could not hold their procession on March 3 on Pennsylvania Avenue. Heartened, Alice, Lucy, and their volunteers quickly confirmed various arrangements that had been only tentative until then, but after two days passed without any official word from the superintendent, Alice and Dora, increasingly dubious, called at his office. A clerk informed them that the superintendent, who was too busy to receive them, had no intention of issuing the permit.

"But Mr. Eustis had no objection," Dora lamented as they headed back to headquarters.

"General Johnston said that he would seek Mr. Eustis's opinion," Alice reminded her, tucking her chin into her wool scarf as a cold gust of wind left her nearly breathless. "He didn't promise to order Mr. Sylvester follow his recommendations."

Since General Johnston's intervention was apparently a lost cause, Alice would apply pressure from other angles. She next wrote to Treasury Secretary Franklin MacVeagh, and tallied another small victory when, "with great pleasure," he granted the committee permission to use the south plaza of the Treasury Building for their allegorical pageant. Soon thereafter, Genevieve Clark, an active volunteer at headquarters and the wife of Speaker of the House James Beauchamp Clark, persuaded her husband to allow them the Peace Monument at the foot of Capitol Hill as the staging ground for the parade.

"Is permission even his to give?" asked Lucy doubtfully, studying his letter.

"I'm not entirely sure," said Alice, "but let's take what's been offered and hope for the best. We'll bring his letter to the procession and present it to anyone who objects."

Yet even with other pieces falling into place, Superintendent Sylvester still denied them the essential cornerstone of their plans—a permit for Pennsylvania Avenue.

Hopes dimming, anxiety making sleep elusive, Alice created an alternative plan to march on Sixteenth Street, if they had absolutely no other choice. She wrote out the arrangements in the solitude of her boarding-house bedroom and confided in no one but Lucy. For everyone else, she kept up the brave, resolute front that as long as they did not relent, they were certain to prevail.

With less than two months to go, and Superintendent Sylvester as obdurate as ever, Alice realized she had no choice but to put her case before the public. She reached out to sympathetic journalists, as well as a few others who did not sympathize but relished a good squabble. Within days, reports of the committee's quest for Pennsylvania Avenue and Superintendent Sylvester's repeated, unreasonable refusals had appeared in every Washington paper and countless others throughout the nation. Alice laughed aloud from astonishment when she read Superintendent Sylvester's response in the *Washington Post*. He claimed he had been told that the suffragists intended to hold their procession at night, and that he had never formally refused to grant the permit but had simply advised the women of the dangers they might encounter, including the potential for riots. "I am perfectly willing to help the ladies in every way possible," he had told the reporter, "but want to avoid any trouble."

His claims were utterly ridiculous, outrageously so. The only part that even remotely resembled the truth was his desire to avoid trouble. He had certainly not gone to any trouble on the suffragists' behalf.

Alice could not allow the commissioner's comments to go unchallenged. Working swiftly, she and Helen Hamilton Gardener wrote an appeal to Cuno H. Rudolph, president of the Washington, D.C., Board of Commissioners, whose opinion both General Johnston and Superintendent Sylvester would surely heed. "All we ask and expect is a fair hearing, and the same consideration which would be given to a great organization of men, an organization of national scope and size," their letter explained. "We are proposing to bring to Washington the leading women from every State in the Union. Women of splendid standing and dignity, college women, professional women, homemakers, mothers, and workers. The demonstration is to be one of fine dignity, picturesque beauty, and serious purpose." As for Superintendent Sylvester's fears and objections, "We do not and have not asked for a night procession and pageant. This seems to be some misapprehension in the mind of Superintendent Sylvester, who we in no way wish to antagonize and embarrass. There will be nothing in this demonstration to call forth hostility or antagonism, as it will be dignified and serious, just as much so as a procession returning from church on Sunday. No one would dream of attacking such women or insulting them. We need police protection simply to keep the street open for a time in the afternoon while we form our ranks and pass from the starting point, down the historic Avenue, past the Treasury where our pageant will be staged, and westward to Continental Hall."

"We are not asking too much," Alice told her volunteers as she passed the letter around the office so that all who wished to add their signatures could do so. "Pennsylvania Avenue would be granted to a similarly respectable, well-established, political organization of men as a matter of course. All we want is fair and equal treatment, to be given the same consideration, regardless of sex."

And yet Alice put the letter in the post with a sinking feeling that she had exhausted her last option. If this too failed, she would have no choice but to unveil her plans for an alternate route on Sixteenth Street.

Finally, in the second week of January, the police commissioner acquiesced. The Congressional Committee received a permit for the entire length of Pennsylvania Avenue, east to west, from the Capitol to Memorial Continental Hall on Seventeenth Street, a block past the White House, where they would hold an indoor rally after the procession. In celebration, Alice and her volunteers unfurled a brilliant purple, green, and white banner outside their headquarters, announcing their triumph to all who passed by.

But Alice could not pause to savor her victory. The battle for Pennsylvania Avenue had lasted more than a month, leaving her fewer than eight weeks to plan and prepare before the procession could set forth upon the hard-won route. With the help of her able volunteers, and in consultation with suffrage groups throughout the country and overseas, Alice's visions coalesced, assumed tangible form. With the exception of one bemusing encounter with a self-described "general" who sought the committee's endorsement for her plan to lead a group of "pilgrims" on an implausible trek from New York City to Washington before joining up with the official procession, ideas for the pageant, floats, costumes, and bands enriched and made more splendid the themes that Alice had imagined months before. The suffrage procession would be a tableau vivant in motion, with floats depicting women's triumphs through the centuries as they fought for equality. The first floats would honor foreign countries where women had already won the ballot. Next would come a series of floats depicting the history of the American suffrage movement, from the pioneering matriarchs of the 1840s into modernity. Following after would come floats escorted by marchers representing the vast breadth of women's work and professions, from farmers and homemakers to nurses, scholars, lawyers, doctors, social workers, teachers, writers, clerks, factory workers, and more. In the final section, women would march behind banners bearing the names of their states, and the men's division would walk behind a banner of its own. Interspersed throughout would be bands comprised entirely of women, inspiring onlookers and marchers alike with lively, stirring tunes.

Alice was confident that no one who observed the procession on March 3 could fail to realize that half of the population—millions of vibrant, intelligent, loyal, patriotic citizens who actively contributed to the nation's prosperity—had been unfairly excluded from participating in the election that had chosen the man who would take the presidential oath of office the next day.

A week later, Alice was typing a letter to the editor of the *Woman's Journal* when a young volunteer tasked with sorting the mail rapped on her open office door. "I thought you should handle this one personally," she said pensively, handing Alice an unfolded page.

At first Alice merely skimmed it, but by the end of the first paragraph, its significance struck home. The author, a Mrs. Clifford who resided on Ninth Street Northwest near Howard University, had written to inquire whether colored women would be permitted to take part in the parade. "Mrs. Clifford," Alice mused, struck by the familiarity of the name. "I don't suppose she is Carrie Williams Clifford?"

The younger woman shook her head, puzzled. "I don't know who that is."

Alice studied the letter again, front and back, but did not find any details that would have answered her question. "Carrie Williams Clifford is a well-known suffragist and equal rights advocate from Ohio. I wasn't aware that she had moved to Washington, if this is indeed the same woman. She was in the Niagara Movement, and she's been very involved with the NAACP and the National Association of Colored Women." The pieces fit; that Mrs. Clifford would be quite likely to inquire about marching in the suffrage procession. It was a simple request, one which ought to have had a simple answer, but in a nation struggling with the terrible legacy of slavery, the ongoing horror of lynching, and the injustice of Jim Crow laws, Alice knew her ruling could be fraught with unforeseen complications.

"The answer is obvious, don't you think?" Alice said nonetheless as she returned the letter. "I trust you to write a cordial reply."

"Certainly," said the younger woman, looking quite uncertain indeed. "And that reply is . . . ?"

"Yes. The answer is yes. Colored women are welcome to march in the procession."

"Of course they are." Relieved, the volunteer allowed a brief smile and backed out of the doorway. "I'll get on it right away."

Alice nodded and turned back to her typewriter. She had just finished her letter and was turning the dial to release the paper when another quick knock sounded. "May I interrupt for a moment?" said Mary Beard, one of the committee's executive officers. "Since colored women are permitted in the parade now, I'd like to consult Mrs. Clifford about recruiting a group of marchers from the National Association of Colored Women. What do you say?"

"'Permitted now'? Colored women have always been permitted in the parade." Alice wondered how any assumption to the contrary had ever developed. "But yes, absolutely, please do recruit a delegation from the NACW."

Smiling, Mary nodded and strode off as quickly as she had appeared.

Alice's thoughts turned to other matters—a multitude demanded her attention—so she had all but forgotten the two inquiries when, a few days later, a troubling letter addressed to Mary Beard arrived at headquarters. Mary immediately brought it to Alice and Lucy, who were more disappointed than surprised to learn that the writer, a doctor's wife from Georgia and a proud member of the United Daughters of the Confederacy, had read in the paper that colored women would be marching in the procession. She found this quite offensive, and hoped it was not true, but if it was, she would decline to participate.

"Well, good riddance to her, then," said Lucy. "We don't need her."

"Perhaps not," said Mary dryly, "but I can't put that in my reply."

"Tell her that all women are welcome, regardless of race," said Alice. "We hope she'll turn out to march with us nonetheless, but if she declines, she will be missed."

"That's not entirely true," said Lucy. "I won't miss her one bit."

"It's true enough," said Alice wearily. "Let's do our best to keep these objections quiet. Our procession must be about suffrage, in its entirety, uncomplicated by other issues. It cannot become a demonstration for every problem afflicting the country."

She saw her own worry reflected in their faces. Would they be able to hold themselves apart from other conflicts? Each kind of discrimination, it seemed, was entwined with every other.

In the days that followed, more letters echoing the Georgia woman's concerns arrived in the post, all written by white women, mostly from the South. With varying degrees of indignation or outrage, they declared that under no circumstances would they march in a procession with Black women. Some promised that not a single white woman from their town or state would participate if Black women were included.

Soon thereafter, at their regular staff meeting, a few volunteers tentatively worried aloud about the threats of defections from the ranks. "It would be a problem if droves of southern women refused to join in," Alice acknowledged. "Their absence would suggest that southerners oppose suffrage, and that would give their elected officials an excuse to vote down any legislation supporting a national amendment."

"Fair point," said Lucy, "but if we exclude colored women—which I believe would be a serious ethical lapse—we would anger and offend women who should be our allies in a common cause. Keep in mind too that if they are banned from the parade, *that* will be the story in all the headlines—not equal rights, not the vote, not any other part of our message."

Alice sighed and pressed the back of her hand to her brow, where a faint headache had taken root. "There's no just cause to exclude women of color, and I have no intention of doing so. We'll simply disperse them among friendly white women from the North. They will be safe, and southern women could not reasonably take offense."

"What is ever reasonable about racism?" asked Lucy.

"What if the colored ladies want to march with their states or their professions?" asked Dora. "What if the NACW delegation wants to march as one group, behind their own banner?"

Alice paused to think, but the perfect solution eluded her. "We'll sort it out when the time comes. For now, let's continue to answer individual inquiries individually, and avoid any public announcements that might be construed as a formal policy."

Her colleagues nodded, but their expressions were full of doubt.

Later, when Alice was alone in her office, another volunteer came to speak with her privately. "I think we should run the question by Mrs. Blackwell at the *Woman's Journal*," Miss Hunt said, lifting her chin. "Her opinion carries weight."

"That would be imprudent," said Alice, concealing a pang of sudden worry. "As the editor, Mrs. Blackwell may feel compelled to write about the controversy, and I'd rather keep it out of the papers, even the National's own."

Miss Hunt frowned, but she nodded abruptly and returned to her desk.

Yet letters from angry white women kept coming—only a trickle, never a flood, but enough to render Alice distracted, apprehensive, and increasingly doubtful that an integrated parade would be possible. When Miss Hunt implied that she might write to Mrs. Blackwell herself, since Alice had refused, Alice reluctantly sent a letter after all, in strict confidence. "Be forewarned that many of the white women who have intended to march will refuse to participate if women of color, in any number, form a part of the parade," she wrote, heart heavy. "As a Quaker, I am predisposed to side with, and not against, the Negro in any question of racial difference. But racist sentiment in Washington is so pervasive and bitter that, as far as I can see, I cannot simply do as I please but must put the needs of our cause above all else." As for how to prevent the conflict from escalating, Alice urged the editor to say nothing about the controversy in public, and to keep it out of the press.

To her relief, Mrs. Blackwell promptly replied that she found Alice's judgment sound, and she agreed not to mention the conflict in the *Woman's Journal,* nor would she discuss it with her counterparts at other papers. "I am glad that colored women are allowed to register for the procession—it would be a shame if they were not," she confided, "but I agree with you in hoping that not many will do so in view of the wicked and irrational color prejudice so prevalent in Washington."

Alice hoped that the flames of controversy would be allowed to burn out quietly while plans for the march proceeded, but a letter from Mary Ware Dennett proved that the dispute was still churning through the rumor mill. "You must not even *think* of rejecting any application from colored women applying to march in the parade," the secretary of the National warned. "The suffrage movement stands for enfranchising every single woman in the United States."

Alice inhaled deeply, folded the letter, and tucked it away in a cubbyhole of Susan B. Anthony's desk. She did not need Mrs. Dennett to instruct or to command her. Alice knew the suffrage movement would never be righteous if it excluded women of color, nor was she willing to compromise her own moral principles to appease racists.

But she could not bear to make the perfect the enemy of the good, to allow the suffrage procession to fall apart because certain people in their human imperfection could not cast off their prejudices swiftly enough. She and her colleagues had worked too hard and had overcome too much to look on and lament as suffragists splintered into squabbling factions. Everyone must sacrifice; no one would be entirely happy. Yet in the end the procession *would* happen, and it *would* work for the greater good, and it would move the cause ever forward.

She could not let herself believe otherwise.

# 17
# January 1913
## CHICAGO, ILLINOIS

### Ida

On the evening of January 30, Ida stood in the foyer of the Negro Fellowship League welcoming women of color from throughout the Chicago area to the first meeting of a new suffrage club dedicated entirely to them and their unique concerns. The response to her announcements had been overwhelming and gratifying, and the consensus was that it was high time Black women had an organization of their own. Too often they had been excluded from white women's suffrage clubs, in practice even if segregation was not written into the bylaws.

Ida knew what far too many white suffragists did not: that women of color had been involved in the suffrage movement from its inception, and that their participation had been omitted from the historical narrative told about the struggle. Sometimes they had been deliberately excised, such as when a sketch alongside a magazine article depicted only white faces in the crowd at a rally, or when a newspaper photographer carefully cropped out the dark-skinned woman on the end of a row of marchers. Sometimes indifference or the habitual underestimation of Black women's contributions left their stories untold. This sort of neglect, Ida believed, was what accounted for their exclusion from the celebrated four-volume history of the suffrage movement Miss Anthony and Mrs. Stanton had published, although to be fair, numerous white suffragists from rival organizations had also failed to make the editorial cut.

Sometimes women of color had been left out of the historical account of a significant suffrage event because they had been quite deliberately excluded from it. No Black women were mentioned in the stories of the momentous suffrage meeting of 1848 in Seneca Falls, New York, because none had been invited. Frederick Douglass had been, but not Sojourner Truth. Mrs. Stanton had often insisted that she fought for the right to vote for every woman, but her speeches and writings suggested that her foremost concern was to gain enfranchisement for women like herself—white, middle-class or higher, educated, propertied, Protestant.

But although women of color barely merited a footnote in white women's suffrage history books, that did not mean they had been idly sitting by, waiting for someone else to win the ballot for them, or that they had been too consumed by other important causes to make suffrage a priority. Ida knew well—and made it her business to educate others—that Black women had been engaged in the struggle for equal suffrage all along. Excluded from most venues available to their white counterparts, they had instead worked through channels that pumped lifeblood through the Black community: antislavery societies, churches, newspapers, women's clubs, and civic groups. "Votes for Women" meant votes for Black women, and equal suffrage promised greater influence over the civic institutions that determined the quality of their lives and their children's futures.

With so much at stake, many women of color, including Ida herself, still endeavored to work with white women's suffrage groups in hopes that their combined strength would benefit all women. Sometimes their overtures met with rejection, but not always. Many local chapters of the National American Woman Suffrage Association welcomed their African American neighbors who wished to join, while others regarded Black applicants with chilly disdain, and some were so obviously segregationist that women of color knew better than to waste their time on them. Sometimes Ida feared that the National's inclusion of women of color had peaked in 1898, when Mary Church Terrell had been invited to speak at their annual convention. "My sisters of the dominant race," Mrs. Terrell had challenged them in her address, "stand up not only for the oppressed sex, but also for the oppressed race!" Unfortunately, and predictably, the white suffragists of the National had not rushed to answer that clarion call, but had carried on as before, balanced on the untenable divide between supporting Black women and appeasing racist whites. Yet Ida had several dear friends and numerous respected colleagues in the group, including Jane Addams, so she was determined to consider them allies rather than rivals.

Even so, a suffrage club for Chicago women of color was long overdue.

Ida tallied each guest who crossed the threshold of the Negro Fellowship League with increasing satisfaction as the total soared past one hundred and kept climbing. She greeted the women cordially, showed them where to find the cloakroom, and directed them down the foyer to Belle Squire, who stood behind a table near the entrance to the meeting hall. There, with the help of Ida's sixteen-year-old son, Charles, Belle encouraged guests to sign their names and addresses to the roster so Ida could contact them later. Another friend who had helped organize the event, Virginia Brooks, a Chicago native nicknamed "the Joan of Arc of West Hammond" for her impassioned activism, was already inside the hall distributing programs and showing guests to seats in the rows of chairs arranged before the dais. Ably assisting her were Ida's other three children—Herman, fifteen; Ida Jr., eleven; and Alfreda, eight. Ferdinand would have been there too, lending his air of elegant, dignified authority to the scene, but he was at home preparing for an important extradition trial scheduled to begin in the morning.

With five minutes to go before the program would begin, Ida estimated that nearly two hundred women had passed through their doors, many of them her own friends or acquaintances. Sometimes three generations of a family arrived together, young mothers with babes in arms, white-haired grandmothers holding the hands of bright-eyed granddaughters.

Mindful of the time and trusting that any latecomers could find their own way, Ida left her post and went to confer about the agenda with Belle, whose eyes shone with anticipation. They had hoped for an excellent turnout, but this abundance exceeded their most optimistic expectations.

"Herman and I set up all the extra chairs," Charles told her as she strolled the length of the table, examining the rosters to see how many pages had been filled. "I can watch over the table if you and Mrs. Squire want to go inside."

"Thank you, honey," said Ida, and was rewarded with his cheerful grin, which never failed to warm her heart.

Inside the hall, nearly every seat was occupied, and Ida's three younger children were busy helping guests find the few empty chairs scattered among the rows. A low murmur of voices punctuated by the occasional happy squeal of a child rose from the audience, and an air of expectation and urgency filled the room. Ida recognized many of the women from the meeting earlier that month, when she had realized that the best way to help colored women organize themselves into suffrage groups was to lead one city-wide, encompassing club herself.

Ida had no doubt that most of the women present had found their desire for the ballot newly rekindled by the recent actions of local white women's groups, whose alarming mission seemed to be to ban colored folks, men and women alike, from voting. That was something Ida might have expected in the Jim Crow South of her childhood, but not here in Chicago, where, of all the cities in the nation, Black men had received something akin to adequate political recognition. And yet, with a few exceptions—including Belle and Virginia, who were waiting on the dais to introduce her—white women invariably cast their lot with white men rather than Black women, choosing race over sex when they had to take sides, even when it seemed obvious to Ida that this went against their own best interests. Unfortunately, more often than not, old habits and prejudices outweighed common sense.

When she heard the clock in the foyer strike the hour, Ida caught Belle's eye and nodded, their signal to begin. As Belle took the podium and began a glowing introduction, Ida gazed out over the audience and was struck by the number of wives and mothers in attendance, their numbers equal to or perhaps greater than the young, unmarried suffragists who were typically the most ardent of the movement. That was to be expected; they enjoyed the abundant energy of youth and had not yet assumed the demanding responsibilities of marriage and motherhood. Ida's fledgling suffrage club would need young women like them if they were to take flight and soar.

Yet Ida would never count herself among those who

assumed that wives and mothers were too encumbered by other duties to contribute to the cause. Indeed, she believed that mothers had a particular stake in the future that compelled them to work tirelessly to create a better world, a better future, for their children to inhabit. Although Ida thought she herself struck a good balance between her commitments to her family and to her activism, some of her acquaintances contended that it was impossible to perform both roles well.

Miss Anthony, who had never married but had devoted herself entirely to the cause, had been among the skeptics. Ida had discovered this about her friend quite abruptly one day when she was four years married, a stepmother to Ferdinand's two children from his first marriage and mother of her own two sons.

It was August 1899, and Ida was thirty-seven, happily married and settled in her adopted hometown of Chicago. Hundreds of miles away, Thomas Fortune, the editor who had hired her to write for the *New York Age* after her abrupt exile from Memphis, had decided to resurrect a national equal rights movement that he had once led under the auspices of the Afro-American League. To that end, he had invited many distinguished leaders of the Black community, including Ida herself, to attend an organizational meeting in New York. Mr. Fortune avidly wanted Ida to attend, and her colleagues in Chicago eagerly urged her to go, and so she agreed. She had recently weaned her youngest son, and Ferdinand's mother had offered to watch the boys while Ida was away. When Miss Anthony learned she was coming, she once again invited Ida to be her guest during her visit.

It was Ida's first trip without the boys since she had become a mother, and although she missed them dearly, she thoroughly enjoyed the luxuries of unbroken sleep, intellectual rigor, and uninterrupted adult conversations. Over breakfasts and evening cups of tea at Miss Anthony's home, she delighted in catching up on the news of mutual acquaintances, discussing the progress of various state suffrage campaigns, and debating the strategies and policies of national suffrage organizations. Miss Anthony was as cordial and insightful as ever, and yet as the days passed, Ida noticed that she tended to bite out Ida's married name whenever she was obliged to say it, as if she had to force herself to call her "Mrs. Wells-Barnett." Twice she corrected herself after mistakenly calling Ida "Miss Wells."

Eventually, Ida became so perplexed that she asked, "Miss Anthony, is it my marriage in particular that you disapprove of, or do you object to marriage in principle?"

"Oh, I believe that marriage is fine for some women,"

said Miss Anthony, a faint flush rising in her cheeks, "but not women like you who have a special calling for important work. I too might have married, but that would have meant abandoning the work to which I had set my hand."

"I don't believe I ever abandoned my work," replied Ida, surprised. "It's true that I gave up the newspaper after Herman was born, and this is the first time I've traveled or lectured in quite some time, but that's only because I believe it's essential for a mother to be present in the home during a child's formative years. My withdrawal from an active public life was never meant to be permanent." She spread her hands and managed a smile. "As you can see, I'm here. I answered Mr. Fortune's summons."

Miss Anthony smiled wanly in return. "Yes, but soon you'll withdraw to home and hearth again, and it hasn't been only for your children's sake that you've stayed away. Ever since you married, your agitation in the press and in the public square seemed to have practically ceased, even before your sons came along."

"'Seemed' and 'practically' being the important qualifiers to that judgment," said Ida mildly. "Even if you don't see my efforts or read about me in the papers, I've been working just as hard as I ever have for all the causes that matter most to me."

"Yes, you're here, helping Mr. Fortune revive the Afro-American League, all the while knowing that your eleven-month-old baby needs your attention at home. You cannot deny that you've been distracted by the thought that maybe he isn't being looked after as well as he would be if you were there. That makes for a divided duty."

"I'm confident that my boys are perfectly safe and content with my husband and his mother." But Miss Anthony made a fair point; Ida nonetheless did wonder and worry, but only out of maternal instinct, not any real doubt. "You're right. My attention has been divided between my work and my family, and it will likely continue that way for the near future. But don't mistake that for diminished interest in my work. I care more about equality between men and women and Black and white now than I ever did. Someday my children will leave home to make their own way in the world. I want it to be a kinder, fairer world than the one I was born into, than the one I set forth in after my parents died."

Miss Anthony seemed to accept her impassioned declaration, for she did not question Ida's commitment again for the duration of her visit. What would Miss Anthony say, Ida wondered, if she were among them that evening, nearly fourteen years and two more children later? As Ida took Belle's place at the podium and prepared to address an audience of nearly two hundred women of color, all of them determined to organize and fight for the vote, she decided that Miss Anthony would have had the good grace to admit her mistake. She never should have doubted Ida's resolve.

"Welcome, everyone," said Ida as she looked out over the crowd of upturned faces, all those beautiful dark hues, their expressions so similar in hopeful determination. "Welcome to the inaugural meeting of the Alpha Suffrage Club, the first suffrage club for women of color in Chicago."

An unexpected burst of applause, thunderous and glad, met her words. She nodded her thanks and waited for the joyous sound to diminish before she spoke again. "Too many of us have found ourselves excluded from white women's suffrage clubs, or have been allowed to pay dues and sit at meetings only to discover that their goals did not align with ours—which is, first and foremost, to obtain the vote for every woman, regardless of race or state of residence."

The nods and murmurs of approval heartened her. "We shall be a nonpartisan organization," Ida continued. "Just as our brothers are Black men first, and Republicans, Progressives, and Democrats second, so too shall we be Black women striving for the greater good of our people regardless of party lines. Our purpose will be to educate women of color—ourselves, our sisters, our neighbors—about our civic responsibilities, and to organize so that we may help elect candidates who would best serve the interests of Black folks. We will seek the vote for ourselves, and we will advocate for the election of people of color to public office, from alderman on up."

"All the way up to president?" a woman called out from a back row.

"Why not?" Ida countered, smiling. "Tomorrow, city hall. Someday, the White House!"

Laughter and applause and cheers rang out until Ida, shaking her head and laughing along, had to wave them to silence. "Well, why indeed not?" she asked. "Everything is impossible until it finally happens—such as the end of hundreds of years of slavery. Such as women of color like us marking ballots and choosing a president."

"That's right," called out a silver-haired woman in the front row, nodding emphatically so that the ostrich feathers on her hat bobbed assent.

Ida went on to describe the proposed structure of the Alpha Suffrage Club, how the members would organize themselves by blocks, meet to discuss the issues confronting their own neighborhoods, and gather together once a week as a unified club to exchange ideas, work on solutions, and invite guest lecturers to advise them about political matters and civic duties. At some future date, they would elect officers, and in the meantime each woman present should consider whether she would like to seek office or nominate some other worthy acquaintance.

After Ida concluded her remarks, Belle and Virginia helped her organize the attendees into smaller block or neighborhood groups, then encouraged them to exchange names and addresses and to schedule their first meetings. Ida and her colleagues mingled among the groups that had spread themselves throughout the hall, answering questions, offering advice, and collecting latecomers' signatures for the roster. The women lingered, their voices rising and falling with earnestness and excitement and the occasional burst of laughter. As the evening waned, Ida told Charles to escort the younger children safely home while she remained to tidy up and to see the last visitor to the door.

"Our block group has already chosen a regular day and time to meet," a young woman informed Ida happily as she and a companion collected their coats and scarves from the cloakroom. "Those of us who have space in their homes will take turns as hostess."

"We also discussed officers for the club," said her companion, giving Ida a significant look. "We are unanimous in our favorite for president."

Ida hid a smile. "Sounds like you accomplished quite a lot for one night."

"That's not all," said the first young woman. "At next week's meeting, we're going to propose a first official group undertaking for the Alpha Suffrage Club."

"And what is that?" asked Ida, pleased by their ambition.

"We're going to suggest that the club raise enough money to send you to Washington for the grand suffrage procession before the inauguration," said the second young woman, clasping her hands together over her heart as if bursting with her secret. "Who better than you to represent Chicago's suffragists and women of color before the nation and the world?"

"Say that you'll accept the appointment," implored her friend. "Promise that you will."

Ida had to laugh. "There is no appointment, not yet," she said. "You'll have to put the idea before the club first."

What she did not say was that she found the idea very appealing. If the Alpha Suffrage Club offered to sponsor her to represent them in the historic procession in the nation's capital, she would proudly accept.

# 18

# February 1913

## NEW YORK, NEW YORK

### Maud

When Colonel Craft unexpectedly scheduled an additional strategy meeting for the Army of the Hudson, as General Jones had christened their spirited band of marchers, Maud set out for Brooklyn as soon as she finished her shift at the library. Her trepidation rose with every block, for the army's last meeting had ended on a disconcerting note. When Rosalie had described her recent visit to Washington, it had become apparent that her meeting with Alice Paul had not gone smoothly. Although Miss Paul had not openly disparaged the pilgrims' intention to trek from New York to Washington before joining the inaugural procession, her frown had deepened and her voice had grown chillier as Rosalie had described their plans. It had occurred to Maud then that perhaps Rosalie should have consulted Miss Paul before leaping ahead to organize the pilgrimage and announce it to the press. Yet what was done could not be undone, so Maud had kept her misgivings to herself. Perhaps Miss Paul considered their uninvited intrusion into her parade disruptive and unwelcome, but she had not asked them to disband, nor had she forbidden them to join the official procession. If the pilgrims acquitted themselves well on their journey, and if they served the cause nobly and garnered favorable reports in the press, Miss Paul might warm up to them.

The parlor in the Brooklyn town house had become familiar to Maud, and so too the crowded quarters and amiable greetings of the more than two dozen suffragists who had become her comrades. They conferred in hushed voices while they waited for General Jones and Colonel Craft to make their entrance, but while several of them shared theories about the impetus for the meeting, no one knew for certain.

Promptly at the appointed hour, the two leaders entered, and when Rosalie smiled broadly, Maud breathed a sigh of relief. "I have wonderful news that could not wait," the general proclaimed. "Notwithstanding the chilly reception I received from the leader of the Congressional Committee last month, the National has officially sanctioned our march, and has assigned us an important mission." Rosalie withdrew an envelope from her dress pocket and brandished it overhead. "This is a letter from Dr. Anna Howard Shaw with a message from the National to the new president of the United States—and we are to deliver it to him personally!"

Maud gasped, astonished, while all around her, her companions cried out in surprise and triumph. "What does the message say?" Maud called above the din.

Rosalie held her gaze, eyes shining. "It's a request for Mr. Wilson to discuss his position on suffrage in his inaugural address."

Maud had to laugh. To speak on suffrage was all she had ever asked of him over the past year. She had gone to jail for it. "Better late than never, I suppose," she said. Several women chuckled ruefully and shook their heads, and someone patted her shoulder in sympathy.

"It should be Maud who places the letter in his hands," said a red-haired suffragist, planting a hand on her hip. "Wouldn't that be delightfully ironic?"

Maud felt a thrill of anticipation, but as other voices clamored to second the idea or to propose other names,

Rosalie good-naturedly waved them to silence. "We have time to sort out all that," she said. "What's important is that we've received the National's blessing. Now any internecine conflict, implied or imagined, must be disregarded. We have too many other matters requiring our immediate attention."

With that, she gestured to Colonel Craft, who cleared her throat and began reading a rather long list of those matters, beginning with a status update. General Jones had met with numerous suffrage leaders from towns along the route from New York to Washington, and their local clubs were happy and eager to welcome the pilgrims as they passed through. The number of volunteers who had asked to join the Army of the Hudson was rising weekly, and it was possible that they might yet reach their goal of at least one pilgrim from every state.

"Some of our new recruits intend to march with us for the entire journey, some for a few days, others only when we pass through their counties," Rosalie broke in to explain. "Our policy is to welcome anyone who wishes to join us, for as long or as little as they can."

"Anyone?" someone piped up. "Including men?"

"Yes, even men, as long as they call themselves suffragists," said the general, over a ripple of laughter.

"Furthermore, a number of journalists have asked to travel with us, and I consented. That will assure us publicity for the cause, if they can keep up with our pace."

She gestured for Colonel Craft to continue, and she did so, reading off some directives regarding the purchase of their uniforms, which included matching weatherproof pilgrim cloaks with hoods, knapsacks, and walking staffs. They were advised to wear their own coats beneath the cloaks for added warmth, and roomy, soft leather shoes with rubber heels, sturdy but not too heavy, with woolen stockings to avoid sores and blisters. "Evening dress will not be required," she noted dryly, evoking grins and laughter, and a few sidelong glances for Rosalie, who loved a fine evening gown, though not for marching.

Every marcher was required to carry her own first-aid kit, the colonel continued, which should include absorbent cotton, adhesive plaster, and a roll of gauze. Each pilgrim would be permitted a single small bag or suitcase, which would be transported from town to town on a baggage wagon. "Each of us is responsible for paying her own expenses, including lodging and meals," said Colonel Craft, looking around the group expectantly, eyebrows raised. "Is that understood?"

Maud tried not to wince as she nodded along with

everyone else. It would be costly, but she could afford it, thanks to her lovely librarian friends who had volunteered to cover her shifts.

Next Colonel Craft read the tentative itinerary, which would begin with their departure from Hudson Terminal at nine o'clock on the morning of February 12 and would lead them through numerous cities, towns, and villages over the two and a half weeks that followed, with rest days scheduled in Wilmington, Delaware, on February 20 and in Baltimore on February 27. "Unless otherwise announced, you should expect to rise early, march all morning, break for lunch, march through the afternoon until we reach our designated overnight stop, and hold a suffrage rally," the colonel said. "Only then shall we settle into our lodgings, find victuals, tend to our sore feet, and retire early so we may be well rested for the next day's march. There will be the occasional morning or afternoon when we'll pause at a town along the way to hold an open-air rally or to meet with the local press, but you shouldn't count on such rest breaks every day. Be prepared to march for hours and miles at a time, or you may fall behind the group."

"What if we do?" asked one young woman anxiously. "What if we lose sight of the group and get lost?"

"Then you're done for, sister," an older woman remarked. "Abandoned by the side of the road."

A few nervous laughs followed, but Rosalie shook her head, smiling. "We'll send the scout car back for anyone who isn't accounted for when we stop for the night. Make it easier on us, though, and tell someone if you can't go on. It might be a while before we can come for you, so find someplace safe to sit and wait. Better yet," she added pointedly, "do your best to keep up."

A nervous frisson passed through the gathering, as if the audacity of their mission had only just then struck home. Even Maud, a prodigious walker—or so everyone said—felt a brief flicker of worry that she might be prevented by injury or fatigue from completing the journey. She must and she would see it through, she told herself firmly. The thought of placing Dr. Shaw's letter into President Wilson's hand would compel her ever forward, even if her feet ached and lungs burned and muscles begged for rest.

In the days that followed, Maud prepared for her brief sabbatical from the library, clearing her desk, rescheduling appointments, and handing off assignments to willing colleagues. On evenings and weekends, she assembled her uniform, packed a small bag with essentials, and took long, brisk walks all around Brooklyn in fair weather and foul, to acclimate herself to the conditions she might face on the road. On the night before the pilgrims' departure, she turned in early and slept well, assured that she had done all she could to prepare.

At a quarter to nine o'clock on the morning of Wednesday, February 12, Maud arrived at the Hudson Terminal Station on Fulton Street, clad in her uniform, brown cloak, and sturdy shoes, suitcase in one hand, walking staff in the other. After leaving her suitcase at the designated spot, she joined more than four dozen of her fellow pilgrims on the concourse, nervous excitement churning in her stomach. A large crowd had gathered to witness their departure, but whether the onlookers' intention was to jeer or cheer remained to be seen. Maud was heartened by the great multitude of yellow "Votes for Women" badges pinned to coats and scarves of many in the throng, their smiles and proud, shining eyes. Only last December, she had stood in a similar crowd watching joyfully, wistfully, as Rosalie's suffrage pilgrims set out on their long trek to Albany. Now she herself was about to embark on an even more remarkable journey that would have wondrous consequences for the cause—or so she hoped.

A stir passed through the assembly as General Jones and Colonel Craft climbed onto a bench near the trains, raised their arms, and called the pilgrims to order. The Army of the Hudson snapped to attention, and much of the crowd also fell silent, riveted, but others muttered rude remarks and jeered. Ignoring the hecklers, the leaders each in turn made a rousing speech that inspired applause from the audience and enthusiastic cheers from the marchers.

"Remember," General Jones concluded, gazing out upon her companions, "we are resolved to see this pilgrimage through to the end. Let those who must fall out do so without embarrassment, but for those of us who stay the course, remember our motto: 'On to Washington!'"

Maud joined in the shouts of acclaim, raising her voice to drown out the men's jeers and applauding until her palms stung through her gloves. Then Rosalie drew a small whistle from her pocket and blew a short, sharp blast. "Get your tickets for Newark," she ordered.

The pilgrims advanced on the ticket office and formed a neat queue. Maud's cheeks grew warm when the onlookers, slow to disperse, murmured in bewilderment as one by one, the suffragists boarded the train to New Jersey. Maud was glad to climb aboard and settle into her seat, where she could better ignore the hecklers' catcalls and rude jokes about women who did not know the difference between marching and riding, and how such dimwitted females should never be trusted with the vote.

"As this is to be a *march* from New York to Washington," said Colonel Craft from the row behind Maud, her voice so low she could barely discern it, "we pilgrims should walk all the way."

"The bridge is dangerous on foot, and the roads across the meadows on the other side are impassible," replied General Jones, with such practiced patience that Maud was certain that it was a reprise of an old argument. "We must make our start on foot from Newark."

The steam whistle sounded, and the train began to chug out of the station.

"Hello," said a young woman in the aisle. Distracted, Maud glanced up to find Phoebe Hawn, the young pilgrim who at the last meeting had expressed concern about falling behind. Phoebe smiled brightly and indicated the seat beside Maud. "Is this seat taken?"

"It's all yours," said Maud, moving her cloak out of the way and straining her ears to pick up the threads of conversation behind her.

"It's the only reasonable course," Rosalie was murmuring to her second-in-command. "Besides, we can't get off the train now."

Colonel Craft sighed. "Well, then, we must march in the train."

"You can't be serious." Rosalie paused, and Maud

imagined Colonel Craft nodding emphatically. "No. I will not issue that order."

A creak of leather and a rough whisper of fabric told Maud that the colonel had risen from her seat. "Then I will walk alone."

She stepped into the aisle, and then, as the train carried them over the Hudson River and to New Jersey, Colonel Craft began pacing the length of the train, opening and closing doors between carriages along the way, letting in gusts of wind laced with frigid sleet. The conductors looked on in surprise as she strode forward and back, while the other passengers muttered indignantly and regarded her with ire, sparing a few irritated glances for the pilgrims sitting nearby, though they were disturbing no one.

After three trips through the train, Colonel Craft dropped heavily back into her seat. "This will never work," she told the general, defeated. "Mathematically it isn't possible to complete the same distance in a single journey. I would have to repeat this trip several times, and walk each time, to accrue enough mileage. Only then would the walk be a fair one."

"It doesn't matter," General Jones consoled her. "If you're concerned that it's cheating to ride, you can calculate the distance and add the miles on at the end by taking a few laps around the Washington Mall."

The colonel liked this idea immensely, and thus peace between the two longtime comrades was restored. Maud was relieved to hear it, for it wouldn't bode well for the rest of the journey if their leaders had a falling-out twenty minutes into it.

When the pilgrims disembarked in Newark, they transferred their bags to the luggage wagon and formed up ranks outside the terminal. A row of mounted policemen comprised the head of the parade that would escort them to the city limits, led by a handsome lieutenant with a yellow "Votes for Women" pennant fluttering from the pommel of his saddle. Behind them came the scout vehicle driven by Olive Schults, whose duty was to ride ahead of the group and circle back with warnings of hazards in the road, suitable waysides, and local dignitaries awaiting them just ahead. Next followed Elisabeth Freeman, driving a yellow wagon covered with suffrage banners and painted slogans. Then came General Jones and Colonel Craft, side by side, leading the brown-cloaked suffragists who marched two by two in a line that stretched the length of a city block. Throngs of cheering onlookers crowded the sidewalks as the pilgrims passed, waving banners and flags and holding up signs inscribed with witty suffrage epigrams. Marching along, nodding and waving her thanks to the supporters on one side of the street and then the other, Maud could have laughed aloud from sheer joy and pride.

The wind blew cold, the gray clouds above threatened snow, and more than two hundred miles of uneven terrain stretched ahead of them, but they were on their way.

# 19
# February 1913

## WASHINGTON, D.C.

## Alice

In early February, rumors that local college students intended to disrupt the suffrage procession became alarmingly credible when a *Washington Post* headline announced, "Mice May Cause Tumult During Suffrage Parade: Students Plan to Liberate Thousands of Rodents Along Line of March."

From the story that followed, Alice learned that mischievous college students had vowed to spend every spare moment until March 2 catching mice and rats and offering bounties to anyone willing to supply them. On March 3, they planned to carry the squirming rodents in baskets and bags to strategic locations along the parade route, await the start of the procession, and, at a given signal, rush into the rows of marchers and liberate their pests. The college men gleefully predicted that in the ensuing chaos, "the marchers will forget woman's advance through centuries, forget man's oppression, forget the privileges for which they struggle, and, harking back to traits of prehistoric ancestors, will break for nearby trees and lampposts."

The *Post* reporter remarked that the scheme was certain "to turn the well-arranged suffrage parade of March 3 from a dignified triumph into a farcical rout," but city authorities insisted that they were prepared to intervene. "This plan must be nipped in the bud," Commissioner Rudolph had said when asked to comment. "The women have a perfect right to march through the streets, and this right must be safeguarded. It is very well for the young men to have fun, but they are not proceeding in this instance in the proper manner."

Ignoring the reporter's irksome tone of amused condescension, Alice found some reassurance in the commissioner's statement. Although she wouldn't call any part of the college men's plot "fun," at least Commissioner Rudolph seemed to be taking the matter seriously. It vexed her that she had to waste any of her increasingly limited time responding to ludicrous threats, but she and Lucy and the other executive officers agreed that they could not let the insults stand unchallenged. So Alice and Helen Hamilton Gardener swiftly composed a stern press release, emphasizing, "The idea that any of the women would desert and run for shelter is absurd. All would walk bravely on, merely for the principle of the thing, if for nothing else. It will take more than rats and mice to break up this procession."

Privately, Alice and Lucy agreed that the college men, and perhaps other anonymous opponents, were already mulling over what, then, *would* break up the procession, if rodents wouldn't suffice. "Our marchers need police protection," Alice said. "Not merely a police presence to keep the route clear, but officers watching out for behavior more malicious than juvenile pranks."

She wrote to Superintendent Sylvester about her concerns, including a clipping of the article, although she assumed he had already seen it. A few days later, he replied that he was mindful of potential threats to the march and the marchers; she might recall that he had tried to dissuade her from staging the event, but she had persisted. To help preserve order, he had inquired about enlisting Boy Scouts to help with security, and Washington's head scoutmaster had agreed to post several hundred scouts as lookouts and guards along Pennsylvania Avenue.

"Never underestimate the Boy Scouts," said Lucy

when Alice expressed misgivings that the marchers might have to rely upon children for their safety. "Those lads are remarkably capable."

"Perhaps the older boys would be," Alice conceded, "but I believe it's reasonable for us to prefer trained police officers."

The entire affair was a thoroughly unnecessary distraction from the essential work of preparing for the march, squandering increasingly limited time. Every day Alice managed dozens of volunteers at headquarters, delegating various tasks such as soliciting donations, stuffing envelopes, distributing literature, and selling suffrage pennants, banners, and pins to raise funds. After regular business hours, Alice often remained behind to attend to her correspondence, but at least two evenings a week, volunteers returned for a sewing bee to produce the marchers' costumes. From the beginning Alice had envisioned a simple, classical ensemble, and a volunteer designer from New York had brought her ideas to fruition: a Portia cap, round and tight-fitting; a simple dress suitable for walking; and a full, knee-length cloak with fitted sleeves and a hood. The cloaks would be made up in waterproof fabric in a variety of hues to correspond with the wearer's division in the parade.

A different style of costume had been chosen for

the pageant. In keeping with the classical theme, one hundred women and girls would perform the balletic tableau on the steps of the Treasury in ethereal white Grecian gowns and sandals. Hazel MacKaye, an acclaimed pageant producer from a famous theatrical family, had agreed to direct, and women noted for their beauty and grace had been cast in the allegorical roles—Columbia, Liberty, Justice, Charity, Hope, and Peace. Miss MacKaye intended to choreograph the dance so that the climax would occur just as the procession reached the Treasury, where the allegorical figures would assume regal poses and review the marching women, courageous troops in the war for equality.

Miss MacKaye assured Alice that the tableau would be breathtakingly beautiful as well as politically symbolic, something Alice had repeatedly emphasized would be essential to the pageant's success. To anyone who might sneer that her emphasis on beauty indicated something superficial or shallow about her priorities, Alice would explain that the procession would be an utter failure if no spectators turned out for it. It was a simple fact that people would be more inclined to attend a production that promised beauty and fascination than one foreseen to be plain and dull. Even so, Alice winced whenever the press emphasized the beauty of individual participants rather than the ensemble, or when they invented contests between so-called "rival beauties," pitting one marcher's "flashing dark eyes, mass of dark brown hair, and dazzling smile" against another's "lustrous violet eyes and Grecian profile." Some impudent reporters reveled in rumors that suffragists were offering pretty young women two dollars if they agreed to march, while their opponents promised them three dollars apiece to stay home. The rumors were absolutely false, but evidently newspaper editors considered that insufficient cause to exclude them from the papers.

One of the most admired of the suffragist beauties made headlines when Alice appointed her to lead the parade from atop a magnificent white stallion. Lawyer Inez Milholland—the wealthy, popular socialist activist who had been the first woman to graduate from the New York University School of Law—was regarded almost unanimously in the press as the most beautiful woman in the suffrage movement. Alice could think of no one better suited for the prominent role. Not only was Inez intelligent and assured, a natural leader, but her stunning beauty would overawe the spectators and command their attention for all that followed after.

Alice remained determined to arrange for the most distinguished of those spectators to view the procession from the grandstands the Wilson inaugural committee was constructing at Pennsylvania Avenue and Fourteenth Street. Again and again she appealed to Mr. Eustis to allow her committee to rent the stands for the day, but again and again he refused, with increasingly feeble excuses. The grandstands must be in pristine condition for the president's inauguration, he insisted, or the honor would be diminished. If the suffragists' guests damaged the grandstands, there would not be enough time to repair them for the more important event the next day. The grandstands had not been constructed with ladies' skirts in mind, and they would have difficulty managing the stairs. For every problem Mr. Eustis advanced, Alice parried with a pragmatic solution. Her volunteers would scrub the grandstands clean after the procession. They would repair any damage well before Mr. Wilson's dignitaries arrived. Ladies had managed staircases in sweeping gowns for centuries; the suffragists' distinguished guests, which included gentlemen as well as ladies, would be attired appropriately for an outdoor event in early spring and could manage a few sturdy wooden steps. Nevertheless, Alice's requests were rejected. She realized Mr. Eustis was being stubborn merely for spite—perhaps at the insistence of his superiors, a group that might include Mr. Wilson himself—when he could not explain his reluctance to recoup some of his expenses by accepting rental fees from her committee. Alice intended to press that point home until the morning of the procession, if necessary. By then, as his bills were piling up and coming due, Mr. Eustis might be grateful for the chance to earn funds without any additional effort.

As preparations for the march surged ahead, the ordinary work of the suffrage movement continued. Lucy Burns organized daily meetings on street corners and in private residences. Elizabeth Kent and a few companions held an open-air demonstration in front of the State, War, and Navy Building next to the White House, making speeches to the midday passersby, selling "Votes for Women" badges, and urging women to defy their husbands if necessary to march in the suffrage procession. Volunteers at the Fourteenth Street headquarters eagerly followed the progress of state suffrage campaigns, especially New York and Illinois. Although Alice was committed to the belief that only a federal amendment would guarantee woman suffrage throughout the land, she fervently hoped the state measures would succeed. States that had granted their own female citizens the ballot would surely ratify a constitutional amendment extending that privilege to all women.

To Alice, all women meant precisely that—rich

women and poor, Black and white, privileged and disadvantaged. Yet she knew with discomfiting certainty that not everyone shared her convictions.

In mid-February, Alice received a letter from Miss Nellie Quander, president of Howard University's Alpha Kappa Alpha Sorority. "There are a number of college women of Howard University who would like to participate in the woman suffrage procession," she wrote, "but we do not wish to enter if we must meet with discrimination on account of race affiliation." Before Alice responded to the first letter, Miss Quander sent a second, repeating her inquiry and requesting that the Howard University contingent be assigned to "a desirable place in the college women's section." Soon thereafter, a similar letter arrived from Mary Church Terrell, an alumna of Oberlin College, cofounder of the National Association of Colored Women, and charter member of the NAACP. She wanted to encourage women of color from various women's clubs and university alumni organizations to register for the march, but first she sought confirmation that they would be permitted to march as white women's equals in their preferred academic or professional sections. Nothing less would do.

Alice wanted to respond with two swift letters assuring both women that they and their companions were more than welcome to join the procession and march in whatever section suited them best. But that was what Alice's heart implored; her head cautioned that she must carefully consider the unintended consequences of her decisions. After the monthslong, arduous struggle to get permission for March 3 and a permit for Pennsylvania Avenue, expanding the mission of their demonstration to include the country's fraught racial issues might cause the committee to lose all that they had gained and then some. It would be impossible to include women of color in the procession without upsetting southern voters, which would be disastrous for the suffrage movement just when they needed the approval of three-quarters of the states. Yet Alice would not be true to herself or to her Quaker faith if she segregated the procession or excluded Black women altogether.

Conflicted, she sought advice from executive committee member Mary Beard, who had handled the inquiry from Mrs. Clifford and the NACW so gracefully the previous month. After mulling over several options, none of them ideal, Alice asked Mary to meet with Miss Quander, Mrs. Terrell, and other Black women who had inquired about participating, in hopes of working out an arrangement that would promote the greatest benefit and cause the least offense.

As soon as the invitations were sent, Mary contacted suffrage leaders in her native New York to explain the dilemma, hoping they would propose solutions. Her efforts bore fruit; at the meeting a few days later, Mary listened to the Black women's concerns, assured them that the procession was open to all suffragists regardless of race, and told them they had been invited to march with the New York City Woman Suffrage Party.

"Mrs. Terrell accepted on the spot," Mary reported at the next meeting of the executive officers. "Several others followed her lead, and some requested more time to think before they decide, but a certain faction was adamantly opposed. They insisted that it was wrong to allow a southern minority to terrorize the northern majority, and that they wanted and deserved to march where they belonged."

Alice's heart sank. "Where would they be content to march?"

Mary shook her head and shrugged. "They didn't specify. I'm sure we can assume that they want to march with their professions, colleges, or state delegations."

"It'll be impossible to please everyone," said Lucy. "Speaking for myself, I'm not inclined to appease racists in the vain hope of winning their fickle support. I'd rather find steadfast allies among women of color who truly believe in the cause."

"Lucy's right," said Dora, nodding. "We must take the high road."

"Even when the high road winds along the edge of a precipice?" Inhaling deeply, Alice planted her hands on her hips and paced the length of the room, thinking. "I will not issue an order excluding Black women from the parade. Those who wish to accept the invitation to march alongside the New York City Woman Suffrage Party may do so. Those who wish to join a different section will be obliged to make the necessary arrangements with the respective section leaders." Alice let her hands fall to her side and looked around the circle, spying doubt and worry in each woman's expression. "If you're aware of other potential solutions I've overlooked, I'd welcome them."

No new flashes of inspiration struck, so by an informal show of hands, they agreed to carry on as discussed and hope for the best.

Later, as she and Lucy walked back to the I Street boardinghouse, where Lucy too had taken a room, Alice brooded over the discord within the suffragist ranks. Conflict beset them from within and without, and more ominous threats than college students unleashing rodents could be stalking them.

Suddenly she felt a chill of fear. Would women of color among the marchers draw the attention of malicious spectators? Would they become the particular targets of verbal abuse or physical violence? She had long worried that Superintendent Sylvester was not adequately preparing the police to control the crowds and protect the marching women, but her concerns suddenly took on a new urgency.

Once more she would have to go over Superintendent Sylvester's head. As soon as she reached the boardinghouse, she bade Lucy good night, raced upstairs to her room, took out paper and pen, and wrote an appeal to the district commissioners.

*February 15, 1913.*

*To the Commissioners of the District of Columbia.*

*GENTLEMEN: On behalf of the procession committee of the congressional committee of the National American Woman Suffrage Association and the suffrage societies of the District of Columbia, I have the honor to request that a sufficient military force be*

*asked for by the commissioners for use on the occa-*
*sion of the suffrage procession at Washington, D.C.,*
*on the afternoon of March 3, 1913.*

*Very respectfully,*
*Alice Paul,*
*Chairman, Procession Committee.*

In the morning she had a volunteer hand-deliver the note, and she received an almost immediate reply via the post. "Dear Miss Paul," William Tindall, the secretary of the Board of Commissioners, had written, "The commissioners direct me to inform you that they have transmitted to the Secretary of War, with the following endorsement, your request that a sufficient military force be requested by the commissioners for use on the occasion of the procession in the city on the afternoon of the 3d proximo." Specifically, the commissioners urged the War Department to provide the largest possible police detail, supplemented by United States troops, preferably cavalry. They included a recommendation from General Anson Mills, United States Army, retired, to station the force along the route of the procession rather than acting as an escort.

It was all Alice could have asked for and more, but her hopes were dashed three days later, when the secretary of war had his subordinate notify her of his decision:

WAR DEPARTMENT,
*Washington, February 20, 1913.*

*To the Chairman, Procession Committee,*
*1420 F Street NW, Washington, D. C.*

*DEAR MADAM: In reply to your communication of the 15th instant, which was referred by the President of the Board of Commissioners of the District of Columbia, in regard to the detail of United States troops on the occasion of the suffrage procession on the afternoon of March 3, 1913, I have the honor to inform you that owing to requirements of the following day and other contingencies of the military service, it will not be practicable to furnish the forces for which request is made.*

*Very truly yours,*
*ROBERT SHAW OLIVER,*
*Assistant Secretary of War.*

Appalled, Alice crumpled the note in her hand and sank down heavily at Susan B. Anthony's desk. The secretary of war intended to do nothing to provide security for what was likely to be the largest peacetime demonstration in the nation's history.

It was almost too much to believe, and definitely too much to accept.

That same day, Alice and Lucy chose a small delegation of eminent women and sent them to call on the secretary of war himself, Henry Stimson, to plead their case in person. He cited several vague legal technicalities to defend his decision and sent the suffragists on their way. Later Alice learned that he had also written to the commissioners to remind them of a budget allocation that would allow them to hire more police, which ought to be enough to maintain public order and protect life and property in the District. Since the commissioners had adequate resources already, Secretary Stimson concluded, "and also for other and much stronger reasons, it would be improper to order a contingent of the Regular Army to report for the duty in question."

Alice could only hope that the commissioners would heed his advice and swiftly hire more police officers, for the suffragists could expect no help from the federal government. It wasn't that the men in power wanted the women to be threatened or injured, or so she hoped. More likely, they assumed that if the suffragists feared for their safety, they would fail to turn out on March 3, and the procession would be over before it had begun.

If that was what the men in power believed, they were sadly mistaken. Generations of women had suffered too much for the suffrage cause for modern women to quit in fear when they were so close to achieving their goal. Alice herself had endured worse at Holloway Prison than scurrying rodents and jeering mobs.

She would continue to pressure city authorities to provide security for the procession as their professional duties required. The Boy Scouts, dutiful and well-meaning though they were, would almost certainly not be enough.

Ultimately, if it came down to marching into danger or staying at home, they would march.

# 20

# February 1913

## CHICAGO, ILLINOIS

### Ida

On Abraham Lincoln's birthday, Chicago civic organizations representing both white and Black communities united to celebrate the fiftieth anniversary of the Emancipation Proclamation with a glorious Jubilee at Orchestra Hall. Ida's primary responsibility on behalf of the Negro Fellowship League had been to organize the Emancipation Chorus, a choir of one hundred African American voices under the direction of the renowned composer and choral conductor James A. Mundy. Among the illustrious speakers were Governor Edward F. Dunne, Ida's friend Jane Addams, and her longtime colleague Dr. W. E. B. Du Bois, who had traveled to Chicago from New York for the occasion. On that clear, starry winter night, an audience of more than 2,500 commemorated slavery's end with a rich musical program, a reading of the Proclamation, and several eloquent, inspirational speeches that celebrated the progress of the past half century while somberly observing that true racial equality had yet to be achieved.

Jane Addams, in a speech titled "Has the Emancipation Act Been Nullified by National Indifference?," offered a strong critique of the steady rise in racial prejudice in the United States, as well as the unconstitutional exclusion of people of color from the political process. One troubling factor allowing injustice to grow so stealthily and ruthlessly was the mistaken notion that since slavery had been abolished by law, the problem was solved, the task completed. This willful ignorance manifested among southern whites as denial that the promises of Reconstruction remained unfulfilled, and in the North as cool indifference. "What has been and is being lost by the denial of opportunity and of free expression on the part of the Negro is difficult to estimate," Jane warned. "Only faint suggestions of the tragic waste can be perceived. Shall we finally admit that the old abolitionist arguments now seem flat and stale; that, because we are no longer compelled to remove fetters, to prevent cruelty, to lead the humblest to the banquet of civilization, it is no longer necessary to consider the concepts of right and wrong in government affairs, but may substitute the base doctrine of political necessity?"

Jane's challenging words met with sustained, vigorous applause—all the more remarkable given that the audience was equally divided between white and colored folks, all intermingled from the first seat in the pit to the most distant row in the balcony.

"In the broadest sense, franchise is only an implement for justice," Jane continued. "It is for that reason that a band of us women, known as suffragettes, are now striving to attain this instrument. It was public sentiment and opinion which, to a large extent at least, was responsible for the issuance of the Emancipation Proclamation. Today this same public opinion exists in another cause, and through it we will win what we strive for."

From her seat upstage, Ida clapped heartily along with everyone else, although she offered one silent caveat to Jane's remarks. Although President Lincoln had waited until public opinion in the North was strongly behind him before he issued the Emancipation Proclamation, he could have done so regardless. Suffragists, on the other hand, could not triumph without the goodwill and consent of the people—in particular, legislators who alone could ratify or condemn new suffrage measures, and the voters who elected them.

As the evening passed, Ida observed that all of the speakers echoed a similar refrain: those who yearned for and fought for equality had achieved much in the fifty years since Emancipation, but much work remained to be done, not only so that the formerly enslaved peoples and their descendants might move ever forward into a more peaceful and prosperous future, but also to prevent a resurgence of the evils of the past.

Much work remained, Ida agreed, and yet one of the most effective tools—the vote—was withheld from more than half of the population, from Black men in the South and from women almost everywhere. The inescapable conclusion was that the powerful men who held the key to enfranchisement in their clenched fists did not want that work to continue.

After the program, Ida and Jane met in the wings and were catching up on the news of work, family, and mutual friends when Du Bois joined them. "If I recall correctly," he mused in his mellifluous baritone, "the last time we shared a stage, it was shortly before the presidential election, and we were debating the merits of the candidates."

"And if I recall correctly," said Ida, smiling, "I won the debate, but your candidate won the White House."

Jane feigned puzzlement. "I believe I won that debate."

They shared a laugh, but Du Bois's smile quickly faded. "I regret to admit that in the months since, I've come down with a case of buyer's remorse."

"You can't mean you're sick of Mr. Wilson already," Ida exclaimed. "He hasn't even taken office yet."

Du Bois shrugged and managed a pained half smile. "The symptoms come and go."

"But you left the Republican Party to vote for him," said Jane, brow furrowed.

"The party left me first," said Du Bois. "I abhorred Taft, and Theodore Roosevelt had already proven himself a capable president. I knew he was not a perfect man, but he advocated for woman suffrage, worker's rights, and other progressive reforms, so when he broke away to form the Progressive Party, I followed."

"As did I," said Jane.

"Then came the Progressive Party's convention." Du Bois grimaced at the memory. "I wrote a civil rights plank and offered it to Roosevelt in hope that he would include it in the party platform. Not only did he reject my work, but he instructed his subordinates not to seat any southern Negro delegates, because he suspected them of being Taft loyalists. It was an outrage. I felt entirely betrayed."

"I remember," said Ida, nodding. She and Ferdinand had agreed that the incident completely vindicated their decision to remain with the Republican candidate, although, of course, only Ferdinand had been allowed to cast a ballot. "So, despising Taft, and no longer able to support Roosevelt, you turned to Wilson as the only remaining option?"

"I would never squander my vote so lightly," he replied, a hint of apology in his voice, knowing that Ida and Jane had no votes to squander. "Wilson courted the Negro voter—sincerely, or so I thought, for he risked losing white voters by doing so. He had convinced me that he would do right by the Black community, and I trusted that he would keep his campaign promises. Now, however—" He shook his head. "I fear my trust was misplaced."

"But Mr. Wilson hasn't broken any campaign promises," Jane protested. "He hasn't even assumed office yet. Give him time."

"He *has* had time, more than three months since the election, to chart a progressive course," said Du Bois. "What has he done? He continues to dodge the question when asked to express an opinion about woman suffrage, and historically, his misogyny has been thinly veiled at best. He's filling his cabinet with avowed seg-regationists. Worse yet, he believes that slavery was a beneficial, civilizing influence on Africans and their American descendants."

"That's a dreadful accusation," said Jane, appalled.

"Dreadful but true," said Ida. "Wilson has said as much in more than one speech. He has also defended Ku Klux Klan violence against people of color during Reconstruction—I believe he called it a necessary evil. I have to wonder what he thinks of violence against colored folks in our own day and age. If he's ever de-nounced lynching, I've never heard it."

"I don't believe he ever explicitly denounced lynch-ing," said Jane, discomfited, "but in all fairness, that doesn't mean he condones it."

"What's preventing him from condemning it to-day?" Ida countered. "I'll settle for tomorrow, or better yet, on the fourth of March, in his inaugural address."

Jane sighed, and Ida understood that she shared Ida's concerns, but she did not expect Wilson to men-tion lynching in the first major speech of his presi-dency, the one that would announce the agenda for his administration. Nor was he likely to use the occasion to finally reveal his position on woman suffrage. Instead, Ida predicted, he would continue to demur and defer to states' rights until some inescapable confrontation forced him to state his opinion plainly.

Perhaps the NAWSA suffrage procession would be that catalyst. What it might do to advance the cause of racial equality remained to be seen, but Ida had reined in her expectations after friends on the East Coast had warned that Black women's participation was being carefully managed.

Officially, women of color were allowed to participate, and the alleged scores of southern women who had threatened to withdraw rather than march in an integrated parade had apparently changed their minds, if their threats had ever been genuine. But that news had come through the grapevine; Ida had heard nothing through official National channels. She knew that her longtime friend and fellow activist Mary Church Terrell was sending out letters encouraging Black women's clubs and alumni organizations to participate, but none of the officers of the National had made the effort, nor had any representatives of the Congressional Committee who were running the show. In such fraught times, without a clear, unmistakable invitation from the event directors, their inclusion of women of color seemed half-hearted at best.

Other friends on the East Coast had mentioned

a meeting in New York, a negotiation of sorts that had resulted in an agreement that Black women who wanted to participate could march with the New York City Woman Suffrage Party. It was nice of the group to offer, Ida supposed, but why should it have been necessary? For that matter, why was it considered appropriate? Ida was no longer a New Yorker, although she had lived there briefly, and she had never been a member of the Woman Suffrage Party. It would make much more sense if she marched with the journalists, or the Illinois delegation, or among academic women, wearing a banner with the colors of Rust College or Fisk University. Ida respected Mary, and she understood well what a powerful statement the presence of women of color would make on such a momentous occasion, but she recoiled from such restricted participation so grudgingly offered. The Alpha Suffrage Club had offered to pay all of Ida's expenses, but she had no desire to participate in a segregated parade. Either women of color were full participants in the suffrage procession or they were not. Ida would not endorse any half measures of equality, for that was not equality at all.

A few days after the Jubilee, Ida made a return engagement to the Women's Party of Cook County, this time to offer a lecture titled "Lincoln as the Nation's Emancipator." The College Room at the Hotel La

Salle welcomed an overflow crowd of eager members and guests, and at the reception that followed, several women mentioned that they had attended the Jubilee and had been deeply moved by the speeches and music. Many sought her opinion on the Illinois state suffrage campaign, but although Ida freely shared her views, she was troubled by the implicit suggestion that she spoke for all Black women, or indeed for the entire race. No white person would accept the notion that one person out of millions represented them all, but they seemed to assume that was true for people of color. Ida gave them credit for caring about the Black perspective at all, but she was not sure they entirely grasped how many diverse and occasionally conflicting opinions this perspective included.

At the conclusion of the evening's program, which also included a performance by a contralto soloist and a literary reading, Ida enjoyed a happy reunion with her friends Virginia Brooks and Belle Squire. They had last spoken at the launch of the Alpha Suffrage Club, and they had all been so busy during the interim that they had much catching up to do.

Sometime later, just as Ida was about to bid her friends good night, Belle raised her eyebrows inquisitively at Virginia, who brightened and nodded, bubbling over with some secret. "All right," said Ida knowingly, planting a hand on her hip. "Out with it. Do you have gossip to share or a favor to ask?"

"Neither," said Virginia, but then she paused to think. "I suppose it could be considered the latter, because we very much hope you'll consent."

"It's an invitation," Belle clarified. "We realize that at this late date—"

"Practically the eleventh hour," Virginia broke in.

"You may have already made other plans," Belle continued. "In the event that you haven't yet committed to another section, we've been authorized on behalf of the Illinois delegation to invite you to march behind our state banner in the suffrage procession in Washington."

For a moment, Ida was rendered speechless. "Are you certain I'm wanted?"

"Of course we're certain!" exclaimed Virginia. "We didn't know you were planning to attend until the Alpha Suffrage Club newsletter mentioned that they had raised enough funds to send you, or we would have asked sooner."

"I didn't mean to question whether you two want me," said Ida warmly, reaching for their hands. "You're my friends, and I know we'd have a grand time marching side by side through the capital on such a historic day." She paused to study her friends' expressions, curious. "But surely you're aware that certain factions within the National would prefer to keep Black women on the sidewalk with the other spectators."

"You're no mere spectator," said Belle. "You're one of the most prominent suffragists in Illinois—in the United States, for that matter. The delegation would be honored if you would march with us behind our state banner."

"You speak for the entire delegation now?" asked Ida, skeptical.

"I trust I speak for the majority," Belle replied. "If any lady refuses to march alongside you, she is free to join another section, if they'll have her. Better yet, she may stay home."

"Mrs. Trout herself said she hoped you'd accept the invitation," Virginia added.

"Did she, now?" Ida was pleased in spite of herself. Grace Trout, the leader of the Illinois delegation, was the former president of the Chicago Political Equality League and the current president of the Illinois Equal Suffrage Association. She had proven herself remarkably successful in both offices, increasing membership, strengthening organizational structures, and developing a forceful lobbying committee. She played the press brilliantly, and over the years she had fomented a strong groundswell of public support for woman suffrage. Several friends whose opinions Ida trusted had said that if the Illinois suffrage measure passed the state legislature, Mrs. Trout would deserve a significant amount of the credit.

"I never did like to avoid a gathering because racists and segregationists said I didn't belong," Ida mused aloud. "Quite the contrary. I've made a point to show up in order to prove that I have a right to be there."

Votes for Women meant votes for women of color. All the little Black girls watching the suffrage procession from the sidewalks along Pennsylvania Avenue needed to see Ida marching for her right to vote. They needed to see themselves in her. How else would they learn that they too had the right to speak up, to be present, to demand equal treatment before the law?

"You may tell Mrs. Trout that I accept your invitation," Ida told her friends.

She would march *with* the Illinois delegation, but she would march *for* all Black folks wondering when the American promise of liberty and justice would include people who looked like them. She would march for her own daughters, who had witnessed their mother toiling on behalf of their race all their lives, persisting even when progress came only in frustratingly small increments. She would march for her mother and grandmothers, who had taught her courage, strength, and forbearance, who had lifted her up on their shoulders so she could reach opportunities they had only dreamed of.

She would march for herself, so that one day she too would have the power to hold her elected leaders accountable for all they did and all they failed to do. They could not ignore her then, she and all her sisters. Alone their separate ballots would make them the equal of any man, and together they would create a rising tide that would sweep away the last cruel vestiges of slavery.

# 21

# February 1913

BURLINGTON, NEW JERSEY,
TO CHESTER, PENNSYLVANIA

### Maud

Maud carefully affixed plasters to her fresh blisters, pulled on warm wool socks, and slipped her callused feet into the new pair of sturdy black leather boots she had purchased to replace the shoes she had worn out sixty miles into the pilgrimage. "Today," she cheerfully predicted as she paced the length of the hotel room, testing the fit, "I shall march in relative comfort."

"It's unfortunate you don't have more time to break them in," said Martha, observing her from the other bed, where she sat yawning and pulling on a thick pair of stockings. Corporal Klatschken, as Maud's fellow

New Yorker was also known, had quit her job as a stenographer in order to devote herself to the suffrage cause full-time. She was in charge of fundraising for the pilgrimage, and everyone appreciated her willingness to take on the tedious, thankless clerical tasks that no one else wanted to do.

"I'll break them in on the road," Maud replied. Her own role had never been officially defined, nor had she been assigned an honorary military rank, but she was naturally drawn to speaking with local reporters whenever the marchers held open-air meetings in the towns along their route. She had also taken on the duty of defusing potentially threatening encounters by engaging hecklers in amusing banter, but those techniques worked only when the onlookers were merely condescending and mocking. If the Antis tried to block the marchers' way or shouted hostile insults or massed on the sidewalks and glared menacingly, she kept her mouth shut, fixed her gaze straight ahead, and marched past with her comrades, breathing easily only after they had left the threat behind.

Maud and Martha joined their fellow pilgrims in the dining room off the lobby, and while they fortified themselves with coffee, eggs, sausages, and toast, General Rosalie Jones read aloud from a letter that had arrived in the morning mail. The pilgrims' itinerary had been widely advertised, so well-wishers and critics alike had figured out how to intercept them with notes, postcards, children's drawings, the occasional bitter scolding, and romantic missives that made the recipients laugh and cringe, often at the same time.

"I have seen your picture in the papers, and I read what you're doing to further a great cause," the latest amorous author had written to Rosalie. "I lost a leg at Chancellorsville for another great cause, so I sympathize with you."

Several of the pilgrims applauded those lines.

"I know how tired your little feet must be," the writer continued. "When this march is over I should like to have the chance to smooth the road before them for the rest of our lives. You may say I am old and you are young—but what of that? I may have but one leg, but my heart is bigger than the heart of any two men. Why don't you rest your tired little head upon it?"

A chorus of groans went up from her listeners. "He should have quit while he was ahead," someone called out. Maud nodded agreement. What had begun as a thoughtful, encouraging message had taken an awkward turn, but that was hardly a surprise. This was the third marriage proposal General Jones had received since setting out from New York, and such unexpected, uninvited overtures from strangers had become almost commonplace. Maud herself had received a proposal after the Utica *Saturday Globe* published a witty interview. Phoebe Hawn, the youngest and prettiest of the marchers, had so enchanted a Princeton student when the pilgrims passed through campus that he had marched alongside her for the rest of the day, wooing her more ardently with every mile until they reached the outskirts of Trenton, where he had proposed. Phoebe, suspecting it was a Valentine's Day joke, had told him that if he joined the pilgrimage she would give him an answer when they reached Washington. Apparently daunted by the long road ahead, her suitor had glumly returned to school.

"'Just say the word and I am yours,'" Rosalie continued reading, looking more pained than amused. "'Other men might be afraid of you because you have so much nerve, but I can understand you. We are both soldiers. Say, little one, if you will join forces with me I will give you anything your little heart desires.'"

"Fresh socks," Colonel Craft called out.

"Sturdier shoes," another pilgrim added. "Liniment for my sore ankles."

"That must be why we're still unmarried," one of Maud's table companions remarked, nudging her with her elbow. "We're just like the general. We have too much nerve."

"I dare you to call Rosalie 'little one' to her face," replied Maud, elbowing her in return. "Honestly, why can't these men just admire our dedication and courage without becoming so infatuated? We're marching for the vote, not for husbands."

"I think it's sweet," Phoebe protested from the other side of the table. "This fellow appreciates the general's strength, and he supports our cause. Wouldn't you prefer more of that sort of talk, and a lot less of the catcalling and mockery we usually get?"

Everyone at the table murmured agreement. After four days on the road, they had all had their fill of the opinions of jeering onlookers. When they had marched into Burlington the previous day, of the enthusiastic crowd of more than 1,500 awaiting them, an alarming percentage had shouted blistering insults and made menacing gestures. They might have done worse had the mayor not sent a local Boy Scout troop to deliver a letter welcoming the pilgrims and offering them the key to the city. The suffragists had proceeded to the town's only theater to accept the key and make speeches, but the increasingly belligerent crowd had shouted them down until General Jones had been obliged to end the meeting early. Disappointed, they had trod off wearily to their hotel for a well-deserved rest.

Today's march would have to be better, Maud told

herself, but before she finished the thought, Rosalie sighed and put the letter away, her pensive expression telling Maud that their leader was about to deliver unpleasant news.

"I know we were all looking forward to crossing the Delaware from here in Burlington this morning," the general began, as all conversation ceased. "Our suffrage sisters across the river in Bristol, Pennsylvania, had planned a warm welcome, with as much fanfare and publicity as we could desire. Regrettably, ice dams in the water will prevent us from crossing by boat, and there is no suitable bridge."

A rumble of dissatisfaction rose from the group. "What's the new plan, then?" someone called out querulously.

"We're going to follow the river on the New Jersey side and take the ferry from Camden to Philadelphia."

Maud felt a pang of worry. "Camden is full of anti-suffragists," she said. "Word of our approach will reach them hours before we do. Antis on both sides of the crossing will have time to gather and prepare a rude welcome. If we have to wait for the ferry, we might have to stand there for quite some time and endure whatever abuse is hurled at us."

"We'll be sitting ducks," another pilgrim chimed in, alarmed.

As a murmur of worry rose, Rosalie held up her hands for silence. "I'm afraid we have no other choice. We have a schedule to keep, and we can't afford to go any farther out of our way. Besides," she added, smiling, "Olive has scouted ahead, and she assures me the walk will be a pleasant one, not like yesterday's eighteen miles of mud."

Maud joined in the rueful laughter. The last four miles had done in her old shoes completely. If the cobbler across the street from their hotel had not had a perfect pair of boots in her size at a reasonable price, she might not have been able to continue on foot—and she would have felt utterly disgraced if she had been forced to ride in the scout car or the baggage wagon.

By nine o'clock, the pilgrims had assembled on the street in front of the hotel, Olive in the lead at the wheel of the scout car, Elisabeth Freeman directly behind her at the reins of the suffrage wagon pulled by Lausanne, the geriatric draft horse Rosalie had purchased for a song in Newark. General Jones, Colonel Craft, and Corporal Klatschken were next, carrying the large yellow suffrage banner, and behind them were the pilgrims, a few loyal men acting as support staff, and several members of the press, who had taken to calling themselves "war correspondents." Only a handful of the original Army of the Hudson remained of those who had set out from Manhattan; some had never intended to march the entire way and had left when other obligations beckoned, while others had been obliged to quit due to injuries or exhaustion. Fortunately, day hikers joined them at nearly every town along the way, from a few members of a single farm family to an entire suffrage club numbering in the dozens. That morning, the temporary recruits included nearly two hundred women from New Jersey and Pennsylvania, as well as the troop of Boy Scouts who had brought them the mayor's message the previous evening. The women looked proud and determined in their new brown cloaks, the boys smart and capable in their uniforms, and all seemed eager for adventure.

A few curious onlookers milled about on the sidewalks as the pilgrims prepared to leave. It made for a less than inspiring sendoff, but Maud supposed that was better than the raucous mob scene that had marred their arrival. The general called the troops to order, the colonel blew her whistle, and off they set on the fifth day of their long march to Washington.

The morning was bright and sunny, with calm winds and temperatures in the low forties with the promise of increased warmth as the sun climbed to its zenith. Maud bit her lips together to stifle groans until her stiff muscles warmed up and she could stride along at her usual brisk pace, or nearly so. The new boots felt warm and sturdy on her tender feet, and the road south, while not the route they had originally intended, was quite lovely, taking them along the western edge of the New Jersey Pine Barrens, where tall conifers stretched to the sky from sandy soil.

About six miles southwest of Burlington, they paused at Bridgeboro for an open-air meeting with speeches and songs attended by a small but enthusiastic crowd. Afterward, they continued marching southwest until they reached a scenic spot on the shore of a lake fed by a swift, narrow stream known as Swedes Run, where they broke for lunch. As Elisabeth Freeman and a few assistants unloaded provisions from the wagon, the Boy Scouts bustled about gathering timber and wood for a campfire, where coffee was soon prepared to accompany their sandwiches and hard-boiled eggs. It would have been a restful woodland picnic if not for the hundreds of sightseers who had come by motorcar, on bicycles, and on foot to gawk at the brown-cloaked suffragists. Sensing an opportunity to convert others to the cause, Maud quickly finished her lunch and joined Rosalie in working the crowd, offering suffrage banners and badges and the occasional sandwich to anyone who asked. Several dapper young men eagerly requested to be introduced to the "Brooklyn Baby," as the press had dubbed Phoebe after the Princeton incident, but she had been in a dreadful mood all morning, grousing about the food and the uneven roads, and rhapsodizing to the war correspondents about all the wonderful delicacies she intended to indulge in as soon as they reached Philadelphia. Most of the older pilgrims had grown quite exasperated with her, and perhaps sensing their mood, she had wrapped herself in a fur coat and settled down for a nap in the suffrage wagon.

The youngest pilgrim did not have long to rest, for they were soon on the road again, passing a line of gawkers' vehicles one hundred yards long as they set out toward Palmyra. Maud usually strode near the front of the group, a few paces behind General Jones and the tall, lissome, athletic, indefatigably cheerful Mary Boldt, but that afternoon she hung back just ahead of Colonel Craft and Corporal Klatschken so she could keep a watchful eye on Minerva Crowell. The thirty-five-year-old was usually quite vigorous, but over the past few days she had acquired a slight limp. At the moment she was breathing heavily and moving at a fraction of her usual pace, so Maud was prepared to offer an arm to lean on should she require it. Minerva had been with the pilgrims from the beginning, and Maud knew how disappointed she would be if she had to accept an honorable discharge and take a train home.

Soon after the troops resumed the march, they acquired a charming escort—two girls, one aged seven and the other ten, who marched alongside them for three miles. The friends wore matching red sweaters and yellow suffrage badges, and they assured General Jones earnestly that if they were "growed up," they would accompany the pilgrims all the way to Washington.

Just north of Palmyra, not long after the girls had wished them good luck and darted off back down the road for home, the pilgrims passed Manless Farm, so named because Anna and Sally Hunter were proud of how successfully they managed their acres without the help of any man. The two sisters declared that they had long approved of woman suffrage, and the sight of the Army of the Hudson filled them with joy. Privately Maud thought that the sisters would have been even more impressed if the army were not stretched thin over nearly a half mile, the brisk striders taking the lead while stragglers trailed along after them, valiantly endeavoring to keep up so Olive would not have to circle back in the scout car to collect them. "I'm sure women can run the country without the help of men," Maud heard the elder sister call out as she marched past, "and they'd do it more successfully than men too!"

All the hikers within earshot cheered.

Although the warm encouragement of the women and girls they passed heartened them, by midafternoon, even the most strong-willed and athletic marchers had grown weary. It was at this time every day, when they were most susceptible to temptation, that wealthy Antis typically went on the offensive, sending their drivers in luxury cars to offer the pilgrims rides to their next destination. Apparently the Antis hoped to take advantage of the pilgrims' fatigue to lure them into abandoning the march, exposing them as weak, hypocritical, and uncommitted to the cause, all while the "war correspondents" looked on, taking notes. Thus far their strategy had failed, but the daily attempts had become annoying and dispiriting. It particularly irked Maud that the culprits were reportedly privileged women who haughtily insisted that they did not need the vote and didn't want any other woman to have it either. If they didn't want to exercise an inherent right of citizenship, that was their business, but why must they prevent Maud from doing so?

The pilgrims sang songs to lift their spirits as they approached Camden, a town known for its hostility toward woman suffrage, but where just enough supporters resided to justify holding a rally. No sooner had they turned onto Cooper Street than they discovered unexpectedly large crowds lining the sidewalks and spilling into the streets, forcing the marchers to draw closer together to pass through. Hundreds of onlookers gathered around as General Jones, Colonel Craft, and several local suffragists spoke from the broad covered porch of a private residence, but the crowd's jeers often drowned out applause. Afterward, as the pilgrims made ready to leave, unruly men and boys crowded in so closely that the police had to be summoned to clear the road ahead. Even then, the women were jostled roughly all the way to the harbor, and some of the pilgrims were knocked off their feet in the struggle to board the ferry.

"We can rest on the crossing," Rosalie assured her troops as they settled in, but it was not to be. The journey across the Delaware River proved rougher than anticipated, the frigid winds rendering them breathless as the ferry crunched through the thin layer of ice on the dark water. Maud took heart from General Jones's relentless good cheer as Rosalie stood in the bow, flanked by Colonel Craft and Corporal Klatschken, holding an American flag that whipped and snapped from the top of a slender staff.

"Why do you carry that flag, General?" one of the war correspondents asked.

"Why? Because I believe this crossing of the Delaware will prove to be as important in the history of the struggle for equal suffrage as another famous crossing was to the struggle for American independence," Rosalie declared.

A few men guffawed, but the general lifted her chin and smiled as if she possessed some insight into the future they could not possibly understand.

When the ferry docked in Philadelphia, Maud and her companions discovered a crowd of more than two thousand awaiting them, and they seemed no friendlier than those who had seen them off in Camden. Maud's heart thudded as six policemen struggled to hold back the crush of the mob so the pilgrims could disembark. The throng of mostly men and boys seemed in good spirits and more curious than hostile, but their numbers were overwhelming. As the brown-cloaked women made their way down the pier, the crowd closed in on them from all sides, shouting ever louder, breaking up their lines and threatening to sweep them away. Constance Leupp shrieked and clutched Maud's shoulder; instinctively Maud steadied Constance, grabbed hold of Phoebe on her right, and linked arms with them both, drawing them close so they could plow their way through the shouting, churning mob past the ferry house and on toward the city.

"Votes for women!" Colonel Craft shouted from somewhere up ahead. "On to Washington!"

Maud could barely hear her piping voice above the din, but she homed in on the sound as best she could and steered Phoebe and Constance toward it. Up ahead, someone had managed to unfurl the familiar yellow suffrage banner that had preceded them for most of the journey. Maud called out encouragement to rally the troops and determinedly shouldered her way forward, ears blistering from the barrage of insults, interrupted by an occasional, distant cry of "Votes for women!" from some safe place beyond the surging throng.

Eventually the pilgrims managed to gather around the two marchers who held fast to the banner's staffs. Buffeted by men who had managed to push past the police, they struggled to form up lines and press onward. Although there was a moment when Maud feared that they would not be permitted to leave the wharf, eventually they reached an intersection where at least twenty additional policemen maintained some semblance of order. With the road ahead sufficiently clear, the pilgrims picked up speed until they were able to march along two by two at a fairly steady pace.

At long last they reached the suffrage headquarters in the Hale Building on Chestnut Street, where local suffragists swiftly ushered them inside, offered them comfortable chairs, and served them restorative cups of tea and plates of sandwiches. "We're all so sorry we couldn't meet you at the wharf," one stout matron around Maud's age said, abashed. "You see, rumors of mob violence—which the scene outside proves were worth heeding—kept us away."

Maud, vexed and exhausted, accepted her apology and others like it with forced smiles and curt nods, but Rosalie was more sanguine. "You made the prudent choice," she assured their hostesses, smiling. "No harm has been done or feelings hurt."

Maud didn't necessarily agree, but the general often spoke for them all, so she held her peace and took another sandwich. After a brief rally to recruit new marchers and to give the crowd outside time to disperse, the pilgrims quietly set out for the Hotel Walton, their haven for the night.

After a hot meal and a bath, Maud sank gratefully into her warm, comfortable bed, too exhausted and footsore to fully appreciate the stylish accommodations. The next morning, in an echo of other mornings in other hotels, she woke at first light, washed, dressed, breakfasted with her comrades in the hotel dining room, listened intently as General Jones described their itinerary, and prepared herself for another long day on the road.

Soon thereafter, thick, wet flakes of snow descended from a steel-gray sky upon Maud and her fifty-two companions as they stood in neat rows of four in the intersection of Broad Street and Locust. Despite their heavy brown cloaks and hoods, they shivered and stomped their feet for warmth as they waited for the signal to depart, heartened by the cheering crowds who had come to see them off, in a bewildering contrast to the raucous, belligerent thousands who had met them at the wharf. It was as if the good citizens of Philadelphia had been embarrassed by the newspaper reports of the rough welcome they had given the pilgrims and wanted to show the harassed marchers their more genteel, hospitable side. The *Evening Times* had hired a fife and drum corps to lead them through the city, and dozens of mounted police officers would keep the route clear. A cornet sounded, the signal to begin, and so they set out, past city hall, down Walnut Street with its elegant homes, all to the sound of stirring music, encouraging cheers, applause, and the occasional shouted marriage proposal. Flowers were tossed in their path; yellow suffrage pennants waved farewell and good luck. Amid all the fanfare, Maud could almost forget her fatigue and the many miles she had to go before she could again rest for the night.

The Army of the Hudson had not gone far when they were met by nearly five hundred young men, students from the University of Pennsylvania who had come to escort them to campus. Nearly one thousand more gave the pilgrims a wildly enthusiastic welcome upon their arrival, obliging the police to clear a path so they could enter the law school. There Rosalie and the other leaders gave speeches to a crowd of more than three thousand, frequently interrupted by thunderous applause, raucous cheers, and chanting of suffrage slogans. Maud was so overwhelmed by the outpouring of support that tears filled her eyes and her jaw ached from smiling. If these young men, present and future voters, believed this strongly in woman suffrage, the prospects for the cause looked bright indeed.

After the rally, five hundred of the students and nearly two thousand more Philadelphia citizens on foot, as well as hundreds of automobiles with their horns sounding merry blasts, escorted the pilgrims through the thickly falling snow to the road to Chester, their next destination, fourteen miles southwest on the bank of the Delaware River.

The snowstorm slowed their progress, reducing visibility and rendering the ordinarily passable roads treacherous underfoot. As previously arranged, fifty representatives of various Philadelphia suffrage groups accompanied them as far as Darby before wishing them well and turning back for the shelter of home. Maud longed for the safety of greater numbers when, soon thereafter, they came upon about thirty men lining both sides of the street, each clutching a snowball in a fist. As the pilgrims approached, the nearest man drew back his arm and hurled his missile against the side of the suffrage wagon; it struck with a harsh thud, startling Lausanne, and fell into a snowdrift, nearly intact.

"That's not snow," Martha murmured at Maud's left. "That's solid ice."

Maud's heart sank. Elisabeth steadied the horse and proceeded ever forward at the same resolute pace, so the marchers too continued on. Maud felt her breath catch in her throat as they passed through the gauntlet, the men standing silently, glaring menacingly, as the women walked between them. In her peripheral vision, Maud saw some testing the weight of their icy spheres and eyeing prospective targets among the brown-cloaked women, while others tossed their weapons from hand to hand as if awaiting a signal to unleash a barrage. The signal never came. In the end, the men only stood and glowered while the pilgrims made their way down the road, rounded a bend, and left them behind. And yet it was not quite true to say that the men had done nothing, for the threat was enough to frighten them.

There were other hazards still to come. The snow-fall diminished by the time they reached Ridley Park, where a gang of boys shot firecrackers toward them, again spooking poor Lausanne, requiring all Elisabeth's skill as a horsewoman to calm her. The pilgrims arrived in Leiperville just as school was getting out, and they immediately found themselves swarmed by nearly fifty boys who pelted them with snowballs. General Jones ordered her troops to smile and march on through the aerial assault, but the missiles, though not as potentially harmful as ice, still stung, so eventually Colonel Craft ordered the women to return fire. Before long the startled boys abandoned the field, chastened in defeat.

The waning day took a brighter turn when they reached the crossroads town of Crum Lynne, two miles northeast of Chester. Four generations of suffragists—an eighty-one-year-old woman, her sixty-two-year-old daughter, a granddaughter, and a great-granddaughter—welcomed them with hot tea, raisin buns, and kind words. They had been waiting hours and would gladly have waited hours longer, the daughter said, for the chance to shake their hands. "You're doing the right thing," the matriarch of the family assured them. "We American women must win the vote by persuasion and not by violence."

The pilgrims parted from the four women much encouraged, and at General Jones's urging, they increased their pace in the homestretch. The heavily overcast skies had created a false twilight, and Rosalie was eager for the pilgrims to reach the sanctuary of their overnight lodgings before the Chester factories let out and thousands of potentially hostile men poured into the streets.

Increasingly wary, Maud marched along the narrow, uneven roads that had been churned into mud and slush, lined by dingy frame dwellings with grimy windows and peeling paint. The women's brown cloaks had turned black from mud and melted snow, their feet ached, and their stomachs rumbled, but they quickened their pace and spared no breath for shouting slogans or singing suffrage anthems. Minerva limped along in old slippers because her swollen feet and bandaged ankles could not squeeze into her boots. Constance hobbled on an injured knee, wincing in pain, and Maud herself felt light-headed from exhaustion.

They had barely crossed the city limits when curious citizens began to emerge from their houses to stare at the marchers. "Why don't you go home and make the beds?" a man called out.

"Who's watching your babies?" a woman shrilled.

A man fell in step beside Phoebe, grinning lasciviously. "Say, miss," he drawled, "I'd walk to Washington too if I could walk alongside you." She ignored him, but he lingered, matching her stride for stride.

Then a woman appeared on the sidewalk ahead of them, clutching a handkerchief, holding her threadbare coat closed at the neck for warmth. "God bless you," she cried, waving the handkerchief, beaming, ignoring her neighbors' glares. "God bless you!"

"God bless you too," Maud called back, waving.

Suddenly, they heard the clattering of hooves and discovered several young cadets in sharp gray uniforms approaching them on horseback. "Welcome to Chester," the leader proclaimed, halting a few yards ahead. "We're to escort you to the Washington House."

Phoebe's unwanted suitor disappeared into the gathering crowd as the cadets flanked the narrow line of marchers and led them down Madison Street toward their lodgings. As they passed St. Paul's Church, the bells pealed a joyous welcome, and Maud felt her spirits rising once again.

After a wash and a change of clothes, the pilgrims reconvened in the dining room to enjoy a hearty, nourishing meal for which they were all sincerely grateful. Before they parted company to seek a restorative night's rest, General Jones congratulated them on reaching an important milestone. As of that afternoon, they had completed one hundred miles of their journey—one hundred fifteen, to be more precise, an astonishing achievement in the best of conditions, all the more remarkable in the cold and the mud and the snow.

"We're almost halfway to Washington," she praised them, her eyes alight with pride. "The worst is surely behind us, and nothing will prevent us from reaching our destination. On the third day of March, we will be in the capital to parade with thousands of our suffrage sisters down Pennsylvania Avenue and demand the vote. Let the new president and the Congress never doubt our resolve. On to Washington!"

"On to Washington!" Maud chorused with her comrades.

They had come so far. They would never turn back.

# 22

# February 1913

## WASHINGTON, D.C.

### Alice

With little more than two weeks to go, Alice continued to appeal to Mr. Eustis to let her committee rent the inaugural grandstands, and to Superintendent Sylvester to increase the security forces assigned to the parade route. The men remained politely intransigent.

"No doubt they hope we'll cancel the event if we can't absolutely guarantee the safety of our dignitaries and marchers," said Lucy, pensively toying with a loose thread on the cuff of her dark green wool walking suit. She leaned against the closed door of Alice's office as if to bar it against more bad news.

"That's a futile hope," said Alice, resting her elbows

on Susan B. Anthony's desk and cupping her chin in her hands. "Canceling is absolutely out of the question. The procession would be more dangerous without the precautions we seek, but it will proceed."

Soon thereafter, just as the committee officers were confirming the final roster of dignitaries, one of the most illustrious women on their list accepted their invitation to review the procession from a place of honor—Mrs. Taft, wife of the outgoing president, who had agreed to attend as one of her last official duties as First Lady. Alice had invited President Taft too, but he had sent his regrets, citing prior commitments for concluding his administration and the current session of Congress. Alice and Elizabeth Kent decided that they could no longer wait for Mr. Eustis to have a change of heart, and so they arranged for a special state box to be constructed near the grandstands opposite the south plaza and the steps of the Treasury, an excellent vantage point both for reviewing the procession and for watching the pageant. Helen Hamilton Gardener issued a sparkling press release announcing the casting coup, and within hours after the story ran in the Washington papers, Mr. Eustis sent word to their F Street headquarters that they could rent the inaugural grandstands after all.

"All we needed was a little presidential glamour,"

remarked Lucy. "Mr. Eustis is too politically savvy to treat an event with contempt when the wife of the president attends as an honored guest."

"Let's hope Superintendent Sylvester is likewise inspired to assign more officers to Pennsylvania Avenue," said Alice. "How could he bear the disgrace if any harm came to Mrs. Taft due to his neglect?"

They waited for a note from the superintendent's office, and waited, until hope gave way to frustration as it became evident that not even the presence of the First Lady would compel him to augment his forces.

Alice's stalemate with Superintendent Sylvester was only one of many concerns plaguing her as the days sped past, busy and full, and February drew to a close. The ever-present, burdensome necessity to raise funds grew more urgent as bills came due. A few of Alice's most prestigious volunteers reached out to the wealthy patroness who subsidized the National's New York headquarters, but Mrs. Alva Belmont hoped for some special recognition in exchange, a role in the march that would not require too much actual marching. Lucy was on the case, inquiring with several float directors about allowing her to ride along, but until a suitable arrangement could be made, the committee could not expect a donation.

Before that matter was resolved, officers from the

National sent word that they did not approve of the color scheme Alice had selected for the banners and bunting. The offensive colors were the same ones that appeared on the flags displayed outside the Washington headquarters—purple for dignity, green for hope, and white for purity. No one had ever objected to them before, but now Mary Ware Dennett complained that these were the hues brandished by British suffragettes, whose appalling behavior seemed to worsen every day. "They sow chaos and destruction," Mrs. Dennett argued, "smashing windows, setting fires in parks, and destroying mail by pouring ink and acid into public postboxes. We cannot afford any imagined association with such unruly, unlawful women."

Dr. Anna Shaw concurred that law-abiding American suffragists dared not become conflated with their reckless counterparts across the pond. "I shall never march under the suffragette flag," the president of the National wrote to Alice crisply. "Better to embrace yellow, a traditional color of the American movement, or blue, which adorns the National's letterhead, or both."

Alice preferred purple, green, and white, but she did not have time for another debate, so she dutifully ordered two thousand yellow pennants and complementary bunting.

Objectionable colors also became an issue with costumes, which had already run alarmingly over budget. The librarians from the Library of Congress were unhappy with the shade of very light blue that had been selected for their dresses and capes, but the darker blue they requested had already been assigned to social workers, who refused to give it up, since their members had already acquired their costumes. Mrs. Dennett insisted that the members of the National would wear sashes and carry banners in their assigned hue, but they had no intention of draping themselves in it from head to foot. Some participants were reluctant to wear costumes of any color or kind, and they clamored for Alice to create a special division "for persons who do not care to march in disguise," as one vexed Washington suffragist put it. Then there was the Ohio suffragist who planned to march draped in chains, which would not only ruin the aesthetics of the beautiful, glorious spectacle Alice was trying so hard to create but might also be injurious to the woman's health.

Drawing ever closer was another source of consternation, the self-proclaimed general Rosalie Jones. To Alice's regret, she had not been discouraged by Alice's tepid response to her proposed pilgrimage from New York City to Washington, and at that moment was trudging along at the head of what sounded like a bedraggled herd of limping suffragists, so-called "war correspondents" from the press, and a surprising number of men. According to news reports of the Army of the Hudson's antics, some of the men fancied themselves pilgrims, a role that Miss Jones had promised Alice would be limited to women, while others served in support roles and a few tagged along, starstruck, in hopes of winning a suffragist bride. It was evident that Miss Jones intended for her increasingly weary band to march as a unit in the official procession, which obliged Alice to write to her and establish firm guidelines. As tactfully as she could, Alice explained that if the men marched alongside the pilgrims down Pennsylvania Avenue, the procession would take on the character of a lark rather than a serious crusade. Needless to say, the war correspondents also did not belong in their section; they could cover the event like every other reporter, from the sidewalks or grandstands. The only pilgrims who would be permitted to join the procession in Washington would be those who had departed New York City with Miss Jones and had accompanied her every step of the way.

Alice had no sooner mailed that letter than the National sent her new instructions about the letter Dr. Shaw had given Miss Jones to carry to Washington. The original plan called for the general to deliver it to

President-Elect Wilson herself, but the officers had re-
considered, and now desired a more formal presenta-
tion of their request that he include woman suffrage
in his inaugural address. Alice agreed that it would be
more appropriate for her Congressional Committee to
carry out this important duty, and she promptly replied
that she would intercept Miss Jones on the road before
she and her pilgrims entered the capital and take possession of the letter. "Miss Jones would likely be disappointed," Alice reminded the officers in her carefully
phrased letter. "I trust that Mrs. Dennett shall inform
her of the new arrangements so that there will be no
misunderstanding when the time comes."

So went Alice's endless and perpetually replenished
to-do list. There were simply too many people with too
many changes of heart or trifling complaints and not
enough time to satisfy them all. Alice did the best she
could, but she heard the grumbling and observed the
disgruntled frowns, and she had to pause now and then
to take a breath and remind herself that the vast majority of suffragists were behind her, that they were united
in a noble purpose.

Ironically, it was on a day when harmony reigned
over their headquarters and her volunteers were particularly enthusiastic and industrious that Dora Lewis
rushed in, breathless and wide-eyed, and announced

that a new sign hung above the entrance to 1306 F Street Northwest, where they had noticed movers carrying in furniture a few days before. The National Association Opposed to Woman Suffrage was moving into a suite of offices barely two blocks away.

A clamor of outrage and indignation filled the main room. "Why do they have to set up their headquarters here, on our street?" lamented a young suffragist.

"Why do they need to exist at all?" retorted another sharply. "What sort of woman joins an organization whose sole purpose is to harm other women?"

As conjecture and condemnation flew back and forth, Alice stood silent and still, thoughts racing. The Antis could have moved into any number of vacant office suites in the capital; their choice was an obvious attempt to bait the suffragists. "I'd like to see this for myself," she announced over the din. "Lucy, Dora, would you join me?"

They quickly pulled on their coats and scarves and walked east down F Street, crossing at the corner so they could observe their opponents from the opposite side. Little more than a tenth of a mile separated the two offices, a few minutes' walk; rivals could almost shout to one another from their front stoops. Alice and her companions tried to blend inconspicuously with the passersby as they studied the Antis' front window, where antisuffrage banners and pennants and neat stacks of literature were prettily arranged. A notice was posted on the front door, but the smiling, well-dressed ladies who passed in and out, alone or in pairs, did not pause to read it. The distance was too great for Alice to make out more than the headline: "Let It Be Known."

Alice knew she and Lucy would be recognized on sight if they drew any closer. Muffling a sigh, she led her companions back to 1420 F Street, where she reported to her anxious, angry comrades the little she had observed. She then asked for volunteers to undertake a quiet reconnaissance mission to the enemy camp. Hands shot up all over the room; Alice selected two women known for their grace under pressure and sent them off with instructions to gather as much information as they could about the Antis' plans and numbers.

The pair set off, and everyone who remained behind tried their best to get back to work.

Less than an hour later, the women returned carrying several leaflets and reported that considering how recently the Antis had moved in, they were remarkably well organized, well staffed, and ambitious. When they passed around the leaflets for all to examine, Alice recognized them as copies of the notice posted on the Antis' front door. "Let It Be Known: Miss Minnie Bronson will have complete charge of affairs until the arrival of Mrs. Arthur M. Dodge, president of the association, who will be accompanied to this city by more than two hundred workers for the cause," Alice read. "They are coming down on a special train, but it will be the ordinary kind. While the suffragists delight in 'hiking,' we are satisfied to arrive on the scene in the usual manner."

She could not be sure whether the snide remark about hiking referred to the March 3 procession or Rosalie Jones's pilgrimage, but either way, it was an unnecessary detail with no other purpose but to disparage.

"They hope to distribute volumes of literature," the elder of the two spies reported. "Not only to the general public, but also to elected officials. They're planning to descend on the Capitol, buttonhole every senator, congressman, and cabinet officer they can, and proselytize on behalf of their opposition to suffrage."

Her partner brandished one of the leaflets. "This has already gone out to every newspaper in the city, and no doubt there are more, and worse, where this came from. They have so many typists pounding away, churning out press releases, that it sounds like a piston factory."

"I know this Miss Minnie Bronson," said Helen

Hamilton Gardener, crossing her arms and frowning as she leaned against the nearest desk. "She presented the Anti argument at the same hearing when Dr. Shaw, Mrs. Catt, and I addressed the House of Representatives' Committee on Woman Suffrage last December."

"What did you think of her?" asked Lucy.

Helen shrugged. "She's a formidable opponent— intelligent, a skilled orator, an effective organizer. She packs halls on speaking tours around the country. She's also an experienced educator. Honestly, I don't understand why she's chosen to be on the wrong side of history in this."

"She was in the news recently," Elizabeth Kent mused aloud, making her way through the rows of desks to the bookcase where newspaper clippings were filed. After searching a moment, she retrieved an article and held it up, nodding. "Yes, here it is, from the *New York Times*. 'Women Gain More Without Suffrage. Miss Minnie Bronson Tells What Women Have Done in the West. An anti-suffrage meeting held last night at the Berkeley Theatre on West Forty-fourth Street by the New York State Association Opposed to Woman Suffrage drew a large crowd, mostly women, who enthusiastically applauded the speakers as they assailed the arguments of the suffragists.'"

"Isn't it bad enough that men oppose us, without having to endure this betrayal by other women?" a volunteer groused.

"'Miss Minnie Bronson, Secretary of the association, took the suffragists to task by asking what they had accomplished in the States where they had the franchise.'" Elizabeth fell silent as she skimmed ahead, frowning. "She says that as far as legislation on behalf of children is concerned, western states where women don't have the right to vote surpass those where they do."

"Where's her evidence?" Helen demanded, as others chimed in with their own exclamations of denial.

"She doesn't offer any," Elizabeth replied, studying the page. "'Woman suffrage, according to Miss Bronson, was, after all, only a question between two kinds of women, those who believed their cause meant progress and those who believed it a dangerous experiment. Finally she denounced woman suffrage as one of the alluring deceptions of the Socialist Party, for which woman, if she yielded to it, would have to suffer just as she suffered for her meekness against the first temptation in the Garden of Eden.'"

A chorus of groans and jeers went up from the group.

"She insists that antisuffragists aren't feeble-minded, as *we* suggest, nor are they wealthy elites who wish to be protected from the unwashed masses." Elizabeth allowed a small smile. "I'm paraphrasing. She said, 'society.'"

"But she *meant* the lower classes," said a middle-aged woman, frowning. "You were right the first time."

"Then what is their objection?" asked Dora.

Elizabeth read silently for a moment. "She says they are opposed to doubling an already overlarge electorate with a vast multitude of people who haven't had any experience with the vote."

The room rang with angry retorts and derisive laughter. "No one has experience with voting until they have the ballot," protested a younger volunteer. "If our country follows that logic, women will never be allowed to vote."

"Not necessarily," said Lucy dryly. "We could all move to California or Idaho, practice voting there for a few years, and then return to our home states with all the required experience."

Her ironic suggestion met with bitter laughter.

"There's more," said Elizabeth. "'Miss Bronson said statistics would show that only eight percent of the women of this country either publicly advocated or privately supported the cause of woman suffrage. She asked her hearers if they thought it was fair for the other ninety-two percent of their sex to have the vote with its responsibilities forced on them by the minority of eight percent.'"

"Again I ask, where's her evidence?" Helen demanded. "Where did she get that number, eight percent? Did she poll only her own acquaintances? I could believe that only eight percent of her closest friends want the vote, but she can't extrapolate from that to include all women everywhere."

"If the Antis don't want to vote, no one will force them," said the younger volunteer, tears of frustration in her eyes. "Why deny us that right?"

"That's the eternal question, isn't it?" said Alice.

"Miss Bronson has an answer," said Elizabeth, sighing. "She says, 'The suffragists argue that we don't have to vote unless we want to, but we will have to vote unless we wish to be represented by the type of women who espouse the cause of woman suffrage.' She goes on to explain what precisely is so offensive about that type of woman—"

"She means us," someone called out sharply.

"Of course she does. Apparently, we are morally reprehensible because every one of us supports Mrs. Pankhurst, who has inspired attacks on shopkeepers, an attack on the prime minister, scattered acts of arson—the list of her offenses goes on."

Alice and Lucy exchanged a look. They knew Emmeline Pankhurst, had marched with her, had languished in Holloway Prison with her and her daughters, but that did not mean they shared all of her beliefs or endorsed all of her tactics. Indeed, the very essence of the suffrage procession as Alice envisioned it was beauty, grace, intelligence, justice, and wisdom, not violence, not destruction. She would not deny that there was a place in the movement for the Pankhursts' more aggressive measures, but to argue that all American women should be denied the ballot because they all admired Mrs. Pankhurst was simply ludicrous.

"As painful as that was, at least we now know who we're up against," said Elizabeth, placing the article on a central table so that anyone who wanted to read it in full could do so.

"We need to learn more about this Mrs. Arthur M. Dodge, their president, too, if she's going to be taking over for Miss Bronson," someone piped up from the back.

"Josephine Jewell Dodge," said Elizabeth, nodding. "Her father was the governor of Connecticut and later became postmaster general. Her husband is the son of a wealthy New York congressman."

"In other words, she's got money and connections,"

said the sharp-voiced volunteer. "There must be dirt on her somewhere, if we dig around for it, and on Miss Bronson too. If we discredit them—"

"No," said Alice, her voice low and firm. "This is a women's movement, and we will not attack any woman, even with words."

The volunteers regarded her uncertainly, some hopeful, others deeply skeptical.

"We can and should discredit their positions, their arguments," Alice clarified, "but we will not dig up dirt or sling mud. Understood?"

A moment passed in silence before a murmur of assent went up from the circle. At least some of it, Alice knew, had been only grudgingly given.

The next morning, she arrived at headquarters before any of her comrades and got right to work, filing reports and writing letters. Sometime later, she was typing up a letter to the editor of the *Washington Post* when Elizabeth and Emma Gillett, the committee's treasurer, interrupted with the news that the Antis' storefront windows had been smeared with mud overnight. Alice sat back in her chair, thunderstruck. "Was this a deliberate, literal rejection of my plea not to dig up dirt or sling mud?" she asked.

Elizabeth's brow furrowed. "Surely you don't think it was one of us who did it."

"I don't know. I hope not." Alice sighed, braced her elbows on her desk, and rested her head in her hands. "I think I made my expectations clear. I suppose it could have been anyone in the city."

"Well, it's not likely to happen again," said Elizabeth. "They've hired the largest, burliest private watchman I've ever seen to keep an eye on things. He has arms like a stevedore."

"He's standing sentry outside their front door as we speak." Emma hesitated. "I've heard rumors that we should expect retaliation."

"But they don't know that any of our women was responsible," said Alice. "*We* don't even know that."

"It's just something one of our volunteers overheard at a coffeehouse this morning," said Emma. "It could be nothing."

Perhaps, but Alice could not take that chance. Since the largest, burliest private watchman was already employed by their rivals, she settled for hiring the second largest and burliest. As she might have predicted, the sight of two large, muscular men guarding the competing headquarters barely a block apart proved too enticing for the press, and reporters soon came around seeking a quote. Lucy and Helen seized the opportunity to ply them with news about the upcoming procession and recent advances of the movement, but they would not be satisfied until Alice answered their queries about the animosity between the suffragists and the Antis.

Eventually Alice told them what she had told her volunteers, that theirs was a woman's movement, and they would not engage in attacking other women. "If the women opposed to suffrage choose to attack us, that is their business," she added. "We have our plans arranged and intend to carry them out, despite opposition, but we have no time to engage in controversies with anyone."

To dispel any doubts that she meant what she said, after the reporters left, Alice sent Emma, Dora, and Elizabeth to pay a formal call on Miss Bronson at her new offices. They took flowers and wore their yellow suffrage badges, and according to Elizabeth, they had a rather pleasant chat.

"Miss Bronson did express bewilderment about why we find it necessary to adopt the methods, manners, and attributes of men," Elizabeth acknowledged, "and she made quite a passionate case for why it is impossible for women to work for the betterment of mankind and to vote as well. We can do one or the other, but not both."

Alice was so astonished that she laughed. "Impossible? Rather she should say essential. We seek the vote precisely so we can work to cure the many ills that plague society." Sometimes the Antis' threadbare logic made her head hurt. She could not understand why so many women worked so hard to preserve their own subjugation.

It was a subject she longed to discuss in earnest with Miss Bronson—and Mrs. Dodge too, when she arrived soon thereafter to assume command of the Antis' headquarters—but although Alice had asked her peacemaking delegation to invite the two women to visit the suffragists' offices, they never paid the perfunctory return call. Occasionally a suffragist and an Anti would pass on F Street, recognize each other by the badges pinned proudly to their chests, and exchange a curt nod, but otherwise the rival factions could have worked on opposite sides of the city, so little did they interact. No more mud was thrown, at least not in the literal sense. Although heated exchanges sometimes appeared in the papers, no windows were shattered or literature stolen.

The two burly watchmen were either very effective or very unnecessary. Alice could not be sure which.

# 23

# Late February 1913

## CHICAGO, ILLINOIS, TO WASHINGTON, D.C.

### Ida

Two days before the Illinois state delegation's scheduled departure for Washington, Ida and her fellow marchers met at the headquarters of the Illinois Equal Suffrage Association to review travel details and rehearse their steps. First they gathered in a meeting room so Mrs. Trout, commander in chief of the delegation, could advise them what to pack, when to meet at the train station, how much money to bring for food and necessities, and where they would be staying during their visit to the capital. It had been quite a challenge to book accommodations for all sixty-five members of their party, as nearly all the hotels in the city had been claimed by people planning to attend Mr. Wilson's inauguration the following day. Fortunately, Mrs. Trout's clever assistant had thought to inquire with several women's boardinghouses, and by doubling them up, she had found just enough rooms for everyone.

"You and I are sharing," said Virginia, squeezing Ida's arm. "I hope you don't snore."

"Ferdinand has never complained," Ida replied, smiling.

Next the women went upstairs to a spacious gymnasium that spanned the entire length and half the width of the building. Athletic equipment had been pushed to the side to make room for the marchers to practice, and light streamed in upon the parquet floor through high west-facing windows. Clara Barck Welles, chairman of the Illinois committee and their parade major, strode to the front of the room, called for attention, and held up a gleaming brass baton. "This was presented to me a few days ago by an Illinois veteran who carried it at the Battle of Gettysburg," she explained proudly. "I shall carry it as I lead our delegation down Pennsylvania Avenue on March third."

Gesturing with the baton, Mrs. Welles began to train them in the art of marching, lining them up four abreast and teaching them the signals for attention, forward march, right turn, left turn, and parade rest. For the next hour she led them through their paces, keeping time with the brass baton and calling out orders. At first their neat, orderly rows collapsed whenever they marched more than a few steps, and there was much embarrassed laughter whenever someone confused the direction of their turns. They persevered, and before long the entire contingent was breathless from exertion, but they knew the cues by heart.

"We're going to represent Illinois proudly," Mrs. Welles declared when she granted them a respite. "No other state delegation will be as smartly turned out as us, I'm sure of it."

While they rested, she went over the order of march. She would lead the way, of course, with the state band following immediately after. The North Side branch of the Illinois Equal Suffrage Association had generously agreed to pay the band's travel expenses, and Mrs. Welles was confident that they would be one of the largest and best musical groups in the entire procession. Mrs. Trout would appear after the band, and directly behind her, marching side by side, would be a representative of the Chicago Political Equality League and the president of the Suffrage Alliance of Cook County, each bearing the banner of her organization. Next, the remaining Illinois suffragists would march in several rows of four. Ida's assigned spot was a few rows from the rear, with Virginia on her left and

Belle on her right. She could not help noticing, as they marched and turned and marched again, that with the exception of one woman who appeared to be of Latin American heritage, she was the only person of color in the delegation.

After rehearsal, the women returned downstairs to the meeting room, where in their absence Mrs. Trout's assistant had set out the matching stoles, hats, and pennants that would comprise their uniform, to be worn with one's own walking suit in dark gray or black. Delighted, the women rushed forward to collect the separate pieces, trying on the ensemble, walking and posing to test the fit, admiring one another. The stoles were made of white trig cloth, about eight inches wide and sixty inches long, tapered to points on the ends and bound with a border of blue. On one end were nine five-pointed blue stars in three rows of four, three, and two; on the opposite end was the word ILLINOIS in blue capital letters, arranged so that when the stole was draped around the neck and shoulders like a scarf, the stars hung down the back and the name of their state ran vertically down the left side of the chest, over the heart. The hats were an intriguing design, round and close-fitting, with a turned-up brim split in the front and adorned with more blue stars. A small peak on the crown gave the appearance, in profile, of a Phrygian cap, a traditional symbol of freedom and the pursuit of liberty. The motifs on the stole and cap were echoed on the pennants, which were made of the same white trig cloth and attached to a slender wooden staff topped by a spear finial. Mrs. Welles, a graduate of the School of the Art Institute of Chicago and founder of the popular Kalo Arts Crafts Community House in Park Ridge, had designed the costumes herself, and she basked in the marchers' compliments.

As the meeting concluded, Ida made a point to thank Mrs. Trout and Mrs. Welles for inviting her to join the state delegation. "You may be courting controversy by including me," she told them frankly, "but it's important to the Black community, even more than it is to me personally, that I march alongside you."

"Our instructions were to include as many of our state's most prominent suffragists as we could," said Mrs. Welles, glancing to Mrs. Trout for confirmation. "You may be the only colored woman in our section, but you won't be the only colored suffragist in the parade. Isn't that so, Mrs. Trout?"

"Yes, indeed," said Mrs. Trout, but then she hesitated. "As far as I know."

"I've heard that there will be a group from Howard University, and I have several friends from other states who intend to march," Ida reassured them, but then she too paused. Why was *she* reassuring *them*? They had invited her; she had not solicited an appointment. The onus should be upon them to assure her that she belonged.

"Perhaps we should telegraph the parade headquarters in Washington just to be sure," Mrs. Trout said, her expression clouding over with doubt. "It would be a shame if you traveled all that way only to be denied a place."

Ida stiffened, but before she could speak, she felt an arm slip through hers. "She already has a place in our section, right between me and Virginia Brooks," said Belle, smiling as she fixed the two leaders with a level gaze.

"Of course she does," said Mrs. Trout hastily.

"Still, it wouldn't hurt—" Mrs. Welles hesitated. "I'll look into it."

"Don't worry," Belle urged after they bade Mrs. Welles and Mrs. Trout good evening and left the meeting room, their uniforms tucked beneath their arms, carefully folded and wrapped in brown paper. "The National insists that women of color are welcome. You will be allowed to march."

"I dare anyone to try to stop me," Ida replied evenly, betraying none of her anger or disappointment. She didn't want her presence to be tolerated graciously by benevolent whites. She wanted to be welcomed gladly, appreciated for her contributions, and valued for her perspective and experience.

The next day, as she packed and prepared for the journey, she waited, vexed and uneasy, for a messenger to appear at the door with a final ruling from the Congressional Committee, whether it was a note from Mrs. Trout or a telegram direct from Washington. No word came.

Ida's eight-year-old daughter, Alfreda, joined her in her bedroom as she was placing her stole and pennant carefully in her suitcase on top of her other clothing. "I wish I could go with you," she said, wistful.

"You have school," Ida reminded her, rolling the cloth of the pennant around its staff and tucking it along the side of her case. "Nothing is more important than your education."

"I know." Alfreda heaved a sigh, then brightened. "Don't you think this suffrage march would be educational?"

Ida laughed. "I do, but you still have to go to school." She closed the suitcase and snapped the latches shut. "Listen. If the Illinois Equal Suffrage Act passes in June, I'm sure there will be a glorious parade right here in Chicago to celebrate. You and I and your big sister can put on our finest dresses and march in that parade, together."

"Promise?"

Ida drew her in for a hug. "I promise." She kissed her daughter on the top of the head, inhaling deeply of her fresh, clean fragrance of soap, hair oil, and a faint trace of apples—Alfreda and her sister had spent the afternoon making applesauce. "I'll tell you all about the suffrage demonstration when I get home from Washington."

"Charles says they might not let you march," said Alfreda, her cheek pressed against Ida's midsection, her voice slightly muffled.

"Did he, now," said Ida. "Well, I disagree with your brother. The two ladies in charge of our state delegation have personally assured me that I am not only welcome, but essential." Pending a reply to that telegram to Washington, of course, but there was no need to burden the child with that detail.

"Really?"

"Really. What's more, Mrs. Terrell will be marching, as well as other colored ladies I know. So don't you worry, and you can tell Charles not to worry either."

Beaming, Alfreda nodded and darted off to tell her eldest brother how mistaken he was. Sighing, Ida sat down on the edge of the bed, wondering what more she should do. Perhaps nothing. Perhaps no news from the Congressional Committee was good news. And yet Charles had ample reason to be skeptical, to suspect that she might be excluded not only from the procession but from the woman suffrage amendment itself. She and Ferdinand and their sons had been following General Rosalie Jones's march in the papers, and on February 19, while the pilgrims spent a day resting in Wilmington, Delaware, two businessmen from the South had called on her. Declaring that they represented many thousands of southern white men, they had asked her to affirm the Army of the Hudson's position on the matter of suffrage for Black women, a question of vital importance throughout the South. The men had acknowledged that white women ought to have the right to vote, but they could not support granting that same right to Negro women.

Like so many white folks before her, the general had tried to dodge the question. "This matter is one that has to do largely with certain states," she had replied. "The men and women of those states must solve their own problems."

Perhaps emboldened by her demurral, one of the white businessmen had said, "Miss Jones, if you advocate votes for Negro women, you will indeed find that your way to Washington passes through enemy territory."

The papers had not reported what reply, if any, General Jones had made to that.

Yet less than a week later, as the pilgrims were in Maryland marching from Baltimore to Laurel, a reporter traveling with the group queried General Jones about rumors that when the pilgrims passed through a certain small town, several representatives from the Colored Women's Suffrage Club there intended to march with them part of the way along the route to Washington. When asked if the Black women would indeed be permitted to join them, the general replied simply, "Yes, they will." Later, when the Army of the Hudson reached the town, six Black women bearing a suffrage flag and the banner of their club joined up with the troops and completed part of the twenty-two-mile advance with them. If General Jones would welcome women of color so soon after receiving a blatant warning from southern men not to do so, was it not likely that the leaders of the Washington procession—a much larger affair organized under the auspices of the National—would be equally resistant to intimidation?

Ida was counting on it.

The following morning, her children saw her off at the front door with hugs and kisses, and Ferdinand escorted her to the train station. He gave her all the usual husbandly warnings and assurances along the way, but his manner was tense and apprehensive as he summoned a porter to tend to her luggage. They parted with a kiss on the platform, where she soon joined Virginia, Belle, and other members of the state delegation, ebullient with anticipation for the adventure ahead.

Soon after Ferdinand departed, Mrs. Trout began distributing train tickets as they awaited a few latecomers. Ida examined her ticket and was satisfied to see that it would admit her to the first-class carriage, exactly the same as any other delegate. Yet even as she boarded the train and found a seat beside her friends, she half expected the conductor to single her out for scrutiny. The steam whistle blew, the train chugged out of the station, but although Ida made an outward show of perfect ease, smiling and chatting with her companions, inside she rang like a taut wire struck by a hammer. At any moment, a white man in a uniform might demand her ticket, might ignore the fare printed upon it and order her to decamp and make her way through the cars to the third-class carriage or the smoker or worse. Even Belle and Virginia, who knew about her history of rough treatment aboard the railroads, seemed oblivious to her heightened tension. What a privilege they enjoyed, to take for granted that they would be treated

like ladies there, that they would be accorded the respect due any human being and the courtesy given to
valued customers. If anyone wronged them, they could
indignantly complain to the wrongdoer's superiors and
could expect profuse apologies and restitution. If Ida
complained about the most egregious ill treatment,
even threats upon her life, she could find herself invol-
untarily disembarked at the next station.

It was as if there was an unwritten law that the train
belonged to the white world, and white folks permitted
Ida to ride—graciously or grudgingly depending on the
individual—as long as she knew her place and kept to
it. And that unwritten law held true not just aboard that
train, but in the station, and on the streets that led to it,
and in the predominantly white neighborhood in which
the Wells-Barnett family resided, and in the state, and
throughout the country. The implicit understanding
in every interaction with white folks was that although
Ida had been born and raised in the United States, this
was not her country. It did not belong to her the way
it belonged to her white traveling companions, who—
rich or poor, educated or not, beloved or lonely—could
breathe easily in their native land the way Ida could
not, not when lynching was commonplace and tolerated, not when her breath caught in her throat every
time her dark-skinned children left the shelter of their

home and ventured out into a world that did not consider them fully human, that did not value their lives, that did not consider their souls as sacred as any other.

Every woman in the Illinois delegation wanted the vote—longed for it, demanded it, fought for it—but Ida and other women of color needed it with an urgency that was beyond measure. For them it was, in every sense of the phrase, a matter of life and death.

# 24

# Late February 1913

## LAUREL, MARYLAND,
## TO BLADENSBURG, MARYLAND

### Maud

The previous day's twenty-two-mile hike from Baltimore had been daunting, their reception in Laurel coldly indifferent. Throughout the day, temperatures had risen into the high forties and sunshine had dried most of the mud from the macadam roads, to the relief of the exhausted, blistered, and footsore Army of the Hudson. Colonel Craft's feet had been badly swollen, with blood seeping through the gauze bandages she had carefully wrapped around them. She and General Jones had barely spoken all day, keeping a chilly mile between them as the line of marchers stretched out between the vigorous striders and the stragglers. General

Jones had been irritable and grim, smoldering over the Congressional Committee's instructions to exclude from the official procession the male pilgrims, war correspondents, and any woman who had not been with their group since they set out from Hudson Terminal. Before they departed Baltimore, she had sent a defiant telegram to the Washington headquarters rejecting the command, stating, "Either my entire Army of the Hudson marches with me or I do not march."

"Aren't you worried that they'll call your bluff?" asked Maud, who had accompanied the general to the telegraph office.

"It's no bluff," Rosalie had replied, "and it's Miss Alice Paul who should worry."

At the end of the day, four uniformed postmen had met them on the outskirts of Laurel to lead them into the city, but otherwise the town had mustered a poor welcome. There had been no cheering crowds of suffragists, no beaming mayor offering the key to the city, and, to the women's dismay, no friendly inn offering a hot meal and warm beds. Instead, the keeper of the town's lone hotel had insisted that he could accommodate only ten marchers, and he would choose the lucky few he deigned to admit. "The rest of you can fend for yourselves," he added, his mouth in a thin, sour line.

With the help of the war correspondents and a pilgrim who had a cousin in the town, the marchers had made a hasty cold supper from their packed rations and managed to find beds or sofas in boardinghouses and private homes. Maud had spent an uncomfortable night on a horsehair sofa in a home that smelled of kerosene, burnt grease, and boiled cabbage, but she had been grateful to have a roof over her head at all.

She had drifted off to sleep hoping that the next day would be better, but when she woke to the sound of rain drumming upon the roof, she knew that another long, difficult footslog awaited them. Even so, she dressed briskly and cheerfully, determined to make the best of things and to kindle optimism among her comrades once they reunited outside the hotel. They would reach Hyattsville before nightfall, and the next day, they would march into Washington.

Shortly before nine o'clock, the pilgrims formed up ranks in the main square. All wore rubber caps and boots, and most had pulled raincoats over their brown cloaks. Lacking more suitable clothing, Elizabeth Aldrich had cut a hole in the center of a white oilcloth tablecloth and slipped it over her head.

"You look like a pantry shelf," Phoebe teased. Elizabeth smiled wanly, and a few pilgrims managed half-hearted laughter. Others glanced about to confirm that the general and colonel had not yet appeared, then hurried off to the nearest dry goods store and quickly returned attired as Elizabeth was.

Moments later, General Jones and Colonel Craft approached from different directions. They took their customary places between the vehicles and the troops, and, without exchanging a word and barely a glance, they called the army to attention and gave the signal to begin.

The pilgrims set off in a downpour, their boots slick on the cobblestones. Townspeople lined the sidewalks, staring at them dispassionately from beneath dripping umbrellas. The marchers trudged along the road south toward the District, spreading out according to preferred pace far less than usual, as if driven by an instinct to huddle together for comfort and protection. By the time they crossed the city limits, the road was thick with mud and morale had sunk to a new low.

Progress was sluggish, and no onlookers hung on the fences of the farms they passed to offer a restorative cup of hot tea, a kind word, or a hearty "Votes for women" cry, encouragement they had been so grateful to receive at other hamlets. Then again, no one came out in the driving rain to heckle or scold them for not being at home to tend to the mending, cooking, and diapering either, so Maud decided the good outweighed the bad.

There was little conversation in the ranks, preoccupied as they were with holding their heads just so, both to keep the rain from obscuring their vision and to prevent the runoff from their caps from coursing past their collars and down their backs. With every step, Maud took care to pull her feet out of the sticky mud without losing a boot, and to plant them carefully on the road ahead so she did not slip and fall. Several of her less sure-footed companions already bore the signs of past stumbles in thick streaks of mud on their coats, capes, skirt hems, and hands, which gradually trickled off them in thin red-brown streams beneath the onslaught of the rain.

"Maud," a voice spoke behind her, low and urgent.

She paused and glanced over her shoulder, and, seeing it was Martha Klatschken, she halted and waited for her friend to catch up. "How did you sleep last night?" Maud asked as they fell in step together.

"Dreadfully, but breakfast was quite delicious." Raising her eyebrows and inclining her head, Martha indicated Rosalie marching a few rows ahead of them. "How does she seem to you?"

"Tired, like the rest of us." Maud studied the general for a moment. Despite the weariness they all shared, Rosalie looked prepared to address a rally on the spur of the moment, in the unlikely event that a crowd might appear. Instead of her brown pilgrim's cloak, she wore a trim black suit and black cap, little besmirched by the mud. Her cheeks were ruddy from the chill, and her dark hair curled prettily in the damp. And yet there was a tension in her shoulders, and when she glanced to the side, strain was evident in the tight set of her jaw. "She seems preoccupied. Maybe it's the rain and the mud. That would be enough to quell even her indefatigable spirits."

Martha frowned thoughtfully. "I think it's something else."

"Maybe it's this quarrel with Colonel Craft. Or maybe she's scheming how to include our entire group in the grand procession without bringing the wrath of the Congressional Committee down upon us."

"Maybe," said Martha, but she looked dubious.

They marched on.

An hour southwest of Laurel, a group of eight Black women from Rossville met them near the Muirkirk Furnace, and with great dignity and politeness asked if they might accompany the pilgrims part of the way. Brightening for the first time all morning, General Jones readily consented. The new recruits unfurled a long banner bearing the slogan VOTES FOR NEGRO WOMEN, fell in step behind the regular troops, and marched along with them through Ammendale and on to Beltsville, where together they broke for lunch beneath the thick, sheltering boughs of oak trees along Indian Creek.

The rain diminished while they ate, though it did not cease entirely, and afterward, the Rossville contingent headed back the way they had come while the pilgrims continued on toward the capital. The roads were slightly better there, allowing the brisk striders to pull ahead and stretch out the lines. Concerned about Minerva Crowell and Mary Baird, both of whom were struggling, Maud hung back toward the rear to keep an eye on them, roughly equidistant between General Jones and Colonel Craft, who still were not on speaking terms.

Suddenly the wind howled and the rain intensified; breathless, Maud ducked her head against the gust, braced herself, and kept her feet. Beside her, Mary Baird faltered; Maud caught her beneath the arm and held her upright.

"Over there," the general called, gesturing to a structure barely visible a few yards ahead, set back from the road in a stand of ancient evergreens. It was an old brick kiln, long abandoned from the look of it, with just enough room for the dozen or so trailing marchers to squeeze in for a brief respite from the storm.

Maud assumed the need for shelter was the only reason the general had called them to a halt while the rest of their army trudged on ahead, but then Rosalie announced that they needed to hold a council of war, the term they had adopted for any serious meeting.

"Shouldn't we wait until we're all together?" asked Maud, glancing down the road where the other pilgrims had disappeared into the mist and the trees.

"Colonel Craft is here, and by my count we have a quorum if not a majority." The general pressed a gloved hand to her heart as if its heaviness pained her. "I have difficult news that cannot wait until this evening. The Army of the Hudson will not have the honor of delivering Dr. Anna Shaw's suffrage letter to President Wilson after all."

Maud was too shocked to speak, but all around her, other pilgrims cried out in anger and disbelief.

"How can this be?" Minerva protested.

"Who have they chosen instead?" Maud asked. She suspected she knew, but she wanted to hear it.

Rosalie inhaled deeply and adjusted her dripping rain hat, stalling for time to compose her thoughts. "Ten days before we set out on this historic pilgrimage, I called on Dr. Shaw and asked her if she would like to entrust us with a message from the National for the president-elect," she said. "Dr. Shaw was intrigued, but also concerned that it might intrude on the Congressional Committee's jurisdiction if I—if we—were the messengers. I heard no more from her on the matter for almost two weeks, but when I visited the National's headquarters in New York just before we set out, Mary Ware Dennett, the executive secretary, personally gave me the letter, signed by Dr. Shaw, Miss Jane Addams, Mrs. James Lees Laidlaw—all the members of the board. Mrs. Dennett specifically said that our group was to give this letter to Mr. Wilson."

"So what happened?" asked Mary hoarsely, turning her head to cough, her face pale with pain and exhaustion.

"A week ago, much to my surprise, I received a letter from Mrs. Dennett informing me that Dr. Shaw wished to lead the delegation that would present the letter to Mr. Wilson," said the general. "Apparently some members of the board were very displeased that Dr. Shaw would even consider asking us to return the letter after we've carried it on their behalf all these many long miles. I had hoped that those few ladies might persuade Dr. Shaw to let us follow through as originally planned. Unfortunately, this morning I received a telegram stating that the board voted to present the letter themselves, accompanied by representatives from the Congressional Committee."

A clamor of outrage echoed off the brick walls of the kiln. "Those high-and-mighty ladies in Washington are jealous of the publicity our pilgrimage has received," one woman called out above the din. "They want to claim all the attention for themselves."

"Surely you aren't going to consent to this," said Constance Leupp. "You can't possibly mean that after we've walked two hundred miles, you're going to let them snatch this honor away from us?"

"You owe it to yourself to deliver that letter to the White House after carrying it this far," said Maud, her own hopes of meeting her longtime adversary swiftly fading.

"You owe it to all of us," said Colonel Craft indignantly. "How you could take that slap in the face so calmly, I just don't know."

"It's a mean trick, that's what it is," someone called from the back.

"After we plodded through all that mud last week and today," said Martha, gesturing to her boots, which were newly caked with so much thick mud that she could hardly lift her feet, "only to have Dr. Shaw and those other ladies roll into Washington in a Pullman car and take the message from us! They don't know what it means to walk as we have walked. They only seek to bask in stolen glory!"

A debate broke out as several pilgrims argued that they ought to disregard these new orders and deliver the letter themselves as planned, or perhaps return the National's letter but then carry their own message to President Wilson. Maud observed that rather than joining in the discussion, General Jones and Colonel Craft stood back and quietly conferred between themselves. Eventually the general nodded, faced her agitated troops, and held up her hands to quiet them. "There are quite a few things I could say about the Washington and New York suffragists, but I cannot condone mutiny," she said. "The most dignified and soldierly thing to do is to obey our superior officers. We will turn the letter over to the committee."

As a chorus of protests rose, Colonel Craft raised her voice to be heard above the din. "General Jones is right," she said, fixing her gaze upon each of the most outspoken dissenters in turn. "We've all made our objections known, and now we must come together, unified around our common goal. It doesn't matter who delivers the message to Wilson as long as he receives it."

"What is most important is that we've brought attention to the suffrage procession and we've promoted the cause in towns from New York to Washington, or so we will have done by tomorrow afternoon," said the general. She then called for a vote. In the show of hands that followed, the majority supported her decision and the rest resigned themselves to it.

The rain had tapered off to a light drizzle, so Colonel Craft urged them back on the road. Maud was pleased to see the general and colonel walking together, conversing in low, earnest voices, their feud apparently mended. Before long they caught up with the rest of the party, who had also taken shelter from the sudden squall and had not gotten too far ahead of them. When they learned of the change in orders, they were indignant, and some complained about missing the vote, but eventually the grumbling subsided. The Army of the Hudson must resign themselves to the National's decision, so there was no point in brooding over it, especially since they had more immediate problems awaiting them only a few miles ahead. They were approaching College Park, and according to their scout's reports, they had every reason to expect an unruly welcome from students at the Maryland Agricultural College. Although the rain had ceased and the macadam road was well suited for a brisk pace, the pilgrims held a close formation, their apprehensions rising with every mile as the forests and fields gave way to the outskirts of the town.

The pilgrims heard the rumble of the mob before they saw them. Striding boldly down the main thoroughfare, the suffragists rounded a corner and discovered at least two hundred young men clustered around the main gates to campus. A sudden crescendo in their gleeful shouts and jeers edged with malice told Maud the students had spotted them. Swiftly the men lined both sides of the street to form an all-too-familiar gauntlet, but this time, instead of the customary rebukes that the suffragists ought to be at home tending to women's work, their adversaries shouted blistering, vulgar insults that made Maud's ears burn and cheeks flush. Her heart thudded as several men rushed forward to shove against the army's support vehicles, rocking them from side to side, spooking Lausanne and forcing the cars and wagon to slow to a crawl. Swarming, hollering, letting out an occasional piercing rebel yell, they tore the banners and pennants from the cars and attempted to reach inside the baggage wagon to steal the pilgrims' suitcases. Then they closed in on the marchers, catcalling and jeering, breaking up the lines, jostling some pilgrims, sending others sprawling. Glimpsing Mary Baird on her hands and knees, Maud pushed through the mayhem to reach her, and a war correspondent helped her haul Mary to her feet. Somewhere ahead, their herald sounded the trumpet in a rallying call; buffeted on all sides, the pilgrims doggedly pressed forward, Maud half carrying her dazed and weeping companion. Behind her came the sound of an exchange of rough, angry accusations and mocking retorts; she risked a glance over her shoulder to discover some of the male war correspondents trading blows with the college men.

It seemed an hour before the suffragists were able to fight their way through the gauntlet and away from the campus gates, but it could not have been more than twenty minutes. Maud assisted Mary into the lead car and walked along beside it until they were in the clear. She watched warily over her shoulder for the students, who had been beaten back by the surprisingly forceful defense from the war correspondents. When she realized the students were retreating to their campus, she took a deep, shaky breath to steady her racing heart and strode forward as quickly as she could without breaking into a run. She would feign courage she did not actually feel rather than give the young hoodlums the satisfaction of knowing they terrified her.

Once they had left College Park behind, the badly shaken pilgrims paused to assess their injuries and the damage to their vehicles. They mourned the theft of their cherished suffrage banner, but they considered themselves fortunate to have avoided serious injuries. As one, they thanked the war correspondents for throwing themselves into the fray so the pilgrims could make their escape.

"If that doesn't prove that they deserve to march

with us in the procession in four days' time, I don't know what will," Maud overheard General Jones declare to Colonel Craft.

Maud wholeheartedly agreed. Their goal was within reach, and every one of them who had survived the day deserved acclaim for it. Tomorrow they would enter Washington to great fanfare, and in four days, the footsore but triumphant pilgrims would march down Pennsylvania Avenue in the greatest peacetime demonstration ever witnessed in the United States.

Exhausted and unnerved by the raucous assault, the Army of the Hudson continued on the road south to Hyattsville, where they trusted a friendlier welcome awaited them. The Prince George Businessmen's Association had promised to celebrate them in fine style with a feast, music, and an enthusiastic crowd to address. Although there was a significant Anti faction among the citizenry, supporters and detractors alike were so eager to impress the pilgrims with their hospitality that they had stationed scouts at various points along the road to apprise them of the army's advance.

The rain had ceased entirely by the time they reached the main square, and beams of sunlight broke through the clouds to illuminate the bell tower on the town hall. Inside, two long tables laden with a wonderful assortment of sandwiches, salads, pickles, ice cream, and beverages had been arranged for the famished marchers. As a smiling white-haired matron ushered them inside and showed them where to wash up, other ladies hurried forward to take their coats and to fuss over how brave they were and how tired and hungry they must be. All would be well, they murmured kindly, they were among friends now. Maud was so overcome with gratitude that tears sprang into her eyes.

The town band serenaded them while they ate, and afterward, they moved outside to the front steps, where a crowd of at least one thousand had gathered. The mayor gave a speech so fulsome in its praise that Maud, embarrassed and delighted, struggled to hold back laughter. Then General Jones and Colonel Craft, looking much refreshed, took turns addressing the crowd, which rewarded them with loud cheers and sustained applause.

Maud would have been delighted to spend the night there among such warmhearted people, but arrangements had been made for them to stay two miles south in Bladensburg. When the cornet signal sounded, it was difficult to coax her muscles into motion again after sitting for the feast. Her feet ached and throbbed, but she told herself it was only forty minutes more on the road until she could rest for the night—and prepare herself for their glorious entry into the capital the next day.

Too tired to speak, she concentrated on maintaining forward motion and merely listened as others conversed. The excellent meal had done little to help Mary Baird regain her strength after her collapse; she rode in the suffrage wagon with Elisabeth, and the scout car had gone ahead to arrange for a doctor to meet her at the hotel.

Maud also overheard that Rosalie had found a telegram awaiting her in Hyattsville, a warning from a concerned friend. The general's mother and sister—passionate antisuffragists, proud members of the National Association Opposed to Woman Suffrage, and close friends with the group's president—were en route to Washington, where they intended to intercept her before she entered the city and prevail upon her to abandon the march.

"As if I would, so close to our destination," Rosalie scoffed.

Yet they absorbed the news somberly, for the threat was all too believable. Weeks before, on the road to Albany, Mrs. Jones had conspired with their family doctor in a thwarted plot to kidnap Rosalie and transport her home. Her schemes never failed to make headlines, and the Antis loved to seize upon the conflict as evidence that the suffrage movement destroyed family harmony.

For her part, Colonel Craft was in much better spirits than Maud had observed in days, chatting earnestly with the war correspondents as they strode along. One reporter noted that at least a dozen local ladies hoped to join them on the march from Bladensburg to Washington the next day, and among them were several women of color. "Will they be permitted to enlist in the Army of the Hudson?" he asked, pencil poised to take notes.

"Certainly," Colonel Craft declared. "There will be no discrimination against any women who wish to complete the last leg of the journey into Washington. We welcome all willing and able recruits. This is a great cause and needs the support of as many respectable women as it is possible to get."

Maud was so pleased to hear this that she fell in step beside them and added that working women and immigrants were also included among the ranks of respectable women encouraged to enlist in the march. The war correspondents jotted notes, nodding, their expressions revealing intense concentration.

It was four o'clock when they reached Bladensburg, the late-winter sky clouding over and creating a false twilight as a steady drizzle resumed. A delegation of local suffragists met them with umbrellas and flowers and escorted them to the town armory, where they were offered hot coffee and doughnuts and entertained with speeches and a performance by a local children's choir. Afterward, they dispersed to several different hotels to rest and prepare for the momentous day that would commence in the morning. Maud found herself in the group staying at the famous Palo Alto Hotel, which included Martha Klatschken, her usual roommate, as well as General Jones, Colonel Craft, and several others.

They were all still comfortably sated from the midafternoon feast and the refreshments offered upon their arrival, but it was too early for bed, so they gathered in a small parlor off the lobby and ordered coffee and tea. "Do you think your mother and sister will find you here?" Martha asked the general.

"No," Rosalie replied grimly, "but only because I planted rumors that I'm staying in Hyattsville. I am expecting another visitor, however." With a sigh, and before Maud could query her, she addressed the table, saying, "I have some good news from Washington. Olive drove the scout car into the capital today, and she reports that we needn't worry about being arrested for violating any traffic laws tomorrow. Superintendent Sylvester has granted us a permit for our march into the city and for the open-air meeting in front of the F Street headquarters."

"That's a relief," remarked Colonel Craft. "Our budget doesn't include sufficient bail."

"The superintendent has promised us immunity from arrest as long as there is no disorder of a violent nature." Rosalie smiled, wryly amused. "I assured him there would be nothing of that nature. We are gentlewomen, and we trust that the good people of Washington will receive us with respect."

"I hope you're right." Martha shuddered. "I never in my life want to repeat that ugly scene from College Park."

They all nodded soberly, then gave a start at the sound of a knock on the parlor door. "I hope I'm not disturbing you," said a slender, dark-haired young woman as she entered the room. Her eyes were large, dark, and luminous, her voice low and rich, and she wore a gray wool coat over a dress of deep purple. After a moment, Maud recognized her from photographs as Miss Alice Paul, chair of the Congressional Committee.

Instinctively, the pilgrims rose, and they exchanged purposeful glances as Rosalie went forward to greet Miss Paul and shake her hand. The general introduced her companions, and Miss Paul nodded and murmured politely to each one. Then she turned her attention to General Jones. "I've come for the letter you're carrying."

"Of course." The general's expression was fixed and pleasant, betraying none of the misgivings Maud knew she must feel. "I'm a loyal soldier, and if the board of the National believes that it's better for the Congressional Committee to deliver the letter, there seems little else for me to do than to bow to its wishes."

Miss Paul put her head to one side and studied her for a moment. "This request comes directly from Dr. Shaw and Mrs. Dennett."

"Understood." The general managed a tight smile as she took a folded letter from her pocket and handed it to Miss Paul, ceremoniously, with both hands. The paper appeared so crisp and dry that Maud knew she must have retrieved it from her luggage only recently. "May it always be said that I'm willing to make any sacrifice for the cause."

"I'm sure everyone appreciates your sacrifice," said Miss Paul kindly. "From what I've been told, the board concluded that Mr. Wilson would be more likely to give an audience to the National's executive officers, since they are recognized authorities. He doesn't support woman suffrage, and he's expressed disapproval of your pilgrimage. The board was concerned that he might refuse to admit you to the White House."

"Well, he certainly wouldn't welcome any delegation that includes me," said Maud lightly, hoping to dispel the tension. "Mr. Wilson and I aren't exactly old friends."

Miss Paul offered her a brief smile before returning her calm gaze to the general. "On behalf of the Congressional Committee, I do hope that you'll still join us for luncheon after the open-air meeting tomorrow, following your triumphant entrance into the nation's capital."

"We're all looking forward to it," the general replied, her tone a trifle warmer.

"One more note: please be sure to enter the city by way of Rhode Island Avenue."

"But that's a side street," said Rosalie, brow furrowing. Maud understood her objections. Their numbers were growing by the hour as suffragists from Hyattsville, Bladensburg, and surrounding villages enlisted to complete the last leg of the pilgrimage, and dozens more marchers were expected to arrive from the capital by morning. They would need a road of more ample proportions to accommodate not only the Army of the Hudson but the great many well-wishers and curiosity seekers they hoped—they expected—would turn out to welcome them into the city.

"I've come to know the streets quite well while planning the procession, and Rhode Island Avenue is the best approach," Miss Paul replied. "A delegation of ladies, including myself, will meet you there with a car and small cavalry squadron, and we shall escort you to headquarters."

"We shall see you in the capital tomorrow afternoon," said the general, smiling. Maud exchanged a knowing look with Martha. They recognized Rosalie's deflection when they heard it, but apparently Miss Paul did not.

General Jones and Miss Paul conferred a few minutes longer over details for the next day's events, but soon Miss Paul wished the pilgrims good luck and bade them farewell. Then she departed, the precious letter tucked safely in her coat pocket.

The room seemed disproportionately emptier without it.

After a moment of disconsolate silence, General Jones inhaled deeply, squared her shoulders, and forced a smile. "We'll enter the city in our own way," she said briskly, looking around the circle of companions. "In the meantime, this is too somber a mood to mark the last night of our pilgrimage. I've written a poem in honor of the occasion—that is, I intend to read it tomorrow to the Army of the Hudson before we embark on the last few miles of our journey, but if you're willing to hear it, I'd like to share it with you few tonight."

Naturally they all insisted that she share her poem.

They settled back into their chairs as their general resumed her place at the head of the table, and standing, began to read.

> Oh sisters, my sisters!
> The trip is nearly done;
> The hikers slowly plod along,
> The towns pass one by one.
>
> The weary miles are left behind,
> The Capitol draws near;
> And soon our lengthy march will end,
> Amid a deafening cheer.
>
> Oh sisters, my sisters!
> The walk was long and hard;
> 'Twas up a hill and down a dale,
> Across God's dewy sward.
>
> While women laughed and men have jeered,
> At us and at our cause;
> Yet every step brought near that time,
> When we shall make the laws.

Her words warmed them, rekindled their hopes, reminded them anew of their purpose. Even without delivering the message to President Wilson, after many days and nearly 250 miles, through mud and storms and heckling and threats of violence, they were poised to successfully complete their mission. Nothing could diminish the golden glow of their achievement.

# 25
# February 28–March 2, 1913
## WASHINGTON, D.C.

### Alice

Despite the difficulties, annoyances, and inconveniences Mary Ware Dennett had created for the Congressional Committee over the past half year, Alice harbored no grudge against her. Thus on the last day of February, she was genuinely dismayed to learn that the National's New York headquarters was being inundated with letters and telegrams condemning Mrs. Dennett for relieving Rosalie Jones of the letter to President-Elect Wilson. Evidently it was not well known that the decision had been made by Dr. Shaw and approved by a vote of the board, while Mrs. Dennett had only been the messenger, and Alice herself merely the agent chosen to carry out the command. Alice too had been stung by a few barbs in the press for her part in the fiasco, but nothing on the order of what Mrs. Dennett suffered. The self-proclaimed General Jones had become a folk, hero, her exploits embellished and immortalized by the adoring "war correspondents" who had accompanied the pilgrims on their long, arduous hike. Thousands of readers who had eagerly followed their adventures in the papers were outraged by the insult to General Jones and demanded an apology on her behalf.

Astonished by the outcry, Mrs. Dennett scrambled to redeem herself and the National in the eyes of the public. "Everything is just as it always was," she insisted to the reporters who hounded her at the National's Fifth Avenue offices. "Rosalie is a darling, and I'm sure she realizes we are all her friends. There has been some misunderstanding." She then offered a meandering explanation that, to Alice at least, clarified little except that the outpouring of anger had caught the board entirely by surprise, and that Mrs. Dennett was too flustered to offer a convincing defense.

According to the morning papers, sometime after Alice had left Bladensburg the previous evening, Mrs. Dennett had sent General Jones a second telegram partially retracting the first: "Regret misunderstanding. Board with you from the beginning. Delegation to present message to consist of national officers, Congressional Committee, and pilgrims if interview with Wilson is secured." Alice already knew about the important caveat—*if* an interview was secured—because her committee had been tasked with arranging it.

"If they don't succeed in getting an interview," a reporter from the *New York Times* had asked, "will General Jones be allowed to deliver the message herself?"

"I don't know," Mrs. Dennett had retorted. "Miss Addams thought it wouldn't be dignified to trail him about the city or thrust it at him in the railroad station."

Alice winced at the graceless reply, which only added insult to injury. Perhaps General Jones did hope to make a public spectacle while delivering the letter—her entire march had been a public spectacle, and there was at least one notorious heckler among her pilgrims—but to accuse her of undignified behavior before the fact was unfair and unkind. Miss Addams was preparing for a trip abroad and was unavailable for comment, and as for Mr. Wilson, he had said nothing publicly about the controversy. Alice assumed that the president-elect, now forewarned, would endeavor to avoid receiving the letter from anyone, making her job to arrange a White House meeting all the more difficult.

Alice's sympathy for the embattled secretary diminished somewhat when a telegram from Mrs. Dennett arrived later that morning. Interrupting Alice's work when she could least afford it, Mrs. Dennett ordered her to instruct the parade marshals and registration clerks not to exclude women of color. She went on to chastise Alice for having "so strongly urged Colored women not to march that it amounts to official discrimination which is distinctly contrary to instructions from National headquarters."

The accusation stung. Alice could not imagine what had prompted it, unless it was somehow connected to the telegram she had received two days before from Clara Barck Welles, chairman and parade major for the Illinois delegation. "We have application from a colored woman to march," she had written frantically four days before the procession. "Will Negro women be admitted to the suffrage parade—answer—quick." The telegram had been sent in the evening, so Alice had not seen it until the following morning. She had responded promptly, all the while knowing that her reply might not arrive in Chicago until after Mrs. Welles and her delegation had departed for Washington. Perhaps, mistakenly believing that Alice had ignored her question, Mrs. Welles had complained to the National. Even so, Mrs. Dennett's admonishment was unduly harsh, for Alice had never urged Black women not to march. Yes, she believed the procession should focus on woman suffrage rather than racial equality, but she had welcomed the National Association of Colored Women, the sorority from Howard University, and other delegations of Black women to join in that effort. And although she had strategically assigned them certain places in the lineup outside the usual categories, that was more to surround them with friendly, supportive delegations to help ensure their own protection than to deflect the anger of southern white women.

She wished, too late, that she had done more to encourage women of color to join the procession, and that she had invited Mrs. Terrell, Mrs. Clifford, Mrs. Wells-Barnett, or another distinguished Black suffragist to join the Congressional Committee back in December. The omission, so obvious in hindsight, embarrassed her, but there was nothing to be done for it now. March 3 was swiftly approaching, and woman suffrage must come first and foremost on that day of all days. Still, Alice obeyed Mrs. Dennett's order without complaint, and sent notes to the volunteers in charge of registry clerks and parade marshals strongly emphasizing that all registered marchers must be allowed to participate in their assigned sections, regardless of race. She considered writing to the leaders of the various state delegations to remind them as well, but she doubted her letters would reach them in time, or at all, since most of the delegates were already traveling to Washington. In the end she decided such reminders from the Congressional Committee were unnecessary in this case, as the state delegations had been organized well ahead of time, and by now the leaders would have sorted out any conflicts.

Alice hoped that would be enough to satisfy Mrs. Dennett and put the controversy to rest. She had no time to ponder a better solution, for it was almost noon, and if General Jones's troops had departed Bladensburg on schedule, they had already crossed the Anacostia River and were marching into the capital.

While most of the volunteers remained at head-quarters to prepare for the open-air rally, Alice and a small welcoming party set out to meet the Army of the Hudson. Two women on horseback led the way, clad in white corduroy riding habits and large white plumed hats with the brim turned up on one side. Behind them came a car carrying Alice, Dora, and Margaret Foley, a Boston suffragist known as "the Suffrage Cyclone" for her remarkable ability to project her powerful voice the distance of three city blocks. Proceeding at a decorous pace, they rode north, turned east onto Rhode Island Avenue, and halted at the intersection of South Dakota Avenue, where General Jones had agreed to meet her escort. A squad of mounted policemen awaited them, as previously arranged, but the pilgrims did not appear at the appointed time, nor ten minutes later, nor were they visible in the distance toward the Maryland border. When the pilgrims were twenty minutes overdue, one of the horsewomen offered to ride ahead and seek them out. Fifteen minutes later, she returned from the south at a brisk trot. "The Army of the Hudson took a different route into the capital," she reported, breathless.

"Where are they now?" Alice asked, confounded.

"They're proceeding along Maryland Avenue," the horsewoman replied, "basking in cheers. The sidewalks are packed with spectators."

Some of Alice's companions grumbled about the general's inability to follow orders, but Alice put a stop to that, although she too was annoyed. Accompanied by the policemen, they quickly turned the car and the horses around, backtracked along a parallel course, made a sharp left south, and intercepted the marchers at Maryland and Tenth Street Northeast, where they had paused to admire the view of the Capitol, whose white dome glistened like alabaster in the sunlight.

Mindful of the many curious onlookers and the war correspondents hovering nearby, Alice assumed a serene expression as she left the car and approached General Jones, who stood at the head of the forma-

THE WOMEN'S MARCH · 437

tion draped in her brown hooded cloak, grasping a tall
birchbark walking staff and smiling broadly.

Alice managed a smile in return as she extended her
hand and General Jones shook it. "I apologize if my
instructions were unclear," she said mildly. "We were
expecting you to enter the city on Rhode Island Avenue and meet us at the intersection of South Dakota,
as we agreed last night."

"We took Bladensburg Road instead," the general
replied, "and entered the city at the old toll gate at Fifteenth and Maryland."

"I see. Was Rhode Island Avenue obstructed in
some way?"

The general shrugged, eyebrows arched in surprise.
"Not as far as I know."

"Then may I ask why you disregarded instructions,
knowing we planned to meet you elsewhere?"

"The Army of the Hudson required a more spacious
route." General Jones swept an arm to indicate the
steadily increasing crowd. "I think you underestimated
our popularity."

Alice thought the general overestimated her own authority. "Now that we've met, would you permit us to
escort you the rest of the way to headquarters?"

"Certainly," the general replied gallantly. Abruptly
turning away, she called her troops together and issued

commands for the order of march. Keeping a pleasant smile fixed firmly in place, Alice returned to her
companions, quickly briefed them, and climbed aboard
the car. Already more onlookers had gathered, men
and women and children, some waving handkerchiefs,
others shouting the names of General Jones, Colonel
Craft, and some of the more famous pilgrims. A cornet
blast signaled the order to advance, and so the entire
formation set forth, the mounted policemen first, followed by Alice and her companions in the car, then
the two white-clad horsewomen. After the escort came
General Jones, followed immediately by a row of thirteen pilgrims, those who had accompanied her every
step of the journey. Next came a line of women who
had marched most of the way, then several lines of more
pilgrims who had marched only part of the way, in de-
creasing order of distance traveled. After the marchers came a wizened horse pulling the yellow suffrage
wagon, most of its banners and bunting long gone,
claimed as trophies by raucous college students. Next
came a smaller cart pulled by a donkey, and the baggage wagon last of all. At the general's request, the war
correspondents strode alongside as her personal escort.

Perhaps the general had been wise to select a
broader avenue, Alice thought, noting with increasing
alarm that the number of spectators was swelling into

the thousands as they rode along the two blocks between Seventh Street and Ninth. The people seemed to
appear out of nowhere, pouring out of residences and
businesses, and street peddlers selling flags, pennants,
balloons, and bags of confetti stoked the carnival atmosphere. Superintendent Sylvester had promised to
have four hundred District policemen on patrol for the
pilgrims' arrival, but as the army and its escort turned
onto Pennsylvania Avenue and the roar of a crowd of
nearly one hundred thousand rattled the windows of
the car, Alice could not imagine that such a force would
suffice.

"Three cheers for General Jones," someone bellowed, and the cry was taken up with thunderous
reverberations. As the crowds spilled over from the
sidewalks into the street, the defenses did not always
hold. A woman would break through the police ranks
and attempt to present General Jones or Colonel Craft
with a bouquet of flowers; or a man would rush forward
with hand outstretched, eager to shake the general's;
or a mother would dart into the ranks with a child in
her arms and hold up the little one to the general for a
kiss. Every time, the war correspondents would swiftly
intervene, hustling the excited admirers away from the
marchers and thrusting them back into the crowd. At
times the throng was so vast that the mounted police

escort could hardly keep the way ahead clear, forcing the escort and troops to slow to a crawl.

All this, thought Alice pensively, for a parade of a few dozen suffragists. What greater difficulties could they expect on March 3, when thousands of marchers and dozens of floats and bands would process down Pennsylvania Avenue, past hundreds of thousands of visitors in town for the inauguration?

At last they reached F Street. Thousands of people massed around the front stoop of headquarters, easily identified by the purple, green, and white banners adorning the windows and doors. A volunteer was waiting to take charge of the car so Alice and her companions could promptly attend to General Jones, whom the crowd welcomed with vigorous applause and enthusiastic cries. Small flags in suffrage colors waved frantically, and yellow suffrage badges were pinned proudly to many a coat lapel. As Alice made her way to the front door flanked by Dora and Margaret, she spotted a cluster of bright-eyed, beaming women in identical white caps with upturned brims embellished by blue stars. Some distance beyond them, a gleaming black car was parked in the intersection; Alice would have guessed it was a police sedan, except that it was draped in bunting in the hues claimed by the Antis. A dark-haired woman dressed in sumptuous furs leaned halfway out of the front passenger window, scanning the Army of the Hudson, and when her gaze fell upon General Jones, her face lit up and her small, gloved hands applauded so swiftly they were almost a blur.

"That wealthy woman adores the general," Alice mused aloud. "We should find out who she is and solicit a donation for the procession."

"She won't give you a dime," said Margaret shortly, her voice barely audible in the din. "That's Mrs. Jones, the general's mother. She's a card-carrying member of the National Association Opposed to Woman Suffrage. Likely she's here for the Anti rally they're holding later this afternoon. What you see is a mother celebrating her daughter's triumph while fervently hoping her cause will fail."

Alice barely had time to ponder that contradiction before she realized that the crowd was closing in around the pilgrims, and even with the able assistance of the war correspondents, their leader could not force her way through to headquarters, where she was supposed to deliver her remarks. Suddenly two of the reporters helped her scramble onto the hood of a car, a pilgrim handed her a megaphone, and she waved her arm for attention. "I am so very glad to be here in

Washington," General Jones declared, smiling, and was rewarded with hearty cheers. "We have come through, and we thank you for this welcome."

Her rapt audience drowned out her next few lines. Alice politely joined in the applause but soon stopped, the better to hear the speaker. "It has been worth all it has cost," the general was saying, "the hardships and privations, the disappointments and foot-aches, and maybe at times a little heartache."

The crowd murmured sympathetically, and Alice felt a pang, certain she was referring to her abrupt dismissal as the courier of the letter to Mr. Wilson. Keeping her expression studiously pleasant, Alice let her gaze wander over the rest of the pilgrims and saw on their faces, in addition to fatigue, excitement, and pride, unexpected traces of anger and indignation, especially whenever they glanced away from their general to the Congressional Committee volunteers who had emerged from headquarters to observe the speech from the front stoop.

"We have reached the hearts of the American people," the general continued, cheeks flushed and eyes bright. "We have set people thinking, and we will win!"

A roar of approval went up from the crowd, so powerful that Alice instinctively took a step back. She quickly composed herself as Colonel Craft took the general's place on the hood of the automobile. In a loud, full voice that carried well, she emphasized the historic nature of their journey, which she declared was the most tremendous thing that had been done for suffrage since 1870. "I am convinced that we have converted thousands of skeptics," she concluded. "We have penetrated the conservative states and have given them an object lesson in the earnestness of those who fight for the cause."

The audience was so enthralled and excited by the speeches that after the colonel stepped down, the pilgrims were obliged to wait twenty minutes for the crowd to disperse before they could approach the front entrance to headquarters. Even then, they seemed reluctant to come inside. General Jones was cordial enough, albeit with iron in her smile, but most of the pilgrims accepted the volunteers' greetings coolly. Even so, they did seem relieved to have a place to sit and rest before luncheon, and they gratefully accepted the hot coffee and tea the volunteers offered.

Hoping to improve their mood, Alice quietly asked Dora to read aloud the second telegram Mrs. Dennett had sent the previous evening. She hoped to remind the pilgrims that General Jones and a few companions would be included in the delegation to deliver the letter that, unbeknownst to anyone but Alice, was securely stored in Susan B. Anthony's desk only a few feet from where they mingled. In sharp contrast to Dora's bright smile and enthusiastic reading, most of the pilgrims listened stoically and looked away, as if it were old news and poor consolation. As for the general, both at headquarters and at the luncheon afterward at the Cafe Republique, she was too busy chatting with her pilgrims and war correspondents to ask Alice about the delegation—how many pilgrims would be included, when they would call on the new president—all the details Alice would have wanted to know in her place.

At the luncheon, the food was delicious, but the mood was more civil than friendly. Alice would have attributed the pilgrims' aloof manner to fatigue, but she had observed that fewer pilgrims had rested at headquarters than had marched into the capital, and their numbers had declined even more on the way to the café. Concerned, Alice approached one of the friendlier pilgrims, a pretty, auburn-haired woman who spoke with an Irish lilt, and mused aloud about her absent comrades.

"They didn't get lost in that great crowd, if that's what worries you," said Miss Malone, smiling tentatively. "Some of them live here in the capital, and they were eager to return home after three weeks away. No doubt a few friends begged to accompany them, to freshen up and rest."

"I see," replied Alice. "That's perfectly understandable."

She suspected Miss Malone was merely being kind, and the next day's papers confirmed her worries. According to the *New York Times*, only minutes after delivering her speech, General Jones had declared that neither she nor her pilgrims would help deliver the National's message to Mr. Wilson. "I am through," she had said flatly. "I was asked to relinquish the message that I had received in New York to deliver to President Wilson. I have done so. It is now out of my hands, and as far as I am concerned, that ends the matter." Jealous local suffragists wanted to diminish the glory of their achievements, other pilgrims insisted, and no half-hearted efforts to include them now could make up for the shocking insult to their leader. A few declared that while they were in the capital, they would decline any hospitality from the Congressional Committee, including the luncheon and the banquet scheduled for the evening of March 1.

Their accusations were so numerous and persistent that reporters called at headquarters seeking a response, which Alice felt obliged to give. "We are doing all that we can to entertain the Army of the Hudson," she said, wishing she could speak directly and confidentially with the offended women rather than reach out to them through the press. "I can assure you that we do appreciate the wonderful walk they have made, and the great aid they have given the cause by their efforts and bravery." She added that she regretted that any misunderstanding should exist between them. As far as she knew, the pilgrims would indeed present the letter to President Wilson; the only change to the original plan was that some officers from the National would accompany them.

Alice hoped that her attempts to reconcile would mollify the general and her ardent troops. Suffrage women would never be taken seriously if they obsessed over petty personal quarrels. Men and Antis loved to contend that women were too jealous and competitive to work together to any common purpose, which was one more reason why they should not be entrusted with the vote. It was all so unnecessary and wasteful. Suffragists could not afford to help their adversaries defeat them, especially on the eve of such a momentous historic event, when they were poised to advance the cause miles ahead of where they stood today. Meanwhile, two days before the suffrage procession, Congress established a subcommittee to investigate and to report to the House whether the question of equal suffrage in presidential elections should be left to a constitutional amendment or to the actions of individual states. The essential purpose of the Congressional Committee was on the verge of fulfillment, no doubt due to the attention the suffrage procession had already brought to the matter. They dared not splinter off into warring factions so close to achieving their goal.

There were so many far more important things to worry about than slights and hurt feelings. The final details of the glorious procession were all falling into place, thanks to the tireless efforts of Alice, Lucy, Dora, and their wonderful, devoted volunteers, but General Jones's march into the capital had confirmed Alice's worst fears: Superintendent Sylvester's police forces were woefully unprepared to manage security for the suffrage procession. On March 3, the participants' numbers—nearly five thousand, according to their most recent estimate—would be many times that of the Army of the Hudson. Visitors arriving for the inauguration would swell the city's population, so the number of potential spectators would certainly far surpass those who had turned out to welcome the pilgrims. General Jones's troops had been forced to push their way through a mob just to make it to headquarters, and that crowd, charmed by the general's folk hero status, included relatively few hecklers and Antis. It was unlikely that Alice and her comrades would be so fortunate.

With increasing apprehension as the days passed and dwindled to mere hours before the procession would set forth and claim its moment in history, Alice strove to persuade any authority who would listen to send reinforcements. The White House passed her request along to the Department of War, but Secretary Stimson insisted that he was powerless to help, since he was legally prevented from sending in troops unless local authorities requested support. Alice doubted any such request would be forthcoming. Superintendent Sylvester downplayed her concerns in the press, noting that he had deputized special officers for the procession, increasing the size of the deployment to 575 men, far more than would be assigned to the inaugural parade itself. With the last few miles of General Jones's march still vivid in her memory, Alice was not appeased. As a last resort, she implored Governor William Sulzer to bring in the contingent of New York militia assigned to the inauguration one day early so that they could cover the suffrage procession as well. He rejected her appeal.

Alice had exhausted every option. She could only hope that some eleventh-hour insight would compel Superintendent Sylvester to augment his forces, or, if he failed again, that decency and mutual respect would rule the day, rendering his protection unnecessary.

# 26
# March 3, 1913

### Ida

The morning of the suffrage procession dawned bright and clear, the sunlight streaming through Ida's boardinghouse window promising blue skies and mild temperatures. The trees lining the street outside were already lush with pale green new leaves, and the breeze carried a faint scent of distant blossoms amid the pungent city odors. How pleasant it was to enjoy a taste of spring so early in March, since Chicago's bare-limbed trees and brown fields still vulnerable to frost awaited the turning of the season beneath gray, over-cast skies.

As she rose, washed, and dressed, Ida hoped that the fair weather of the morning would endure until the last marcher completed the final mile of the suffrage procession. The parade would go on regardless, rain or shine, and she certainly would not allow a little wind or rain to prevent her from demonstrating. But warm, sunny weather would encourage more spectators to turn out, more witnesses to note her presence, a proud, dignified Black woman marching behind the banner of her state.

Virginia and Belle had invited her to join them for breakfast and some sightseeing before their final rehearsal, but Ida declined on account of an important prior commitment. Miss Nellie May Quander, a recent magna cum laude graduate of Howard University and the first international president of the Alpha Kappa Alpha Sorority, had organized a brunch reception on campus at the Founders Library, where Ida looked forward to meeting the bright, ambitious students and reuniting with several dear friends and colleagues. Mary Church Terrell had been invited to offer the keynote address, and Ida too would speak. She anticipated a fine meal and the excellent company of distinguished women of color from the District as well as some who had traveled to the capital to march in the procession or to attend the inauguration.

The sidewalks were already bustling and the streetcars packed as Ida made her way to the university campus. The red, white, and blue bunting draped upon nearly every building and lamppost in honor of the next day's inauguration gave the city a festive, anticipatory air. Ida had always felt a frisson of pride and sublime joy whenever she visited Howard University, and that morning the sensation was more intense than ever. Any one of the students she observed strolling along the quad engaged in earnest conversation or departing the library with an armful of books could be a future business leader, poet, teacher, lawyer, doctor, journalist, politician—the possibilities seemed limitless now in a way that would have been scarcely imaginable to her parents' generation. She suffered no illusions that the road ahead would be smooth and clear, but change was coming, and universal suffrage would speed its arrival.

The atmosphere at the reception was warm and enthusiastic, the speeches challenging and inspiring in equal measure. Afterward, Ida found herself surrounded by students eager to query her about the NAACP, the Alpha Suffrage Club, and her experiences as a journalist and activist, and the young adults anticipating graduation and the pursuit of promising new careers respectfully sought her advice. She took advantage of a momentary lull in the flattering attention to chat with longtime friends and make new acquaintances, including the sculptor Mrs. May Jackson;

the musician and writer Mrs. Harriet Gibbs Marshall, founder of the Washington Conservatory of Music and School of Expression and the first Black woman to have graduated from Oberlin Conservatory with a degree in music; and Dr. Amanda Brown Gray, a Howard alumna, pharmacist, and the first Black woman to own and manage a pharmacy in Washington. Each of them intended to march in the procession later that day, but several mentioned troubling rumors that at the last moment, the parade would be segregated, or worse yet, women of color would be excluded altogether.

"I hope those rumors prove false," said Ida, an all-too-familiar mixture of anger and wariness stirring in her chest. Turning to Mrs. Terrell, she asked, "In what section will you be marching? With the teachers or the college women, or under the banner of the District?"

"None of the above," Mrs. Terrell replied, smiling. "I'm an honorary member of Delta Sigma Theta, and I'll be marching with the sorority. And you?"

"I'll be with the delegation from the great state of Illinois," said Ida proudly. "We'll be the ones in the white caps with blue stars, marching with remarkable grace and precision. We've been practicing."

"We haven't," said Mrs. Terrell. "We'll have to rely on our natural grace and ability. Fortunately, we have ample quantities of both. We'll be more than a match for you ladies."

They shared a laugh, but the conversation reminded Ida that the time was drawing near for the Illinois delegation's last rehearsal before they reported to their staging area. Bidding farewell to her friends and a few admiring students who had lingered, she hurried off to catch a crowded streetcar to the intersection nearest the Congressional Committee headquarters on F Street Northwest.

Several members of the Illinois delegation had visited headquarters a few days before to welcome General Rosalie Jones and her troops to the capital, but Ida, Virginia, and Belle had not expected the vast crowds that had swept in seemingly from out of nowhere, and they had not left their boardinghouse early enough to make it within two blocks of the building. As Ida approached now, she spotted Virginia waiting on the front stoop, clad in her procession uniform and carrying Ida's stole, cap, and pennant, as they had previously arranged.

"You made it," Virginia called, waving, visibly relieved. "The city is so busy this morning, I wasn't sure you would."

Ida climbed the stairs to the front stoop and accepted

her uniform from her friend, and together they entered the building, shutting out the noise of the street. They did not have time to tour the committee's offices, where women clad in suffrage colors and badges and sashes were visible through the windows, bustling about with tense, excited expressions as they attended to last-minute procession details and emergencies. Instead the two friends followed the sound of voices and a cadence of footsteps upstairs to a large meeting room on the second floor, where the rest of the delegation mingled. Most, like Virginia, were already clad in their uniforms. No sooner had Ida donned her cap and draped her stole around her neck and shoulders than Mrs. Welles held her brass baton aloft and called them to order.

Proudly, with keen focus and joyful hearts, they went through their paces, marching, turning, and halting with crisp precision according to Mrs. Welles's commands. Several newspaper reporters, distinguished by their slouch hats and pads and pencils, observed them from the edges of the room as they marched. Before long the strike of the women's footsteps on the wooden floor drew curious volunteers upstairs from the offices below, and they stole into the room or peered in through the doorway, smiling in admiration. Occasionally Ida felt eyes linger on her with particular curiosity, but she was accustomed to the stares of white folks who thought she looked out of place, and she ignored them.

When Mrs. Welles called for a five-minute break, Mrs. Trout, who had been coming in and out of the room throughout the rehearsal, hurried over to Mrs. Welles and engaged her in a brief, hushed, and fervent conference. Then, wringing her hands, Mrs. Trout called for the marchers' attention. "I have some concerning news," she said, her glance alighting on Ida for a moment before darting away. "Evidently there is some question whether Mrs. Wells-Barnett will be permitted to march with our delegation."

Ida felt her heart plummet as a murmur of bewilderment and indignation passed through the room. She sensed Virginia and Belle drawing nearer to her, closing ranks.

"Many women from southern states greatly resent that so many colored women have been included in the various delegations," Mrs. Trout continued, a faint flush rising in her cheeks. "Some have even gone so far as to say they will not march if Negro women are allowed to take part. Some representatives of the National have advised us to keep our delegation entirely white."

A murmur of astonishment went up from the marchers, and Ida felt her hackles rise and her jaw tighten.

"What representatives?" Belle demanded. "Who advised this? Give us their names."

Mrs. Trout hesitated. "Well, it was Mrs. Claude Stone who informed me." She gestured weakly over her shoulder, which Ida interpreted to mean that Mrs. Stone had been among the women observing their rehearsal earlier. "She's a member of the Illinois delegation to the National, and of course, her husband is the congressman from the sixteenth district."

"That doesn't give her any authority over us," Virginia protested.

Ida agreed, but she smoldered in silence, waiting for more.

"Well, not directly, of course, but she's—she's a congressman's wife." Mrs. Trout placed a hand over her heart and cast a beseeching gaze over the group. "As far as Mrs. Welles and I are concerned, we should like to have Mrs. Wells-Barnett march in the delegation, but if the National has decided it is unwise to include colored women, I think we should abide by its decision."

She paused, wringing her hands, awaiting their approval and bracing herself for dissent.

Mrs. Welles drew closer, grasping her baton in both hands, brow furrowing. "Are you sure this comes from the Congressional Committee and not just Mrs. Stone?"

Mrs. Trout looked taken aback. "I can't imagine Mrs. Stone would take it upon herself to issue recommendations without the National's approval."

"Either way, it's the right decision," another marcher called out. "It will prejudice southern people against suffrage if we take the colored women into our ranks."

Her voice carried a distinct southern accent, and when Ida searched the crowd and traced it to its source, she recognized the speaker as Mrs. Brandt from Oak Park, originally of Georgia, who often expressed nostalgic fondness for an idealized version of southern folk and southern customs.

"But that would be entirely undemocratic," Virginia protested. "We've come here to march for equal rights. It would be autocratic to exclude women of color."

"Hear, hear," Belle seconded her.

"I believe we must allow Mrs. Wells-Barnett to walk in our delegation," Virginia continued, her voice rising. "If the women of other states lack moral courage, we should show them that we are not afraid of public opinion. We should stand by our principles. If we do not, the parade will be a farce."

A chorus of agreement went up from the gathering, and the many nods of affirmation heartened Ida. Even so, she felt heat flooding her cheeks and she took a deep breath to steady herself before she spoke. "Southern white women have evaded the matter of racial equality time and again, and the National and its state branches have allowed it," she said, clearly and firmly, fighting to keep a tremor of emotion from her voice. "If the women of Illinois don't take a stand against racism now, in this great democratic parade, then colored women are lost."

Mrs. Trout mulled this over. "It is indeed time for Illinois to recognize the colored woman as a political equal." Looking directly at Ida, she added, "Mrs. Wells-Barnett, you shall march with the delegation."

A murmur of approval rippled through the room. Virginia put an arm around Ida's shoulders, and Belle patted her encouragingly on the back. But before Ida could breathe easily, a woman she did not recognize strode into the room, drew Mrs. Trout aside, and whispered in her ear. Mrs. Trout nodded uneasily, gnawed at the inside of her lower lip, and announced to the delegation that she would have to confer with some of the National's officers before a final decision could be made.

With that, she and the other woman—whom Ida suspected might be Mrs. Stone herself—hurried from the room, leaving a storm of consternation and bewilderment behind.

"I can't believe this," said Virginia to Ida and Belle,

planting her hands on her hips, shaking her head. "The procession is only a few hours away, Ida has traveled hundreds of miles to participate, and they expect her to gracefully withdraw without a fight, all because some southern women resent her presence? Well, I resent *their* presence!"

Ida threw her a grateful look.

Belle shook her head, incredulous. "What right does the National have to dictate whom the Illinois committee includes in our state delegation?"

"It's their parade," a woman standing nearby pointed out.

A woman in the center of the room spread her hands helplessly. "It'll be undemocratic if we don't let Mrs. Wells-Barnett march with us, but we shouldn't go against the decisions of the National. We're only a small part of the great line of march, and we mustn't cause any confusion by disobeying orders."

"Oh, yes, disobedience must be avoided at all costs," said Belle acidly. "The only 'confusion' we need to fear is moral confusion. To me, our choice is very clear: let Mrs. Wells-Barnett march with us, and accept whatever reprimand the National wishes to bestow on us afterward, if they dare do such a disgraceful thing."

"That's exactly what we must do," someone cried. "Isn't Illinois the land of Lincoln, the Great Emancipator? If we don't stand up for our colored friends, who will?"

"Now, ladies, please," Mrs. Welles called out, holding up her brass baton as if to resume rehearsal, but it was to no avail. The delegation had broken apart into smaller groups, debating or arguing, or whispering while casting furtive, disapproving glances Ida's way. Tucking the baton under her arm, Mrs. Welles heaved a sigh and went in pursuit of Mrs. Trout.

Stunned and bitterly disappointed, Ida made her way to an empty chair against the far wall and sank into it, clasping her hands together in her lap. Virginia and Belle hurried after her. "It'll be all right, I'm sure," Belle said, resting a hand on her shoulder. Virginia said nothing, her eyes glistening with tears of outrage.

Eventually Mrs. Trout and Mrs. Welles returned, their expressions chagrined. Steeling herself, Ida rose. She held Mrs. Trout's gaze steadily, daring the leader of the Illinois delegation to look away.

"I'm afraid that we shall not be able to have you march with us," Mrs. Trout announced, wincing and holding up her hands for silence as a chorus of protest drowned out a light smattering of applause. "Personally, Mrs. Wells-Barnett, I should like nothing more than to have you represent our Illinois suffrage organization, but we must answer to the national association and cannot do as we choose. I shall have to ask you to march with the colored delegation at the back of the parade. I'm sorry, but I believe that it is the right thing to do."

Ida's anger and frustration threatened to boil over. "I shall not march at all unless I can march under the Illinois banner. When I was invited to join this delegation, I was assured that I would march with the other women of our state. I intend to do so or not take part in the parade at all."

Mrs. Welles shook her head, regarding Ida in utter bewilderment. "If I were a colored woman, I should be willing to march with the other women of my race."

"There is a difference, Mrs. Welles, which you probably cannot see," Ida replied, an edge to her voice. "I shall not march in a segregated section. Either I march with the Illinois delegation beneath our state banner, or not at all. I assure you, I'm not taking this stand out of any desire for personal recognition. I'm doing this for the future benefit of my whole race."

Mrs. Welles and Mrs. Trout merely looked at her, speechless and disbelieving. Ida felt her expression hardening into a mask of grim determination. She was not bluffing, if that was what they hoped.

"If you walk in the colored delegation, I shall walk by your side," said Belle, linking her arm through Ida's.

"And I shall join Mrs. Wells-Barnett and Mrs. Squire," declared Virginia. "It would be a disgrace for the women of Illinois to allow Mrs. Wells-Barnett to march in a segregated section—indeed, that a segregated section should exist at all—when this glorious procession is intended to show woman's demand for the great principles of democracy."

Her words met with so many vigorous nods that for a moment, Ida imagined half the marchers defecting from the state delegation in order to join her, Belle, and Virginia in the colored section at the rear—but that would be a well-meant but wasted gesture, for Ida would not be among them. Years before, she had fought the conductors who had put her off the train to Woodstock when she would not exchange her seat in first class for one in the smoker. All these many years later, she refused to settle for anything less than what she deserved, than what she had been promised, in this suffrage procession.

Tucking the wand of her pennant under her arm, Ida murmured farewells to Belle and Virginia, nodded to the few women who stood awkwardly nearby regarding her with stricken sympathy, and turned a steely gaze upon those who looked at her in smug triumph, their cheeks flushed, their mouths set in curved, hard lines.

She strode to the open doorway, chin raised, shoulders back.

"Where shall we meet you for the procession?" Virginia called after her. "Ida?"

She could not bear to linger long enough to reply.

"Meet us at the assembly point for our delegation at New Jersey Avenue," Belle called, more urgently. "We'll walk to the colored section together."

No, they would not, Ida resolved as she passed through the doorway, descended the stairs, and exited onto F Street. She had said that she would not march in a segregated section, and she meant it. Let no one doubt that she was a woman of her word.

# 27

# March 3, 1913

## WASHINGTON, D.C.

### Alice, Ida, Maud

At one o'clock, clad in her University of Pennsylvania robe, doctoral hood, and mortarboard, Alice left the F Street headquarters and hurried to the Treasury Building for a last-minute conference with Hazel MacKaye, who was leading a final rehearsal for the allegorical pageant. Alice had seen the costumes displayed on dressmakers' models weeks before, but the way the lightweight fabrics glowed in the sunlight and shifted with the dancers' graceful movements took her breath away. Hazel assured her that although it was a bit cool for such diaphanous gowns, the performers would not be standing still outdoors long enough to catch a chill, and the exercise would warm them.

Satisfied that her cast knew every step by heart, Hazel ushered them into the Treasury lobby to await their cue to take the stage, forty-five minutes after the procession began. In the meantime, Alice walked down Pennsylvania Avenue inspecting the parade route in reverse, every sense alert in anticipation. The profusion of American flags unfurled on storefront staffs and the red, white, and blue bunting adorning nearly every building gave the scene a patriotic, celebratory air that suited the suffrage march as much as the inaugural parade for which the decorations were intended. Earlier that morning, Superintendent Sylvester had ordered his officers to line the sidewalks with half-inch steel cables threaded through solid, heavy stanchions, a temporary barricade to hold back the crowds, which had already begun to mass by the thousands on the sidewalks and side streets. Alice hoped this new line of defense would suffice. The suffrage procession must not be disrupted by overly enthusiastic spectators as General Jones's entry into the capital had been four days before.

By the time Alice reached the Peace Monument near the Capitol, so many more spectators had arrived that she had to wend a circuitous path down the crowded sidewalk, taking one step sideways for every two forward. Female newsies clad in purple, green, and white sashes mingled among the sightseers, selling the *Woman's Journal*, while other girls sold yellow suffrage badges and pennants. From several yards away, Alice spotted the lovely Inez Milholland, the procession's herald, holding the reins of her majestic white stallion, Gray Dawn. A gold tiara with a single star in the center of the ornament held Inez's long dark curls away from her beautiful face, a light blue cape flowed down her back from her shoulders to her ankles, and a silver trumpet hung from a belt at her waist. She stroked her horse's flank as she chatted with May Walker Burleson, the Texas debutante and military wife serving as the parade's grand marshal. May brightened when she saw Alice approaching, exchanged a quick farewell with Inez, and hurried over to meet her.

"First thing this morning, I checked in with Superintendent Sylvester," said May. "He assures me that the police are prepared for whatever may come."

"I certainly hope so," said Alice. "I'm glad to see the stanchion wires, but I'm still not convinced he's taking our security seriously enough."

"Fortunately, others are," said May. "One of our marchers is the sister-in-law of Secretary of War Henry Stimson—"

"Elizabeth Rogers," Alice broke in, nodding. "She volunteers at headquarters. She's often asked her brother-in-law to assist us, but he's always brushed our concerns aside, on every issue from securing permits to reinforcing the police detail."

"Not anymore. Just this morning he checked in with the city commissioner. General Johnston told Secretary Stimson that he doesn't anticipate any serious problems, but he'd like a troop of cavalry from Fort Myer to be prepared to assist, just in case. Stimson agreed."

"Finally!" Alice exclaimed, much relieved. The secretary had said all along that he could not intervene without a specific request from local authorities; now, at the last moment, General Johnston had given him one. "I'm glad they'll be prepared. I only hope we won't need them."

May fervently agreed, and they parted with mutual good wishes for the day ahead.

Mindful of the hour, delighting in the air of rising expectation and jubilance all around her, Alice continued along the staging area, greeting acquaintances, answering questions, and accepting congratulations, which she hoped were not premature. To her relief, it appeared that the few changes to the order of march they had been obliged to make at the eleventh hour had not caused any confusion. Everyone bustled about cheerfully as they made ready to set forth, and at the head of the parade, the vanguard seemed only moments away from completing their final preparations. As grand marshal, May would lead the procession, accompanied by four aides, only steps ahead of the color guard bearing the Stars and Stripes and the flag of the National. Next would come Inez astride Gray Dawn, representing the nobility of the cause and the dawn of hope for its fulfillment. Ten ushers would follow in a line, carrying a blue-and-gold banner announcing the occupants of several cars directly behind them: the officers of the National and several distinguished women who would speak at the rally at the Daughters of the American Revolution's Continental Hall after the procession. Next were the first of several women's bands, whose musicians were tuning their instruments and rehearsing measures in a merry cacophony of lively marching tunes. Forty more ushers would follow, clad in gold and light blue and carrying yellow-and-blue pennants. The Mounted Brigade, Washington Division, would close out the vanguard.

As Alice continued past the First Section, which was introduced by a large banner bearing the slogan WOMEN OF THE WORLD UNITE, she was pleased to see how many marchers attired in the native costumes of their foreign lands had assembled and were already forming orderly lines. Another herald with a trumpet led the Second Section, which would begin with another women's marching band. Next, two horses would pull a cart adorned with a great banner. Its bold words, though familiar to Alice by now, warmed her heart anew: WE DEMAND AN AMENDMENT TO THE CONSTITUTION OF THE UNITED STATES ENFRANCHISING THE WOMEN OF THE COUNTRY.

The entire procession came down to that simple, profound, and essential statement of purpose.

Alice walked on, past mounted brigades and bands and floats depicting scenes from the history of women's quest for equal suffrage. Before long she came to the Third Section, which was designated for various professions; after the In Education float, she found the College Women, capped and gowned like herself, and lined up behind the banner of her alma mater. She was welcomed with warm smiles and kind words, and immediately felt at home.

At last, the moment she had worked for over the course of many long, grueling months was at hand.

**From the** Congressional Committee's headquarters, Ida had walked alone to the Washington Mall, angry and disconsolate. She deliberately avoided Pennsylvania Avenue with its trappings of patriotism, those proud colors and flags and banners celebrating the victor of an election in which she had been forbidden to cast a ballot. And she was not the only one. A vast multitude of people of color had been disenfranchised, perhaps enough to have changed the outcome of the election.

Ida knew that her exclusion, while morally wrong, was shamefully legal. The same could not be said for the disenfranchisement of countless thousands of Black men throughout the Jim Crow South who had found themselves thwarted at the polls by convoluted and farcical local laws designed to dismantle what the Fifteenth Amendment had enshrined in federal law. Now even Ida's right to peacefully demonstrate had been denied her, thanks to the collusion of racist southern whites and timid northerners unwilling to confront them.

Mrs. Trout, Mrs. Welles, and their cohort would likely protest that Ida had not been excluded from the procession; she could march, as long as she contented herself with a segregated section. She would be among her own people, Ida imagined them saying; if those distinguished colored ladies did not object, why should she? Ida would not judge her Black sisters for their choices, but neither would she blindly follow along if those choices contradicted her principles. She would march as an equal or not at all. If she accepted segregation now, if she accepted second-class status now, if she settled for less than she deserved or agreed to relinquish any of her inalienable rights now, what would white suffragists expect her to sacrifice tomorrow? Would they segregate the suffrage amendment itself, altering the language so that white women and white women alone would win the vote? Would they beg her to be patient, to let them secure this partial victory for themselves rather than risk losing everything by insisting upon the controversial inclusion of women of all races? Would they promise to use their new political power, once attained, to secure the vote for Black women, only to defer again and again as new, more important causes demanded their immediate attention?

Ida had seen all this before, and she would not entrust her future and the future of her children and her race to the ephemeral security of empty promises. If her ostensible allies refused to acknowledge her right to march with them as an equal, how could she expect them to recognize her as an equal at the polls?

"Votes for Women" meant "Votes for Black Women." It had to, or Ida and her daughters and her people would find themselves drawn ever backward into the injustices of the past—if not into slavery itself, then into something barely distinguishable from it.

Ida inhaled deeply, steeling herself, and turned north along Seventh Street toward Pennsylvania Avenue. Her college degree qualified her to march in a cap and gown with the College Women. Her professional accomplishments as a journalist, essayist, and author earned her a place among the Writers in their costumes of white and purple. But she had come to Washington as a member of the Illinois delegation due to her status as one of the leading suffrage activists of her state, and she had the stole, cap, and pennant to prove it.

Block by block, the sidewalks grew more crowded, the distant murmur of tens of thousands of voices and footfalls ever louder, more compelling.

She had said that she would march with the Illinois delegation or not at all, but upon reflection, she would amend that vow.

She would march with the Illinois delegation, full stop.

**The Army** of the Hudson had been honored and feted ever since they had arrived in Washington, so when they gathered at the Capitol reflecting pool for a debriefing before marching as a group to their parade staging area, they were astounded to learn that the order of march had been changed. Although they had originally been given a prestigious spot in the Second Section between the Great Demand Banner float and the Baltimore Mounted Brigade, at some point they had been reassigned to the fifth and final section with the state delegations and other miscellaneous groups.

General Jones could offer them no explanation for the last-minute change, since the Congressional Committee had not provided her with one. Some of the pilgrims, indignant and annoyed, protested that the order of march had already been published in all the papers; their many admirers expected to see them in the Second Section, and there the Army of the Hudson must be or their absence would create untold confusion. Almost everyone agreed that their place in the lineup, directly behind the National Men's League for Equal Suffrage, was particularly insulting—to trail behind men, in a women's march for woman suffrage! A few firebrands declared that they must find Dr. Shaw or Miss Paul wherever they might be lurking in the staging area and demand to be reinstated to the Second Section. General Jones and Colonel Craft managed to talk them out of it, reminding them that their duty as loyal soldiers was to obey orders.

"If nothing else," General Jones pointed out, "our new position will put more distance between us and those persistently vexing officers of the National."

After a moment to consider, Maud and her companions conceded that the Fifth Section might not be so dreadful after all, and they would comply with their new orders.

Yet not everyone was happy about it. "Fifth Section," Phoebe fumed as they strode off in neat rows four abreast to find their new staging location. "Our redeployment was motivated by jealousy and spite. This is yet another attempt by the National to diminish our importance and to steal our glory. They cannot bear that we—and the general, especially—have become more famous than they, and so they stick us at the end where they hope we shall escape notice."

"Hey there, Brooklyn Baby!" a young man shouted from across the street, waving his hat in the air to draw Phoebe's attention. "Will you marry me?"

She offered him a quick, tight smile before pulling the hood of her brown cloak forward to conceal her blond curls. "When all this is over and I return home, I hope never to hear that nickname again," she grumbled.

"It doesn't sound like you're entirely happy with your newly acquired fame," Maud observed, hiding a smile.

"Oh, dear me, no. I wish all of the attention would go to General Jones instead."

"She's received an abundant share too."

"And she deserves every word of praise and not one of censure. As for me, I only ever wanted to bring attention to the cause, never to myself." Phoebe waved a hand over her shoulder as if shooing away a pesky fly. "And honestly, what decent young woman has ever accepted a marriage proposal from a brash stranger who shouts at her from across a street?"

"My guess would be very few," said Maud solemnly, struggling not to laugh. Despite their demotion to the tail end of the parade, she was in excellent spirits and would not allow small disappointments to ruin her day. The sidewalks were packed with spectators; the bands were tuning up their instruments, filling the air with merry music; and the Army of the Hudson basked in admiring glances and adulation wherever they turned. They were immediately recognizable by their long brown cloaks, somewhat faded and worn after nearly three weeks of hard use and exposure to the elements, but freshly laundered and charmingly distinct from the other marchers' costumes.

"Perhaps we're looking at this the wrong way," Maud ventured, glancing to her right to include Martha in the conversation. "We're assuming that the reassignment is meant to diminish our importance, to humiliate us. What if it's instead meant to honor us? Saving the best for last, so to speak, so the crowd sticks around for the entire show. Perhaps we're not the footnote, but the grand finale."

Martha nodded thoughtfully, but Phoebe glared, profoundly skeptical. "They put us behind the *men* in a *women's march*," she said, emphasizing each word so there could be no mistaking her meaning.

She made a fair point, so Maud let it go. She was simply glad to be there, in the nation's capital among her sister suffragists beneath clear, sunny skies, marching for a cause she believed in with all her heart.

**At three** o'clock, Alice strained her ears for the silvery trumpet note announcing that the procession had begun, but the appointed hour came and went, and the marchers and bands and floats ahead of her section did not budge. All around her, the College Women held their lines, adjusted their mortarboards, and chatted among themselves, apparently unconcerned with the delay, but after ten agonizing minutes, Alice could not be content to wait and hope. With apologetic smiles for her nearest companions, she withdrew from the lines and quickly strode alongside the forward sections toward the head of the parade. The delay was probably nothing serious, but it wouldn't hurt to check. Fortunately, Hazel knew that her cue to begin the pageant was not the clock but the last note of a relay of trumpet calls sent down Pennsylvania Avenue from Inez's heralding peal. A brief delay at the outset should not throw off their carefully coordinated timing. The vanguard of the procession would still arrive at the Treasury at the climax of the dance, precisely as Alice and Hazel had planned.

As Alice made her way toward the Peace Monument, for a moment she was rendered breathless at the sight of the vast crowds packing the sidewalks, barely held back from spilling over into the streets by decorum and stanchion wire: men, women, children, a great many of them waving flags and holding up banners in suffrage colors—hecklers too, no doubt, but Alice dared hope they would be in the minority. How could President-Elect Wilson fail to take note of everything this unfolding scene represented? How could any reasonable man not see from this marvelous turnout that the tide of public opinion was shifting, that he must ride it or be swept away? Where the people led, the president and Congress must follow, or be tumbled from their high offices.

Alice hurried, but one harried section marshal after another spotted her and begged her to help sort out urgent logistical problems. She dared not refuse, or her neglect could worsen the situation and prolong the delayed start. She listened in vain for Inez's trumpet, hoping that the unknown issue would resolve itself without her, but the thrilling peal never sounded; the procession did not move forward. Perhaps the trumpet itself was the problem, she thought fleetingly as the white marble figures atop the Peace Monument came into view above the milling throng.

Suddenly someone cried out her name and seized her arm; turning, Alice was dumbfounded to discover Glenna Smith Tinnin, the theater director and playwright who had helped Hazel choreograph the pageant. "Shouldn't you be at the Treasury?" Alice asked, glancing past Glenna's shoulder to her assistant, Patricia, breathless and red-cheeked from running to catch up to them.

"I couldn't get my car through the crowd, so I parked it with the committee's." Glenna waved that off, impatient. "There's a problem with the police. Come."

Still grasping Alice's arm, she broke a winding trail through the milling sightseers, past Inez astride Gray Dawn and May with her four elegantly robed aides, to a gathering of about a dozen mounted police officers. Nearby, Lucy Burns, clad in the costume of the New York delegation, stood before a black police sedan, engaged in a heated discussion with a uniformed officer. For one heart-stopping moment Alice feared that their permits had been revoked and they had been ordered to shut everything down. Her heart was in her throat as Glenna plunged ahead, pulling her after, leading her to Lucy and the officer.

After a quick introduction to Police Commissioner Johnson, Alice learned that the procession had not been banned; the delay centered on contradictory instructions given to the police escort about their role, and the commissioner and Lucy were trying to sort it out. Alice had brought along Superintendent Sylvester's most recent letters, and after she showed Commissioner Johnson the relevant sections, they quickly resolved the issue.

"Thank goodness you came along when you did," said Lucy, raising her voice to be heard over the din. "Will you go back to the College Women now?"

"I think not," said Alice, rising up on tiptoe to watch as Commissioner Johnson strode ahead and joined the mounted police, who were apparently awaiting his instructions. "I'll stay here and join them as they pass."

"Then I'll keep you company until the New York delegation arrives," said Lucy.

Alice glanced at her watch. It was almost twenty-five minutes past the hour—a late start, but not irredeemably so, not yet. A quick glance ahead confirmed that the mounted police had moved into position. A low roar of excitement and expectation passed through the nearby crowd. Alice's heart pounded, but although Lucy laughed aloud from sheer delight, Alice kept herself contained, watchful. So much could still go wrong.

Then Inez nudged her magnificent steed forward, poised at the center of Pennsylvania Avenue, the parade marshal and her aides motionless in formation several yards ahead. Inez raised the silver trumpet to her lips and sounded one long, haunting, beautiful note. Its echo lingered as Gray Dawn walked gracefully forward, Inez radiant and regal in the saddle, her long cape cascading down her back, the star on her headpiece glimmering in the late-winter sunlight.

After a momentary pause, the vanguard moved forward, the gleaming black automobiles, the forty ushers in light-blue-and-gold regalia, the first mounted brigade. Behind them, the banner bearers of the First Section gathered themselves as if ready to take flight.

The procession had begun.

**As the** Presidential Special chugged into Union Station, Woodrow Wilson felt entirely content, even serene, humbly aware of the profound responsibilities that would soon be his, but confident in his ability to master them. Although he looked forward to crossing the threshold of the White House—inspecting the Oval Office, convening his cabinet in the Blue Room, basking in his wife's proud, loving gaze as they strolled through the Colonial Garden—already he felt a pang of nostalgia for Princeton. Upon his departure earlier that morning, the students had serenaded him with a stirring, heartfelt rendition of "Old Nassau," their beloved alma mater, as well as other cherished college songs. Next, 560 students and faculty, eight railcars full, had boarded the train to accompany him on this journey and to witness his inauguration. A ninth car was packed with members of the press, an inescapable and occasionally useful encumbrance. Accompanying him in the luxurious state car were his family, members of the inaugural committee, advisors and potential cabinet members, and other dignitaries. The campaign had accustomed him to traveling with an entourage, and his years as governor had prepared him for a certain excess of ceremony, but sometimes he longed for an academic's relative anonymity, to once again be able to stroll a quiet, leafy quadrangle on his way from library to lecture hall, recognized by few others aside from his respectful colleagues and worshipful pupils.

The train halted at the platform. Wilson rose and offered his wife his arm, and she rewarded him with a radiant smile. They lingered in the state railcar while the Princeton contingent disembarked and formed two parallel lines facing inward, a corridor through which he would pass as he disembarked, a symbolic transition from one significant role in public life to another, even greater one.

He helped his wife and daughters down from the train, nodded to his gentlemen companions, and paused for a moment at the head of the two lines while the Princeton men removed their hats and placed them over their hearts. Moved by the solemn gesture, with great dignity Wilson led his family, his advisors, and his companions through the lines, down the platform, and into the station. Glancing ahead to the tall double doors of the exit, he reflected that when he passed through them, he would step out into the grand capital of the proud and glorious nation that had chosen him to lead it through the next four years.

As the liveried doormen opened the doors in perfect unison, he braced himself for thunderous applause and earsplitting cheers, reassuringly patting his wife's hand where it rested in the crook of his arm to prepare her as well. She was so gentle and delicate, as befit a woman; she would have to learn new courage as First Lady.

He stepped outside to meet the public and accept their welcome. Moving from the dimly lit building to the bright afternoon sunlight, he was momentarily blinded; he blinked, confused by the polite smattering of applause that greeted him. He blinked again; only a dozen or so smiling, clapping citizens stood there, at a respectful distance from the foot of the stairs. He descended in a daze, remembering to nod to the gentlemen and tip his hat to the ladies.

He and his entourage climbed aboard a trio of gleaming black automobiles that would carry them to the Shoreham Hotel, their home until the inauguration, after which they would move into the Executive Mansion. Overcoming his stunned speechlessness, Wilson asked the driver, "Where are all the people?"

"Everyone's on Pennsylvania Avenue," the younger man replied, with a bemused shake of his head. "They're all watching the suffragists' parade."

Wilson felt his mouth twitch, but he quickly masked his annoyance. "How long will—"

He broke off as the police superintendent leading his security detail approached the vehicle, his various insignia, brass buttons, and gold epaulets indicating his exalted rank. "I beg your pardon, sir," Superintendent Sylvester greeted Wilson through the open window. To the driver, he added, "Follow me and stay close. We're going to have to take a roundabout route to Fifteenth and H Streets. Pennsylvania Avenue is packed."

"Because of a suffrage parade?" queried Wilson, incredulous and irritable.

"Yes, sir, but it's nothing for you to worry about," said the superintendent. "I've called in the cavalry from Fort Myer to assist."

"Might not be enough," the driver replied, adjusting various knobs in preparation for departure. "I hear the women won't be able to get through."

"They'll get through," the superintendent said grimly. He offered Wilson a curt bow and strode off to his own vehicle, and soon they were under way.

As his wife and daughters peered through the windows, eagerly taking in their first glimpses of Washington and marveling at this and that, Wilson kept his gaze fixed firmly on the road ahead, jaw tight from the effort of concealing his perturbation.

**Alice and** Lucy had climbed to a higher vantage point as they awaited the arrival of their respective sections, and they watched in consternation as a few yards ahead of the parade marshal and at numerous more distant points as far as they could discern, men were leaping over or slipping under the stanchion wire, spilling onto Pennsylvania Avenue, undeterred by the Boy Scouts' outstretched arms and gestures and shouts to keep back. Slowly the procession crawled ahead two blocks, then three, then four. Suddenly the crowd of men surged forward on both sides around

May, her aides, and the color guard, cutting them off from the rest of the vanguard.

Beside her, Lucy gasped and seized Alice's arm. "The escort, they don't see—"

"I know," replied Alice, heart thudding in her ears. Thirteen black police sedans in a V formation like migrating birds were slowly proceeding west along the avenue just ahead of the mounted police escort, wedging the crowd aside and leaving a clear path for the suffrage procession in their wake. But no sooner had a space been cleared behind them than the milling throng filled it, whooping and shouting just ahead of the procession vanguard, forcing May and her companions to a halt while the police escort forged ahead, oblivious.

White-hot sparks of anger and indignation fired Alice into action. "Come on," she urged Lucy, pulling her forward. "Let's get to the cars."

"Cars?" Lucy echoed, hurrying after, but Alice did not have time to remind her of the committee's vehicles parked southwest of the Capitol in anticipation of emergencies requiring swift trips back and forth to headquarters. They ran as swiftly as they could, dodging spectators, Alice keeping her mortarboard on her head with one hand and holding up the edge of her academic gown with the other. When they arrived, breathless,

Alice was relieved to discover Glenna and her assistant climbing into two of the cars, apparently inspired by the same thought that had struck Alice.

Alice and Lucy claimed the third car, and after a quick shouted conference, the four women sped off on a course parallel to the Avenue, then cut sharply north to intercept the front of the procession. They arrived in time to witness Inez charging the crowd on Gray Dawn, struggling to clear the way through to the police escort. Glenna, in the lead car, pulled in front of the parade marshal and her aides, while Alice and Lucy in their car and Patricia in the other maneuvered into flanking positions. Slowly but relentlessly, they drove forward, herding the men, most of them drunk and all of them obnoxious, out of the way, the earsplitting roar of their harsh, belligerent cries an almost physical force against them. Steadily they gained ground, giving the vanguard space to regroup. With Lucy behind the wheel, Alice leapt from the passenger side and strode ahead, pushing stragglers out of the way with her bare hands; they were so astonished that they instinctively drew back. On the other flank, Patricia had been forced to halt rather than run the men over, so she parked her car, stood on the running board, and shouted through a megaphone for them to move aside.

Some obeyed, but most did not. Glancing back over

her shoulder, Alice discovered that the First Section had caught up with the vanguard, and the procession was once again whole, but the crowd was pressing in from all sides, slowing them down to a crawl, forcing them from lines of four abreast in some places to three in others, or two, or single file. The mob roared with taunts and insults and vicious laughter. A cry of pain rang out above the din. Alice turned in time to see an usher pressing her hand to her cheek, already glowing red from the sting of a slap; a man who had dealt the blow stood before her, jeering; a police officer looked on from the sidewalk with cold eyes and a chilling, arrogant smile. All around, red-faced men were shouting expletives at the marchers, pinching them, groping them, tearing off their suffrage badges and sashes, ripping banners from floats and from marchers' hands and trampling them underfoot.

So much beauty and dignity spoiled at the hands of these wretched men. Smoldering with outrage, Alice climbed back into the car and urged Lucy onward. They would hold together and fight for every inch of the length of Pennsylvania Avenue if it took them all day.

**Standing on** the southeast corner of Pennsylvania and Seventh, nearly the midpoint of the parade route, Ida watched in dismay as men gleefully circumvented the flimsy wire barriers and dodged the brave but over-matched Boy Scouts, swarming into the avenue, tens of thousands of them as far as she could see in both directions. She searched in vain for the police who ought to sweep in at any moment to restore order, but the few officers she spied hung back, some looking queasily afraid, others indulgently amused.

Perhaps the mob would move off as the procession approached, Ida thought uneasily. Perhaps the police escort was keeping the avenue clear immediately ahead of the parade, so although they were doing nothing in Ida's vicinity, by the time the vanguard arrived, the chaos here would be quelled. She thought of her friends in the Illinois delegation, of the many hours they had spent perfecting their maneuvers. Her heart sank to imagine them forced to wend their way through that vicious crowd, single file, holding hands in a brave attempt to maintain some semblance of their lines.

Craning her neck and rising up on tiptoe, Ida peered down the avenue, hoping for a glimpse of the approaching procession in the distance. Perhaps even now they were moving forward in regal splendor behind the shield wall of their police escort, safe within the eye of a hurricane, calm amid chaos. But it was no use. Although she imagined she heard a low roar in the distance, like a roll of thunder beyond the horizon, she saw no sign of the herald on her magnificent white steed, no flags or banners aside from those on the buildings.

"I beg your pardon," a man spoke behind her, his accent reminiscent of her adopted midwestern hometown. "Are you Mrs. Wells-Barnett?"

Wary, she turned to discover a handsome young Black man peering at her hopefully. He wore an impeccably neat but modest dark suit, and his charcoal-gray felt hat was adorned with a green feather tucked into a purple band—a nod to the suffragists' colors, perhaps, or merely happenstance. He looked to be no more than ten years older than her eldest son, and he carried a notebook and a pencil, those ubiquitous tools of the journalist.

"I am," she replied. She did not flatter herself that he recognized her from a lecture or an author portrait. Although she was standing among the spectators, her white trig stole and blue-starred cap identified her as a member of the Illinois delegation, and she was, or had been, the only Black woman in that group.

He smiled, pleased by his chance discovery, but then his brow furrowed. "Why aren't you marching in the procession? I see you're dressed for it." He gestured past her to the rowdy white men carousing in the middle of Pennsylvania Avenue. "Did these charming fellows make you change your mind?"

"Not at all," she said. "I've faced worse than these in my day."

"I know you have," he said, nodding emphatically, as if he was familiar with her exploits. Although he didn't open his notebook, his grip tightened around his pencil, and she knew he longed to take notes. "I'm Caleb Jackson with the *Detroit Free Press.* Do you mind if I ask you a few questions?"

Ida glanced east down the avenue, but there was still no sign of the procession. "I suppose I have time."

"Thank you, ma'am." He hesitated. "Is it true that Miss Paul and Dr. Shaw segregated the suffrage parade? Is that why you're standing here instead of marching in the colored section?"

Ida chose her words carefully. "Someone at the National wanted to segregate the parade, in deference to southern white women's demands, but I don't know exactly who made the decision and who merely delivered the message."

"I see," he mused aloud, opening his notebook.

"Be that as it may," she continued, "the Illinois suffragists want me to march in their section, and so I shall. I don't believe the land of Lincoln is going to permit Alabama or Georgia or any other state to begin to dictate to it now."

He nodded, glancing up at her appraisingly as he

wrote. "And yet, ma'am, the parade has begun, and you aren't with the Illinois delegation."

"I await them here," she said, as if it were eminently reasonable and did not require explanation. "When the Illinois delegation comes along, I'll join them."

He smiled and thanked her for her time, looking both satisfied with her answers and pleased with himself for acquiring them exclusively. She turned her attention back to the parade route. Where *was* the Illinois delegation? She glanced at her watch; forty-five minutes had passed since the trumpet relay had announced the start of the procession. Several blocks to the west, at the Treasury, the allegorical pageant was surely well under way.

Despite the delayed start, the vanguard of the procession really ought to have reached her by now. Apprehension swept over her as she checked her watch again, and again glanced east down Pennsylvania Avenue. What was keeping them?

**A full** hour passed before the Army of the Hudson, inching forward one moment and forced to an abrupt halt the next, reached the Peace Monument and the official launching site of the procession. From her new vantage point Maud suddenly understood why: a sea of people, virtually all of them men, had flooded

Pennsylvania Avenue as far before them as her eye could see. Shouting, snarling men seized marchers by the arms and shoulders and flung them to the pavement, or reached up and grabbed their ankles and tried to yank them off their floats. They ripped down banners and snatched at horses' reins, knocked instruments from musicians' hands and tore marchers' clothing.

Then the pilgrims stepped onto the Avenue and were suddenly swept up into the fray, shoved closer together by the crush of the mob, their lines collapsing, so that every stumbling step forward was an effort. Maud had faced belligerent crowds before, all along the road from New York to Washington, but none that frightened her as this one did. Their numbers were immeasurable, their malice gleeful and inexhaustible. Occasionally a rioter would recognize their brown pilgrims' cloaks and let out a cheer, but it would be swiftly drowned out by the surging waves of catcalls, jeers, threats, and cursing. A few yards ahead, Maud thought she spotted a clearing just after the Men's League cars. The pilgrims could regroup there if they could only reach it—but as they doggedly pressed on, the spot of calm moved ahead of them with the pace of the procession, unobtainable.

A bullish man plowed into their ranks, sending two

pilgrims sprawling. Farther ahead, Maud saw a large, red-faced man spit a long stream of tobacco juice into the face of a gray-haired Quaker woman.

"Why are you just standing there?" Maud shouted frantically to a nearby policeman. "Help us!"

"I can't do anything with this crowd," he shouted back from the sidewalk, smirking as he folded his arms over his barrel chest. "And I ain't gonna try. No one asked you girlies to come here."

Gritting her teeth, Maud watched as a young man shoved a woman from the Oregon delegation in the back, knocking her to her hands and knees in the path of several companions, who stumbled over her and nearly fell themselves. Growling low in her throat, Maud broke ranks, shoved her way alongside the marchers, and hurled herself at the man, pummeling him with her fists and screaming at him to leave them alone.

Suddenly she felt hands seize her, heard fabric tear, felt herself hauled backward. "Go home, girlie," the barrel-chested policeman yelled, giving her a teeth-rattling shake, his face inches from hers, spittle flying. "Go home!"

She wrested her torn cloak free from his grasp, spun about, and dove back into the ranks of pilgrims.

"Forward," General Jones shouted at the head of

their column, gesturing with her walking staff. "Forward, pilgrims! Forward to victory!"

*Victory?* Maud wondered, exchanging a bewildered glance with Phoebe. Yet the general's shout inspired them, and newly determined, they slogged on, the way forward more treacherous than the worst of the muddy, ice-slicked roads they had traversed on their long hike to Washington. Suddenly, glancing ahead down Pennsylvania Avenue, Maud understood the general's jubilant cry. Though the suffragists were beset on all sides by the mob, those who had escaped injury continued ever forward. Their lines had been knocked asunder, but they had not quit the field; though many of them were bloodied and battered, their clothing torn and nerves shattered, they had not fled. Well aware that the worst of their trials might yet lie before them, they nonetheless persisted. They refused to scatter, to abandon cause and comrades.

Suddenly Maud heard Phoebe shriek in alarm. "Not them," she lamented, her voice high and trembling. "Not now!"

Maud followed her line of sight, and her heart plummeted to discover about twenty young men in the coats and scarves of Maryland Agricultural College forcing their way through the crowd toward them. The bullies of College Park had returned to torment them anew, when they were already on the ropes and exhausted from the struggle.

"Hurrah for General Jones," one of the students shouted, and his companions took up the cry.

Breathless, astonished, Maud watched as the students fell into formation ahead of General Jones and alongside their ragged lines. Chins down, shoulders braced, forearms raised to chest height, the young men rushed the crowd, forcing the rioters back, shouting and shoving, reforming their offensive line and plunging forward again, driving back the mob, clearing the way for General Jones to stride ahead unimpeded as the pilgrims quickly fell into ranks behind her.

Maud could hardly believe it.

Catching her breath, lengthening her stride, she marched on with the Army of the Hudson. "Votes for women," she called out, and laughed aloud from wonder and delight as the reformed and redeemed young college men echoed her cry.

**Fighting for** every inch of ground, Alice and Lucy and a handful of brave Boy Scouts strode between the embattled police escort and the vanguard, hearts pounding from exertion, throats hoarse from shouting, ever watchful for new incursions into the vulnerable clearing they created a few paces before the procession.

They had just crossed Fourteenth Street when suddenly the mob ahead surged toward them with a new, almost fearful urgency. Beyond them, Alice perceived a disruption in the swirling ebb and flow of the crowd—and then, moments later, she saw men on horseback swiftly approaching. It was the cavalry from Fort Myer, she realized as the troops sped past the District police, charged into the mob, turned the horses about, and charged again, sending the rioters scattering.

At last the parade route was clear.

Consternation warred with relief in Alice's heart as the procession completed the last few blocks unimpeded. If only the cavalry had arrived earlier. If only they had been deployed from the outset. Alice glanced over her shoulder and saw that the marchers, floats, and bands were quickly falling into order, regaining much of the splendor that had been so beautifully displayed in the staging area. It was some consolation to know that the rest of the procession would pass before the grandstands almost as gloriously as she had imagined, except for the torn banners and damaged floats.

They approached the Treasury, where Alice figured the pageant must have concluded more than an hour before. As she passed the plaza, silently lamenting the loss of the magnificent spectacle that should have been, the performers dashed from the building, took their

places, and assumed their regal poses. Alice's spirits
rose. It was not the choreography nor the timing she
and Hazel had planned, yet the scene was profound
and moving nonetheless.

They marched on, around the north side of the
Ellipse and past the South Lawn of the White House.
Would she and the suffragist delegation meet President Wilson there in the days ahead? Would he be impressed by what they had accomplished that day, and
by all they had endured in the years before, they and
all the generations of women who had fought for equal
suffrage since the founding of their republic?

Would President Wilson heed their clarion call for
justice and equality, or would he take the easy path of
callous indifference, like all the other powerful men
who had preceded him in that place?

**A murmur** of excitement passed through the spectators on the sidewalk from west to east, and by the time
it reached Ida, it had swelled into a roar. She watched,
astonished, as the cavalry rushed onto the scene, scattering the raucous men before them, sending them
scrambling into the gutters or leaping for the sidewalks.
In a few minutes, Pennsylvania Avenue was clear, and
for the first time the procession could move ahead unimpeded, as should have been possible all along.

"Better late than never," Ida murmured, shaking her head, eagerly searching the procession for the banner of the state delegations. Passing before her at the moment were the sections devoted to various professions—floats and marchers representing nurses, homemakers, women in the law and in education and in business, teachers and social workers, and so many others. Ida found the implicit argument difficult to refute: If women contributed so much to society and the economy, should they not also have a voice in selecting their government's leaders?

The procession passed, dignified and marvelous now that the marchers no longer need struggle for every step forward. At last the state delegations came into view, the nine states where women already had equal suffrage given pride of place in front, with the others following in alphabetical order behind a banner declaring them STATES WORKING FOR EQUAL SUFFRAGE.

Murmuring apologies, Ida made her way through the spectators to the edge of the sidewalk. Women from Florida marched proudly by, then ladies from Georgia, and then the familiar banner of the Illinois delegation appeared. Drawing herself up, Ida boldly stepped out onto the avenue, matched her strides to the marchers', maneuvered between the lines, and assumed her rightful place between Virginia and Belle.

Her friends cried out in surprise and joy. "Where have you been?" Virginia asked. "We waited for you. We wouldn't have let you march alone."

"We thought perhaps you joined the authors or teachers," said Belle. "Our worst fear was that you had gone home to Chicago."

"And miss all the fun?" replied Ida, more loudly than necessary. She glanced around defiantly, waiting for any of her fellow delegates to challenge her right to be there. Some of them smiled brightly back at her; others were too embarrassed to meet her gaze. *As well they should be,* Ida thought as she marched on, flanked by her friends. As for the women who had preferred to exclude her rather than stand up to the National, Ida would accept their apologies later, if they were brave enough to offer them.

For the moment, marching exactly where she deserved to be was satisfaction enough.

**Striding briskly** down Pennsylvania Avenue, the way before them clear at last and the Treasury now in sight, Maud and her companions basked in the cheers of the crowd. Now when spectators ducked under the stanchion wires and rushed forward, it was to offer bouquets to General Jones until her arms fairly overflowed with them. Women and men alike tossed flower petals in their path, and the air rang with applause and glad shouts.

Happy tears filled Maud's eyes, and she quickly blinked them away. They were coming to the end of the march—and somehow, after so many miles and blisters and jeers, she could not bear for it to be over.

Soon thereafter they came to the Ellipse, where they discovered hundreds of marchers from the first four sections lining both sides of the street, showering them with applause. Their own difficult march finished, they had lingered to welcome the pilgrims, who had endured so much just to get to Washington. And yet every difficulty and confrontation along those 250 miles had prepared them well for what they had faced on Pennsylvania Avenue that day.

They had reached the end. Colonel Craft called them to a halt, but before they disbanded for the last time and headed off to the rally at Continental Hall, General Jones indulged them with one last speech, bidding them farewell and thanking them for their cooperation, devotion, and loyalty.

Maud would have done it all again, every grueling mile of it, for the cause of woman suffrage, for the noble ideals of equality and liberty, and for the brave women who had marched by her side.

# 28
# March 1913
## WASHINGTON, D.C.

### Alice

Long after the last marchers completed the route, Alice remained at the disbanding area to supervise the removal of the floats from the Ellipse, to confer with section leaders, and to respond to questions from the press. When prompted, she readily offered her opinion of the shockingly inadequate police response and the last-minute, partial rescue by the Fort Myer cavalry, but as for the number and nature of the assaults and injuries, Alice could only describe what she herself had observed. A thorough understanding of what had happened that day would have to come later.

After the procession was fully disbanded, instead of reporting to Continental Hall for the celebratory rally, where she was expected to address a full house of marchers and supporters, Alice made her way alone to 1420 F Street Northwest. The front door to the Congressional Committee headquarters was locked, the lights extinguished, but she knew from the loose stacks of flyers scattered on a table and the piles of suffrage banners and sashes strewn on desks and chairs throughout the main room that many of her volunteers had stopped by after the march, perhaps to tend minor wounds and repair torn clothing before hurrying off to the rally.

Over the past six months, whenever Alice had contemplated the aftermath of the procession, she had expected to feel proud and satisfied with a job well done. Now that the moment had come, she felt drained, numb, ineffably weary. The suffragists had completed the march, and widespread publicity for the cause was all but certain, so in that sense, the procession had succeeded. Yet the chaos and ugliness that had erupted where she had endeavored to evoke beauty and dignity had stolen any sense of triumph she might have taken from the day.

She would have to shake off her disappointment, take a deep breath, and carry on. She had no other choice, not with so much work to be done.

There were letters to write, reports to file, so Alice

withdrew to her office, unpinned her mortarboard, and sat down at Susan B. Anthony's desk, soothed by the unexpected solitude and the familiar rhythms of reading, writing, contemplation. Not knowing whether the dispersed mobs would seek new targets, she had locked the front door behind her and quickly became absorbed in her work. More than two hours later, a persistent knocking broke her concentration. Caught unaware by twilight, she carefully made her way through the cluttered main room, flipped a light switch, and answered the knock. Standing on the stoop was Winifred Mallon, correspondent for the *Chicago Tribune,* whose Washington bureau was just across the street.

"We were expecting you at the rally," Winifred said, hands in her pockets, brow furrowed from concern. "I thought perhaps you had been injured in the mayhem."

"I took a few bumps and bruises, but I'm fine." Alice opened the door wider so the reporter could enter. "I had some work to do, so I thought I should take advantage of having the whole office to myself."

Winifred looked skeptical, but she forwent the opportunity to probe deeper. "The conduct of the police was an absolute disgrace," she said instead. "I myself witnessed an officer tear down the stanchion wire at Fifteenth Street to allow the mob to fill Pennsylvania Avenue. Others just stood on the sidewalks, smirking, doing absolutely nothing as women were being groped and pinched and shoved to the pavement right before their eyes! As for the mounted police, they seemed absolutely powerless to hold back the rioters."

"They weren't, though," said Alice shortly, showing Winifred to a seat, taking one for herself. "Powerless, I mean. I spent most of the procession on foot near the vanguard, walking up to the crowd and pushing people back with my hands. That was all there was to it. The police could have stopped the disorder immediately if they had been determined to. The Boy Scouts were the only ones who did any effective police work today."

Winifred studied her. "You don't mean that the officers intentionally failed to do their duty?"

"You saw it yourself," Alice replied. "Failure was inevitable. It was meant to happen."

"Well, you're not alone in that opinion." Winifred retrieved a notebook from her coat pocket, leafed through it to a half-filled page, and read aloud. "When Dr. Shaw addressed the rally, she said, 'Never was I so ashamed of our national capital before. The women in the parade showed wonderful dignity and self-respect by keeping cool in the midst of insults and lewd remarks.'"

"I wholeheartedly agree."

"Mrs. Catt called for a congressional investigation. After the last speaker, a resolution condemning the police for their conduct passed by a unanimous vote."

Alice could well imagine how Superintendent Sylvester would react to that. She had tried to warn him. She could not imagine what more she could have done to convince him that his forces were inadequate, and it gave her no satisfaction to have been proven right.

Alice and the reporter spoke for a few minutes more, but eventually Winifred hurried off to file her stories. Alone again, Alice considered resuming her work, but decided instead to close the office and return to her boardinghouse. She ran into Lucy in the parlor, and over cups of tea and sandwiches, they reflected on the events of the day. Not shying away from their own shortcomings, they mused aloud about what their next steps should be.

The next day, the newspapers laid the facts bare: Five thousand marchers and an estimated quarter of a million spectators had come to Pennsylvania Avenue for the procession. One hundred women had been hospitalized, including more than two dozen with fractures or deep wounds. Eight men had been treated for drunkenness, and eight more arrested for disorderly conduct. Eyewitness reports were filled with praise for the marchers—seasoned with the usual condescending, stereotypical depictions of women as overly concerned with hairstyles and fashion even in a moment of crisis— and with blistering condemnation for the police. "No inauguration has ever produced such scenes, which in many instances amounted to little less than riots," the *Washington Post* noted. "Police Must Face Charges," the *Fort Wayne Sentinel* declared. "Failed to Protect Suffrage Parade Against Hoodlums. Scene Was Shameful." The *Detroit Free Press* condemned the rioters and police almost in the same breath: "Hoodlums Ruin Splendid March of Suffragists. Several Thousand Women in Gorgeous Costumes Bravely Battle Rowdies in Riotous Washington. Skirts Torn Off Marchers by Drunken Assailants Whom Many Police Fail Utterly to Restrain." Winifred's *Chicago Tribune* concurred. "From beginning to end the police mismanagement was the worst in the world," an editorial noted. "To say that Major Sylvester, superintendent of police, is being criticized here would be putting things mildly."

Later that day, after Woodrow Wilson took the oath of office and became the twenty-eighth president of the United States, the police maintained perfect order at his inaugural parade. The spectators who lined Pennsylvania Avenue on Tuesday, March 4, were practically the same people who had disrupted the suffrage procession the previous day, which proved conclusively to

Alice and her comrades what Superintendent Sylvester's forces could have done for the women's march if they had applied themselves. She said precisely that to the reporters who sought her out for comment.

If there was a silver lining to be found, Alice surmised, it was this: As far as press coverage was concerned, in comparison to the woman suffrage march, Woodrow Wilson's presidential inauguration was barely an afterthought. Although she knew the rowdy hoodlums and indifferent police had generated most of the headlines, so many of the articles also mentioned the impressive floats, the beautiful costumes, and the steadfast courage of the marchers that she dared hope the true message of the procession had gotten through. Perhaps it would even reach citizens who had never before paid much attention to the suffrage cause.

The procession had not turned out as Alice had hoped and planned, but perhaps it had still accomplished its purpose.

Even as Vice President Thomas Marshall was enjoying a ball in his honor—President Wilson had refused one—and much of Washington was celebrating the inauguration at public festivals throughout the city, Alice, Lucy, and a few select volunteers were ensconced at headquarters, preparing to send a delegation to the White House, in optimistic anticipation of a meeting with President Wilson, although he had not yet consented. When Alice read a transcript of his inaugural address in the evening paper, she was disappointed but not surprised to learn that he had not mentioned woman suffrage. He had spoken of change, and of looking critically upon old habits and customs "with fresh, awakened eyes," and of being "refreshed by new insight," but this was in the context of his campaign promises to overhaul corrupt and oppressive American business practices. And yet perhaps there was reason to hope. Perhaps woman suffrage could fit into his agenda of national reform somehow.

As for the letter Alice had taken from General Jones in Bladensburg, the message from Dr. Anna Shaw urging President Wilson to mention suffrage in his inaugural address had become obsolete. There was no point in delivering it now, but Alice would pursue a meeting between the president and the officers of the National nonetheless. They could instead ask President Wilson to recommend an equal suffrage amendment to the Constitution when he addressed a special session of Congress in April.

Early the next morning, the U.S. Senate passed two resolutions regarding the events of March 3. The first called on the commissioners of the District of Columbia and Superintendent Sylvester to explain why they had not carried out a congressional resolution of March 1, which had ordered them to halt all traffic on Pennsylvania Avenue from the Peace Monument to Seventeenth during the parade and "to prevent any interference with the suffrage procession on that day." A second resolution provided for an investigation of "the failure of the police to clear the avenue and preserve order." In the House, Alabama representative Richmond P. Hobson declared his intention to request a House investigation into the police department's failures. To that end, he requested that all members of the public who had observed police neglect or mistreatment of the marchers file affidavits with his office or with the National's Congressional Committee at 1420 F Street Northwest.

With very little notice, Alice, Lucy, and their volunteers scrambled to clear away the detritus of the march and to arrange the main office to best accommodate the interviewing of witnesses in the presence of a notary public. They had already taken more than a dozen statements by the time the afternoon mail arrived, bringing Alice a surprisingly warm, supportive letter from Dr. Anna Shaw praising her for her "splendid work" in arranging the procession. "Too much credit cannot be given to you and Miss Burns and the others who are responsible for all this," Dr. Shaw had written. "While it may seem to you that the work of all these months was lost in the fact that the parade as a spectacular display was destroyed, nevertheless I think it has done more for suffrage and will do more for suffrage in the end than the parade itself would have done."

Alice wanted to believe her. If some greater good came from the senseless ruin of the march as she had envisioned it, she must consider the sacrifice worthwhile.

A steady stream of witnesses eager to share their stories called at headquarters throughout that day and the next. Letters and telegrams began pouring into the offices as well, some offering testimony, others simply expressing indignation or outrage over how the suffragists had been treated. Sympathetic messages arrived from all corners of the nation, not only from proud suffragists but also from people who confessed that they had never really given much thought to woman suffrage before, though they were certainly thinking about it now. Except for a few male Antis who wrote to brag that they had joined in the mayhem and had no regrets, the people seemed unanimous in their belief that the police should have protected the marchers better. The officers' personal disdain for the movement was no excuse for failing to do their jobs.

As for the female Antis down the block, on the morning of March 5, Mrs. Dodge announced to the press that the National Association Opposed to Woman's Suffrage had decided to cease campaigning in the city for the time being. They would close their headquarters that very day.

"Washington is sick of hearing of suffrage," she told the *Evening Star*. "We will give the people here a rest for a time. We feel that the exhibition put on by the suffragists on Monday has helped our cause. At some later date we will reopen, but in the meantime, we shall begin immediately to collect facts to fight the attempt of the suffragists to get a constitutional amendment."

By late afternoon, the Antis had cleared their front window of literature and had locked their doors for the last time.

Soon thereafter, Alice received word that she would be called upon to testify before the Senate.

For the next few days, Alice and her volunteers raced to gather evidence for both the House investigation and the Senate hearing. The hearing before the Senate subcommittee opened on March 6, and throughout the twelve days of questioning and testimony, the chamber was packed with observers, mostly women, with nearly one hundred more crowding the corridors outside the room and begging for admission. One by one, Superintendent Sylvester, former secretary of war Stimson, General Johnston, and other men responsible for security in the District were compelled to account for their preparations before the procession and their actions during it. Many suffragists who had participated in the march, including the official historian of General Jones's Army of the Hudson, testified about the abuses and neglect they experienced. Their testimony was confirmed by many spectators who took the stand and described the outrageous scenes they had witnessed. A great many police officers who had been on duty that day were also questioned under oath about their own behavior as well as their commander's.

Alice was astonished on March 8 when, during two and a half hours of testimony, Superintendent Sylvester repeatedly disavowed any personal responsibility for the breach of the peace, blaming the failure on ineffective officers who had not carried out his orders. "I did my duty," he declared, evoking sardonic smiles and eye rolls from the suffragists in the gallery. "I exhausted every effort I could as an official, the head of the police department, to furnish the paraders the protection which should have been theirs. My conscience is clear."

Superintendent Sylvester went on to explain, in minute detail, the procedures he had followed to ensure the safety of the procession, including a vast number of specific duty assignments and his repeated emphasis during roll calls that the police must not allow their personal opinions about woman suffrage to interfere with their duties. When he had finished, Senator Wesley L. Jones frowned bemusedly. "How, then, do you account for their failure to preserve order?"

"I cannot account for it," the superintendent replied. "The failure of the police to protect was contrary to discipline, contrary to law, contrary to justice, contrary to my orders, and any man who failed to do his part to protect these women should be instantly dismissed."

A murmur arose from the gallery, but Senator Jones raised a hand for silence. "Then if the Avenue was not properly cleared by three o'clock on the day of the parade," he queried, his gaze fixed on the witness, "in your judgment, the men and officers on duty did not do their jobs?"

"Yes, sir, that is my judgment," Superintendent Sylvester replied firmly. "I was surprised and shocked when I reached Pennsylvania Avenue, after escorting the president-elect to his hotel, to find that the crowd had overflowed into the street all along the line, instead of only at the point where the ropes had broken."

Alice exchanged a pointed look with Lucy, who had accompanied her to the Senate for moral support. They had personally seen what an ineffective barrier the stanchion wire had been. It strained credulity that a man of Superintendent Sylvester's experience would not have known how inadequate it would be to the task of restraining a quarter of a million people.

Soon thereafter, Alice was called to the stand for the first time. A standing-room-only crowd hung on her every word as she informed the committee that in the months leading up to the march, she and her colleagues had repeatedly appealed to Superintendent Sylvester and the War Department for sufficient police protection. "The District authorities would refer us to the War Department," she said, "and the War Department would tell us that if there was any trouble, the fault would be with the District authorities."

Even earlier than that, Alice explained, when they were seeking a permit for Pennsylvania Avenue, Superintendent Sylvester had attempted to discourage them from holding the procession at all by warning that the vast numbers of men in town for the inauguration would be disorderly, and that he had too few men at his disposal to sufficiently protect the suffragists. "When we finally were granted a permit, I reminded the superintendent of these statements, and I urged him to request aid from the War Department," Alice said, keeping a level gaze fixed on the presiding senators so she would not be tempted to glare accusingly at Superintendent Sylvester. "This, he did not do."

Her remarks seemed to be well-received, but Superintendent Sylvester's decision to blame his men and to accept no responsibility for himself did not play well in the Senate chamber or in the press. Nonetheless, supporters hastened to defend him. Over the next few days, several respected businessmen, politicians, and military officers vehemently argued that he was a truly exemplary officer and an honorable man, but to Alice, it seemed that they convincingly lauded his character without absolving him of wrongdoing in this particular case. From what she observed, his strongest defense, ironically enough, came from the very rank-and-file policemen he had blamed for the fiasco. When called to the stand, the men naturally began by defending their own actions, but each also insisted that their superintendent had issued reasonable orders well in advance of the procession, called for reinforcements when the need became apparent, and been active and in command on the ground. No one could have anticipated the size of the crowd or its unruliness, they argued, and if Superintendent Sylvester had been unable to maintain order, that was only because it was an impossible task.

On March 17, the special session of Congress concluded, bringing the hearing to an end before a verdict was reached, even before all witnesses had been called. When the committee adjourned, Senator Jones said that the next meeting would be at the call of the chairman, which indicated that there would be no additional hearings until the first session of Congress opened in mid-April.

Alice was less disappointed than many of her colleagues and volunteers. She wanted those responsible for the lawlessness on Pennsylvania Avenue to be held accountable, but she could not spare any more time for the hearings and investigations at the expense of the Congressional Committee's central mission: advocacy for a constitutional amendment.

Then, unexpectedly, on the same day the hearings concluded, Alice and her comrades were given reason to hope they had moved much closer to their ultimate goal.

President Wilson consented to meet with their delegation at the White House on March 17.

Representative John E. Raker—a Democrat from California's Second District, an ardent suffragist, and a good friend of William and Elizabeth Kent—had agreed to introduce the delegation to the president. Dressed in modest, dignified suits in somber colors, the five women—Anna Kelton Wiley, Alma Marie Stone, Mary Dixon, Ida Husted Harper, and Alice herself—walked together from their F Street headquarters to the White House, where at eleven o'clock Representative Raker met them outside and escorted them through the front portico and upstairs to the reception room outside the executive offices. A group of photographers found them there—by chance or by prior arrangement, Alice did not know—and convinced them to pose for a portrait.

Soon thereafter, the women were led into the East Room, where five chairs had been placed in a row in the center of the room, with a sixth chair facing them. Alice had little time to ponder the arrangement before President Wilson entered, accompanied by an aide. He was tall and thin, with a long, narrow face; Alice's first impression was that his high forehead and protruding jaw were more pronounced in person than in photographs. His lips were thin and unsmiling, and his cold blue-gray eyes regarded them sternly through round, rimless spectacles.

Introductions were made and he invited them to sit, his manner chivalrous but vaguely amused. As he took the chair facing them, Alice had the sudden, fleeting sense of the delegation as unruly students called before a professor for a scolding. The women had agreed beforehand that she would be the first to speak, and after thanking the president for consenting to see them, she got right to the point and requested that he recommend the submission of a constitutional amendment providing for equal suffrage in his upcoming address to Congress.

"I have no opinion on woman suffrage," President Wilson replied. "I've never given the subject any thought. My priorities at the moment are my campaign pledges to revise the currency and reform tariffs."

Alice could not believe that he had never given woman suffrage a single passing thought, but she did not call him out on his duplicity. "Mr. President," she said instead, "we represent several million voters and other women, currently disenfranchised, who wish to vote. One-eighth of the Electoral College is now chosen partly by women. One-fifth of the Senate and about one-ninth of the House represent equal suffrage states. It is time for our country to make those fractions whole, and that will require a constitutional amendment. If you mention this in your remarks to Congress, they will be obliged to consider it."

President Wilson's expression hardened as each of her companions addressed him in turn. Mrs. Wiley spoke as a wife, mother, and homemaker, explaining the plight of mothers who struggled to raise their children as they wished because they had no voice in making the laws. "Woman suffrage helps to improve society and civilization," she said, but the president barely nodded in reply.

Next Mrs. Stone spoke on behalf of the women of western states, who had benefited greatly from suffrage and thoroughly understood how it would benefit their disenfranchised sisters, as well as the states in which they resided. "A constitutional amendment is necessary to guarantee voting rights to every woman, regardless of her state of residence," she insisted, but the president only regarded her dourly.

Miss Dixon offered the perspective of suffragists from the south, but when she alluded to the potential benefits to race relations if Black women had the vote, President Wilson's frown deepened. Sensing a new antipathy in his demeanor, Alice was relieved when Miss Dixon quickly changed the subject to the potential benefits to his political party if thousands of southern women joined the electorate, but the president remained unappeased.

Mrs. Harper spoke last, and she began by summarizing suffragists' long struggle for the same equality before the law and independence that men took for granted. "Since 1869, efforts have been made to prompt Congress to act, but nothing has been gained." Glancing wistfully about the room, she added, "I was one of a group of women who spoke with President Roosevelt in this same room in 1905, and he took no action. The situation is different now, Mr. President. Women have the vote in nine states, and the cause is swiftly gaining ground. The time has come when woman suffrage is a question of national importance, and the president and Congress may well afford to recognize it as such."

After giving President Wilson a moment to respond, which he ignored, Mrs. Harper took a book from her satchel and began reading excerpts from his most recent work, *The New Freedom*. "If you substituted 'women' for 'men' in some sections," she remarked as she closed the book, allowing a small, knowing smile, "it would be the best argument for woman suffrage I ever heard. All we ask of you is that you take every word of what you have written in regard to the political liberty of men and apply it to women."

President Wilson's expression had become increasingly stony as the women spoke, and after about ten minutes, he abruptly rose. "I am still deciding what to say in my address to Congress," the president said, returning to Alice's opening request as if nothing that had been mentioned since then mattered, or had even been heard. "If I do not include the recommendation you have asked for, it will not mean that I am opposed to woman suffrage. Bear in mind that Congress can consider the question without any prompting from me."

"We're aware of that," said Alice, "but your endorsement carries with it the profound authority of your high office. If you supported woman suffrage, the Congress would follow your lead."

"Indeed they would," he said, bowing slightly. "Good afternoon, ladies."

The aide hurried over, his arms slightly outspread as if to prevent the delegation from following Mr. Wilson from the room. Evidently the meeting was finished, although they had been granted only a third of the half hour that had been promised. To protest would have been undignified, so they thanked the president for his time and allowed the aide to escort them from the White House.

"I've never met a more condescending and didactic man," fumed Mrs. Harper as they strode from the White House grounds.

"He won't mention the cause in his address," said Mrs. Wiley, close to tears. "He'll never support woman suffrage. He will never see women as men's equals."

"Probably not," said Alice, smiling faintly.

Her companions regarded her in astonishment. "How can you be in such good spirits?" asked Miss

Dixon. "Our words today were wasted, and so was all the work we put into the procession. We have nothing to show for our efforts."

A few paces ahead, Alice halted and turned to face them. "That's absolutely not true," she said, emphasizing each word. "Our courage and persistence impressed everyone who witnessed how we refused to be daunted by adversity. We have more sympathy and respect from the public now than ever before."

A glimmer of hope lit up their faces, but Miss Dixon shook her head, dispirited. "But the procession was ruined," she said, gesturing over her shoulder to the White House, "and we have four more years, at least, with *that man* as our president, and he will never do anything to help us."

"Thankfully, our future is not in his hands, but in our own." Alice took one of Miss Dixon's hands, and one of Mrs. Harper's, and looked around the circle of faces in which she saw new resolve taking hold. "We have a long, hard fight ahead of us, and we will endure many dark days, but the outcome is certain. We *will* triumph, we *will* win the vote, because we will not give up until we do."

It was only a matter of hard work and time—as long as they kept marching, ever forward.

# Author's Note

Twice more in March 1913, Alice Paul and a delegation of suffragists called on President Wilson at the White House to implore him to use his upcoming address to Congress to recommend a constitutional amendment guaranteeing woman suffrage. From her home in Brooklyn, Maud Malone chimed in via a letter to the editor of the *New-York Tribune*:

> *I would offer the Democratic party a kindly word of advice. The suffragette party in this country is still young, and you have but just come back to power. You have an opportunity before you to make good your claim that you are fundamental, not partisan, Democrats. The test is: "Are you for woman suffrage?" If you are not you will be swept out of office*

*at the next national election by men and women*
*voters of the free states. No tariff revision, no Mexi-*
*can policy, no plan of independence for the Filipinos*
*can keep you in if you fall down on woman suffrage.*

*Will Mr. Wilson be kind enough to recommend to*
*Congress the submission of an amendment to the fed-*
*eral Constitution? This is the constitutional method*
*of gaining our vote. We are asking him to do this.*
*The responsibility rests on him. Will he do it?*

It probably came as no surprise to Maud that he
did not.

Despite Wilson's lack of support, on April 3, a federal suffrage amendment was introduced in the House
by Representative Frank Mondell of Wyoming and in
the Senate by Senator Joseph Bristow of Kansas, two
elected officials from equal suffrage states. About two
weeks later, Alice stunned the leaders of the National
by announcing her intention to create a new suffrage
organization, the Congressional Union for Woman Suffrage, to focus exclusively on advocating for the constitutional amendment. Although the new organization
would not be affiliated with the Congressional Committee, it would operate out of the same offices and
include many of the same volunteers. Alarmed that
the new Congressional Union would compete with the

National for membership and fundraising dollars, Dr. Anna Shaw sent word to Alice through their mutual friend Dora Lewis that the Congressional Union must have no official affiliation with the National, nor could it use the National's letterhead. Thus began a split between the two groups that would, over time, become an intense and often bitter rivalry.

In late May 1913, the Senate Committee on the District of Columbia released its report on the conduct of the police before and during the woman suffrage parade. They concluded that while traffic on Pennsylvania Avenue should have been halted by noon and the crowds could have been controlled more effectively, there was insufficient evidence "to single out any particular individual for reproof or condemnation":

> While we felt that with more earnestness and with a more systematic effort on the part of some of the officers better protection could have been afforded the line of march, we at the same time think that the conditions were so unusual, extraordinary, and difficult, that the police force as a whole should not be condemned. The many officers who proved faithful ought not to be discredited by those who proved faithless to their duty.
>
> There is no proof whatever that any negligence or

indifference upon the part of members of the police department was warranted by any suggestion or act of the superintendent or those in higher authority; nor was any officer, whether uniformed or special, justified in believing that any dereliction upon his part would be either excused or overlooked by his superiors. On the contrary, all the officers who testified said in substance, that they fully understood that all orders issued were to be obeyed literally and that anyone neglecting his duty was alone personally responsible therefor.

All reasonable precautions were taken in issuing proper orders and in detailing and assigning the police along the Avenue, considering the number available for duty.

"On the whole," the *Washington Times* predicted, "the report of the committee will be regarded as a victory for Major Sylvester and the Commissioners in view of the severe criticism of the police department made by the suffragists and their friends."

As disappointing as this outcome might have been to equal rights activists, more important battles were being waged in the Illinois state legislature. In April 1913, while the long-awaited state equal suffrage measure was being debated, several racially discriminatory bills were introduced: one that would permit white unions to replace nonunion Black employees in certain railroad positions, a Jim Crow transportation bill for Pullman cars and streetcars, and anti-miscegenation measures that would prohibit interracial marriage and sexual intimacy. Ida B. Wells-Barnett was fundamentally involved with an unprecedented effort to organize vast numbers of African American women from all parts of the state to gather in Springfield to lobby state legislators to vote against the bills. Eventually all of the measures were defeated, and the impressive effort of "so many brilliant persons of color" compelled the author of one of the racist bills to declare that he was sorry he had ever proposed it. Afterward, when the African American newspaper the *Chicago Defender* published an honor roll of fourteen activists who were most responsible for the victory, Ida's name was listed first, and was the only one to appear in all capital letters. "The name of Mrs. Barnett stands alone," the *Defender* explained, "because that constant and fearless champion of equal rights was on the firing line all the time. Her eloquent pleas in private conferences with the legislators and in open session were eloquent and forcible. Ida B. Wells-Barnett has again endeared herself to the world."

On June 26, Ida enjoyed another victory for equal

rights when the Illinois Equal Suffrage Act passed and was signed into law. Women in Illinois, regardless of race, would be permitted to vote in presidential elections as well as those for certain local offices, although they were still forbidden to vote for state and federal legislators. Even so, the success of the Municipal and Presidential Voting Act of 1913 was a triumph worth celebrating. On July 1, 1913, Ida and her daughters participated in a grand "Woman's Independence Day" parade beginning on Michigan Avenue and proceeding down Monroe, La Salle, and other boulevards, and ending at Grant Park. The Chicago *Inter Ocean* reported that more than two thousand women participated in the "triumphal parade of 500 automobiles, two military bands, and a line of march along which thousands of men, women, and children cheered themselves hoarse." Of the eighteen suffrage organizations represented in the automobile fleet, the Alpha Suffrage Club appeared twelfth, comfortably in the middle, a placement which one hopes indicates that they were regarded as the equal of the white women's organizations.

After helping to win presidential and municipal suffrage for the women of her state, Ida continued to campaign for the suffrage amendment to the Constitution, which had been introduced to both chambers of

Congress on June 13, 1913. Ida also continued to write, to lecture, and to work tirelessly on behalf of anti-lynching campaigns and other important civil rights causes whose missions were to improve the lives of people of color.

Within the first few months after taking office, President Wilson, who was a virulent racist as well as a misogynist, began segregating the government, ruthlessly purging federal agencies and departments of African American civil servants—ruining careers, impoverishing families, and destroying lives. Apparently unaware of his direct involvement, Black civil rights leaders formed a committee to visit President Wilson to "call his attention to the segregation enforced in the departments of the government," and to ask him "to use his influence as president of the United States in abolishing discrimination based on the color line." Ida was among the delegation that called on him at the White House, and as she recalled in her memoir, *Crusade for Justice,* her impression at the time was that he "gave careful attention to the appeal." After the delegation's leader, William Monroe Trotter of the National Equal Rights League, finished speaking, President Wilson claimed that "he was unaware of such discrimination, although Mr. Trotter left with him an order emanating from one of his heads of the department, which forbade colored and white clerks to use the same restaurants or toilet rooms. The president promised to look into the matter and again expressed doubt as to the situation." As the only woman on the committee, Ida was asked to comment. "I contented myself with saying to the president that there were more things going on in the government than he had dreamed of in his philosophy," Ida recalled, "and we thought it our duty to bring to his attention that phase of it which directly concerned us."

A year passed in which President Wilson failed to enact reform or even to contact the delegation. When William Monroe Trotter made a second visit to the White House, Ida wrote, "the president became annoyed over Mr. Trotter's persistent assertion that these discriminations still were practiced and that it was his duty as president of the United States to abolish them. President Wilson became very angry and he told the committee that if they wanted to call on him in the future they would have to leave Mr. Trotter out."

Sadly, it is not surprising that Wilson fiercely refused to listen to the Black leaders who confronted him about systemic racism in his administration. As Gordon J. Davis wrote in his 2015 *New York Times* op-ed, "What Woodrow Wilson Cost My Grandfather," Wilson "was not just a racist. He believed in white supremacy as government policy, so much so that he reversed decades of racial progress. But we would be wrong to see this as a mere policy change; in doing so, he ruined the lives of countless talented African-Americans and their families."

Maud Malone was one of the first, the most public, and the most persistent of those who criticized Wilson for evading questions and feigning ignorance when questioned about his opinions on matters he would rather ignore. It is less certain, however, whether she actually did join the Army of the Hudson on the long march to Washington. Evidence in the historical record suggests that she was not one of the few pilgrims who accompanied General Jones on the entire journey, but like many others, she may have joined in for part of it. Since Maud was renowned as a "prodigious marcher," since she certainly would have been with the pilgrims in spirit if not in fact, and because it made for a better story, I took some artistic license and included her in the entire pilgrimage.

Soon after the Woman Suffrage Procession, Maud was in New York working through the long-delayed appeal to her misdemeanor conviction for interrupting Woodrow Wilson's speech in October 1912. On the afternoon of March 13, 1913, she appeared before five judges of the Appellate Division of the Brooklyn Supreme Court in Brooklyn Borough Hall. Two weeks later, in a unanimous decision, the court upheld her earlier conviction, concluding that her disturbance at the Academy of Music was willful, intentional, and designed. "I do not doubt her belief," wrote the presiding justice, Almet F. Jenks. "Thoughtful men and women recognize that the principle of woman suffrage is supported by cogent argument." However, he said, Maud had been tried for her behavior, not for her beliefs, and she had violated the law. "If the law should blink at little things which are unlawful, irresponsible enthusiasts might be encouraged to commit grave offenses," Jenks warned, adding, "There is no question of free speech or of oppression involved in this case."

The next day, beneath the headline "Sauce for the Goose," the *New-York Tribune* declared that Maud "might just as well take her medicine." In fact, the author noted archly, she ought to be pleased by the equal treatment she had received under the law, for she "has been treated just exactly as if she were a male offender with a full-fledged vote." It's difficult to take this claim of equality before the law seriously. The author apparently did not consider, or perhaps deliberately ignored, that unlike the hypothetical male offender, Maud had had no part in choosing the lawmakers under whose regulations she had been convicted.

Never one to let the press have the last word, Maud

wrote a letter to the editor, which appeared on April 3. "I do not admit I have lost," she declared, adding,

> This decision decides nothing. It is only the opinion of five men. Our American theory is that even judges make mistakes. They have done so when they say: "There is no question of free speech or of oppression involved in this case." Now, this case is solely one of the denial of political free speech to an American citizen.
>
> "What is sauce for the goose is sauce for the gander." Will the Tribune point out any gander who was arrested, imprisoned, tried and fined in the last campaign for asking a political question of a candidate? Many ganders held conversations with Roosevelt, Sulzer, and even Wilson himself and were answered.
>
> From the learned argument of the Appellate Division it is plain that the decision might have been different if the judges had not felt it their duty to punish me for the "militant suffragists who are producing a reign of domestic terror in England," as they put it. The case was not tried on its merit, but on a fear of an English invasion.
>
> The decision also says: "It must be borne in mind that the defendant did not seek to interrogate the

*speaker upon another subject, but persisted to push the inquiry upon the same topic." From this it seems the judges admit that the same person may ask two questions on different subjects in a meeting, but not two on the same subject. If two, why not three or four? They might allow any number, so long as the suffrag[ist] was sidetracked and the candidate saved.*

Although the justices urged Maud to refrain from heckling politicians in the future, she refused to promise to do so—certainly not before women won the vote. She continued to work for suffrage, women's rights, and workers' rights throughout her career, and in 1917, she became a founding member of the Library Employees' Union and served as their spokesperson. Her activism eventually led to her firing from the New York Public Library, after which she was employed as the librarian for the *Daily Worker,* a newspaper published by the Communist Party of the United States of America.

After the historic Woman Suffrage Procession of 1913 where their lives briefly intersected, Alice, Ida, and Maud continued to work for woman suffrage, but it would be seven long, arduous years before the Nineteenth Amendment to the Constitution granting women the right to vote was ratified on August 18, 1920. The abuse and torment suffragists endured in that time equaled—and arguably surpassed—anything Alice Paul, Lucy Burns, and the British suffragettes had experienced in Holloway Prison.

Unlike the founding mothers of the United States suffrage movement, Alice, Ida, and Maud lived to cast their first ballots. In 1951, Maud Malone died in New York City at the age of seventy-eight. One week after her death, she was remembered in the *Daily Worker* as "the first militant suffragette in the United States." When she marched alone for suffrage in Albany, her "signs were startling and caused people to stop, read and discuss." "She antedated the Pankhursts of England by several years," the eulogist noted, "and was over a decade ahead of the militants of the Woman's Party who went to jail in Washington shortly before the National Suffrage was won in 1920 . . . Many who knew Maud Malone, this smiling willing librarian of the *Daily Worker* office who worked there nearly five years, did not know of her early tempestuous history and her extraordinary contributions to the women's movement." It is unfortunate that memory of her exploits faded so quickly and that her role in the suffrage movement has been largely forgotten today.

Ida B. Wells-Barnett died in 1931 at the age of sixty-eight after a lifetime of activism. In May 2020, she was awarded a posthumous Pulitzer Prize for her investigative journalism, which exposed the horrors of lynching and undermined the false cultural narratives constructed to justify it. "Of the dozens of Black female journalists in the 19th century, few ventured into political topics as fearlessly as Wells," wrote history professor Sarah L. Silkey in the *Washington Post.* "An early muckraker, she attracted the ire of those who benefited from the unjust systems she exposed. Wells's campaign against lynching, for which she won recognition, brought unprecedented scrutiny to American mob violence. She published numerous investigative newspaper reports, editorials and pamphlets denouncing lynching as a form of racial terrorism."

In 1923, Alice Paul offered a version of the Equal Rights Amendment to Congress, only to see it swiftly buried. She continued to campaign for it, and twenty years later, during one of many appearances before the Senate Judiciary Committee, she presented a revised version that read, "Equality of rights under the law shall not be denied by the U.S. or any State on Account of sex." Congress was no more receptive than before, but Alice persisted.

On March 22, 1972, the Equal Rights Amendment finally passed Congress, which imposed a seven-year deadline for ratification. Well into her eighties, Alice worked alongside a new generation of feminists (many of whom were members of the National Organization for Women instead of Alice's group, which they considered outdated), to win the required number of states for ratification. But new generations of Antis had sprung up too, and the opponents of the ERA eventually triumphed, as the deadline for the amendment ran out one state short of ratification.

In 1974, Alice was hospitalized for a head injury incurred when she suffered a stroke. For two years she resided in a Connecticut nursing home, while her nephew, her closest living relative, plundered her estate. By the time concerned friends became aware of the exploitation and arranged for him to be removed as conservator and replaced by a court-appointed guardian, Alice's savings were gone. On November 4, 1975, a startling announcement appeared on page twenty-one of the *New York Times:*

### Mother of U.S. Equal-Rights Measure Nearly Penniless in Nursing Home at 90

RIDGEFIELD, Conn., Nov. 3—On the eve of the vote on Equal Rights Amendments in New York and New Jersey, the author of the original Federal version is near destitution, recovering from a stroke at a nursing home here. Dr. Alice Paul, now

90 years old, nevertheless continues to push for the amendment that she drew up in 1922 and keeps abreast of the states that have ratified the equal rights amendment to the Federal Constitution.

On July 9, 1977, Alice Paul died of pneumonia in a New Jersey nursing home at the age of ninety-two.

In the four decades since Alice's death, women's rights activists have continued to advocate for the Equal Rights Amendment, arguing that despite the advances women have made through the years, until the United States Constitution is amended to explicitly state that "equality of rights cannot be denied or abridged on account of sex," the legal and political victories women have achieved could be undone, if current laws offering women protection from discrimination are replaced by laws voiding those protections.

In January 2020, Virginia became the thirty-eighth state to ratify the Equal Rights Amendment. Seventeen days later, on February 13, 2020, the U.S. House of Representatives voted 232–182 to pass H.J.Res. 79, a joint resolution to remove the original time limit imposed to ratify the ERA. At the time of this writing, June 2020, the amendment is facing political and legal challenges to the ratification process that must be resolved before the Equal Rights Amendment can become part of the U.S. Constitution.

One hundred years after the Nineteenth Amendment granted equal suffrage to women, it remains to be seen whether Alice Paul's last great ambition will be fulfilled.

# Acknowledgments

I am deeply grateful to Maria Massie, Rachel Kahan, Jade Wong-Baxter, Alivia Lopez, Julie Paulauski, Kaitie Leary, Elsie Lyons, and Laura Cherkas for their contributions to *The Women's March* and their ongoing support of my work. Geraldine Neidenbach, Heather Neidenbach, and Marty Chiaverini were my first readers, and their comments and questions about early drafts of this novel proved invaluable. As ever, Nic Neidenbach generously shared his computer expertise to help me in crucial moments.

The Women's March is a work of fiction inspired by history. I am indebted to the Wisconsin Historical Society and its librarians and staff for maintaining the excellent archives on the University of Wisconsin campus in Madison that I rely on for my research. The sources I found most useful for this book include:

Adams, Katherine H., and Michael L. Keene. *Alice Paul and the American Suffrage Campaign.* Urbana and Chicago, IL: University of Illinois Press, 2008.

Baker, Jean H. *Sisters: The Lives of America's Suffragists.* New York: Farrar, Straus and Giroux, 2005.

Bernard, Michelle. "Despite the Tremendous Risk, African American Women Marched for Suffrage, Too." *Washington Post*, March 3, 2013.

Cahill, Bernadette. *Alice Paul, the National Woman's Party and the Vote: The First Civil Rights Struggle of the 20th Century.* Jefferson, NC: McFarland & Company, 2015.

Davis, Gordon J. "What Woodrow Wilson Cost My Grandfather." *New York Times*, November 24, 2015, A27.

Feimster, Crystal N. "Ida B. Wells and the Lynching of Black Women." *New York Times*, April 29, 2018, SR11.

Fry, Amelia R. *Conversations with Alice Paul: Woman Suffrage and the Equal Rights Amendment.* Berkeley: Regents of the University of California, 1976.

Jack, Zachary Michael. *Rosalie Gardiner Jones and the Long March for Women's Rights.* Jefferson, NC: McFarland & Company, 2020.

National American Woman Suffrage Association. *Proceedings of the Annual Convention of the National Ameri-*

can *Woman Suffrage Association,* vol. 44. New York: NAWSA, 1913.

Roessner, Lori Amber, and Jodi L. Rightler-McDaniels, eds. *Political Pioneer of the Press: Ida B. Wells-Barnett and Her Transnational Crusade for Social Justice.* Lanham, MD: Lexington Books, 2018.

Silkey, Sarah L. "Ida B. Wells Won the Pulitzer. Here's Why That Matters." *Washington Post,* May 7, 2020.

Staples, Brent. "How the Suffrage Movement Betrayed Black Women." *New York Times,* July 29, 2018, SR8.

Walton, Mary. *A Woman's Crusade: Alice Paul and the Battle for the Ballot.* New York: St. Martin's Press, 2010.

Wells, Ida B. *Crusade for Justice: The Autobiography of Ida B. Wells.* Edited by Alfreda M. Duster. Chicago: University of Chicago Press, 1970.

I consulted numerous excellent online resources while researching and writing *The Women's March,* including the archives of digitized historic newspapers at Newspapers.com (www.newspapers.com); the National Women's History Museum website (https://www.womenshistory.org); and census records, directories, and other historical records at Ancestry (ancestry.com). Digital archives of the *New York Times, Washington Post, Chicago Tribune, Broad Ax, Inter Ocean,*

*Brooklyn Daily Eagle,* and *Washington Times* were especially useful and informative.

As always and most of all, I thank my husband, Marty, and my sons, Nicholas and Michael, for their enduring love, steadfast support, and constant encouragement. You are the best quarantine crew I could ever wish for. Thank you for the long walks, the kayak adventures, the many loaves of fresh-baked bread, the homemade pasta, the movie nights, and the endless supply of warm hugs and laughter. I will always be grateful for your courage, optimism, resilience, and humor in difficult times. You make everything worthwhile, and I could not have written this book without you.

# About the Author

**JENNIFER CHIAVERINI** is the *New York Times* bestselling author of numerous acclaimed historical novels, including *Resistance Women, Enchantress of Numbers,* and *Mrs. Lincoln's Dressmaker,* as well as the beloved Elm Creek Quilts series. A graduate of the University of Notre Dame and the University of Chicago, she lives with her husband and two sons in Madison, Wisconsin.